"In *Akmaral*, Judith Lindbergh draws a portrait of a fierce, head-strong, yet vulnerable female warrior who lives on the Central Asian steppes in the 5th century BCE. An orphan, descended from Amazons, Akmaral's ascent to power is fraught with conflict both internal and external. Fans of Madeline Miller and Natalie Haynes will relish how Lindbergh weaves fact and fiction. Thoroughly imagined and vividly described, this novel is a gripping saga, a love story, and a convincing portrait of a time and people lost to history."

—Christina Baker Kline, #1 bestselling author of *Orphan Train* and *The Exiles*

"Judith Lindbergh's meticulously researched, deeply imagined *Akmaral* brings the joy and hardship of a nomad woman warrior to vibrant, often aching life. Set against the unfolding drama of an ancient warring tribe of the Asian steppes, the novel captures both the mystery of love and the majesty of the human spirit."

—Cathy Marie Buchanan, *New York Times* bestselling author of *Daughter of Black Lake* and *The Painted Girls*

"Once there were female warriors more powerful than any man, with fierce wills and bodies strong as iron. Born in the ancient steppes of Asia where Kazakhstan, Mongolia, and China now meet, *Akmaral* is the breathtaking story of a mesmerizing female warrior who is well-trained for battle but finds herself confronted and confounded by a man who is just as skilled and passionate. When young Akmaral falls in love with her proud Scythian captive, her role as protector of her clan becomes infinitely more complicated as she is forced to choose between kingdom, family, and her own heart. *Akmaral* delves deep into female power and confronts complex issues about womanhood, motherhood, and the sacrifices women make to protect those they love: issues as powerful today as they were in ancient times. If you love Madeline Miller's *Circe*, you must read *Akmaral*. Lindbergh delivers a breath-taking story filled with vivid characters, haunted landscapes, powerful battle scenes, and a love story you will not soon forget."

—Laurie Lico Albanese, award-winning author of *Hester*

"Judith Lindbergh's magically immersive novel, *Akmaral*, unfolds among an ancient matriarchal tribe of nomads living on the Ukok Plateau, in the Altai Mountains of southern Siberia. The story centers on the life of the anointed girl child, Akmaral, whose extraordinary bravery and fully realized humanity make her into a heroine on a par with the characters of J.R.R. Tolkien. Lindbergh combines her impressive gifts for research with an uncanny ability to evoke an exotic, remote, and meticulously imagined civilization from 2,400 years ago that nonetheless shimmers with authenticity in all its details. You will smell the sweat of the horses and feel the ache of a warrior who is also a mother and a lover. *Akmaral* transported me, night after page-turning night, to a world I would never have been able to experience otherwise, an unforgettable wind-swept world before the dawn of patriarchy."

—Barbara Quick, author of *Vivaldi's Virgins* and *What Disappears*

"I was unable to put down this riveting, rugged journey of a young woman in an almost inconceivable world which vanished millenniums ago. Akmaral may be one of the most fascinating warriors in literature. She loves three things most: her beloved tribe with its relentless god, the silent captured enemy she takes into her life, and the child she bears him. But what if the stranger turns on her because she loves too much? Written with a wild poetry, the author brings to life a strong woman and her unforgettable story amid stark cliffs and green pastures, guided by a mystical exiled old woman and the ghost of her lost best friend. *Akmaral* is pure literary magic."

—Stephanie Cowell, American Book Award recipient and author of *Claude & Camille: A Novel of Monet* and *The Boy in the Rain*

AKMARAL

Judith Lindbergh

Regal House Publishing

Published by
Regal House Publishing, LLC
Raleigh, NC 27605
All rights reserved

ISBN -13 (paperback): 9781646034697
ISBN -13 (epub): 9781646034703
Library of Congress Control Number: 2023942950

Cover images and design by © C. B. Royal

Regal House Publishing, LLC
https://regalhousepublishing.com

The following is a work of fiction created by the author. All names, individuals, characters, places, items, brands, events, etc. were either the product of the author or were used fictitiously. Any name, place, event, person, brand, or item, current or past, is entirely coincidental.

Printed in the United States of America

To my mother
and to all women who must fight to make peace.

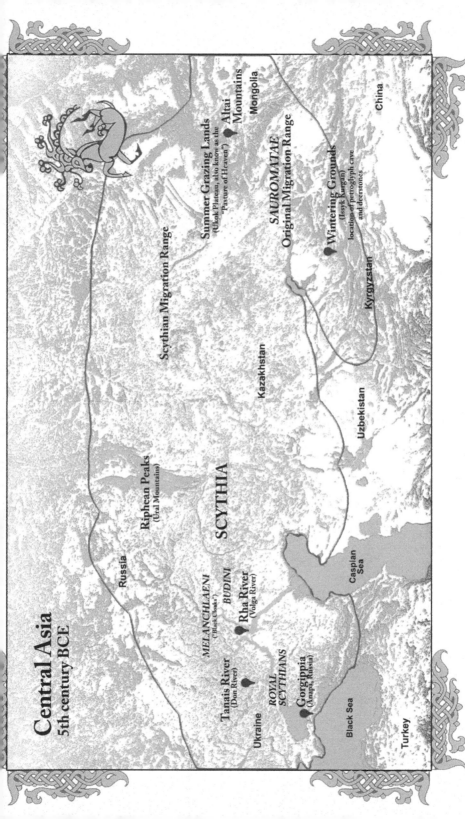

Of the origins of the Sauromatae, it is told that, after their victory on the Thermodon, the Greeks sailed off on three ships, taking with them the surviving Amazons as captives. While at sea, the Amazons attacked and killed the Greek crews. But they knew nothing of sailing and drifted with the waves until they came aground at the cliffs of Lake Maeotis. This was the free Scythians' country. When the Amazons landed, they set out toward their settlements. Seizing the first herd of horses they found, they mounted them and began to raid.

The Scythians wondered where they had come from, and assumed these strange raiders were men. It was only after they had met them in battle, and then examined the dead, that they realized that their foes were women.

The Scythians argued about what to do. In the end, they decided to court them. They moved nearer to the Amazon camps and imitated all they did, fleeing instead of fighting whenever the Amazons approached. Soon the women understood that the Scythian warriors meant no harm. The two camps joined together for raiding and hunts. And some of the women chose the men as lovers.

When finally they had learned each other's languages, the men urged the Amazons to return to their settlements and become their wives. But the women refused. "We could not live with your people. We shoot bows and arrows. We throw javelins and ride. Your women stay in their wagons and do women's work. They never hunt or even travel beyond your encampments. If you wish to be our husbands, let us leave this place and live by ourselves." And the men agreed.

So they crossed the Tanaïs River and rode to the east and to the north until they came to a new land of pastures and mountains. There they settled. Ever since, the Sauromatae women have followed their ancient ways, riding out to hunt with their men or without. They dress and behave in every way the same as their men. And when needed, they go to war.

Regarding marriage, it is their custom that no maiden weds until she has killed a man in battle; and some grow old and die unmarried, because they cannot satisfy this need.

—Herodotus, *The Histories*, Book IV: 110-117, 5th century B.C.E.

AKMARAL

A black stork drifts onto an isle in the middle of the great shallow lake that stretches for miles—a shimmering mirage. The water in some places rises only to the great bird's ankles. It nips at the fishes, swallowing them by lifting up its beak and choking them back whole.

Some say I am like that: stately, yet savage, as easy to call for blood as for silence, as longing for the warmth of a lover's chest as to shove it off at the call to arms. But I do not like battle. Only know that a show of strength is required to keep the peace. Blood is strength which often forms still pools on the battlefield, like this lake or others that are formed by sudden rains. When the sun rises, it dries into the soil and cannot be seen. Blood, passing into memory.

I, too, am passing into memory. I am dying and will lie soon within the earth and be forgotten. For most of us, it does not last long—this life. A warrior's death always comes early. Yet mine has lasted long enough, longer than I would have thought. I should be proud of what I've done, of defending my people, of guiding them such a great distance from where we had begun.

They call us Sauromatae—the Greeks do and the Scythians also—"lizard breasts" for our glittering armor scales. But I remember a time when our people had no name, when we were a disparate multitude of wandering herders—a thousand, thousand isolated clans clustered into petty camps, our wind-rattled yurts scattered like dung clots across the undulating steppes. Half our horses then were wild, raising dust into dry showers; our sheep, goats, and camels tirelessly gnawing at the tall, sharp grass, turning the hapless earth from emerald to amber to ashen.

Out of this I made a nation, though it was nothing I ever

sought, never my intent, nothing I would have chosen. This throng that surrounds me now they call a confederacy; and of its greatness, they name me leader—this, my legacy that will linger long beyond my death, exalting all the mighty strife that I abhor.

For most of my life, I have served the war god Targitai. In his duty, I have worn the pelts of wolves and leopards, and hung the horns of wild boars upon my belt. Many other beasts I have hunted roaming across our grasslands. And I have led my people into battle, and I have regretted it.

What I did was as anyone would do to protect her people, her family, her children.

I have tried to make amends for the damage I have done. If they call me queen, it is little honor for my sorrows. My people gather around me, singing chants and ringing small bronze bells. *Hewana,* they call me—mother of our tribe—but I have been a mother only once, and not for very long. Most of them do not recall.

This has been my journey; and I will leave it—now, or very soon. Though these last breaths before death are anything but sweet. Perhaps no one is proud on the day of their death. All are filled with question and doubt. As am I. As I have been, almost from the beginning.

PART I

THE SNOW LEOPARD

1

The Flying Deer

The Kara Kam foretold that I would be important. I was five winters old and had just begun to learn the skill of sewing felt. I sat beside our fire working at two small patches with a thin wool thread when my mother stepped inside our winter hut, kneeling low to warm her hands.

"It is time," she murmured, cupping her icy fingers around my elbow, looking across at my father who sat on a cushion with his long legs crossed. He'd been sharpening the edge of a new-made dagger, the tools of his craft scattered over the thick felt mat. "Blood moon." My mother gestured toward a sudden light that had broken over the snow drifting through our roof's eye.

My father nodded, put down the blade, then rose to his feet, brushing the bronze filings from his leather trousers. His gaze drifted upward toward the wafting flakes—the air, laced with some foreboding I could not fathom.

I knew better than to question, as my mother pried a spouted jug from the pile of our stores. It was her favorite—made of pounded silver etched with the shapes of warriors, horses, and thick-maned lions, in a style I had rarely seen, unlike anything my father or any other craftsman could have fashioned. Perhaps the jug was bartered from a caravan of Persian merchants along the trade road—*Six sacks of colored ores, I offer you! Add seven blocks of cheese! And three wool felts! No, I must have one of those fine daggers!* I could almost hear the traders' voices as my mother gestured for my attention back. She handed me the jug and helped me polish it with milk and sand, then gave me the small bronze bowl that always lay beside our fire. There, our earthen cauldron steamed with fermented mare's milk—koumiss, the intoxicating drink whose bitter sips bring us closer to our ancestors.

I took up the bowl and ladled the koumiss carefully. When the jug was full, my mother wrapped it tightly in soft leather and bound the bundle with a thin gut cord. She wrapped me, too, in a heavy felt-sewn cloak. Outside, the snow was falling harder as my father loaded up our horses.

So late at night and all the other shelters of our camp already still—I sensed the burden of my parents' silence as we rode single file into the storm. My gaze fixed ahead at my mother's horse's hoof-falls pricking the perfect blanket like small stitches through the white. We traveled eastward to where our narrow valley widened and windswept veils of forgotten spirits danced across a snow-draped steppe. There, beneath an overhanging cliff, stood a single yurt—a low, round tent—not even a winter cabin.

I gasped and reined my horse, but my mother had already drawn up close beside me. "Akmaral, a warrior is never frightened." I nodded, clutching my cloak a little closer.

It was the Kara Kam's yurt, as any child of our aul would know, swathed in felts so dark, they matched the high cliff's walls. My mother had often told me how the Kara Kam could ride on the tails of golden eagles, how she knew the twisting fishes' waters and could swim them out to the distant sea, that she flew between the altars of the stars and had traveled every passage to the heaven realm. But hers was a blackened path. She practiced in darkness, painted with ashes, her yurt filled with acrid smoke—so different from the Ak Kam, our people's priestess, who sacrificed beneath the sky's wide gaze before the aul and all the elders, where everyone could see and hear and understand her meaning.

My mother urged her horse and led us closer, settling our mounts before a frail wood post. My father raised his arms to ease me from my saddle. He clung to me—only for a moment until my mother tugged me off. I willed myself not to linger as I followed, trying not to stumble through the new, thick snow.

I entered last, behind my mother and then my father. They each knelt to give their offerings: a heavy sack of winter meat, small beads carved of colored stone, six pelts each of fox and marmot, the fleece of a yearling sheep, and my father's new-honed blade. I carried the heavy jug filled with the drink my mother and I had prepared. And a tunic of colored felt, carefully embroidered, stretched across my mother's arms. I'd seen her working at it, stitching in the dark, strange murmurs sputtering from her lips—prayers to our ancient ancestors.

The Kara Kam sat alone in her frigid hut before the embers of a failing fire. Her shoulders were slender, stooped beneath a rough silk tunic too large for her fragile frame. Her bare legs stuck out like brittle twigs from a long, thick skirt of crimson wool. Around her waist she wore a woven belt tied with heavy tassels, and from her head arose a headdress as tall as the lattice walls, dangling with fine, carved birds, gilded leaping horses, and twisted lions attacking rams. At its peak protruded sharp-fletched arrows wrapped in strips of gold. They spread like branches, reaching up as if to pierce the roof's eye. Before her lay powders of ochre, cinnabar, and ash, each pressed into oyster shells, though there was no ocean near. Across her bare arms traced the tortured struggles of straining beasts—deer with griffins' heads caught in the jaws of winged snow leopards—etched into her skin as dark indigo tattoos.

I had never seen her properly before. The black kam always lived alone, following our paths, settling her yurt at the distant edge of our encampments. Only sometimes she'd appear in the shadows beyond our fires. All knew her for the sudden flash of her round bronze mirror which she would hold in the dark to capture the hearth goddess Rada Mai's homely light; then, she'd hurl the spark into a startling flare that would tear across the looming darkness. We all would scurry from the light, frightened and blinded.

Now she held the mirror before her face, and I could make out the figures of five stags flying and a single mountain goat caught in an endless whirl. She turned, moving the mirror through the air, softly, slowly, making the thin white smoke before her curl and dance. And she sang—strange, unintelligible chants—her mouth moving, revealing livid gums, pegged teeth between purple lips.

I squirmed to avoid her mirror's cutting light. But my father held me still as my mother bowed low, offering her food. She unwrapped the jug and poured our koumiss into the small bronze bowl. The Kara Kam paused in her incantations, greeting my mother with a hard, quick glance, followed slowly by a guileless, almost tearful smile. She took the bowl and tipped it, scattering the droplets several times in all directions. Then she slurped the last down loudly. My mother poured another bowl and passed it round for each of us to sip. Even me. I choked a bit before I swallowed.

At the black kam's beckon, my father pressed me forward. My mother took my wrapper off so that the icy air rushed around my frame. The Kara Kam did not seem to feel the cold, her shoulders fully bare now as her eyes rolled back deep inside her skull. I willed myself not to turn away as again she chanted, reaching blindly for a tall alabaster jug from which she sprinkled small black seeds over her smoldering fire.

Soon the yurt smelled strange. Another puff of smoke and then a haze. In time—I do not recall how long—the Kara Kam's arms grew wide, then sprouted feathers. Flapping, she began to screech—she had become a bird—a vulture circling, with wings all black and an ashen-colored ruff. Then the stubbled head transformed again into the woman's. I shuddered in mounting terror, for everything around me had transformed—even my mother and my father, who had become long-limbed gazelles.

Then the Kara Kam spoke. "Look down at your feet, Akmaral, my sister's daughter's daughter." I looked and saw the hooves of a powerful steppe deer; then, almost without thought, I leapt through the roof's eye and flew across the open sky.

࿓

When I awoke, I was still shaking.

It was morning. The light shone bluish through the roof's eye, left open to release the smoke that rose coldly from the black kam's fire. She sat in silence, looking feeble and diminished. Her headdress was gone. Her eyes were pale and clouded. She seemed now truly blind as she grinned at a space beyond me.

We left. My mother and my father both seemed pleased, each bending to take an arm, for I could barely stand, my limbs leaden after so much flying. But out of view of the old woman's yurt, I began to feel my feet. They had left me, but now were firm and solid.

"What do you remember, Akmaral?" my mother asked as we rode slowly back. When I told her, she nodded to my father. "I will make you the flying deer."

Some weeks elapsed before a caravan stirred the traders' road. We trotted close, our warriors lowering their weapons so they would know we posed no threat. We offered thick felted mats, raw wool, and cheeses in exchange for unworked ore. In the days that followed, my mother carved a beeswax mold, her nimble fingers paring a graceful shape before casting it in clay. Finally, she set it in the fire to burn away the dross, then poured the metal. When the mold was broken, she withdrew the perfect figure of a deer with tiny, delicate antlers—threads made strong by the wisdom of a thousand generations.

My mother strung the little deer on a leather strand and hung it around my neck. I felt its heat. It was a long time cooling, and the fire left a little scar that I still treasure.

2

HORSES

Of course, I did not start a warrior. I was a girl with long braids running down my back, just like these guileless girls I see on this highland pasture. Here they settle with their families in dome-shaped yurts and are sent to the mountain stream to bring back water. They are sturdy, often laughing, with a rosy flush about their cheeks. When I was young, I recall the skin was chapped and sometimes hurt from the constant, callous touch of the wind.

As a girl I rode horses, as all our people do. As soon as we can speak, we are set atop wool blankets on wooden saddles and taught to grip with all the strength in our calves and thighs. There we wobble from side to side until we fall from the horses' backs into our parents' waiting arms. I remember my mother catching me, warm and lusty as she hugged me to her breast, stroking my ruddy cheek, briskly clutching a thick hank of my sun-washed hair.

"What color is it today, Akmaral? Copper or bronze or almost golden?" she marveled as she plaited it into a smooth, taut braid, catching up the wind-scattered wisps and tucking them behind my ears. "Now you can ride and it won't distract you." She stroked the sleek, long tress which shimmered with a touch of embers. She said it was because of the fire she raised to form her craft: my mother knew the ways of shaping melted gold. She had learned them from my father who had been a captive—a villager, they say, but kept alive because he was useful. He knew the art of smithing. He worked in bronze, she mostly in gold. Each served our people, smelting ores and casting them into tools, armor, finery, and weapons.

When our people raid, we rarely take captives—better to be burdened only with what we need, to travel light and swift as the flash and thunder of the warrior god Targitai. In a nomads' camp, we rarely rest unharried, our aul always moving from place to place, following the good grass with every season, always on alert even as our herds graze, ever ready with our arms. On the steppes, there is no horizon without its dangers. Any advantage we can muster to keep our people safe, we take. So we kept the village smith alive.

My father made swords and daggers, arrowheads, fine-etched drinking bowls, and horse's tack—all beautiful as well as useful. But finest of all were my mother's warriors' plaques: medallions shaped as golden eagles, wolves, and leopards bearing twisted, straining prey. These were the ancient symbols of our clan, given to our warriors in honor of great deeds. In my dim memory, I hear them laughing or talking quietly while they work beside the sparking pit dug beneath our hearth—such comforting sounds as they melted chunks of ores into reddish and golden fire.

I remember, too, that dawn—little different from any other, with its first softening of crickets' song and then the swelling breeze as the sun caressed the horizon's breast. We lay, all three together in the darkness, my eyes cracked open but unfocused, gazing at the smoke-edged rafters rising to the open roof's eye. That is what our people call the smoke-hole, for through it our ancestors look down from the heaven pasture and keep watch on us and all our earthly dealings. From its circular rim, the sloping wood beams reach like a camel's spreading lashes down to sturdy lattice walls wrapped around with felt. I recall that my mother's yurt felts were soft white and, on that morning, slightly raised above the grass to let in the late spring breeze.

I felt, more than heard, the oncoming riders—the earth rumbling beneath us and a pallid smell of dust. They startled me alert and, when I breathed in, made me cough. So I nudged my mother's shoulder. "Mama, horses." She murmured, then softly brushed me off. Next I tried to stir my father. "Horses,"

I whispered. He only squinted at me vaguely. I said it again, this time with more force. "Horses." He opened up his eyes.

My father looked frightened then—I remember that. Since he had been a villager, he lacked the proper skill to defend himself; though my mother had more than skill enough, having served Targitai in the warriors' yurt, as all our people must, before she was allowed to become an ana-woman and bear a child.

When I shut my eyes, still I can hear the strangers' horse hooves skittering and scraping just outside our yurt. The dust they churned rose into chalky, golden clouds. Then came garbled voices, and their leathery shadows blocking the early sun as they tore away our woolen door-flap and stormed into our yurt, tossing back rugs and bedclothes and scattering our embers in search of food or weapons or perhaps my parents' hidden ores.

We would never know why they came, only that they did not find what they sought. The battle raged beyond our yurt as loudly as inside. Soon there rose the scent of burning blanket wool and choking, thick black smoke. They smashed our earthen cauldron—I heard the crack, then felt the sting of boiling mare's milk splashing against my skin. The liquid seeped into the porous soil, mixing to hot mud that slipped between our packing sacks and trunks where my mother had shoved me. "A warrior does not cry out," she'd said. "No matter what, Akmaral, stay hidden."

So I tried. Deep among our bundles, beneath our yurt's low sleeping cot, I held my breath and listened to the clank of my mother's dagger and then her sword. I had never seen her fight before, but now I saw her skill. Again, again came the fierceness of her battle cries, then the strangers' stabbing groans, and then their falls. So I began to hope, but in the end, there were too many. One and then another charged until she could not escape. After a time, each of her weapons clattered down, and then I didn't listen anymore.

My hands pressed against my ears so hard, I could hear the rhythm of my own heart beating as loudly as any thunder Targitai could raise. There was blood pooled on the yurt's grass floor. I remember the smell of it, and when I opened my eyes at last, the color: dark crimson mixing to pink where the cream milk pooled. At its edge were Meiramgul's soft felt boots, beaded and trimmed with fox fur. "Death is the risk of life," she said. "You must learn to accept it." Her words cut like a horsewhip, but her hands on my back were gentle as she raised me up. She said nothing of the thick tears streaming down my cheeks while the Ak Kam tended to my arms and legs—no wounds, but sodden with gore, slightly scorched, and shaking.

My parents were buried in a kurgan mound—only two of half a dozen lost in that dawn raid. It was the first burial that I remember—and how we dug the narrow pits, clearing away hard stones beneath the grass-bound hillock to expose the yellow earth at the center of the open plain. Our people build our houses for the dead to echo the caves that the gods tuck high among the mountains. It is said these cliff-bound hollows reveal one passage to the nether realm, while these kurgans, set deep into the earth, offer another.

I stared into the pit we'd made, searching for a path, but there was none; though I knew too well that the flying deer could only guide the dead. And I was still alive, clutching my amulet as the wind swept across the steppe, my bare hands raw as they warmed the small, cold metal. My eyes shut tight, but still the steppe's dust struck my tears, churning till they turned to yellow mud. With my forearm I wiped them off and continued digging.

"*Alel bam, alal bam.* We are one fire. We are one hearth," the Ak Kam chanted as sacrifice was made—fine horses given to each of the dead to ride to the heaven pasture and, for my parents, the many tools they'd used to shape new blades. Their deaths, she claimed, were an especially hard loss, for no others of our aul knew how to use them. But I did not care for tools as I knelt and touched my mother's and then my father's hands—

their fine calluses made smooth with wax and honey the Ak Kam had smeared, their bodies emptied, stuffed with herbs, readying them to make their journey.

My tears welled up, but I fought them back, my fingers stroking their skin already caked with a thin cast of dust, all of me longing only for my mother's voice: "A warrior," she would whisper, calm, "is not afraid." Though this I could no longer believe, for fear had settled in my own heart's beating; instead, I clung to something else my mother had sometimes told: "A warrior is not alone, Akmaral. She is accompanied always by those who have gone before her."

Finally Meiramgul's gentle fingers drew me off. The niches were covered up and the stones replaced. When the aul rode away before the fall of dusk, few signs that my parents had ever lived remained.

Meiramgul was Hewana, the keeper of our fire and the wisdom of its tales. I had known her all my life. Still I was afraid. Already seven children slept within her yurt's dark heart—most, like me, not born of her womb. They paid me little mind as I stepped beyond the wool-flap door and set down my few things—a cast-off tunic, a pair of well-worn riding trousers, a blanket stained with useless tears, and the goddess Umai's gifts: a tiny bow and sheath of arrows made by my mother's hand. When I clutched them now, wrapped in their bit of charry felt, I could recall only that cursed dawn—how my mother had pressed them into my arms, saying that they would protect me.

Now I knelt and the Hewana's eyes followed, shining beneath her heavy shadowed brows like the heated stones surrounding Rada Mai's hearth-fire. She offered me a bowl of koumiss and watched me, silent, as I gave sacrifice to the hearth before I sipped. "Your mother taught you well." She nodded her approval and leaned in close to take my chin. Meiramgul's teeth shone yellow, a gentle smile rising as she wiped horse milk from my lip. "Do not be afraid"—her whisper echoing my mother's words.

She reached her arm around me and led me toward another girl standing by the wall. "Lay your head down and try to rest. Marjan will stay close and keep you company."

Marjan took my hand and helped me find a place on the thick felt mat. Her face was like the shining moon rising from the dark. "Do not be afraid," she whispered, then tucked me to her chest—"We are one fire. We are one hearth"—and stroked my hair. Her arms were warm and her words were tender—the very same that the Ak Kam chanted, but in her child's voice, light and hush against my ear. For the first time since my parents had been buried, I believed them.

3

The Wild Boar

"One woeful dawn, the world was ravaged by Chaos. Sky pressed into Earth and Earth was split in two. The air became a whirling mass. Storms, black sands, ashes mixed with clouds that tumbled, shifted. The world was seized by thunder. Lightning slashed its silver sword. Hailstones pelted from the sky like arrows. Mountains moved and glaciers boiled. Rivers brimmed beyond their banks. Fires blazed from the forests across the steppes. And in the sky, Moon, Stars, and Sun all lost their tracks. All that had been living began to perish."

The Hewana sat in the shadows of the elders' yurt, her eyes unblinking with the hearth-fire's sparks. Her mouth pulled firmly downward as she shifted on her cushion set against the western curve, the place of highest honor.

"Three seasons, Chaos reigned. Three summers and three winters, Rada Mai suffered. All was misery, grief, confusion, until finally she could stand no more. In a trembling voice, Rada Mai cried out, 'Targitai, go—make war on Chaos!'"

The Hewana's bulk began to sway with the anguish of her words, arms folded tight across her chest, cragged fingertips gripping deep into her shadowed sleeves.

"At her command, Targitai bowed, forever her consort and protector. Faithful to his duty, Targitai set his long spear firmly beside his neck. He went into the world and set sharp eyes upon the raging heavens. Far across the swelling steppe, he ascended high into the icy mountains. There at last he saw his target's course. He set strong legs into a throwing stance and aimed. With one enormous thrust, Targitai plunged his spear-tip deep into the heart of the spinning, devastated sky. Then Chaos stopped. Everything found its place and the world slipped slowly back into its proper order."

The Hewana inhaled deeply and we all did the same. Many times we had heard this tale before. But now we were no longer children listening without thought. Now, we were truly warriors.

Marjan had been the first to be sworn to Targitai's purpose and spent her days in practice and at the hunt. I watched as her fighting grew more fearsome, the wind of her riding rushing past me as a summer storm. Then came the frigid season when ice froze long and hard after dripping down the roofs of our winter huts. We children went out, as we always did, to break them off and use them as throwing spears. That season I hit my mark so well that someone ran to find the war-master Bayir.

Now he sat before us at the Hewana's shoulder while she spread her fingers wide and raised them, shaking slightly through Rada Mai's hearth smoke. "To this day, Targitai's spear still anchors the reeling heavens." She pointed beyond the roof's eye toward the distant stream of stars. "There you see its shaft, steady at the center of the sky, and all the spheres of life and death, of earth and the nether realm, ride dutifully around its axis. Targitai's spear has never lost its grip, though at times the sky does shake and the Earth and all the heavens rattle. At such moments, Targitai's warriors raise their swords and bows again. As Targitai's strength protects Rada Mai's hearth, just so our warriors protect this aul."

The Hewana's breath cast a ripple of brighter light across the coals. As the fragile sparks dispersed, the Ak Kam began to hum. On her wide, flat drum, she pounded and slowly raised the sound of thunder. Then came the shush of rain as she pinched ochre dust from a seashell packed and dangling from her belt. She stood and dropped it onto the instrument's taut skin, tipping it from side to side as she walked around our circle to spread the sacred dust upon our shoulders.

So we left the Hewana's yurt and made our way across frost-nipped grass, slightly tripping from lack of sleep, silent but quivering with expectation. It was not yet dawn and our movement stirred the shallow fog that hung like clumps of un-combed fleece above the tranquil pasture.

From somewhere at my back, I heard soft footsteps and then Marjan. "Akmaral!" She raced up close and took both my arms. "You will join the hunt!" She whirled me gently. Her face shone bright as a late dawn star. "And we will be together, sleep sisters again, as we were before in the Hewana's yurt. It is all arranged—I have asked Bayir—sharing mats and warmth by Targitai's hearth. Now look at you, no longer a child!"

Together we joined the other riders, the youngest, like me, newly fitted with battle gear: hard tunics of boiled leather, soft felt boots, and riding trousers thicker and more sturdy than before. But ours were plain and dull compared with Marjan's. Her vest was covered with glittering, small gold plaques—rewards for her keen hunter's eye, though she had not yet been called to battle.

We made our way past the farthest of Targitai's yurts where the better-tested warriors would stay behind to guard the aul. Now they hung about the door-flap: young men and women murmuring, pointing, sometimes laughing among themselves, occasionally hooting, "Battle virgins!" and other unkind slurs. I cringed as we passed, trying to ignore them as I knew Bayir expected us to do. But Marjan kept beside me, her footsteps steady. "They were once like us." Her lip curled wryly, though her eyes never left them, meeting their taunts with a steady gaze.

We marched until we reached a wooden corral set in the hollow of an open field. There Bayir called us to prepare our horses.

"You will search among the foothills for antelope and boar. Be stealthy at the hunt to be steady and certain in battle." Bayir stood, tall and sturdy, wizened but not yet bent, our master and our general, though this was not a time for war. "Boars prefer rough scrub to open grassland. They are vicious when attacked, swift runners with tearing teeth and curving, pointed tusks. Their scent is keener than their sight. Take close notice of the wind."

I listened, concentrating, feeling Marjan pressed close beside me and my horse's muzzle tucked about my neck, half conscious of her steaming breath as the chilly breezes nipped my skin. This hunt would be my first, now that the wind bore the first sweet scents of spring; the goddess Argimpasa had just opened up her long, thick sleeves to release her many birds. They were returning to the north: brightly colored ducks soaring overhead, broad-winged geese and swans filling the shallow lake with wild squawks and ruffling.

At Bayir's signal, we turned to saddle up our mounts. He led us first over low, gnawed grass, then upward toward some shallow hills. My heart beat a steady rhythm in echo of my horse's trot. We all knew this would be no frivolous hunt. After so many months of winter, our food stores were diminished— little left of meat or cheese, and only a few fresh bitter weeds that we had dug out of the thawing soil. As we departed, the ana-women gathered to see us off, their faces anxious as they bobbled hungry infants on their hips. Just beyond them, the Ak Kam made her offering, flicking a few precious droplets of fresh mare's milk across the grass. "Ancestors, guide them. Rada Mai, watch over them. Targitai, give them bravery and strength. May the flying deer lead them far from death on their path to wisdom."

The Ak Kam's words pressed heavy on my heart, but once we left the sounds of the aul behind, their portent faded. Truly, that day we were only children. We rode off as all young ones do—enthusiastic and naïve. I was just ten winters old. This would be my initiation.

Through that day's bright hours our small band traveled, but we found few signs of prey—only once a herd of antelope so far off that even a hasty arrow-shot did not disturb them. We rode closer, following Bayir's wordless gestures, but the herd sauntered unperturbed, almost as if they knew that we would never come in range.

At dusk we set our camp on a low grass hill. There Bayir had us gather stones. We piled them high. Then around them he kindled fire and chanted in his raspy voice, "Rada Mai, great goddess who keeps us warm, and your sister who is mistress of these grasslands: be generous. Free some small measure of your countless herds so that our aul may eat, so that our people may survive." Solemnly he drained a thin trickle of new milk drawn from one of our young riders' suckling mares. There was little enough when he was done for each of us to sip as we gnawed dried meat, the very last of all the aul had hoarded through the winter.

That night I shared first watch with several others scattered across that shallow hill. The sky faded from dusk to dark as I listened to those who'd been allowed to rest—Marjan just beyond my touch, and her friend Aigul beside her—their murmurs slipping into silence and a steady, rhythmic breathing. I took comfort in their closeness like a shield against the dark. Beyond, at the very edge of the undulating, infinite expanse, I could just make out the distant handful of our yurts. They lay like a pale scattering of tsaagan bones—sheep's anklebones the Ak Kam used for prophecy—just six extended families joined together against the swelling, windswept gloom. Vulnerable and exposed. Now and then their fires flicked through their open smoke-holes, feeble sparks mirroring the countless stars where our ancestors cooked their meat upon the heaven pasture.

With first light we carried onward, now riding together just as Bayir had advised—Marjan on point, me at the rear, and Aigul center, keeping eyes in all directions. For two days more we rode that way, anxious, hungry as we stalked and camped, shooting only a few marmots and two rabbits, and Marjan once a fox. She had a keener eye than all the rest, sighting beasts from far away or at just a spear thrust's distance. Where there seemed to me only a stretch of empty grass, Marjan pointed until finally I noticed the twitch of stalks that moved against the wind. Even then, most often I was too late. Marjan had aimed and shot before I'd even drawn my weapon.

I despaired at each missed chance, but Marjan would not

let me lose heart, speaking softly as we rode, pointing out what clues she saw amidst the grasses.

Then, near dusk of our hunt's third day, we came upon a spiny thicket. Dizzy with hunger and exhausted from the sun, neither Aigul nor I could comprehend when Bayir pointed toward some low-grown scrub. There, crushed, matted grasses and signs of rooting, broken branches and, in one spot, piled pig's dung. We followed forward, now silent and alert, guided by Bayir's subtle waves and glances. His face flashed sternly as one of our horses whinnied. Then, cunning as a dog, he sniffed the air and signaled us to spread into an array.

Our horses' hoof-falls merged with the wind's rustling. We circled wider, Aigul taking up the lead. Then we came upon a still damp wallow and, all at once, heard the shrill of little pigs.

I pulled up sharply.

"Akmaral, calm," Marjan whispered. "Aigul, go fetch Bayir." She tossed a glance across the thicket while we gaped, dumb with fright. "Aigul, quick!" Marjan prodded with her horsewhip, then drew an arrow from her quiver. Aigul's face washed pale, but she coaxed her pony back the way we'd come.

Beside me, Marjan had already nocked her arrow. She wagged her chin for me to follow, nudging her horse with a gentle press of calves and heels.

My heart fluttered in my chest. "We cannot take this beast alone."

"We are not alone." She smiled. "Akmaral, we have each other." But her brows pinched slightly, so I knew she was afraid. Somehow, from Marjan's fear, I took stock of my own strength. I nocked my arrow, too, and prodded my mare forward.

The copse was still. The sow was somewhere close, but we could only hear her piglets snuffling faintly in the brush. We drew our horses wider, shadowing each other's movements around the thicket's densest clumps. I searched as Marjan had taught me, looking for an unexpected rustle, sniffing for a pungent scent. But the wind had shifted and I hadn't sensed it;

Marjan gestured from the far side of the copse, but I didn't understand. Then a sound—I thought it was Bayir's shrill, the noise he made when he signaled from afar, that he'd tried to teach us all to copy. The sound came again. I turned—"Bayir?"—my voice barely above a whisper.

Suddenly the huge sow charged.

Her tusks were curved, pointed, sharper than Bayir had described, longer than I'd ever realized—like the slashing sickles farmers used against us when we attacked their settlements. Never before or since have I seen a sow's tusks grow so large. She aimed them toward my horse's fetlocks. I tugged at my arrow, already nocked into my bow. Its springy, curving tips pinched sharply back, like an eagle's wings before a dive. But my aim was shaky, my fingers fumbling, my breathing short and gasping, still untrained.

Death comes riding when a warrior falters, Bayir had warned often, though I did not fully learn it until then.

She was a suckling sow defending her little pigs, taken by surprise in her nest, not snuffling alone among the roots as we'd expected. A mother's rage. I shot, but my arrow veered. The sow struck hard at my mare's shanks. She rose up in anguish and sent me hurtling backward.

With nothing to hold my feet or strap them down, my legs sprang from my wooden saddle. I clung with all my strength to my dangling reins, but still I couldn't keep my seat. Suddenly I was falling. Head tucked, I released my grip and landed, dazed, rolling off my shoulders, scrambling low and crouching in the muck as the raging boar tore across the trampled grass.

"Akmaral!" Marjan shouted.

The sow had turned her path and prepared to strike again. Her eyes were beady, black, too small for me to read their full intent. My mare reared wildly above me, dark horse blood spattering the earth and my riding trousers. My bow dangled where it had been flung onto a nearby branch and all my arrows lay scattered among a knot of thorns. As quickly as I could, I rolled and reached for the dagger on my belt—my father's short blade, barely a hand-span's length, but sharp enough because I'd whetted it that morning—

The blade. I felt about, but it was gone.

There were voices, shouting, though I could barely hear them. My heart rattled in my ears like rough-struck drums. All the other sounds around me grew mute as fresh snowfall. I listened to that silence and found it calmed.

A charging boar has a strange, clipped tempo, not the rhythm of a cantering horse or the loping gait of a well-laid camel. It is an awkward beast, yet surprisingly fast when it runs. Its snout looms first with its ripping tusks agape—not white but a dingy yellow, splayed as they open broadly.

The furious boar gored hard. I tried to spin out of its reach, but its tusk pierced sharp into my calf. The shock of it, as the sow began to raise me up, shaking me by my leg like a broken twig tangled in its jaw.

There was no time for fear or pain. With all the power that was in my waist, I wrenched around and clamped hard fists onto the sow's stiff ears. I clung with all my might as it tried to fling me off. My own red flesh hung from the boar's long tusk, scarlet flowing, the strange spike poking through my leg like a knife through uncooked meat. Then from somewhere, an arrow's thud—it flew and barely missed my forearm. A short breath more and I heard the pluck of Marjan's bow—so far away, yet her strike pierced the wild boar's chest. I clung even as it mewled, kicked, and finally sprawled.

The earth came hard and the tusk tore deeper—the boar still gasping, her small eyes pleading. My leg hung high, the other trapped beneath the great sow's hairy ribs. Finally we both lay still. Marjan ran to me, then Aigul, and then Bayir. He knelt, stroked my cheek and the belly of the sullied beast. Shaking his head, he lifted up my calf with his hard hands to try to free me.

When I could stand, I could only hop. Marjan helped me stumble to where my mare lay bleeding. Her tendons were gashed beyond repair, her strong, broad neck twisted round and her great black eyes, hot pools of pain.

I longed to reach to her, to comfort her, but I held back. I bit my lip, knowing well my obligation.

Marjan caught my wrist. "Are you strong enough?"

I nodded, gesturing for my horse's pack which was flung amid the bramble. She ran and brought it quickly while I balanced on one leg; then, using its shaft as a crutch, I withdrew my spear. Without a word, Marjan let me brace against her. I raised the shaft, finding steadiness and a moment's calm. Then I thrust its point deep into my fine mare's heart.

"Now both are sacrificed," she murmured. "The aul will eat well tonight."

I nodded and we stood silent watching the thick red mare's blood surge, then trickle, then finally still.

With Marjan's arms wrapped around my chest, she helped me to the ground and eased my back against my horse's bloody saddle. Then she propped my leg up with a clutch of moss and some leafy branches. All the while Bayir had stood nearby, watching. Now he stooped to wrap my leg, my wound searing, throbbing, where before I'd barely felt my injury. I breathed hard against the pain, staring up through the thicket's lacy bramble. The cold, stark sky bore the brittle brightness of breaking winter. A few thin clouds drifted like horse's breath and then dispersed into the bleak orb of the thawing sun. Marjan knelt beside me. Her arms reached around my waist and mine snaked onto her shoulders. Marjan's cloak was wool, scratchy against my cheek, soaking up my tears.

Four full-grown men were called to move the carcasses to the aul for butchering. But in the end, it was still too much, so several ana-women came and hacked both beasts to pieces in the field. We ushered the meat home with me clinging to Marjan's waist, riding behind her on her spotted gelding, my left leg wrapped tightly in felts torn from my horse's saddle shawl. We followed two slow camels, one carrying the boar's meat, the other the mare's, both caked in purple streams that congealed across their shaggy humps. Meanwhile, Bayir and some others

stayed behind to gather up my lost weapons, and Aigul collected the little piglet orphans.

The piglets became our charges, growing fat with the spring's
slow heat until the season when our cousin auls converged for
Umai's games and feasting. But pigs cannot be herded, so they
were sacrificed one by one. Their meat smelled sweet as they
boiled in the ana-women's cauldrons, and sweeter still as they
burned in the hard sparks of Rada Mai's coals.

In the warriors' yurt, the Ak Kam tended to my calf with
pure white smoke and the mother boar's blood mixed with
moss and fermented milk to make a poultice. It was many
weeks before I could walk again, but Targitai's warriors all were
grateful that, even injured, I could still ride and draw a bow.

They mentioned nothing, but I knew that I had failed
them—not just Bayir, Marjan, or the others on the hunt, but
the gods and the ancestors themselves. The flying deer had led
me near to death. It had tested me and I had faltered. My gold
charm's antlers stabbed bitterly against my chest. I would not
hunt again until the steppes had blossomed.

4

The Choosing

"Your mare was too jittery." Bayir carried me across the wide-stretched fields on his stallion's back. I clung about his waist, his riding steady even as we cantered. "She was a child's horse, too easily unnerved, useful at the hunt but much too timid for battle. You would have outgrown her soon enough, Akmaral. Felling her was Targitai's way."

I nodded into his shoulder, hoping that what he said was true as we swept across the pasture toward our grazing herds. We passed where camels wandered, raggedy and humped; and our goats with wispy chins and swooping horns gnawing on the jagged grasses; and then our sheep that milled about like soft, dark boulders or matted clouds. Finally, our horses—their backs glossy and powerful in the sun. These were our greatest wealth, more valuable than gold. Without a mount, I was no warrior.

Yet I wore the sow's tusk tied tight upon my belt—a gift from Marjan, strung upon a thong. "You survived the boar's attack," she had said. "That took nimbleness and courage. Place this tusk round your next horse's crest and bear it proudly."

Her words were little comfort as we reached the pasture's rise where Meiramgul met us on her thick-boned roan. She trotted closer and beckoned us to follow to the broad corral where half a dozen horses stood restrained. "Here," she murmured as we drew up close. "These are more proper for a warrior."

I stared, wide-eyed, knowing better than to speak. These were far beyond my deserving: fine chargers, sleek and sturdy, two hands taller than the pony I had lost, their coats in measured shades of chestnut, dun, and bay.

From across the steppe, Daniar rode to join us. He was Mei-ramgul's mate and the breeder of our herds. "How does our young boar wrestler?" he taunted. "Still limping?" He reached across Bayir's horse's croup to muss my hair. Now he handed me an *urga* pole, a long bowing shaft strung with a heavy leather cord. "Akmaral, choose any one you want, but choose it wisely."

I took the sweat-smoothed handle. The leather loop dangled above me like a noose. Bayir helped me from his saddle—my calf still weak from my injury. But I knew this was also part of why they all had come: to see if I was strong enough to return to Targitai's duty.

Just then I noticed another warrior approach. Alone, on foot: Erzhan, a hunter and a fighter, some three winters older than I. I knew him well enough. Erzhan was among our bravest riders, strong and keen-eyed, quick with both his hands, daring on his mount. But he was arrogant, even cruel, especially with the young recruits. Since the boar hunt and my wound, more than once I'd felt his scowl like a sharpened barb.

"Why is Erzhan here? He has a fine gray gelding."

"Erzhan's mount was injured on patrol. Sliding down some scree, it split its forelimb. Already it has been slaughtered."

I stared as Erzhan approached, my face impassive—not a glare, for the elders stood close by and everything I did or said would be judged, but a stony glance which Erzhan echoed. We are taught that our enemies all dwell beyond Targitai's hearth but that, within the aul, fidelity is sacred. Still, Erzhan was an enemy; I felt it in his gaze. But I did not reflect it back. Instead, I let his rancor flash like sunlight on the springtime lake, casting sparks but lighting no fire.

When Erzhan sauntered close enough, Daniar tossed him another urga pole. Then he trotted to the pen's far gate and slid back its heavy sinew cord to let us in. "Pick any one that pleases you," he called, then cracked his whip. The horses raced away as if they'd suddenly been made wild.

We both knew the task, as we'd seen other warriors do before. This rite was meant for us to work as one. But as we drew in close, I sensed that Erzhan had little mind to help me.

I stumbled from the horses' rush, their hooves thudding like the pounding of the earth's own heart. Erzhan raced ahead while I kept out of their path, studying them, not knowing yet which to choose or even how to catch one. My leg no longer bled or throbbed, but it was stiff and difficult to lean on. Still, I could walk and sometimes skip as I moved closer into their cloud of dust. Blinking, I raised my hand to shield my eyes.

Each mare and stallion had its own swift gait: some long and low, leaning heavily ahead, others plodding or upright, prancing or sultry as they raced, almost flirting with the wind. Erzhan did not seem to notice as he darted and lunged. But he was bold and much more graceful than I, even without my limp. He waved the urga pole as sinuously as a whip while I could barely manage to steady mine.

One by one the horses galloped past, ringing us around as if this were a game. Two were by far the finest: a mare—lithe, chestnut brown with a golden shimmer, and a stallion of milky white with a stiff fawn mane and a tenacious stare. The mare caught my eye at once with her playful gait and clear intelligence. But Erzhan raised his urga just as he saw me lift mine. Glaring, he dashed into the mare's path so fast that our poles clacked, the leather leads entangling.

Erzhan jerked away and scuttled toward the mare with a heavy, angry stride. I couldn't match it and stood watching as he almost seized her. But then the female raised her limbs, reared back, twisted in midair and raced away. Her move was startling, purposeful as she shifted, darting left and right, almost teasing as she trotted out of reach. From a distance she seemed to appraise me, calm as if she knew I couldn't run. I shook my head and sniffed, set my urga for support into the ground. The mare tossed her mane and pranced in satisfaction.

Now the stallion came, racing hard and snorting. I raised my urga pole almost in defense as it reared up, its forelimbs towering, scraping the heavy air, sifting dust and clots of mud onto my shoulders. Erzhan left his chase and veered toward us instead. He reached up hard and brought the stallion down with a ferocious jerk. The stallion bucked, whinnied, caught by surprise and filled with fury—so vicious, so wild that I barely felt my feet as I moved back. They struggled for a time, both blowing, kicking, grunting, until finally there were only snorts and livid headshakes, but no longer struggles.

I caught my breath enough to speak. "Erzhan, a stallion suits you."

But he tossed me an uncivil glance that said my fair wishes meant little enough to him.

Just then, the mare came trotting. She paused just out of reach, pranced a little, then almost bowed. I crept up, breathed in deeply, and murmured as I raised my urga pole. She let me tuck my dangling loop over her muzzle.

"Well done!" Meiramgul burst with laughter and clapped her hands three times. "As it should be—each horse chooses its own master. Treat them well, both of you. The rest of our aul's fortune you must earn."

I bowed before the elders, humbled and grateful beside my prize.

But Erzhan only clutched his stallion and glared beyond me.

5

KESH-KUMAY

The steppes are not a lonely place. They are vast, filled with spirits that linger and nourish. They take the form of eagles and antelope, hill pigeons that flock, black choughs that inhabit the winds. Foxes roam the flatlands and rabbits tuck into the narrow places. They tickle alive the broad, verdant grasses and the shallow, fragrant valleys. If you watch closely, and listen, you will learn from them.

Still, it is not a human place. If ready companionship is what you seek, you must go to the settled villages. These dapple the shores of rivers, the sheltered sides of hills, the confluences of roads made by hoof-prints of goats and sheep, horses and camels. Our people sometimes visited these villages, for they had fine things to trade. We showed them rolls of felt or crafted rugs or dried meat or cheese, and they gave us glistening beads of stone or glass formed in places we had never heard of, or bolts of nubbly silk or wrought-gold plaques like those my dead mother once knew how to cast. Or tools or blades of bronze and sometimes even iron, like my father's.

Sometimes we stood at a distance watching the strangers who roamed the endless byways: impatient merchants coaxing their caravans—small dots like a trail of ants traipsing to each horizon. They were vulnerable and anxious for a place, forever heading somewhere, while we herders were at home wherever we stayed.

Still, we longed for company, with our kin scattered across the steppes like seeds blown from the tufts of autumn grasses. Our closest cousins might be many days' ride off, lost aunts married to another clan, grandchildren born or dead before an

elder had ever greeted them. That was why, when the moon was
bright in spring or autumn, we would leave our isolation and
wander until we'd chance upon another aul's path. Then we'd
travel to a riverbend and set our yurts together, and for several
days make great feasts with wrestling and games.

Such it was that spring, two full winters since I'd passed
into Targitai's service, when we joined into a crowd, exchang-
ing news, trading goods, and laughter. It was a time of peace
when our auls were well protected. None would dare disturb us
for our very size. It was also the goddess Umai's season, most
favorable for breeding. As our Ak Kam joined with priestesses
from the other auls leading chants and making sacrifice, Daniar
and the cousin herders set about to join our beasts. Just so, all
our multitudes mingled together like tiny rivulets absorbed into
a flowing stream.

There was excitement as the fields filled up with wrestlers
and riders—young braggarts standing high on horseback doing
tricks while others grappled one another to the ground, and
contests of *kesh-kumay* where girls raced off, heeling at their
horses' bellies, teasing while the young men chased them. For
some it was just a game, as we gathered in a round to taunt and
cheer. But for others, kesh-kumay was the dawn of courtship.

That season I was just a child, hovering at the edge of what I
could not understand. I had not encountered love or even true
desire and knew nothing of its hungers or its pains. But Marjan
had begun to sense—I saw it in her face as she headed toward
the riding fields. She sat tall upon her mount with Ruan close
beside her, their shoulders nearly touching, saddles bumping,
reins flicking at a steady pace, almost as if entwined. Ruan was
a fine, strong hunter, experienced at war. But Marjan was still a
battle virgin. Warriors of our aul cannot breed until they have
proved their fighting's worth, and a woman is set free of Targitai's oath only when she's borne a living child.

So when they played at kesh-kumay, it was in innocence—a
game. They rode joking, laughing, Marjan's face full flush with
mischief, and Ruan close enough to catch her waist, then slip-

ping back, purposefully missing as she veered. I darted on the
sidelines cheering until, across the field, I noticed Erzhan. His
eyes fierce, black, his thick arms crossed and judging.

"What business is it of yours?" I called, winding through the
throng to stand before him and block his discontent. But Erzhan only scowled—"She is no warrior"—and stormed away.

The feasting moon had begun to wane when a race was called
among the youngest warriors. It would be our final challenge
before the auls would split apart, and I was bound to use it well
to raise my stature.

"Marjan, hurry! We should be readying our horses." It was
early dawn and she lay groggy on our sleep mat. I nudged her,
but she swatted me away. "Marjan, you must get up." I shook
her more roughly. Even while awake these days, Marjan lingered as in a dream. Finally, she rose, fiddling with her hair. In
her hand was a small gold comb I had never seen.

"From Ruan?" Aigul teased as we gathered horse tack and
saddles. "Better leave it or lose it while you ride."

Marjan sighed and tucked the gift away, at last reaching for
our horse-whips from the yurt's high rafters.

Fog still hovered low above the grass as we ducked outside
to join the others moving toward the horse corral in a quiet
stream. Just ahead, we spotted Ruan, and Marjan sped her pace.

"Do you think that's wise?" Aigul held her back.

"I do as I like," she snapped, but still she stayed.

After a time, I tugged her gently. "Marjan, what's the matter?"

She bowed her head and wouldn't lift her gaze. Then she
turned and cupped my cheeks. "Akmaral, I'm sorry. You are
a good friend to me but much too young to understand." She
kissed between my brows, rubbing away their worried furrows,
but would say no more as we moved in awkward silence toward
the warriors gathering in the field.

When we arrived, already there stood a crowd—some forty
riders, all young and strong, struggling to control their mounts,

eager to prove their skill. Erzhan lingered among them and would have looked quite fine had he not been so smug, sitting on his horse, broad-shouldered, his high-boned cheeks rimmed by smooth, dark hair, his legs muscular and well bowed from years of riding. But his eyes were insolent, scanning the crowd as if for prey. It was not long before his gaze landed on me.

Since our clash with the urga poles, I'd become the aim of his malevolence. On the practice field, Erzhan often called me out, riding side by side, shouting or sometimes whipping my horse himself to drive me faster; or challenging me to draw with him at archery, daring me to beat his aim; or hurling heavy spears; or slashing fiercely with our swords; even at longer, louder battle cries. Now his gaze beat down like two sharp-thrown daggers, so I drew myself up tall, as if my body were a shield. This race would be my first among all the gathered auls. I would not have Erzhan's threats steal my chance away.

"May Targitai show you favor!" the Ak Kam chanted, wafting smoke and dusty powders over the crowd. Before their cloud had drifted, Bayir led us toward the course's start, all of us excited, chattering, laughing as we cantered beyond the many knitted rings of yurts and horses.

I kept a steady pace, resisting the urge to press my mare and waste her strength—as I knew Erzhan expected me to do. He had mocked me for it often—and my mount—inexperienced as we both were. I kept a horse-length's distance, my eyes ever on his back, feeling his ire pique as I finally inched up close and reached the place where the race would start just after him.

The spot was marked by a tall wood post tied with a white felt flag and six bronze bells. They clattered and flapped, incautious in the wind.

"No kicking or rearing," Bayir shouted as we gathered round. "Stay along the path. Don't urge your horse to butt or nip. No lashing your horsewhip against your rivals." As he spoke, he scanned our crowd, but his gaze seemed to linger a moment longer on Erzhan. Though surely Erzhan understood the rules. They were the opposite of when we practiced war.

Finally we all lined up—Marjan at my side, Aigul a breadth away, and Erzhan farther over, though precisely where I tried hard not to notice—all holding back our restless mounts until Bayir let out a short, sharp bark. When he dropped his upraised arm, we drove our horses forward.

Wild as a dust storm, Erzhan set off and passed us all. His horse was a blazing streak, scorching the grass like fire. I caught my breath, hugged my horse's mane, and clutched with both my knees. Striking my silver horsewhip again, again, I bit into my lip. Still I drove her harder. Marjan and Aigul hovered just beside, but their press was nothing—a friendly jaunt. It was Erzhan I longed to beat. Now I aimed to prove my worth, if only it meant that he would finally let me be.

Soon a break appeared in the frantic crowd, but another rider hurtled by on my left—a cousin from another aul. Erzhan was on my right, just half a length ahead. So I let the rider pass and watched as Erzhan laid down traps—cantering so his foe would break into a gallop, then charging harder to force the chase and exhaust his rival's gelding.

Now I understood his tactics. I pushed up closer. Erzhan was in the lead and the other rider just behind when I tucked into their wake, clearly pushing into third, passing Marjan and Aigul to their half-breathed cheers. Still I rode a little harder, but not as hard as my mare could run, coaxing her to keep her pace, squeezing low and tight against her bounding ribs.

Almost shoulder to shoulder—first with the cousin rider's mount, and finally nearly equal to Erzhan's stallion—I could feel my heart and my mare's match pace—

"Back!" Erzhan hissed at me.

I turned and saw his eyes were slits, narrow crevices cut against the rising dust. His skin glistened, dark with sweat, limbs taut, holding strongly around the saddle's cinch. I glared at him, then rallied, hugging my horse's barrel with all my strength, stinging lightly with my silver whip while Erzhan bristled. He clutched his stallion's mane, curling limbs to seize an even tighter seat, peering into the wind like a cruel-shot arrow.

I copied his stance, muttering, "I will not lose!" loud enough for Erzhan to hear.

Just then he charged out hard.

Reaching with his boot, he kicked with all his might into my mare's flank. We both staggered with the sudden shock, my mare bucking awkwardly as I worked to hold her down.

"Erzhan!" I shouted. He steadied at his bit, then turned to see me glare. With a smirk, he pulled back to kick again.

This time I was ready, but my mare was not. She rose—fetlocks dangling, stymied forelimbs flailing from Erzhan's blow. I fought to steady her, but we tumbled sideways into the other riders' path. Hooves flew above our heads as they jumped and swerved, splitting left and right to avoid collision. Then, with a sudden gush of blood, Erzhan and his stallion rolled, nearly crushing us in the dust, snorting and whinnying.

The cousin rider bolted—the leader now without rivals, growing smaller in the distance.

Erzhan rolled onto his knees, raised a fist and beat the earth.

"Why did you kick?" I gasped, struggling to free myself from my cockeyed saddle, but Erzhan had already turned cold fury and pressed his horse to stand. He ignored me as he mounted until I pointed to the gash across the stallion's thigh. "Erzhan, your horse is injured."

He answered nothing, did nothing to staunch the bleeding. He only turned hard eyes on the cousin rider's back and forced his horse to ride again.

My own mare stood startled, dusty but unharmed. As quickly as I could, I righted my seat, then charged off after him. "Erzhan, you'll never catch them!" But he kicked forward sharply and ignored me.

Still, with his stallion wounded, he couldn't keep his pace. So I set out, dodging and darting across his horse's trail—"What does it matter, Erzhan? In the end, we both have lost!"—my words, a certain truth, and yet they mocked him.

Erzhan whipped his stallion until its loins grew raw. I rode harder, calling, "Erzhan, stop! You'll kill him!"

Just so, our chase became a twisted game of kesh-kumay, this time for war, not love; though he would not let me catch him. And when at last we'd reached the race's end, the winners had already received their honors.

To the ranking riders: glittering plaques. Aigul had come in second and Marjan fourth. Aigul stood showing off her gold—a badge crafted as a goat seized by a leopard—and for Marjan, a snarling wolf attacking a writhing doe. Among the crowd I saw how Ruan beamed.

But the winner was the cousin rider. For him there was a living mare, four winters old, of sturdy stock that had already been bred. It was a handsome prize—one that every warrior envied. As Bayir gave the mare over to its champion, his gaze caught roughly on Erzhan. Cloaked in mud and dust, his stallion's leg and thigh crusted with blood, Erzhan cringed beneath the war-master's stern reproach. Then he kicked the muddy earth, tossed me a spiteful glance, and turned away.

6

THE STALLION

Every day we practiced fighting, learning how to ride while bearing bows and spears, our swordplay wild, shouts boisterous as we raced across the broad steppe grass; and the strumming of our bowstrings like ill-tuned music, our barbs plunking feverishly on the wind.

Above that twang and thump, we could hear Bayir's shouting: "If a horseman charges you, take aim at his saddle bow." He crouched beside the practice field, knees tucked tightly into his chest. His face was shriveled as a desiccated fruit, in places furrowed as the settled people carve their fields. "If your arrow swerves up high, it will hit the horseman's chest. Low, and it will pierce his belly." At his call, our warriors charged, our horses' hooves thundering against the distant hills. "Make your aim precise to counter your horse's movements!" Our onslaught reached its peak with bobbing spears and blunted arrows flying, but in the end Bayir only stood, shaking his head.

"Erzhan, come and show them!" More and more that season, Bayir called him out. To be true, Erzhan had long drawn Bayir's attentions. It was an awkward preference, like a herder troubling over an unruly camel. Most said Bayir's heed was reckless, with several other warriors just as strong and keen. But Bayir kept Erzhan closely in his sights, and only he and Meiramgul seemed to know the reason.

Now Erzhan trotted onto the practice ground, his tanned arms bare, though the sun was hardly warm. He cosseted his beast, then whipped its rump to pick up speed, charging toward the small felt rags that hung at a distance on a bobbing sinew thong. He drew and shot, striking every one, then turned, triumphant, to scan our crowd. I felt my courage pummeled like iron beneath a forger's blows. It had been last spring when he toppled me in Umai's horse race. And since that time, he had never stopped: every day needling me harder.

I lamented once to Meiramgul, but she only sighed and stroked my cheek. "Akmaral, some say Erzhan was born of wind. You can see it in his restlessness. Always brawling, bragging, begging for a fight—from you, today, but at any other time, he'd battle another. It doesn't matter who or why. He is an unbridled horse, rearing, bucking against the reins, circling to raise a whirlwind of dust as a feeble shield. But you"—she shook her head and fingered my deer amulet thoughtfully—"you, Akmaral, are the force he cannot break. You are the air."

I'd been bolstered by her words, but now they brought me small relief as Bayir met Erzhan's arrogance with an approving nod. Then he sent us out again to hone our aim—each of us riding in quick succession to try to match him.

By noon in the bright white sun, we practiced angling our arrows high, then releasing in arcade, shooting all as one so they formed a piercing cloud that descended from the blinding heavens. Too, we ran attacks, scattering wide to noose our foe, shooting from our farthest range, then cantering back to just beyond their arrows' reach.

"Avoid their archers! Gain the best defense!" Bayir called until his voice grew hoarse, conducting the play of massing and un-massing as we bounded forward, backward, twisting with our shots, our arrows flying even in retreat. Erzhan countered our attacks, battling as if he were our foe. Ours was a dance as wild and graceful as the swelling flight of a starling flock—and Erzhan, the offending falcon.

"It is one thing to kill for meat," Marjan murmured, "another to kill a man. Or a child."

"Who told you that?" Aigul rolled onto her belly in the bristling grass, watching as Marjan dressed the rabbit she'd shot out of the brush.

It was nearly evening after a long day's practice. We were stationed to the west, a horizon's distance from our camp. It was a novice's place. Raids came mostly with the dawn, when the aul was asleep; or if we were awake, they approached from the east, planning that the sun would blind us.

I peered up from my spear tip, my fingers on the sharp bronze point still slightly warm from whetting. "Why different, Marjan?"

"Ruan says in battle you know the other warriors are afraid, that they fight to protect their families and their aul."

"And what about a beast?" Aigul challenged. "When you shoot, don't you sense its fear? Don't beasts fight back and protect their young?"

"Yes," Marjan stirred, "of course—"

"Then why? Marjan, you don't think twice to shoot a marmot or an antelope. Why should you think again in battle?" Aigul scoffed, but only lightly, resting higher on her elbows as she tossed another berry from the bristle-scrub onto her tongue. "Don't listen to such nonsense. Ruan is kind, a decent fighter even, but he can also be a fool."

I watched the hurt rise in Marjan's eyes, glistening as she pressed her dagger into the rabbit flesh, slicing its skin away to reveal the pinkish muscle, then spreading the rabbit's pelt across some rigid stubs to dry. "This meat I cut—I know it is for food. But a warrior's carcass is left for carrion—its worth wasted on the battlefield."

Aigul rolled her eyes, then pressed another fistful of fruit between her lips.

"Must you always eat?" Marjan snapped.

But Aigul only laughed. "Eating is why we are alive. We fight to eat. We sweat to eat. We starve to eat. We kill to eat. Eating is life, and after that is only love, singing, and dancing!" Now she got up from the grass and began to prance about. "Who has brought a horsehead fiddle? Someone play for me!"

"Hush," I scolded. "You should be still and watching."

"Marjan is afraid to die—the great huntress! But don't you know only the fiddle's song will hold off death?"

"Aigul!" I warned. "You will draw raiders."

"Always so bleak, Akmaral." She grimaced and slapped her palm against her thigh.

"When they come, we will see who is afraid." I pressed down to the ground and set my ear against the soil. The sun already leaned toward the distant mountains.

She nudged me with her foot, as if to loosen up a stone. "Akmaral, you hear nothing."

But I held her off with an upraised palm, then rose, and grabbed my quiver. "One rider"—I took two arrows, plucked up my bow. Both of them gaped, then gazed off, suddenly alert, to where I pointed.

After a breath, Aigul turned and waved indifferently. "It's only Erzhan," she scoffed, wiping berry juice from her palms on some flattened grass.

"Erzhan? How can you—?" But then I saw—the posture of his horse and, through the dusty haze, the white coat of his stallion.

I shook my head, placed my bow back on the ground, and began to test my arrows, making sure their heads were steady on their shafts. But my hands were shaking. Marjan reached and calmed them with her own.

"Bayir probably only sent him here to scout the boundary." But her words were little help. My heart seized inside my chest, so tight that it choked off breath. I stared down at the grass, stiff with bits of earth showing out in clots and patches. From not far off drifted the muffled rumble of our herds: soft whinnies, snorts, and bleats. But otherwise the air was still except for the rising beat of Erzhan's horse's hooves.

Aigul tapped me on the shoulder. Already she'd raised her bow, nocked an arrow, and drawn it back. Marjan quickly did the same, her face imploring. Finally I rose. Erzhan approached us from the west so we squinted hard and could barely see him. Charging out of the late sun's rays, he screeched a savage cry and drew his sword. With a mighty slice, he cut the air.

"Wait a moment longer!" he mocked. "I could have killed all three of you before you'd even seen me."

"We saw you, Erzhan," I called out. "We just weren't much impressed with your fancy riding."

Erzhan sniffed at my reproach, then doubled back, gaining speed for another charge. The other two ran as Bayir had taught, sliding behind their horses' shoulders and taking aim around knees or hocks. But I stood my ground, not even raising my weapon. Finally Erzhan slowed and pulled to a rough halt. His stallion kicked up dust that drifted back, broad and bushy as a fox tail.

He nodded to Aigul, Marjan. "You two passed my test. But not you, Akmaral." He pointed with his sword.

"I will not fight you," I answered as calmly as I dared.

"I do not mean to fight." He curled his lip. "Only practice—only play! Are you afraid?"

"You are not Bayir. I do not take your orders."

Erzhan bristled, raised his eyebrows, then reached his sword slowly toward my waist. With its tip, he plucked my dagger from its sheath. It was far shorter than his weapon—barely longer than a grown man's hand—but my father had made it of trader's iron. It was heavy and very strong.

Erzhan dangled it by its gilded hilt, then flicked it roughly to the ground. "Show me you are ready to serve Targitai."

"I have always been, Erzhan. I'm just not afraid of you."

"That's a shame. You are brave, I've heard, when you are frightened."

I felt the blood surge up my neck, then rush into my cheeks and ears. Erzhan snickered at my rage, his eyes flicking toward where my dagger lay caked in a sheen of yellow dust.

"Fine." I stooped to pick it up and held it ready.

The other two stood, silent. Marjan's face was watchful and

slightly pinched. Erzhan slipped down from his horse, his legs well turned and stocky from gripping at the stallion's barrel, powerful for his sixteen winters.

We circled, bearing weapons cagily, daring not to hurry. "Closer. Akmaral, come! With a dagger, don't hold back or you'll never reach me." His strikes at first were barely taps against my blade. But in my mind, the blood rush fell away and a keenness filled me as it always had the moment I sensed a fight. Keenness and a cool attention.

With every tap, Erzhan grew more brazen, tickling with his sword, almost laughing—arrogant as I'd known he'd be. I pressed away my fury, waiting, watching, measuring his conceit. Soon he'd let down his guard and then I'd take my chance, though I knew no proper enemy would ever let such haughtiness expose him.

We fought. But even as I evaded him, a shadow crossed the far terrain. At the corner of my sight: small and slow, a cloud as soft as breath drifting like a late day mirage.

"Erzhan." I motioned only with my eyes. He laughed, but I pulled back. "There—look."

"So you are afraid!" He jabbed at me, but I leaped out of reach and pointed with my free hand.

"Three—no, seven riders."

Still he wouldn't turn his head. "Akmaral, I wouldn't think you'd stoop—"

"Raid," I murmured, and then again, "Raid," louder, strident enough that Marjan and Aigul started toward their horses.

"There is no raid. Aigul, Marjan, come back!"

But I shoved my dagger into its sheath, grabbed my bow from the dust and all my arrows. "Erzhan!"—I snapped, so emphatic that he turned. The cloud was rising, catching the angled flames of dusk. The riders wore the ruby haze as a cunning veil.

Now all of us flew onto our saddles. Erzhan lashed his horse as we rallied and galloped toward the herds. Together we charged them back and forward, startling sheep and goats and horses. We forced them to raise a twisting storm of dust that would signal our other warriors stationed to the north and south. Soon all the herders and warriors everywhere around were driving beasts into a churning frenzy—sheep and goats hard back, but the horses forward—horses especially to act in our defense, a barrier of powerful hooves to press the raiders back in fear of trampling.

From somewhere out of the rising whirl, Bayir charged, leading our most skilled captains, followed close by more warriors at full gallop—a shimmering front of hoof-scaled armor and short, drawn bows. They raced beyond us and fanned out broadly, their fearsome arrows arcing upward in attack. They gobbled up the distance, their horses' hooves like gnashing teeth. But soon there was no need: the great herd's tumult had warned the raiders off. When the four of us rounded that way again, they had already sunk back beyond the sunset-charred horizon.

That night, on Daniar's orders, we drove our herds closer to the aul. Bayir set a ring of armed patrols so deep and wide that none but ana-women and toddling infants remained to tend the dung coals. I was given an extra hour's rest since I had sounded the alarm. And Erzhan, who had made a fair report of what I'd done, now sat awkwardly beside me.

After the near attack, food tasted sweet—fresh curded cheese and a bit of mutton soaked in mare's milk. We ate in silence, both peering at the dark. Just beyond, the other warriors were already riding, their hoof-falls palpable, resounding through the earth like a hundred pounding hearts. Much more than the usual tremors of our nighttime watch, their pulse turned wilder and strong. Several ana-women and elder men had joined the warriors' ranks—anyone fit to keep their seat and still bear arms.

"You did well, Akmaral," Erzhan finally muttered.

I glanced at him sideways, still sucking on my meat.

"I shouldn't have doubted you."

"Or challenged me. Or threatened me."

"No." He lowered his head and picked uncomfortably at his food. "Never again."

I sniffed and looked away. If he saw me with new respect, I didn't want it. I sipped the milky broth until the bowl was drained.

Around us, the air was anxious, shivering with the sounds of crickets. From inside the Hewana's yurt, the Ak Kam's voice swelled and droned: "Rada Mai, Great-Grandmother, we call to you, sacred fire that keeps us warm—"

Erzhan set down his bowl and so did I. We rose and wandered closer. There came a sudden flash and a heavy whiff of strange-smelling smoke. The Ak Kam's chants grew steadily, drawing other footsteps through the dark—those ana-women who still remained, swaying in the shadows, bearing sleeping infants in their arms.

"Here is horsemeat of a fine white mare. Here, the horse's neck to give us vigor. Here, its stomach for our sustenance. Here, the horse's ribs—as they held the mare together, so may they bind our aul."

A smell rose up of burning meat. Muffled through the yurt's felts, we heard each chunk of flesh drop and sizzle on the coals.

Erzhan grunted, shook his head, and thrust his hand deep into a pouch dangling from his waist belt. He drew out a small fistful of tsaagan bones.

"Erzhan, this is not a game." In the warrior's yurt, we used sheep's anklebones for gambling.

"No," he whispered, "not for the Ak Kam." He rolled them with his thumb across his open palm. They made soft, scratching noises—a dozen, smooth and creamy, faintly shining in the starlight.

Inside the Ak Kam's voice rang out. "We are one fire; we are one hearth!" Her wide round drum began to quake like distant thunder. "Grandmother, I call to you. I call you, Great-Grandmother. I call to you, Great-Great-Grandmother—to all who dwell upon the heaven pasture." Sharp, she struck her drum three times and we barely breathed, waiting for the sound to fade. "Tsaagan mod!" Through the yurt's felts we heard the clatter-fall of bones.

Erzhan squeezed his own small clutch, then opened up his palm. Sticking slightly to his sweaty fingers, the bones dropped down one by one and scattered across the earth in a tumbled pattern.

"Can you read them?" I murmured.

Erzhan shook his head. "Can you?" His gaze turned strangely probing. He reached toward my mother's tiny antlered deer where it hung on its leather thong around my neck. "Some say there is vision in your blood. Is there, Akmaral? Can you see the future?"

I longed to swat his hand away, but there was something in his look—suddenly as fearful as it ever had been cruel. I'd never seen him so before, with a thin trail of sweat tracking along his cheek and his usually still palms quivering. I clutched the golden deer before he drew it from my chest, then stretched my hand above his tsaagan spread.

I searched for some sensation—as I'd never dared before, not since my parents' deaths or the Kara Kam's smoke-filled vision.

After a time, I let my hand drop down. "I sense nothing."

Erzhan sniffed. "What does it matter? We are warriors. We are already meant to die." He shook his head as he snatched the scattered bones away.

7

AMBUSH

I could not help but ponder Erzhan's words: *Some say there is vision in your blood.* I knew what he said was true—had sensed it since I was a child. But never had I heard it said aloud, with such clarity or dread. I could not understand his thoughts, but mine were haunted by a distant memory of a crystal night when the Kara Kam's strange black smoke had sent my spirit flying.

One midnight after some days on alert, the elders' door-flap drew apart and the Ak Kam stepped outside with upraised arms. "The tsaagan bones are scattered. We must travel with the dawn. Take the path to the higher mountains."

The ana-women murmured their assent, tiptoeing from the glow of the elders' fire to pack away their yurts. I sighed my own relief and patted my mare's neck as I settled on my mount, then moved to take my place among the encircling guard.

Always we rode in pairs. Especially in the darkness, no warrior wisely rides alone. So when another sentry joined the rhythm of my mare's hoof-falls, I simply settled on my mount and continued my patrol. Only then I saw that it was Erzhan. I flashed a glare, fearful of what he'd start. But we rode in silence, tracing our herds' milling shape toward its farthest bound. Only there, as we faced the windy, blackened plain, he murmured, "You have never seen real fight, Akmaral, but I have been through many." His coal-black eyes were swathed in a dusky veil. "The risk of life is death. Yet a warrior takes it, even when simply hunting wild prey. You have proved yourself at that, Akmaral. But when a wild boar gores you, it is only in defense. A man strikes always with intent to kill."

He had said so many times before, though usually more

harshly, always as a means to condescend. This time his tone was pensive, his face brooding.

"You think I am not bold enough for war?"

"No." He shook his head. "Not that. Not any longer."

We rode on for a time in awkward silence, peering beyond at the empty steppe, so dark and vast as if we traveled on the edge of nothing. Soon he began to tell of the pain of arrow wounds, of mud-runs slick with blood and the treacherous impediment of riding over corpses. It was the strangest departure, from adversary to confidant, as if I'd passed some test I hadn't known I'd taken. Though sometimes his mood would shift, his face raised to the glittering heavens and his voice so loud even our enemies would hear: "They ride like infants. You should see their ruddy back-sides! They tumble from their horses and can barely draw their bows. Their aim is laughable, always short or digging into dust. And their swords, Akmaral, they can barely manage them. Once one even dropped his weapon to use bare palms, as if they could deflect my slashes!"

"Erzhan, quiet!" I tried not to laugh. "You will draw them here like torchlight."

But Erzhan only snorted, then raised his heavy blade to flay the empty dark. As if that was exactly what he intended.

By morning, we'd both quieted with exhaustion. The sky broke low and clouded. Mist mixed with our breaths and muffled our horses' plods. Strangely we'd grown used to each other's presence, so that when the light shone bright enough, I found that I no longer cringed to see him there.

We headed toward the aul, our saddles and thighs nearly touching for want of warmth. But Erzhan turned his beast just before we reached the corral. "Be glad, Akmaral, that you have not yet seen the flow of human blood." He reached into his pouch and pressed a tsaagan bone into my hand.

In the half-dim light, the aul traveled toward the foothills, but the foreboding mist turned quickly to a heavy fog and then to driving rain. The downpour turned our path into a muddy torrent. The steppe-lands lent no shelter, so our people could not hide. We cowered beneath pounding hail while lightning tore broad cracks across the pallid sky. Our people tell that savage storms are Targitai's fury, so as his warriors hurtled arrows, only infants dared to shriek. Meanwhile our warriors rimmed our herds, working to keep them from startling into a charge. We crouched beneath our shields, bearing the brunt as if we battled our own god.

Through the dousing, I noticed Erzhan. He sat shivering and soaked upon his mount, his gaze as blank as if he stared at death. I thought he must be ill, but when I neared, he held me off. "Stay back! You—you bear the black kam's blood."

I stumbled at his shaking, upraised palm, recalling a rumor someone once had told, that happened long ago when Erzhan was just a boy. It was a dark-moon night when the Kara Kam came with her rattles and her bones. She had warned of Targitai's anger. No one listened. Yet it came—lightning, sudden and furious as this storm. It struck Erzhan's mother's yurt, sparking it aflame. Even as it rained, the fire burned. Both his parents and all his siblings had been trapped inside. But Erzhan, the eldest, had just passed into Targitai's charge, and so only he survived.

Now I looked at him again and somehow understood. The war god's rage had cursed his house and some still said Targitai shunned him. Now I saw why Meiramgul and Bayir kept him closely in their sights. The blow had bruised and left him bitter. Erzhan was afraid.

I backed away but our eyes stayed locked. Erzhan did not cower or even raise his shield for shelter but sat high in his saddle, his back exposed, as if daring Targitai to strike him down. Finally the last thunder eased and he collapsed against his stallion's crest.

Still we moved, bearing sodden yurt felts and dripping woolen rugs, our packhorses and camels plodding. The tempest had subsided, but the sky bore the same dull gloom—still Erzhan would not look at me. Our goats and sheep huddled in tight masses, stubborn, muddy, mewling, as our riders drove them with whips, hard nudges, dogs. It was strange the way Erzhan dealt with me: one moment almost merry; the next bitter with enmity. He was a wild dog, nipping at the hand that offered meat. I would not have thought I could ever pity Erzhan. But I did.

Late that day we reached a narrow valley where we paused to set our yurts down in the mud. Inside the warriors' shelter we huddled, drenched and shivering, barely able to rekindle Rada Mai's flame. I took my place at Marjan's right. Then Erzhan settled next to me.

Marjan eyed us both. "Now you two are friends?"

I mumbled, "Well—I don't...." Erzhan shifted uncomfortably.

I could not explain—Erzhan and me as we lingered close, not through any choice of mine, but simply because Erzhan stayed and I no longer tried to avoid him.

With the dawn we broke camp again, riding higher into mountain passes. These were dangerous tracks with scree and boulders and countless places for an enemy to hide. Bayir sent our warriors off in packs, each responsible for its own direction. Erzhan's was along the lower path while I rode ahead to guide our herds. I took my place near the middle of our band, closest to our beasts, the ana-women, and untried children. They were our aul's heart, like the living coals of Rada Mai's dung fire. But as I rode, I gazed sometimes beyond the open cliffs to watch the warriors far below draw out our defense—a broad blockade across the mountain pass with Erzhan riding tight, then wide, his horse a startling prick of whiteness against the murky gray and swaying grass.

I urged the herd ahead—horses, goats, and sheep, while Marjan ushered lambs and foals and Aigul attended the youngest horseback children. She trotted near each one, making sure they gripped firmly on their reins. She was patient with them, never teasing as she was with us, singing to ease them through the narrowest gaps while I dropped back along the ridge to guide a few elder ana-women who lagged behind.

I rode carefully, wary of the unsteady earth, calm until, from somewhere just above, a soft shush echoed my horse's rhythm. I stopped and turned. The rustle came again, this time softer. I held my breath, urged my mare closer to the high cliff's rise, then dropped silently from her back and tucked into an over-hanging shadow.

Here the barren slope was strewn with shifting scree. The rock wall dripped with damp as I pressed my cheek against it. I listened to my breath, watching the little clouds it made in the mountain air. For a long while I heard nothing, but just as I was about to move, the rustle came again—a scratch harrying the quiet earth. Then, from somewhere close above, a gentle hail of pebbles.

They clattered down around me. My heart thumped like a rabbit struggling in a trap. I stayed silent, reached for an arrow, and set it on my bow. High along the rising cliff, I gazed toward the gray-cloaked heavens. The sun glowed round and cold, a lustrous orb too pale and bleak to burn away its veil, but a slow, faint brightening cast soft shadows from above—a crouching form. My enemy was real.

All at once I stretched and arched, aiming high and pulling taut against my bowstring. I set my sights toward a crevice, dark against the open sky. Shielded by the cliff's damp shoulder, I shot, then tucked in tight again against the stone. I nocked an-other arrow and waited. For a moment, there was silence, then a heavy thud—something falling, tumbling to the ground. It landed hard, then slid across the rubble tract to settle near the next sharp drop some distance from where I stood. Stunned, I thought at first it was a mangy beast covered in thick, ragged fur. But then I saw it move. I saw a hairless cheek. I caught my breath. My victim was a man.

Cold sweat like chilling rain trickled down my back as I slipped across the scree and knelt beside him. I drew my dagger.

The stranger lay, pierced by my arrow through the neck. His eyes gaped, mouth drawn wide, choking at the jaw as he struggled through burbling drool and blood for breath. I felt as if I should know him—he was young, just a few seasons older than Erzhan and in his prime. But gaunt and fierce, his eyes, hollow. Still, beneath his tattered pelts glinted the yellow gold of breast plaques—six sewn to the boiled leather—an honored warrior, though the tunic underneath was made of moth-bit felt in a fashion I didn't recognize.

I swallowed back my dread, bent, and whispered in his ear, "Are there others? Where?"

He glared at me, his dark eyes proud, defiant. He raised a bloodstained hand, leathery across the palm from plying reins. He tried to grip me, but I skittered back. He had no strength and could not hold me.

His face turned stony in recognition of his defeat, his power draining out in a slow red pool. His eyes held mine and I froze in his helpless glare as he gurgled something I couldn't understand. "Speak again." But his eyes rolled back, bulged in pain, then shadowed and dulled.

I rose up, startled by the bluntness of his death—so swift and harsh and yet so simple. I had done this thing—and for a breath I longed to call him back—but then I heard more scuffling beyond the ridge.

Hoping Marjan and Aigul were somewhere near, I whistled loudly. Their answer came in a quick fall of arrows. I charged to join them, finding ana-women already taking up their bows and swords, even children fighting, and Meiramgul shouting from the fore—battle cries and orders scattering our herds, whipping hides of beasts to make them run.

I flew into the fray. Somehow we plucked a second and then a third intruder from the rise. When everything was finished, six raiders had fallen and Aigul and I had both made first kills. Already ana-women bent, stripping the hostiles' bodies of anything they thought worthwhile.

We paused to regroup and survey the damage. Though several of our band had been pierced or injured, and some beasts trampled or lost over the cliff, none of our own people had been slain. There was great relief. Even laughter, singing. We had stopped the raid before they'd struck. With Aigul and me, Bayir seemed particularly pleased.

"To have never seen a battlefield and done so well!" He hugged us, his hard, gruff strength oddly comforting after so much blood. Only Marjan had made no battle kill. Riding near the front, she'd been caught up in the crush and had come to the attack only after all the raiders had been scattered.

We climbed the cliff to find six fine horses tied up neatly— three geldings, two mares, and, on the cliff beneath my first arrow-shot, a tall bay stallion. We added them to our herds, but the bay was given as a prize to me. I was still too short to ride it, but it was mine to breed or trade—the first that I could claim as mine since my parents' passing.

That night Erzhan came to me. I lay almost asleep beside the warriors' fire. "You have sipped the enemy's blood," he whispered as he knelt above. "You are a proper warrior of Targitai now."

Taking my face between his hands, he leaned down, pressing his lips to mine, softly and then more fiercely. I let him, staring up as his tongue probed mine. Strange sensations: the weight of him like heavy tufted felt, the slippery muscle of his probing. All the while around the earthen floor, the other warriors shed their gentle snores, their legs sprawled or entwined across rugs or mats or beneath wool blankets.

I knew it was my right—I had paid Targitai's due. Often enough I had awakened to the sounds of grunts and gasps as other warriors took their pleasures. Wedded in Targitai's blood, their forceful ruts were fraught with little affection but so much yearning, as if joining so would somehow keep us all alive.

Marjan stirred beside us as Erzhan fumbled beneath my tunic. I felt his heat, the hunger of his rough hands, the rising in my own hips as they pressed against his thighs. But something in Erzhan's cheek unsettled me, as he reached to unlash my trousers and then fumbled with his own—his scent, the stippled sweat above his lip, the strange tang of metal that infused his skin. Suddenly I pressed him off. "Erzhan, no. I did not choose you."

He startled, rose onto his knees, straddling me—his stare, hot at first, though I couldn't say if it was with pain or shock or fury. Then slowly he shook his head, his face distorting in a twisted grimace. "You are a true warrior, Akmaral, as I had always sensed."

He backed away, then stood above, towering for a moment, casting wide shadows over me with the dim light of Targitai's hearth. Finally he turned, pulled the door-flap back, and left the yurt. Through the dark I heard him sniff, then a bit of silence before he laughed under his breath, his tone both mocking and amused.

8

THE SNOW LEOPARD

I did not know why I'd thrust him off. Perhaps it was his menace, perhaps his hunger. There came times when I regretted what I'd done. I could have chosen any warrior to take what was my right. Among our people, first joining was an honor; and Erzhan was a worthy choice. But I'd refused him and sought no other since to take his place. It had been three moons since I'd drawn first blood. Still I had not chosen a lover.

Meanwhile Aigul had already joined with several of our warrior band. She mocked me for my restraint. "Would you be like Marjan, suffering for love?"

Indeed Marjan suffered, clinging to Ruan only when she thought no one was aware. But ever in Targitai's service, the elders—like the ancestors and gods—were always watching.

I shut Aigul out. "It is not my time. I will not waste such privilege on frivolity." So I said, but in truth, it was something more. Since I'd been bound to the warriors' cult, I had focused only on what would come, what battle Targitai would call me for and whether I would survive it. I'd never thought before that night what I would do. I had thought only of blood, never of what would come after.

"Long ago, seven suns hovered in the sky. They scorched the earth. There could be no water, no food, no dark. All the people and all the animals were dying." The Hewana began the ancient tale as the Ak Kam rapped softly on her narrow drum. "At that time, there lived a masterful archer: Erkhii was his name. Anything he set his sights on he struck with a single shot. But Erkhii was boastful. He did not honor the thunder god Targitai—"

Erzhan squatted in the shadows beyond Rada Mai's lapping flames. Through that season, he had not come to me again. Instead, he hovered as a wolf drawn to the aul's warm coals, always just beyond its glow, its breath catching yellow light in pants of loneliness and cold. I did not want him—had never liked him. Yet his eyes, his awkward, gruff attempts—there was something in him that I pitied.

"All the people and the animals went to Erkhii. 'Go!' they begged. 'Kill the seven suns!' So Erkhii strode across the dry, parched earth and waited as each sun rose. One by one he took his aim. An arrow flew and a hot sun fell. One, two, three—a sun tumbled from the sky. Four, five, six—each sun rose and the archer's arrow shot it from the heavens. But as the seventh arrow soared, a swallow flew across Erkhii's sight and the barb struck the center of its tail. So now a swallow's tail is always forked. And still they taunt our archers, circling around our heads at dawn and dusk, haranguing, tittering, 'Catch me if you can!' And still there is one sun; for the seventh, seeing how lucky it had been to escape the archer's shot, took refuge beyond the western horizon. So there came to be night and day."

Meiramgul joined her sister softly humming as she motioned to a woman kneeling at the fire's edge: a warrior of our aul, five seasons in Targitai's service. Last spring, she'd made first battle kill. Then Umai's games of kesh-kumay had done their work: now her belly bulged into an expectant round. The woman bowed, as did her consort, before the Hewana while the Ak Kam marked a white chalk circle around them both. Then Meiramgul reached into the fire. With a long bone spoon, she scooped out a living coal. Carefully she broke it and passed around the chunks, one to every elder, then to all the ana-women, then finally one ember to the woman herself who held it gingerly in a small bronze bowl.

"These are the last shattered pieces," Meiramgul continued, "all that are left of those broken suns. Now the world is often cold. Rada Mai's fire warms us. We kindle the hearth-flame as our mothers and grandmothers, as Rada Mai, great-great-

grandmother of us all. Now this woman has gained the right to
join them: to light a hearth and build a yurt for her family and
her child."

The woman's smile bloomed to match her belly as her consort helped her rise. The solemn tones of the Ak Kam's chants
transformed into celebration. Someone played the horsehead
fiddle. Bowls of our strongest koumiss were passed and the
music swelled. Until the moon's descent, we reveled by the river,
where I found Marjan sitting at the edge of the festive crowd.

She was alone, her face in shadows. "Akmaral, leave me."
She shivered as I drew close. But I followed her eyes as they
drifted across the fire toward where Ruan sat, also solemn and
alone.

I wrapped my arms around her, offered her my koumiss
bowl, but she would not even sip. "If only it had been me on
that cliff," she mumbled.

"Marjan, you must be patient—"

"No, Akmaral. I have waited long enough. I have hunted
elk and wolves and boar. I have risked my life. I have proven
myself already. But look—" She pointed to the couple. "Look
at Aigul. Look even at you! Meanwhile I watch, stone-eyed as
a wanting child." She gasped, her words unchecked, her slim,
strong fingers gripping at my wrist like barbs. "I would not have
hesitated—even to kill a man. I would have shot and would not
have missed. Then my waiting would be over." She closed her
eyes, new tears running in a stream.

I stroked the salty rivulets away with my calloused fingers.
"There is nothing we can do. The gods decide when we may
pass from one purpose to the next."

"Yes," she sobbed and pressed my skin to rub away the ruddy gouges she had made. Still she trembled and would not meet
my eyes. "You were wise to refuse Erzhan," she whispered. "He
would only have caused you pain. Still, if you had chosen him,
I would have been happy for you."

I drew my arm away. I hadn't thought Marjan had known—

lying there beside us, awake when the veil of choice had passed my way and I'd blithely refused.

"I am sorry," I choked, but there was nothing I could say. We both knew that Marjan could only wait until Targitai summoned her.

Summer leaned toward waning, and still there were no raids. We scoured the steppes for soft movements among the drifting shadows of the clouds and often brought back foxes, rabbits, sometimes swift, spindle-legged deer. Then one dawn we came upon a track, one I'd never seen before: four broad toes spreading wider than a grown man's hand, thickly fringed on all sides with fur. If there were claws, they barely scratched the earth but still Marjan recognized the print. "Snow leopard," she whispered—and before her words were fully breathed, we had already mounted up to tell Bayir.

A snow leopard—silent, ruthless, a killer stalking through our placid fields. Bayir came at once, calling Daniar to join him. They stood for a time silent, examining the leopard's track, following as it veered in a meandering circle—out of reach but close enough to scent our goats, sheep, horses, even our camels.

"Only one," Bayir murmured. "Somewhat small. Probably a female."

Daniar nodded. "She is hungry. There is snow upon the peaks." We all peered toward where the mountains wore new cloaks of heavy white and the highest crests shimmered through a misty haze. "Leave a few old sheep," he said. "Let them wander and set no guard. We'll move the rest well back, closer to the aul. If she comes, she'll take only what she needs. When she's sated, perhaps she'll leave."

They stood calmly, but in their silence I sensed their dread— Bayir pulling on his scant, gray-flecked beard. Then he turned as if he'd remembered us. He patted us on our shoulders, pressing to move us on. "No need to worry. Leopards are solitary creatures. They mostly shelter to themselves." But he spoke almost too brightly as a darkened veil spread across his hollow cheeks, and the old sharp scars that had always scored them seemed to softly redden.

The herders did as Daniar advised. We waited through the night, our beasts milling close beside our yurts, startling the air with their hoof-scratches and snorting. Their heat congealed the chilly air, warping the light that wrapped our fires set wide as a burning fence to hold the snow leopard off. To keep us all alive.

But by dawn, the old, tough sheep remained, still grazing where they'd been. Three days more we did the same and the snow leopard did not trouble them. We sent out scouts to hunt for tracks but found none fresh and only scat well dried and no places where the leopard might have bedded down among the grasses. So the Ak Kam sacrificed a gold-hued mare, and we let our herds spread wide again.

It was strange, unsettling, to see the beast drift close and then simply disappear. But all animals are spirits as much as they are beasts. The Ak Kam said that when a big cat comes, it is there to teach us.

For half a moon, we let down our guard. The dwindling summer breath grew chill with the first light scent of autumn. Then the snow leopard struck: the boy was two winters old. From the far side of our aul, we heard the mother's screams and then the growling cat, spitting to protect its hard-earned prey. All the warriors tried to drive it off—all of us yelping, shouting, threatening with wide-aimed arrows and rattling our spears. But we couldn't shoot for fear of harming the boy.

Finally the leopard withdrew with a flick of her frosted tail and a pallid snarl. The boy lay alive but mauled; great gashes scored his limbs and gut. The Ak Kam carried him to the elders' yurt, though there was little she could do—only lay a somber feast and sing soft prayers to the goddess Umai who protects all children. She fed him sips of koumiss through the night, covered him with poultices of moss and herbs, tried everything she knew to knit his ravaged flesh. Still the infant moaned and shivered, wrapped within the stuffy cloud of sulfur-colored smoke. With the dawn, lying in his mother's arms, he took one last shallow breath and expired.

The elders called at once to move the aul. We ran to pack our things away in dumb confusion. In Targitai's yurt, I reached for my own saddle packs, my clothes and quiver, arrows, blades. I didn't think to look for Marjan until I glanced up at the barren struts. There her riding tack, her hunting spear, all her arrows and her bow were swept away. Only the leather sash that had held them up still dangled.

I raced to the elders' hearth and handed it to Bayir. He turned the half-torn strap over in his hands. "A snow leopard with a taste for human blood." The strain on his face pressed his stony brow until it cragged and furrowed. "Akmaral, find her. Take Ruan with you. Perhaps she'll come to him. Go quickly. The aul cannot linger long here."

I nodded, stumbled backward, then turned and began to run, shouting, "Ruan!" all around the camp until I found him already mounted.

We galloped for the hills. Marjan must have known we'd try to stop her. Her path led through a highland stream, then across rugged stones where her horse's hooves had left few marks. Soon Ruan and I slowed, stalking in silence for any whisper of her trail, listening to every screech and scratch that might lead us to her. Vultures glided overhead, their wingtips tracing a web of feathered shadows along our path. Just once I raised my bow, intent to strike one down for its lurid stare, but Ruan set his hand against me.

"Save your shot," he said. "The birds may lead us to her."

Knowing what he said was true, I lowered my aim.

Our trail traversed slick slabs of stone, cold, made treacherous by black ice and runoff. Above, a glacier stretched like a lolling, crumpled tongue, in places twisted into heaves, at others melt-carved swells, some desiccated to fragile crystal ribs gnawed clean by the nipping sun.

"What could she have thought?" My anguish hardened to a quiet rage.

"To help," Ruan murmured. "To protect her family and our aul. To save our people, as any of us would. Akmaral, we all do our best as we are called."

I held my breath, then stretched my hand to his, knowing his wisdom churned deeply with his fear. "Marjan knows the ways of beasts. Only she, of all of us, might—"

But Ruan wouldn't look at me. He only sighed a heavy, stricken breath that hung about us like a vapor.

They say the snow leopard is an eerie beast, sudden to appear and then, like fog, to simply fade away. We found no trace of her—of either of them—as the last slim blade of sun cut across the brittle sky. We were left to find our way in bleeding darkness. A new moon hung above, lending no beam of light to help us in our search. Slowly, carefully, knowing that to continue through the night would likely mean our deaths, Ruan and I returned to the half-dismantled aul and waited.

On the third dawn, a doleful form descended from the mountains.

It was clearly Marjan, with her thick black braid and her straight, strong stance riding very slowly on a spotted gelding. As she crossed the valley, the Ak Kam warbled a high, shrill call and all the aul road out in a wild flurry to greet her.

The pelt was caked in blood—Marjan's mixed with the snow leopard's. Meiramgul rode up first, then slowed and stopped, nodding to the child's mother to approach. The ana-woman slid down from her horse and drew the carcass of the beast that had killed her son from the back of Marjan's gelding. Their gazes met, the mother reaching up, Marjan collapsing in a silent rush of sobs.

We all turned back, the mother leading the aul on foot with the leopard's pelt draped heavily across her forearms. All the while the Ak Kam chanted. "Sacred spirit, older than our race.

Your tracks traverse the narrowest paths. They lead to the heaven realm."

Marjan clutched her horse, too weak to hold her reins, wobbling as she tried to keep her seat, her neck and chin deeply scratched, her limbs scored with narrow, sticky rivulets of blood that ran down her arms and thighs and spattered on her mare's fair coat, until both were darkly mottled.

When we reached the elders' yurt, the grief-sick mother laid the pelt before Rada Mai's fire. There the Ak Kam raised the flames, offering the leopard's soul into the smoke and ash, cleansing it and the aul of its hard transgression. Finally Meiramgul offered up a hand to Marjan, but she had no strength even to leave her mount. So the Hewana drew her gently from her horse and carried her.

The Ak Kam bathed her in fermented milk, cinnabar, and ash. For three days, Marjan slept, feverish and ill, but on the fourth, more quietly, and soundly by the fifth. Then on the seventh dawn, the Ak Kam woke Marjan gently and bared her arm. Where the skin had not been torn, she etched a dark tattoo in the shape of a twisting, fearsome leopard.

Marjan lay still and endured the sacred pain, but her eyes filled slowly to their brink with tears. Suddenly she reached toward the ashy stones that ringed about Rada Mai's hearth. "Surely," she gasped, "the snow leopard is enough. I beg Targitai to release me!"

The Ak Kam paused her scoring as the Hewana raised her hand. "There is nothing we can do." She smoothed away the furrows from Marjan's brow. "Such sufferance belongs to the gods who rule our earth and to the ancestors above us, always watching."

Marjan bowed her head, her shoulders suddenly drooping as a two-humped camel who has crossed the steppes but seen no food. The Hewana offered nothing as she bent again over her work tanning the cream-and-dappled fur. But when the Ak Kam's brand was done, she helped Marjan to rise and laid the heavy pelt across her shoulders.

9

DEATH MOON

With the snow leopard's death, the aul stayed on the highlands. Our herds spread wide. Horses cantered hale and sleek. Our sheep grew fat on the thick green grass, nearly ready for the autumn slaughter. There was no need to run, no strangers passing close or raising any dust. Only the ancestors lingered, their spirits a subtle presence hovering above, as if our aul were tucked away on heaven's periphery.

When finally the air turned cool, the elders chose Marjan to lead us through the mountain passage. It was an honor and a danger riding for three days at the fore, usually reserved for those who'd already proven Targitai's favor. In this, at least, the elders seemed to understand. Her presence meant she'd be first to face a foe. But some rumored it would raise the war god's wrath—Erzhan, most stridently, though Bayir restrained him. Through the long, hard trek, he watched her with a gaze like an arrow nocked into a half-drawn bow. Whenever I could, I slipped between them, as if his sight could maim and my back could somehow shield her.

"Erzhan, let her be." I cantered close as we approached a narrow pass. Forced to travel single file, at such places Erzhan tensed, his lips pressed raw, jaw distorted by his scorn.

But he would not stop or even talk until we'd reached a broad, flat hollow. Then, "Tell me, Akmaral, what has Marjan done but kill a beast, as much as any stumbling, half-trained child?"

"Erzhan, the leopard nearly killed her."

"We'd be safer if it had. Targitai demands sacrifice and Marjan gives him scraps. She cares no more for the safety of our aul than the lightning cares for me."

I trembled at his sacrilege and reached my hand to stop his talk. At my touch, his breathing broke, his body shuddering.

For three days more, the aul rode wary—quiet, if quiet is possible amidst the milling din of two hundred head of horses and countless other beasts. We grew hungry, weary, but even the children remained subdued, all the aul alert to any noise or drift of scent, watchful of the shifting clouds for Targitai's bolts, every hoof-step rumbling with the echoed pitch of thunder. But in the end, no trouble came. We emerged on the autumn steppe unscathed. Everyone was relieved except Marjan. Our peaceful passage had gained her nothing.

"It doesn't matter"—Ruan's words came hollow, though they tried to reassure. Marjan only closed her eyes and gripped her snow leopard cape, her fingers fast entwined in its still sharp claws.

I was grateful to slip away from Marjan's sorrow to take my turn on guard. There I could break the dew alone and breathe the morning stillness. It gave me time to ponder—what would I do for love? But the more I thought, the more I had no answers.

Mostly the steppe was dull. In the stillness, I lost myself in the rhythm of my blade stripping sturdy stems, laying willow boughs in rows to shape new arrows. It was careful work, enough to quell my thoughts as now and again I raised my gaze to search for subtle shifts on the horizon. But then a sound arose—a scrape of heels across the stubbled grass. Footsteps. I stopped, clutching my blade, and listened. They came from just behind—from the direction of the aul where there was little chance of threat, wobbling slightly like a loose-dug post too unsteady for holding horses. Somehow I knew that it was Erzhan.

"What do you want?" I kept my eyes upon my task.

He stooped and brushed his palm across the dew, then lifted one of my new-fletched arrows. "We trust our survival to the steadiness of these shafts, to our bowstrings strung with sinew wrapped about these curves." He took my bow out of the grass and stroked its bent-horn limbs, then plucked the string and listened to it sing. "You are not like other girls—too frightened to really fight, always looking to escape, hiding in Rada Mai's protection—"

"Is that what you think, Erzhan? There are ways far worse than battle by which an ana-woman dies." For a moment, he looked away. We both knew too well the sight of a woman lying pale and cold in a pool of her own blood after struggling to bear a child.

Finally I spoke. "Marjan is not afraid. She is braver than I, braver than you by far. It is not her fault Targitai has not summoned her."

He pulled a single blade of grass and tore it between his thumbs. "Targitai chooses those he trusts."

"I trust Marjan with my life, Erzhan. So should you."

He looked at me. "We are not Targitai."

I shook my head and turned back to my chore, fitting arrows' ends with vulture feathers. I reached for the one Erzhan had taken, nocked it to my bow and raised it to my eye to test its aim. "Marjan's time will come. You have no right to condemn her."

He sniffed and tossed a hail of grassy bits. "I only meant that you are different." He lowered my aim and took my chin. "There is fire in your eyes, not the weak kind of fire of Rada Mai's hearth, but the fire of a lighted spear."

I raised my brows, then nudged his hand away. Resetting my aim, I let go my shot. The arrow soared just as the sun broke full across the grass and set the earth on fire.

Erzhan squinted into the orange light as I pursed my lips, nocked, and shot again. "There—you see? Not even blindness daunts you."

I laid my bow across my lap, and Erzhan raised both hands and clutched my cheeks—his fingers cold and rough, holding gently but with an urgency so intense that I pulled away.

"Erzhan"—I plucked a clot of dirt and threw it in his face— "is that what you want from me?"

He sputtered. Some of the soil settled in the hollows of his collarbones. He pinched some up, crushed it between his fingers. "We two are alike," he sniffed, "meant to live brilliant as a flame, and as quickly die."

The way he gazed at me, oddly, curiously, I reached and cupped his fingers with my palm. Pulling him close, I bent my neck and softly kissed him. For a time, our lips and then our tongues entwined, slippery, gritty with the taste of dirt. But then he pressed me to the earth, his body shadowing as he pinned me with his knees. I pushed him off and rolled away. Brushing the dust from my tunic and my mouth, I turned back to my duty.

The quarter moon passed, yet still I tasted Erzhan on my lips and tongue. My hand moved absently to wipe him off but somehow my fingers lingered. Even now the peace of my dawn watch was fraught with anticipation of his footsteps. When they didn't come, I assured myself that I was grateful. Though my heart throbbed slightly and my stomach roiled, the unfamiliar hunger consuming me.

I prayed for some distraction, and after some few days, it came: a bare shadow moving across the steppe, taking shape as a slowly wandering band. It eased in from the west, slipped beneath the gibbous moon, and settled in a shallow basin—some new aul I had never seen before, their yurts sprouting like a spray of mushrooms in the far-off pasture.

There were other bands also settled in that distance—auls we knew, with whom we had feasted or shared some tie of blood. But these new strangers sent no messenger, no horse and rider bringing offerings to our hearth. Their handful of yurts lay gray and huddled on the sunken flat, too close to the others, as if they would intrude. And with them, not so many horses, few goats and fewer sheep, all skinny and unkempt, and some spindly wagons—these, strangest of all, built on bowing wooden wheels so rickety they could only slow them down, and loaded with household goods, all still packed as if ready at any moment to depart. Out of some came the muffled pitch of infants' shrills.

When I first noticed them, I thought it only another camp—
perhaps more impoverished than most—come from somewhere far away. But as I sat in the open field alone, first light
broke and the stranger riders charged. I saw, in the crimson
glow of dawn, their armor scales catching with the tarnished
gleam of bronze. They wore thick cloaks across their backs,
weighty as if made of pelts. And underneath, all were heavily
armed.

From so far off it is odd to see a fight. You cannot hear
the sounds. There is only movement and then the flash of fire,
people scattering and falling. Most battles do not last for long.
But the flames do, rising into lapping columns like scarlet serpents with twisting tails. First the smoke is white, then gray,
then turning black, carrying the scents of wood and wool, then
finally meat and hard bone burning.

Those half-pleasant odors soon carried on the wind, mixing
with dust as the raiders raised their bows and then their swords.
By the glaring dawn, they attacked our distant neighbor's aul,
rounding up their herds, which needed little prodding to run in
panic from the firestorm.

I sang out our own aul's warning: the mimic of a lonely
wolf—though it stuck in my throat so my sound came choked.
I tried again—this time the raven's caw, strident and at a higher
pitch, over and again until finally Bayir came.

"There." I pointed.

But Bayir had already seen: at the horizon's edge, our neighbor's aul engulfed in flames. Several raiders drove the stolen
herds back to where their wagons waited, while another dozen
rode farther to the east—toward another aul some hand's-
length stretch away.

"Two attacks before the sun is even hot," Bayir murmured,
his breath stale and close, his whiskers tickling my shoulder.

"Who are they?"

He squinted, then suddenly rose up. "Akmaral, wake the others. Call the warriors—go!"

"Who?" I begged.

"They are Scythians."

At his words I began to run.

The Scythians were the enemy that filled our legends—a vast, powerful tribe that lived far to the west at the edge of the open steppe. Their homeland bordered the great Black Sea where Greek ships carried off slaves the Scythians captured from the grasslands, even some from the forest steppes and the foothills of the Riphean peaks. In Meiramgul's stories, they were more numerous than the heaven's stars, more powerful than black sandstorms that can destroy a camp in a single hour. Yet they were also kindred. Meiramgul told how once we had been fearsome warriors riding side by side with the Scythian army, joining them at war. Together we had driven out the invader Persians and their king who called himself Darius the Great. We had reveled in our triumph—equals, allies in our western homeland between the Caspian and Black Seas, sharing open grass and the freedom to hunt and roam. Until the Scythians grew proud, filled with plots they had learned from greedy trader Greeks. They turned their force against us, threatened to enslave us, but our great-grandmothers would not bow. Instead they took their herds and horses and swept off to the east as far as they could reach. That was how our people came to settle long ago among these distant peaks of the Altai Mountains.

Now here they were, raising fire to burn away the morning dew. I raced, my footfalls reeling and a tremor in my voice as I spread the news across the aul like terror.

Soon our warriors thundered from Targitai's yurt, rushing to saddle their mounts and don their armor. But the Scythian raiders stayed busy to the south, charging the far horizon while our warriors waited, ready with our arms, tucked up in the north, slightly hidden by the mountains' shadows.

By nightfall we lay still untouched, but wary, wracked with expectation. Even Rada Mai's own fires we had smothered down to coals; they smoldered only in the elders' hearth—even there, burning low as a precaution. We gathered round those embers, hunched into that small, dim space. The press of bodies gave more warmth than Rada Mai's protected flames. Meanwhile the Ak Kam bobbed and chanted, "First, the new white stallion," spooning meat onto the coals. "Second, the ashen mare. Third..." Three horses given to the fire.

As she made our sacrifice, dousing the telltale smoke with a bowl of milk and blood, the last of the nighttime's guard tucked beneath the hanging door-flap and pressed against the lattice walls. Erzhan was among them, head erect, grown taller now to reach where the framework met the beams. He tried to catch my eye, but I looked away and would not greet him.

Finally the bowl was drained and the Ak Kam raised a small bronze mirror. As it dangled from a sinew thread, its sacred glimmer caught the beams of the aging moon. For a long time she drew cold light down from the purpled roof's eye, then with a wafting gesture sent heavenward the heated glow of Rada Mai's coals.

"This is no time for pride," the Hewana murmured. "Targitai strikes a heavy bargain: one darkness we must face, another we would bring. It is not our way to choose attack, only to defend and travel peacefully."

"But these strangers," Bayir murmured through the dark, "are Scythians."

Meiramgul closed her eyes. Her mouth fell slack. "Sister, I beg you. Call the ancestors."

The Ak Kam nodded, her hand already in her pouch drawing out the tsaagan bones. Soon the spread lay scattered across the felts. It glowed in the dim red light as she bent above them, humming softly as her finger stroked her drum, rubbing tightly across its skin until the sound resembled distant thunder.

The Hewana bowed her head and we all understood: tomorrow we would attack. Drive away the Scythian enemy. Free the steppe to make safe crossing before winter. My heartbeat quickened. I reached to Marjan sitting at my back. "At last you will have your chance!"

She squeezed my hand. But in the fire's eerie light, her eyes looked more like a rabbit's caught before a taut-drawn bow than the piercing gaze of a hunter.

We slept fitfully and cramped and were awakened well before the dawn by a rattle and some movement. Then a windy gasp. The door-flap of the elders' yurt blew back and a shadowed figure entered. Odd shapes—a tall, peaked cap jangling over pelts and a rough silk dress that hung in tatters. Long arms, bent and craggy, painted white with talc over deep, wrinkled tattoos. Then a voice coughed low and breathed, "Death moon."

The Kara Kam. When last I'd seen her, she had seemed a dream—I so young, and my parents still beside me. Now I stared in the icy dark, my fingers on my amulet, the flying deer warm against my chest; I pressed it hard into the place where the scar still marked my sternum.

"Death moon," she said, glowering past me, past all of us.

The other warriors groped to find their weapons.

"Go away, old woman." The Ak Kam finally stood. "There is no death moon tonight. Look about, if you are not blind. It rises near to full. Rada Mai has taken all our offerings. She has eaten well. Don't you smell her meat? Targitai prepares his horsemen—"

"Sister, hush." Meiramgul raised her palm.

The black kam began to speak. "The light from your mirror shines falsely, priestess. Plunge Targitai's sword into that flame and have an end. Death moon comes, I warn you." Her voice was coarse, as if ground between rough stones, and a shiver quaked across my shoulders. Around me, warriors, ana-women, ancient men who had lived beyond their final fight—all their eye-whites shone, broad and strained, fearful of the swallowing darkness.

The Ak Kam knelt and fanned the flames until Rada Mai's coals rose at last into angry brilliance. "You see, old woman? The hearth goddess repels you. You serve only darkness. You cannot see the light. Go—get out!"

"I serve the truth, as you know, Khagan."

We had never heard the Ak Kam's proper name before, said aloud as if she were just a child.

The Kara Kam shook her head. She scanned the crowd—first one warrior, then the next. As her gaze neared me, my amulet grew hot, nearly burning when she paused, showing me a gaping, peg-toothed grin. I clutched it with my hand, and Marjan clutched at me. Only for a breath, then the Kara Kam's eyes passed on.

Finally she turned. The last we saw of her that night was a flash from her own bronze mirror, finer than the Ak Kam's but far older and deeply tarnished. I remembered it well—its shapes of five flying deer and the single mountain goat leaping. Now she did not raise it. As it dangled at her bony breast, it caught the fire's light of its own accord and hurtled it first upward toward the sky, then out the yurt's low door.

10

THE BATTLE

"What does it matter? We are warriors. We are already meant to die"—Erzhan's words said so long ago and now again, muted in the wake of the Kara Kam's prediction. *It is unwise to disregard her portents*—my mother's words, a whispered memory. I longed to speak them out, but held my breath. She had held the Kara Kam in deepest reverence, but she had been the only one.

With every step I heard again the murmur, *Death moon*, though my lips stayed taut and sealed, like all the other warriors. *Death moon*, as we made our way across the silent aul. *Death moon*, as we prepared for war. *Death moon*, I breathed against my terror. We would battle Scythians.

We gathered in Targitai's yurt, filling it until its felted frame strained with our pressing backs. I entered near the last, groping to find a place, nearly stumbling across the hearth coals. They lay cold and black with ashes—fragile wisps, delicate and flaking.

But Bayir's footsteps were sure between our tight-tucked limbs. He squatted by the hearth and breathed low across the coals. Then he raised his sword and pierced them through. Fire seeped like new blood from a broken scar. "We will ride when the moon hangs one hand's breadth above the grass. Slow and silent across the steppe. Lie flat against your horses. Then hide among their herds. The Scythians are unused to so many beasts and cannot yet have learned their sounds."

We murmured our assent. The air inside was close, the warriors' faces reflecting dry, hot embers. Pressed against the wall, Erzhan's shadow shifted in the gloom. His eyes were pensive, watchful, dark over hollowed cheeks.

"Keep alert," Bayir warned. "Use gestures calm and small. No words. Not even whispers. At arrow's reach, all our captains rise to pick their sentries off. Yerbol, Madiyar, Jarakal, and Erzhan will lead. The rest, hold back. When their front guards fall, everyone ride forward and let fly."

It was the first time Erzhan had been named captain. His shoulders slightly rose, broader than they'd seemed before. But his face, still stony. I turned to cheer him, raising my gaze. But his eyes skittered off, following instead the pallid curls of smoke rising through the roof's eye.

Iron arrowheads were passed to replace our practice bone and bronze. We fit them to our shafts, checking their points and barbs. When Bayir left, the talk of battle rose, fresh and full of bravado to hide our fear. Then we all lay back, eyes wide and fingers gripped behind our necks, and waited for the call to arms.

At the far side of the yurt, Marjan tucked in beside Ruan. Her head curled down against his shoulder, their fingers fast entwined. They no longer seemed to fear what anyone might say. And no one tried to draw her off. It no longer seemed to matter.

Finally Bayir's signal came: a warbling howl, muffled through thick felts. We rose as one, finding our way into the chill where ana-women had laid great piles of our battle gear: war belts, horsewhips, saddle cloths, shields and extra weapons, and a mound of our warriors' armor—boiled leather stitched with horse-hoof scales, some with golden plaques that caught dull flashes of the moon. I dug to find my own, well hidden with only three small plaques to snag the light: two bronze for hunting wild boars which I owed mostly to Marjan, and one for the mountain ambush—luck bound in a griffin's golden beak. Soon enough, I thought as I numbly put it on, I would die or I would have more.

The hoof-scales jiggled as I walked toward the horse corral, my uncertain stride merging with the other warriors' and the rhythmic croaks of hidden toads and crickets' song. I reached the corral gate, unlatched it, pressed, and entered. Our beasts stood ghost-like beneath a sky stained black but for a haloed moon and a scattered spray of stars.

I clucked my tongue to find my mare. Bayir had counseled us to saddle our mounts calmly, to feed and tie them as we would on any other dawn. But my mare, as if she sensed or feared her fate, hid away as she had never done before, standing reluctant as I placed her rein around her head and tightened her saddle's cinch. She challenged me, refusing to let me mount, and even when I had, she bristled and tried to throw me. I clung with all my might, calves pressed tight into her barrel. Finally she conceded, gruffly snorted, and tossed her head. She had made her point. I did not have to fight with her again.

As I rode to join the others, I saw another mount not far across the dew—a stallion, motionless, tall and pale against the darkness. "Erzhan?"—my sound carried far on the suspended air.

He murmured, "Now you'll see that all I've said is true. This dawn you will prove yourself in battle—"

"I am afraid."

"Warriors revel in the face of death."

"Do they, Erzhan, really?"

"What does it matter? We all die soon enough," he sniffed. But this time I no longer believed his nonchalance. Erzhan cared very much if he lived or died.

"Ride in my wake, Akmaral," he said. "Stay close beside my horse and be my second."

"You trust me now?"

"I trust no one else. Only you—you will not run away."

The others had gone ahead and we stood alone in the darkened field. I rode closer until our horses' necks nearly entwined. Then I took a breath, reached across his saddlebow, and drew his face to mine. I kissed him, this time without reluctance, welcoming the stirring, stabbing heat that rose through my limbs. I savored the sensation, then pressed his hands to me, cupping them against the horse-hoof scales that lined my breasts. Erzhan pulled back, wide-eyed. Then he reached for me again. Even through the armor, I felt his heat. I straightened, slightly gasped. Finally I murmured, "It is unwise to waste Targitai's choice. He has given me a gift that I haven't yet enjoyed."

Both our breaths exhaled as one, wisps threading thinly through the dark. Leaving only our lips to linger and then unclutch, I slipped down from my mare, lay back in the cold, damp grass. Erzhan followed, sliding next to me.

We unfastened our leather trousers, yanking at them hurriedly. He reached and we came together, our war belts clanking. We thrust them off to make smooth ground, then Erzhan pressed into me. As a new-forged sword plunged into the armorer's icy bucket—the shock and then shivering relief—I savored it. But then—his face, suddenly fierce, demanding as his fingers tore at the polished scales that concealed my chest. Snatching at their binds, his hard hands gripped my naked bosom.

Over and over, he pressed into me, his face close to mine, his two arms buttressed beside my shoulders. His breath blew hot across my face, his sweat slowly dripping, gathering in the small, soft pool above my collarbone. I felt him heaving. I lay back and tried to think that I enjoyed this, the pounding, as cold dew seeped between my buttocks and my open thighs. Wind spat a frigid spray as I waited for satisfaction. But no pleasure came, not even when Erzhan was through. He withdrew and fell back across the grass. His chest rose and fell; his breath came in puffs that grasped the light of the unblinking moon. I pressed up, first to my elbows, then my knees, sitting with my chest exposed and my thighs half-bared, letting the sticky wetness seep from me. I looked down at Erzhan. He glanced, then turned away. In that panting, sheepish grimace, I saw the hollowness of our act and could think only of Marjan—of her hopeless, heartfelt longing.

We rode back, silent together for the awkwardness of what had been, and gathered with the other warriors at the aul's south boundary. It was well before the dawn when we cut a path across the muted steppe. I looked for Marjan but did not find her. I was almost grateful not to see her face, there beneath the ample moon, great and full, the time when our people told that an ana-woman should fall pregnant. The thought of Er-zhan's seed seemed no better than an intruding shard that I longed to cast away.

My horse's hoof-steps were noiseless beneath the swath of early morning sky tinged ebony with ochre streaks, indigo, and deepest violet. Bayir chose our path, his gelding's gait always a measured hush. Even when his beast seemed tense, it never snuffed or snorted. But other beasts were not so quiet. Erzhan's stallion trotted before mine, whinnying and grunting as he worked to control him, keeping a sure, firm grip. His leathered back twisted sometimes to check if I saw his skill. I smiled at him mutely, not knowing what to think, feeling a strange, new awareness deep within my body but not welcoming it. Not wel-coming him.

Bayir led us out along the farthest edge of the Scythians' encampment, still too far to see more than the milling peaks of the heads and ears of their stolen herd. There he gathered us around. "Do not cluster," he reminded. "Stay apart to shoot from the greatest range. Aim skyward, then turn and let the next rider take their blows. Counter their attacks, but stay out-side of striking distance. Leave only the closest archer in each round exposed. If you must ride in, keep distant from their yurts and especially from their wagons. They are rickety and strange, but movable concealment. We cannot know what dan-gers they contain."

The captains bowed their heads before we broke apart. Erzhan led our band toward the western darkness. We lay flat against our horses' necks, their manes tickling our noses, moving until we could observe the strangers' camp. Sentries scattered here and there, looking lean and wiry as their back-bent bows and long-tipped spears. Thin smoke rose from soot-edged smoke-holes but gave very little light, near extinguished as our own—if theirs were Rada Mai's flames at all.

Despite their raiding boldness, these Scythians seemed a

desperate clan, their yurt felts in tatters, sheep scrawny as their goats, their horses stolen but for the few they rode. I sensed it and felt odd pity, though there was little time to dwell as Erzhan whispered over his shoulder, "Akmaral, take half our band and scatter among their horses. Dawn is not far off. Stay low and close. Listen for Bayir's call."

I nodded, looking toward the horizon. "Erzhan"—turning, I pointed toward the moon. Our other warriors saw it, too: the bright white disk half swallowed by unnatural darkness.

"Death moon," someone whispered.

All their eyes shone in the shrinking light. The Kara Kam's warning made manifest before our eyes—

"Ignore it. It means nothing." Erzhan prodded me and the others to ride on.

We moved slowly, reluctantly, our hoof-steps barely crushing grass, our breaths blending with the stillness, our horses' reins held tightly in our fists, poised to yank up sharp should any heavy head dip to nip the short, dry stubble. Finally a sound swept in: Bayir's call. Erzhan and the other captains joined him—a wolf pack's howling, their echoes manufactured yet precise.

Our attack began with a single shot. The other captains followed. We listened for the first soft falls of bodies, our arrows raised, precisely nocked, ready to fly off our bowstrings. Our riders rushed in, fired, doubled back, again, again. The sky was soon beset with iron darts like so many stars falling from the heaven pasture.

Erzhan and I raced side by side, leading the widening span of our attack. I clung to my horse's mane, tucked my rear into my saddle's cantle, thrust my heels hard into her bounding sides. My breath filled with our brutal rhythm, forward, back, the tumult and frenzy of my first true charge. It was not long before the Scythians woke to face our onslaught. Their sentries already fallen, their other riders quickly on their feet, scrambling for bows and armor, shouting to find their horses. But Yerbol's band had rounded to their backs, opened their corral, and scattered them.

We held our attack to one hundred paces' distance. The rumble of our horses' hooves raised a shadowed cloud of dust. It hung over the whole encampment as they aimed their bows and shot. Even without mounts, the Scythian archers were impressive.

Our warriors toppled. Some injured, others killed. And horses, racing wild or kicking, helpless in the dust. Still we charged, galloped forward, shooting, pulling quickly back until the Scythians suddenly faltered, then dropped their arms.

Through the haze, a total blackness had fallen across the moon. Now they saw it too.

I looked to Erzhan but already he had resumed his charge, exploiting our enemies' panic, shooting arrow after arrow, yelping to drive us on. We obeyed, unnerved by the shadowed moon but even more, that the Scythians were also. We descended like wildfire, sparking their bare encampment with our unchecked barbs. Their arrows rose to meet ours, more deadly than before as they tried to drive us off. We veered, one after another, risking, taking aim, then riding quickly beyond harm.

We were winning, shouting Targitai's name, battering our shields with our weapons, reveling in our war god's might. But the moon's eclipse cast an eerie glow, livid and unsettling. Out of the gloom, a trespasser suddenly appeared as if from nowhere, creeping in a silent trot that swelled to a proper charge. I turned and nocked my arrow, drew my bowstring, almost shot, but then I saw—

It was Marjan.

She rode up fast behind me, then beyond.

"Marjan! Marjan!" I called.

She could not—would not hear me. She raced ahead and raised her bow, plucking her bowstring again, again.

"Marjan!" It was Ruan now. Flying past me, his captain Madiyar and all their band followed in frantic disarray. "Retreat! Marjan, go back!" Ruan cried, his free arm waving.

He pulled up short beside me. "She followed us, silent as a leopard. The whole way we didn't hear." Cantering, he reared on his horse's haunches, then dug in, turned to rally back his troop.

I followed, calling, "Marjan, get back!" but she paid no heed. She fired wherever she chose, riding closer to the strangers' archers, ignoring Bayir's warning to stay out of striking range. I rode after her as closely as I dared. The Scythians gathered up more arms, suddenly wielding well-made swords, slashing dawn-sparked scythes, vicious daggers, and bounding, bronze-mounted spears.

"Marjan!" Now Ruan galloped from behind, passing us close as he swerved to counter her path. Riding low, he reached and grabbed her rein, their horses' manes whipping in a frantic tussle.

She thrust him off—"One kill!" I heard—striking Ruan's armor with the flat of her sword. Charging toward a tight pass between the strangers' wagons, she pressed her unsheathed blade steady against her thigh.

Ruan followed her into the Scythian camp. I raced after them both as Erzhan roared behind us. "Retreat! Get back! Don't ride so close!"

Amidst the scrabble and confusion, our warriors saw only our charge. They followed, all of us soon caught in a labyrinth of Scythian yurts and carts. Arrows showered from above— theirs, lit now by their hearth coals. The sparks caught our hair and their own felts. Soon even the yurts' lattices burned.

I saw one and then another of us fall—warriors trained together since we were children. I dared not turn as each one dropped. I kept only Marjan in my sights, racing to catch her.

"Retreat!" Erzhan barked again, urging his stallion, cutting and dragging as if to herd us. "Pull back, Akmaral! Marjan, you fool!"

Then an arrow fell into our midst. Marjan buckled. Before our eyes, she lost her balance, collapsing over her horse's neck. She would have dropped had Ruan not raced to catch her.

He held her by the arm, then shoulder. The arrow's shaft rooted in her waist pointed toward the sky. Ruan righted her, grabbed her rein, and whipped her horse to keep on riding; then, they were gone.

Around me, the battle savaged. Horses dashed among the carts and yurts. Bodies raced toward me, spears and arrows flying. I shot, then drew my sword, first at the strangers' men, then at their women. In my ears, everything went still as I battled with sword and shield, my blade now so caked with blood that it slipped and would not cut. I wiped it on my tunic. The woolly black willingly absorbed the red.

I struck one and then another, losing Madiyar in the fray. But Erzhan stayed by me, a stream of mangled bodies in his wake. His blade fell hard to cut a man nearly in half. Hips and legs still held erect as chest, shoulders, and head peeled away.

Erzhan laughed, his eyes on fire.

"Erzhan"—I tried to speak, almost sick, my sword arm suddenly quaking.

"Defend your flank, Akmaral!"

A Scythian woman rose to my right and drew a dagger. So I slashed—forward, backward, my blade cutting through her frame. The woman fell and from her arms tumbled a tiny baby. It lay on its face, too young to roll, and crying loudly. Erzhan bent over his horse, used his point to flip it up, then pressed the blade again—into the infant's heart as if it were nothing. The wailing noise—suddenly it was still.

Behind us, dawn cut the sky in two. The black veil slipped from the moon; its face returned to white, then faded into the new day's glory.

Smoke from the ruined yurts rose in great gray pillars, their long shadows tracking our retreat, stretching across the grass to the distant edge of the Scythians' scattered, stolen herds. There was little left now of their aul but blood and fire. Our warriors gathered and counted ranks. We were diminished by nearly half, with many injured. But amidst the moans and bloody sweat of our exhausted tribe, Marjan and Ruan were nowhere to be found, not among the living or the dead.

11

THE ANGER OF THE GODS

The Kara Kam had foretold well. Death moon had done its
work. Marjan lay, hands clasped across her chest in the shadows of the elders' fire. Rada Mai's red coals mocked the pallid
color of her skin. Ruan had driven both their horses across the
purple dew, lashing Marjan to her mount so she would not fall.

"I thought she'd died at once," he choked. "Slumped over
her horse's withers, she barely made a sound. But then she
reached her hand, trembling, glistening with blood from where
she clutched her wound."

"She deserves what she has wrought." Erzhan scowled. "She
ignored Bayir. She presumed to heed Targitai when she was not
called. Even the Kara Kam warned—"

I tried to defend her until finally Ruan snapped, "Akmaral,
he is right. How did that black witch know?"

The next dawn, the aul packed its goods and prepared to
leave. It was dangerous to stay on the autumn pasture. Gray
light cast insubstantial shadows. The sky hung low with threat.
"Targitai is angry." Erzhan nodded toward the looming clouds.
He seemed almost relieved, watching as they rolled in. Perhaps
he was grateful for what Marjan had done—by piquing Targitai's rage, she'd turned it away from him.

I hushed him with a glare, then whipped my horse to match
his pace. Bayir had sent our band ahead to scout the Scythian
camp, not knowing how or where they'd fled, or how many had
survived. We reached the battleground before the sun was half
a hand's width high and found there several ponies wandering,
some sheep and goats scattered about. We herded the strays
into our flocks and notched the horses' ears to mark them as

our own. But the camp itself was empty. No stragglers or sur-
vivors that we could see—only bodies, or pieces of them. And
vultures.

At the carnage's edge we found uncharred slats from the
strangers' broken wagons. We spent most of the brightest
gloom working to lash them up. When finally the aul arrived,
carrying Marjan wrapped in blankets on four men's shoulders,
they placed her in the makeshift sled, then the aul moved on.
Winter would come soon. We could smell it on the air.

We traveled across the lowland until we glimpsed a familiar,
distant rim of peaks. Just beyond, a gorge of steep, bare stone
cut deep into the pasture. There our people had retreated every
winter for as long as the eldest elders could recall. Its shelters
were our ancestors' places—dank cave floors strewn with straw
tucked beneath jutting rock, wooden cabins set up high on cliffs
built of hewn logs dragged from someplace so far off that no
one living had ever been there. Each season our people patched
them up, stuffed bare cracks with wool and grasses, laid the frozen earth with thick wool carpets, hung the wooden walls with
felts. Our summer yurts we used to store our hay and meat.
Higher still, our sheep would climb, joining mountain goats and
wild rams. Beyond the gorge spread another protected valley
where, if winter did not melt, then freeze, then crust the snow,
our horses could dig through the drifts to graze.

That morning a white frost glittered on the barren cliffs, but
the valley's floor lay in shadows, still dry and hard. We arranged
our camp, dividing the shelters as we'd done for generations—
several among Targitai's warriors, those for the ana-women
and their kin, and the Hewana's cabin where the elders and the
orphans ate and slept. There Meiramgul took the first red coals
from their heavy clay pot and laid them in the cold ring of
stones.

"*Alel bam, alal bam.* We are one fire, we are one hearth," the
Ak Kam chanted as the Hewana set the flames alight, then
shared the glowing embers all around.

Our warriors took their coals and returned to Targitai's hut.

There we lit our fire and watched it rise, then huddled close to wait for Marjan to die.

I could not excuse what she had done—disobeyed the call, riding when she should have stayed. We are trained to follow orders. As Bayir always told, Targitai's oath binds us to the aul; our own fate matters less than that our kin survive. What had she thought—that love would protect her? That her faith would shield her from the war god's rage? I could not understand such love, recalling only the emptiness of Erzhan's touch, the hollowness as we joined before facing death. Such a paltry thing could not be love, but only desperation.

Since the battle, he and I had barely spoken. It was awkward, difficult in such a small, close band, as if a hole had been bored into my sight or a tripping pit had appeared in the midst of level pasture. Often, as duties called, we were bound to ride close and work as one. But even on the practice field our words were clipped and sharp, our glances slipping fast away just as the heavy blades we wielded.

For several days Marjan's sickness bloomed and quelled, her eyelids closed, stretched thin as a close-shorn lamb. Ruan and I stayed by as the Ak Kam set a freshened poultice on her wound. "It is the barb." She pulled the thick felts back to show a great bloom circling the wound's entrance. "Snapped from the arrow's shaft, the iron point is still within. The skin there blazes with its own fire. To cut it out would likely kill her." Still, no amount of unguents, tinctures, or pleading with the gods seemed strong enough to heal. The wound festered, thick with ooze. The malevolence grew powerful within her.

On the seventh dusk came the first hard snow and with it, through the glittering fall, the Kara Kam returned. She staggered into our camp on a twisted leg, lurching though she never stumbled. She went to the warriors' cabin and flung open the door. Baring a jagged grin, she ducked inside as if she had always belonged there.

We all turned and stared. The Ak Kam and Hewana stopped

their hands stirring a great bronze cauldron that sat atop a glowing mound of coals. Appeasing Targitai's fury, they had sacrificed another pure white foal. I stood, my own hands slick with blood and bits of yellow fat from helping with the sacred butchering.

The only sound outside was wind, and within, the rattling of boiling horse bones. The Kara Kam let the wood door slam. It bobbed and creaked as she sucked her lips, then hobbled across the floor to take the honored place at the center of the western wall.

"You," she pointed. "Show me the wanderer." Her finger stretched and wagged at me; her voice, like the scrape of wood before it is smoothed and fashioned.

I rose up, terrified. The shriveled crone stole closer, leaning on a larch staff topped with a shining deer's bust cast in bronze. Even the Ak Kam stepped back as the black kam peeled Marjan's heavy wrap away to show her belly, now distended, the poultice sickly green, crusted from absorbing her wound's ooze.

The Kara Kam shook her head, raised her staff and began to shake it. Its curling antlers flashed, hung with clanging rings and bells. Now she gripped her mirror from where it dangled at her chest. "My sister's daughter's daughter—" She shook until I'd clutched the mirror's handle and, following her bobbling jowl, began to copy her movements, waving its reflection from side to side until the smoky air twined into a plume.

I watched it rise as the Kara Kam struck her drum—again, again with her long larch pole, the bronze bells rattling. Stonily, she began to chant, "Shoo! Shoo! Kak! Kak!" as if to ward off demons, her words growing louder above her drum. The warriors crowded near me, their terror merging with my own. Erzhan, most of all, tucked beneath the shelter's rough timber beam, his face stricken as he watched me—the Kara Kam's bronze mirror wafting, but I could not stop—back and forth, the movement and the Kara Kam's pounding compelling me.

Suddenly the Kara Kam raised her sheepskin cloak, flapping

her arms like a vulture's wings. Out of her mouth came urgent cawing—"Hie! Hie! Kak! Kak!"—as she waved us back and straddled her rattle's pole. She rode it like a mount—the small bronze bust transformed and grown into a deer's head. "To the pastureland where lost souls wander. Hie! Hie!" she cried and galloped round the hearth.

Now she rooted her shaft into the earth and began to climb. "First footstep to the sphere of stars.... Second to the full moon's bosom.... Third to the light called highest of the high.... Fourth in the heaven realm.... Come, my sister's daughter's daughter! Come!"

I tried to draw away, but could no longer see—not the cabin or our warriors or even now the aul. Instead, an open steppe and pale stars brightening—

"Do you see, there? Wanderer, can you hear me?" the Kara Kam cried. "Put me down, you. Hush now! Settle." She spoke to her flying deer as if it were a horse she'd tamed. "We have arrived, my sister's daughter's daughter. Look, child, we are home!"

She patted and stroked the deer's broad antlers, then began again to call: "White Deer, are you here?—Kak, Grandmother, I am here! Black Wolf, are you here?—Kak, Grandmother, I am here! Snow Leopard, are you here?—Kak, I am here! Golden eagle"—for each beast she called, I heard both question and response in her voice, but their pitch completely different, as if many souls filled her mouth to make the sounds.

"Come, my sister's daughter's daughter, find her. Help me." She turned as we ambled through the heaven realm. "The wanderer is lost! She searches for the heaven pasture. They are waiting—all of them—Grandmother, Great-Grandmother, all the ancestors who have ever walked the earth and those who have not before. Ah, she hears the songs of death! Yes"—the Kara Kam nodded—"they are beautiful."

I heard them, too—sounds too strange to be described. Then, in the distance, Marjan walking away from me.

"Marjan!" I tried to call but found I could make no sound.

For a moment I felt my fear, rushing as if I were falling, but the Kara Kam took my arms, and her eyes were suddenly deeply black and clear.

"We must draw her back," she whispered. "It is shame that draws her off—shame that makes her run. My sister's daughter's daughter, call her. Tell her, 'Marjan, we would have you stay!'"

I tried. I tried—

All at once the Kara Kam grabbed at Marjan's body. She gripped her arm and pulled so hard that she shuddered in her sleep and opened up her eyes.

Marjan screamed.

I awoke as if I had been asleep, again in the winter shelter with all the warriors gathered. I dropped the mirror, rushed to Marjan's side, Ruan and I both falling to our knees, trying to soothe her, but the Kara Kam held us off. She grinned and all at once the whole cabin was set awhirl, sharp light glinting off the small pegs that hung from her livid gums. She shook her rattling bronze and all was silent.

Marjan lay as if she had never stirred.

"It is shame that draws her off," she cried, now loud and lucid, her ragged voice oddly smooth and honed. "Shame—Marjan hides away. It is shame. We must set her free—draw her back with gratitude. Give her praises, honors!"

"Praises? Honors?" Erzhan spat on the frozen earth. "Death is what she deserves. She betrayed our hearth, our gods, our oath. Because of her, so many branches are laced with dead." He gestured toward a leafless cluster of distant trees that held the disemboweled corpses of our warriors. "All that wasted flesh for the selfishness of one fool girl."

I stared at him, as the others did—astounded, stricken, while the Kara Kam chewed her gums. Then quietly she croaked, "Young fool, you would have one more?"

Her bare sounds silenced him—silenced all of us with a chill that felt like frost. The Kara Kam began to nod, her head bobbling, jiggling as her eyes drew shut. Her mouth agape, her breath came in hot, dry puffs. She seemed to have forgotten us.

Then slowly her vision lifted—a hollow, haunted look as she climbed again onto her rattle's pole and trotted as if she rode a horse, waggling her drum and picking up the mirror I had dropped. She threw fistfuls of herbs and seeds on the fire until thick smoke wafted through the cabin like a veil. Hard to see. Harder to breathe. And everything around us slightly swaying.

The Kara Kam began to circle, calling, "Spirit of White Deer, you may go! Spirit of Black Wolf, you may go! Spirit of Snow Leopard, you may go! Spirit of Golden Eagle, you go too! Kak! Kak! All of you—you are not wanted. Rada Mai, who is our hearth, you have warmed this body long enough. You may leave, too, daughter of my sister's daughter. Tuck away the light." She slipped the mirror inside her tunic. When I looked into her eyes, I saw only the milky, lifeless gaze I remembered when I'd awoken as a girl.

The roof's eye, too, soon drained of all its smoke. Then, with lips curled and drooping, limping again, the Kara Kam picked her way to the door and left us. All that remained was a thin tendril rising from the coals like a night vine reaching toward the moon. Marjan lay full asleep and all of us sat cold and numb, staring into Rada Mai's enfeebled embers.

Dawn came. The sun drew high up in the sky and the winter glare bore down upon us. We spoke nothing of the night before; but I knew what I had seen, and the vision haunted me. All through that night as I'd lain on our lonely cot, my spirit wandered, searching, though I found the Kara Kam nowhere. Only I heard her speaking, "My sister's daughter's daughter," again, again. Through that mute refrain and the silence of Targitai's winter hut, I kept slow count of Marjan's breathing.

No one dared ask or explain—not even the Ak Kam when I passed her through the frigid dawn. Since I had been the Kara Kam's chosen, she seemed almost to fear me. She slipped her tsaagan bones, busying her hands, her eyes drawn distant and grim. So I joined the warriors' ranks. Bayir sent us on our usual scouting rounds, traveling to the edges of the gorge to watch for beasts or men who might raze our herds. Even Ruan rode, at Bayir's insistence, though he'd argued hard to stay behind; under threat of the war god's wrath, he knew better than to disobey. I rode out beside him but shunned Erzhan just as he shunned me. I did not care if he was afraid or awed by what I'd done. I had found Marjan on the heaven path. She had seen me, too, and—except for Erzhan's bitter words—I might have brought her back with me.

All that day Erzhan stayed silent as a shadow, circling just beyond our horses, camels, watching while we led our sheep and goats toward open patches revealed by windblown drifts. He was not the only one. Our other warriors also kept their distance, as if some wisp of the black kam's smoke still hung about me.

In the weary twilight, as we returned to the warriors' hut, we found Marjan sitting up in bed and smiling.

I stood, astonished, leaning to find my balance against the heavy, splintered wood while Marjan reached out softly and Ruan rushed to take her hand. "The Kara Kam was wrong," she murmured. "I am stronger than any of you thought."

"No." I bent down, too, and hugged her gently. "You are exactly as we've always known."

The Ak Kam helped Marjan sip a healing broth of salt milk tea, while Ruan laid his head onto her lap, exhausted. Tears drained as she cradled him and ran her fingers through his thick dark hair. When the Ak Kam turned to go, I rose, but Marjan grasped my wrist.

"Ruan"—she nudged him tenderly—"I must speak with Akmaral alone."

When they both had gone, a strangeness came into her eyes, a glassy luster as if she'd stared too long and hard into the sun. "Akmaral, it doesn't matter," she said.

"What?"

"The battle. Your weapons. Everything—none of it." She raised her hand. It shuddered as she cupped my cheek. "I am happy for you," she said, nodding toward the door.

"For what?"

"You and Erzhan."

I stammered. "How—"

"And envious, really." She smiled. "You have known what I have not and never will."

"Marjan, hush! The Kara Kam has healed you."

She whispered oddly, "The Kara Kam is gone. You won't see her again until the spring." Then she shook her head as if to thrust the thought away. "Life is in you, Akmaral. You do not feel it, but it's there. Death is shadows. Don't be foolish. Live while you are alive." Then she paused, her eyes heavy with sadness. "I should have been more patient. Ruan would have waited another season for me."

"He will wait again."

"I must rest," she whispered. Then she closed her eyes.

I helped her to lie back on the folded rugs and, for a breath, stood watching her hands pressed against her gently rising ribs. For a time she lay simply breathing, her mouth parted, eyes open, staring wide. Then—"Akmaral"—she reached again. I sensed strange urgency as she squeezed my hands. "In the heaven realm, I saw you riding."

"Marjan..." I tried to laugh.

But her face flushed rosy. The dung light shone against her cheeks. "You rode with many horses—in a great, tall hat. You both wore gold—you and your mare—walking slowly at the lead." Then she stopped and stared, a slow curve rising on her lips as if she were seeing something lovely.

She slept then; we all did. Even Ruan couldn't stay awake for long. And when we roused—his head resting softly on her shoulder—Marjan had already died.

We buried her that spring with solemn ceremony, burning sacrifices and chanting praises high on the mountain steppe. Into the earthen mound where her mother's mothers slept, we carved another niche large enough for Marjan's body. Covered thick with wax and honey, she was fodder for the bees; but her organs were long gone, replaced by mosses, sedges, fragrant herbs to keep her sweet, the incision behind her neck tightly sewn with horsehair. But her face, more peaceful than it had been in sleep, as it had not been in many seasons.

Into that niche, we also laid her warrior's garb, her arrows, quiver, her short, arched bow, the great bridle of white boar's tusks, and the small gold griffin amulet that she always wore. The snow leopard's pelt lay across her shoulders and the spear that slew it rested by her arm. Fresh foal's meat steamed in its round clay pot, enough to give her sustenance and to offer as a gift at the ancestors' hearth.

There I knew Marjan would be welcomed. When she reached the blade-thin beam of heaven's bridge, surely it would spread wide and she would race across it, joyful, laughing. But here on the earthly steppe, we knew well what we had lost. Hers was a virgin death, virgin in battle and in the ana-woman's bond; so as Marjan's spirit flew up toward the nether realm, the youngest children danced and sang and tossed white petals to spread the promise of her lost bounty.

PART II

THE GOLDEN EAGLE

12

PASSAGE

We are warriors. We are already meant to die. Erzhan's words haunted me, as they had that night when first we'd called our truce—as they'd taunted me until the eve of our only joining. Now the full moon had passed and all of it a grave mistake. I sat in the warriors' hut and stared at the crusted soil of my woman's blood. Whatever life he might have thrust inside of me—rich with fear and need and perhaps some want of love—all of it quickly driven out by what had come after.

I was glad of it, as I stuffed myself with new washed wool, then rose to stand beside Targitai's doorway. I parted the thick draped felt. Beyond, the aul was stained with gray. Shadows beneath the moon stood bold: outlines of crossings, so many paths made by people come and gone, our horses, herds, the aul's incessant course. From our many huts came movements, sounds—ana-women hushing cradled babies, bawling, sniveling, nursed to silence with a steady suck while cauldrons clanked, cooking horse meat, boiling butchered bones—all the passion and necessities of living.

Life is in you, Akmaral. You don't feel it, but it is there—Marjan's voice speaking from the path's last turn. It only leads to death; and the way she'd talked, as if from prophecy—*You and your mare—walking slowly at the lead.*

But, no, with my moon-brought blood, there was no lineage to come from me. I was grateful, truly, never having wanted Erzhan or his seed. Only fear had spurred my actions, while Marjan's goad was love. Was it right that she was gone while I stood barren on the forlorn steppe? My woman's blood—a dark red seep between my thighs that promised nothing.

Through those darkest hours, I rode mostly alone, grateful for the cloaking shrouds of snow that rose with the slightest wind. Sometimes, through their veils, Ruan would join my steps, quietly blending his unspoken grief with mine. We rode always one horse's girth apart, as if somehow Marjan's soul would ride between.

Then came Umai's season and the gatherings of spring when the camels had all calved and the ewes had mostly lambed and all around us new babies of all sorts received the fecund goddess's blessing. So came again the rounds of kesh-kumay, the fields rife with thundering horse-hooves and laughter. But I did not ride, for there was no one whom I cared to catch; and whenever Erzhan veered toward me, I avoided him.

Since the Kara Kam's rite, Erzhan had turned from me, too, as if he were afraid—not of what I'd done at the black witch's hand, but of what he could not know that I had seen. Still, he watched me from the shadows. But in daylight, he shunned me and fixed his passions on another girl. Her name was Gulnara, my new sleep-sister, who had taken Marjan's place on our heavy, matted felt. If he'd chosen her to spite me, it mattered little. I did not wrap my arms around her waist as I had with Marjan there. For all her living comfort, Gulnara was unwelcome as a late spring frost. With her every guileless breath, I missed Marjan all the more.

By Thagimisad's season, beside the evening autumn hearth, even Ruan and Aigul had become proper lovers. I could not blame them. Marjan's death had made an opening that Aigul aptly filled. Her light and wit were exactly what Ruan would need.

And I, unburdened, returned to my riding, following the herds across the great breadth of the steppes, no longer prickling like a barb whenever Erzhan ventured close, free to roam to the very edge of the horizon. If I was lonely, it was in mourning for Marjan. Her absence troubled me, though it had been many months now since she'd passed. Though I ached for her, I learned to savor my longing.

It is said to be unwise to hunt alone. And I did not—Marjan hunted with me. Long ago she had given me my skills, taught me how to bring down boar, how to track the mountain antelope, or stalk great wolves who preyed at the outskirts of our sheep. Now Marjan was beside me as I lay quietly in the bristle scrub listening for footfalls and rustling. She was the constant wind that blew—my mask, my protector. I sensed her in the way a beast would turn, in how I knew which direction it would take and how quickly it would run. I sensed when I should wait until a breath or twitch or flicker showed an eye peering coyly or a nose insensible to my human scent. And then the wind would hold its breath as I drew my bowstring, laying my arrow-shaft across my fist. I would take my sight and shoot. My arrow flew and the beast would fall to me.

Again, again—a rabbit or a fox, an antelope or a heavy-antlered elk—each time I'd gut my prey and watch life seep, then whisper praises to the spirit rising in the twisting curl of steam, then to the mistress of our clan's lands, then to Rada Mai who kept our hearth-fires ablaze, and finally to Marjan who, it seemed, watched over me.

But she was not the only one. I found footsteps and sometimes offerings. Bare prints crossed the drifts beside stones piled high and bits of blue torn cloth, or figures scratched in mud that would disappear when the frozen earth would soften. I did not know from where they came, only that I would ride and find them, tracing a line across the boundless steppe, enigmatic and intimate, both at once, as if they walked just beyond me.

One dusk, as I crossed toward the edge of the open gorge, I found myself in a place of tall, tilted stones—great pillars like teeth cutting through the earth's frost flesh, flat and gray, fixed and blunt as they stood against the wind. I had heard of such things: Meiramgul's stories told of stones like these found sometimes at the confluences of rivers or on the rise of shallow hills, left by someone ancient, older than ourselves. I rode in close and bared my palms, then pressed them against their frigid stillness. Beneath a sheen of ice, I felt shapes of an ancient herd—deer, each tucking thin limbs into bowing chests; heavy heads tilted backward to bear the weight of great curved antlers. Each leapt with all its grace and might into the sky. Flying deer. I clutched my amulet as I drew my hands across—they were the same odd shapes, as if they had been guiding me.

I turned, haunted by a distant howl. I twisted toward the sound and caught my glance on something sharp and slight—a thread of twining smoke and, just beneath, a single dugout cabin—no, a single yurt, plain and black, tucked beneath the cliff's hard rise. I knew at once: it was the Kara Kam's yurt, alone as it had stood so long ago—where I had not returned since I was a child.

I mounted my mare and moved off slowly, softly, recoiling with all the ancient fears. But then I heard the Kara Kam's voice and for a breath I saw her face—shadowed, feral, her teeth hanging from purple gums like thorns. "My sister's daughter's daughter!" I shook my head and turned my horse hard about, searching, but she was gone. I saw only the blaze of dusk burning through a whirling squall that sparkled like the stars on the heaven pasture.

Across the quiet steppe, I pressed my mare to leave, tripping swiftly, lightly, certain that, even from this distance, the Kara Kam could hear me. Night had begun to fall as I climbed, ever upward and away, until I had reached the cliffs that rose above the Kara Kam's yurt. I was frightened, panting, as if the black witch herself had chased me there. I had never ridden to this place before, where sheer stone walls were laced with ice, silent even of a breathless wind. Our people say that somewhere near lay hidden caves and that the long-passed spirits of our ancestors dwelled within them—my mother, father, perhaps Marjan—always watching.

It was strange to be so high and the air, so taut, as if drawn upon a well-strung bow, crisp as ice snapping with the weight of breathing. My mare's hooves grew cautious, hesitant, following the thin strand of smoke from the Kara Kam's hearth rising up until it frayed.

It was there, just then, that the snow leopard appeared. Spirit or real, I could not tell, as it paced along the overhanging ledge on silent, padded feet. I did not notice it at first, until a glittering cloud of crystal drifted softly down. The sharp ice grazed my cheeks, then flitted, lit by a heavy orange moon. In such stillness, I glanced up, cautious, moving just my eyes.

Above me, glowing, lucid golden vision shone from a mask of spotted silver, black, and gray. Paws larger than the size of my own boot print—the leopard settled in the snow and folded them neatly.

She did not look hungry or angry or even particularly fierce. Only curious, as if my shape had cast a tone of shadow she had not expected. I did not raise my weapon. There, beneath that ridge where the great power of the leopard's hind legs could be so quickly cocked, any threat I could present would have been pitiful and pointless. I stood, breathing steadily, as she watched me.

I don't know why I knew she was a female. Perhaps I only sensed—in the way she stared, almost daring me to take my right to pass, then granting it. When I did not move, she rose herself and turned to leave, but not before her bobbing cub scrambled through the snow beside her in careful hops. She glanced over her shoulder one last time, gazing directly at me.

I returned to the winter camp and did not speak to anyone of this meeting. Not even to the Ak Kam or Meiramgul. But soon I found the snow leopard haunting my dreams. Sometimes she pounced, and I would jolt awake, knowing that she had licked me—her tongue, coarse but not unkind, her gesture meant to cleanse me of some grit I could not see.

13

THE LION

Spring came and the aul moved on. Yet at every passage that we took, the ancestors and gods seemed to hold us back—boulders shifting, shaking, slippery with springtime ice. On the third day of our journey, a cloak of angry clouds descended across a narrow, treacherous pass, lacing it with the flash and crackle of Targitai's lightning. Suddenly it began to snow. We turned back. Whenever thunder marries snowfall, it is a sign of the god's displeasure.

We made camp in that frozen slush. Then the elders summoned and addressed us. No one knew what had caused the storm. But when it came my turn, the Ak Kam dealt with me harshly. She stripped me of my battle tunic, then tore at the thong that held the small gold amulet at my breast.

"What have I done?"

"You have seen the Kara Kam."

"No. I have not—not since Marjan's death." Yet I knew what she said was somehow true. The snow leopard was no mere beast. She was a spirit, watching over me.

"It is forbidden," the Ak Kam murmured. "The air she breathes is the gasp of demons. It turns green pastures into deserts and brings our newborn herds disease. The black witch's worth is that she lives and dies alone." Her voice was a slap, hard and stinging.

"Why?" A boldness rose up in my throat, though without the courage to raise my eyes.

The Ak Kam ignored my question as she pressed me down and held me by my scalp, then poured black ash across my brow, scooping it still hot from Rada Mai's fire. I bore the pain in silence, knowing that these marks were the harshest punishment any warrior could receive. Then she took her mirror and turned it toward the flames—"It is forbidden!"—scattering its jittery light. Foul smoke wafted toward me—choking—so like the Kara Kam's rite and her reflection, but this one held so little heat....

"Who"—I reached to block her sway—"who is the Kara Kam to me?"

At the edge of the smoky shadows, Bayir and Daniar exchanged a rippling glance. Finally Meiramgul held her stitch and sighed. "She is your elder aunt. Soyun, your mother's mother's sister."

"Soyun?" My body began to quake. I had heard that name only once or twice before. She was an elder, cursed and shunned, driven from the aul for speaking with the dead and dwelling in darkness. I had thought her only legend. "I did not know—"

"Of course." Meiramgul held my wrists. Her touch was warm against my sudden shivering. "You could not have known because we did not tell you." She stroked my temples. Ashes fluttered from my hair onto the waiting lattice of my lashes.

The Ak Kam spoke again. "The Kara Kam is condemned. She walks the path between life and death. Even in battle, it is death that chooses. Akmaral, do not go near her!"

But the Hewana raised her hand. "Khagan, enough. Let Akmaral steady with her new understanding."

The Ak Kam sniffed, then reached and took my cheeks, her touch stinging at the places where the ash still burned. Finally she let me go.

Meiramgul raised her felt again, stitching small, even darts like footsteps across a pure white field. "Akmaral," she said, "sacrifice a newborn lamb. Feed its meat to Rada Mai and pray that the gods protect you. The Ak Kam is not wrong. Beware the Kara Kam—that she does not beguile you."

With the dawn, the sun rose bright. The unsettling snow vanished as quickly as it had come and the mountain's shoulders shimmered with torrents crackling over ice. Argimpasa, the springtime goddess, had put on her jewels and begun to dance. So we followed where she flashed in search of greening pasture.

At the back of our cavalcade, I lulled with the swaying of my mare's hoof-steps, but my heart was troubled. I was no longer alone. The Kara Kam was my aunt. My only blood relation. Yet even with my parents dead, the elders had kept her back. What was this part of me that they all so feared—even Erzhan, our fiercest warrior? I searched our ambling pack, between lines of goats, sheep, horses, camels. I could not find her. Had never thought to look for her before. Had never questioned how or where or why she traveled with us. Always close and yet we saw her nowhere: she was ephemeral as the wind or like the buzzards winging overhead, steady as they clung to a snag of rising air but silent, barely casting shadows.

Too, I sensed, beneath the Ak Kam's ire, some envy or even awe. It brought back how she'd stooped after the Kara Kam's rite: there, beside Marjan's death bed, dropped onto her knees, sifting through the dirt and soot to scrape up fallen seeds which she'd tucked away into a carved stone vessel. I did not smell those seeds again until coldest winter when Bayir's breath turned to a shallow cough and then, as it always did, to a gasping whistle. That season his breathing was far worse. Some called it Targitai's fist, gripped about his lungs in punishment for failing to control his warriors. For days the Ak Kam burned those seeds and pressed Bayir to breathe their smoke until finally he grew strong again. Now I understood—it must have been the Kara Kam's seeds that healed him.

Three days we rode until Argimpasa showed us a place of flowing streams. Bright flowers bobbed beneath the weight of birds and insects. Spring on the steppes is brief. There is abundance; the harsh sun and whipping winds have not yet left their blisters and scars. So we let our horses drift toward the waters' edge. But before they even reached that far, we saw that another band had also settled near.

They seemed not much: just a handful of riders bent against

the wind, their horses' muzzles dipped into the stream. Bayir called a party to go forward and discover their intent, whether to share this field or if they would move on. Yet we had no time to talk. Even as our envoys breached the plain, the strangers whirled about and charged.

They rallied round our herds, circling faster, keen to seize what we had brought. So few on horseback, yet half their number broke with bows from inside flimsy yurts, sticking arrows through holes in the wadded, moth-eaten felts.

I galloped, the fastest I had ridden through our six days' travel. Already the Hewana had veered her course, shouting across her horse's neck, "Back into the hills!" The aul turned at her command while the warriors gathered, then spread out. At Bayir's signal, we began to swarm.

We had practiced many times, in all weathers and every season. Bayir knew our most vulnerable places. He had trained us in attacks and showed us how to prevail when backed against a cliff or on slippery scree. But here in this open field with few obstacles and little need for finesse, our arrows flew and crossed unchecked, falling across the battleground like hail.

Behind us Bayir called, "Forward! Strike! Pull back!" My mare's hooves cut the air as I galloped at another warrior's flank. Then both of us drove wide. Our full host spread out like a fox's tail. We raised our bows and shot. Strangers' arrows battered all around us. Their aim was fierce as stinging wasps, and their attacks, wise, mirroring our own, cutting through our lines, storming over and over with their meager forces. Their arrows flew at twice our speed and pierced almost as often. One skimmed my horse-hoof scales and split my tunic's leather, but it only grazed my upper arm. As I rode on, I felt it bleed.

Between strikes we dashed, ducked, swerved, joined to stretch into an arc. We spread wide, then closed. Bayir shouted, but his voice grew hoarse. He coughed, leaned forward across his gelding's neck as if his breaths were Targitai's last bleak embers. I feared for him, so I prayed to the thunder god: *Please, let Erzhan come!*

Finally, from behind, his white stallion pounded past me. Its breath came hot, mouth sputtering froth as Erzhan seized his rightful place. My heart released as he rode close, then called, "Break wide!"

We all fell into ranks as Erzhan pressed us to rally in renewed attacks. We surrounded the strangers, drove hard, shot fast, then turned in retreat, again, again until we'd forced them into a huddle. With each turn we kept beyond their range, twisted in our saddles, let fly another shot. They were trapped. They should have given up. Yet the strangers' arrows continued.

Suddenly two of our own warriors toppled, their horses pierced through the shoulders, riders crushed in a tumbling of hooves and weapons tossed. We pulled back to avoid collision. The strangers caterwauled and jeered. For a moment we rode in shock. But Erzhan's voice cut through. "Pull back. Shoot them in arcade!"

We did as we were ordered, circling our dead, sending arrows high. They fell and struck in a pointed shower, but clattered, useless, to the ground. I realized then that the strangers' caps were made not of felt like ours, but of rounded, tarnished metal.

I turned for my next retreat, and one of their warriors followed—a ragged brute hunched low against a black-hocked mare. As he gained, I held my breath, drew up, peered low, aimed at his saddle. My bow arched taut. The bent wood squeaked. I let my arrow fly. From a distance, I feared I'd miss, but somehow I pierced his horse's withers. Together they rolled, kicking up dust, tripping others of their pack who reared and doubled back.

Around me, the fighting closed. Warriors fell from their mounts to attack on foot. Swords clanked as loud as sparks and thunder. "Too close!" Erzhan shouted. "Pull back! Ride on!" His words played rhythm for my next strike. Rounding left, I aimed from my bow-seat. Pulled and shot. One, two. More strangers fell. Just beyond their reach, I found a clear path again, turned, grasped another arrow, and charged.

Soon the grass was littered with men and arms and horses. Of those who had attacked, all that remained were a scattered few. Erzhan pulled up short and mocked them. "Watch them—frightened sheep scurrying before our wolves!"

But Bayir rode in close and hushed him. "It is wrong to gloat. The strangers were far outnumbered. They fought bravely."

The stragglers skittered along the river's banks, urging on their injured horses. We watched them for a time, until Bayir slipped from his mare to pick up a shattered point. He examined it. Then he handed it to Erzhan.

"Iron." He pointed. "Trefoil and barbed." They latched eyes, then passed the arrow-tip around.

We all understood, remembering the only other time we had found such points. They had littered the battlefield after the raid when Marjan was shot. They were Scythian.

"Go after them," Bayir said. "Bring them back as captives. Stop them before they can summon more." He coughed, then his hand passed across his lips where a gob of spittle hung. He brushed it from his sparse gray whiskers and wiped the wet across his gore-spattered knee. Then he rode to warn Meiramgul and the others.

Erzhan called his captains to lead small bands after the lingerers across the steppe. The rest of us paced the bloodied field. Many of the Scythians lay still moaning, limbs shattered beneath their horses, horses bleeding but not yet dead. I approached them cautiously, standing just beyond their reach. With my long sword, I pried away their scabbards first, then their quivers, then sliced the sinew of their bows and kicked their weapons off with my upturned boot. Their faces stared at me, gaunt, ill-tempered, desperate in a way that said food had been scarce. So I let my work be quick, driving my sword cleanly through each warrior's lungs or heart or underneath the shoulder.

The bodies that remained, the aul left for carrion. But the strangers' injured horses we butchered and burned. We added koumiss and fresh mutton as Targitai's offerings, their smoke drifting together to the sky. The pasture was our own again, dedicated to Rada Mai with the Ak Kam's chants.

At dusk, just as Targitai's blade tinged the earth with the shades of blood, we saw our riders returning. They brought three captives tied on horses sideways, their spines bare, laid against their saddles, arms and legs spread and bound about each horse's girth. Madiyar led them, dangling guiding reins at a steady pace while some younger warriors charged home with wild shouts. As the sunlight slipped away, the whole aul rode out to meet them.

The night shone new with a slivered moon. The stars wore a windswept veil of clouds. We stayed mounted on our horses, well above and three lengths back. Meiramgul stared down at the captives, paced around them slowly, then gazed at Madiyar. "Only three?"

"Two more we shot as they breached the river's bank," he said. "These are all that were left alive."

The Hewana caught Bayir's grimace. The Ak Kam rattled a fistful of tsaagan bones.

"This is the second time they've come." Bayir pulled at his chin. "What do they want here?"

Weaponless and bound, the strangers could do us little harm. But even in that dim, we all stood afraid.

I could see in their eyes their fierceness. Set wide, unblinking, even laid upside down on their horses' backs, their gazes were defiant, cold, and scheming. By their tunics, they must have been soldiers—littered with war plaques and iron scales. Even their horses wore bridles of griffins' heads and savage dueling rams, all supremely crafted out of bronze. But their stiff black cloaks were mottled, mangy, as if they'd worn them many years without repair. They were made of the fur of bears which are distant forest creatures. They must have come from somewhere north or west, where the trees grow dense as the bristles of fine horsehair.

Erzhan cut one of the stranger's cords and the man slipped hard into the dust. Wrists and ankles still bound, blood from our lashings traced his arms, and across his chest a deep gash from the fight. As he'd lain backward on the saddle, the blood had seeped along his neck and dried in muddy clumps in his coal-black hair.

"Too fine a cloak to waste," an ana-woman shouted. "Cut it from his back!" She had lost her mate to the Scythians' arrows. So a blade frayed the stranger's binds while three riders stood full weight upon his arms, lifting and yanking until the cloak was wrenched away.

We bound the brute again, then stripped the other two down to their skins. Each cloak we gave to the family of someone who had died. Their golden plaques we removed, then turned to kicking, spitting, pelting them with stones and dust. Some warriors brought out horse whips and long urga poles or jabbed at them with half-dulled swords and daggers.

"Do not kill them," Bayir commanded. Still it was some time before the tormentors moved away, leaving the captives with dark welts and bloody gashes.

The Ak Kam cleaned their broken skin so it would not fester, but only so they would live long enough to speak. For three days the elders plagued them. "Why have you come? What do you want here?" The prisoners made few sounds, or when they spoke, their words were garbled, unfamiliar, as if they didn't know our tongue or refused to speak it. We tortured them, but they did not give up easily, even as we tied them to their own horses and yanked them through thorny scrub.

At night we left them in the shadows tied to a rooted horse post, exposed to the chilling breath of early spring; then, with the morning, baking in the sun. It shone high, a cloudless sky where vultures traced dark circles around the Scythians' own fallen. The birds often landed in great clouds to peck at the moldering corpses, our captives' eyes reflecting back the horror.

We set watch and each took turns. When mine came, I settled close—just beyond their bare arms' reach. They kept their faces still as stone, though I knew they eyed the sword I'd left beside me on the ground, the dagger at my right, my bow and

arrows still in their quiver strapped to my horse grazing nearby.
I left them there to test them, to see how much they wanted to
escape; though they could not, all tied together, backs against
backs, hands and arms staked, wrists stained with the blood of
futile trying.

I had never been so close to such enemies before. Unless
they were women fit to breed, our aul rarely took captives. Two
of them were dark, their eyes expressionless, coarse and hateful. But the third stared off evenly and calm, always gazing at
the horizon. There his face often turned wistful as if somehow
he could travel using only his will and eyes. So I murmured,
"It is too far—as far as the heaven pasture. Your ancestors are
closer to you in death than you are to your homeland now." The
way he glanced at me, I knew he hadn't understood, but I said
it again a little louder, then laughed at him cruelly.

Sometimes the stranger's lips would move and I thought
that perhaps in some Scythian way he prayed. Those lips were
cracked and parched, though he refused to drink even when
water was offered. Strangest of all, beneath the grime this prisoner was fair and his eyes a vivid blue. Like the sky.

Meiramgul had always told that there were people from the
west whose eyes were as pale and clear as ice-melt on a springtime lake. Now I looked at his and saw it true. And his hair, so
bright, a shade lighter than the fairest coat of a two-humped
camel. It glimmered in the sun, long and twisted, sparking even
through sweat and grime and blood. I found myself wondering,
twisting the ends of my own long braid around my thumb. It
was bronze instead of dark. But that was nothing. This captive with his thick blond beard that grew around his chin—I
couldn't help but think, the man resembled a lion.

As the captives sat, our children came and pelted them with
rocks. One found a stick and nearly poked at the blond man's
eye, but I pulled the stick away. "If Bayir means to blind him, I
will return it to you."

All the while I occupied myself with my blade and a bit of
narrow willow, crafting a strong shaft for one of the arrowheads

we'd gathered from the fields. Dozens lay about, so we sent the
children to collect them. Bayir spent the night examining their
tips, showing them to the elders and our four captains. Now we
worked to add them to our quivers. I took pleasure in the task,
humming as I worked, knowing that it irked them to see me
studying their finer craft. Our own points were flatter and not
bored hollow, while theirs were neatly shaped to hold the shaft
within the barb. My father would have found them a marvel.

On the third day we drenched them with buckets of river
water to cut their stench. Then we fed them. Erzhan stood
guard while Yerbol loosened their arms from the post but kept
their ankles and wrists still bound. Enough freedom to eat, but
no more. The gristly meat we gave, they gnawed desperately between their teeth. Their fingers glistened with the fat to match
the gleam of water dripping from the stringy coils of their
beards. The blond man sat cross-legged at a slant, awkwardly
leaning his body over his food. He was mostly naked except
for his leather trousers, torn at the knees and cutting sharply
at the bones of his scrawny waist. He didn't seem so fierce
now as he had: the sun had baked him brown, red in some
places, which lent a painful sheen to his indigo tattoos—vicious
beasts poised for attacks or cowering prey. And strange hairs
covered his chest, twisted tightly into curls. I had never seen
a man made so before. Our own men's chests were bare and
completely smooth.

He ate quickly and for a while rested, left to wait while the
other two finished. He straightened out his legs and placed his
fists between his upper thighs. Leaning his bare back against
the rough-hewn post, the blond man stared, as he always did,
toward the horizon. Then he lifted up his coupled wrists. Pressing hands together, thumb-knuckles to his mouth, he blew and
a sound came out—the softest whistle. Low and mournful like
the cry of a black-necked grebe. For a time he closed his eyes,
lost in his own music. When he opened them again, the sun
caught his gaze, bright as if a bit of sky had broken off and
fallen into them.

There was talk of killing. "What is the worth of keeping them alive? They must eat," Daniar muttered. "They must travel with us. They must sleep beside us. Murderers and thieves—they will kill us in the night, take our cattle, horses, sell those who survive on the trader's road as slaves."

Bayir shook his head. "They are most likely scouts. Otherwise, why come so far alone?"

Meiramgul sighed. "So many generations since our great-grandmothers fled the Black Sea's shores—the Persians and the Scythians, the scars still left from endless war—it is hard not to remember."

Bayir nodded. "If these scouts do not return, others will follow. They will be tracked. Either way, more Scythians will come. I will send out warriors to follow in their wake." So he did, each in a new direction.

After three days they returned, having discovered two other nearby camps raided. One aul had driven the invaders off with tribute. "The Scythians took no captives," Madiyar said. "Only food and horses, then moved on. But another aul fought and lost. The bodies left were long since pecked to bone. Of our cousins' yurts, there were only ashen circles."

"But sheep still grazed the fields," Yerbol said. "They bore our cousins' ear-split brands. We brought them along with us. Strange that the Scythians left them."

Bayir threaded his fingers against his bushy brows, then shook his head. "The sheep would have slowed them down."

The Ak Kam spread her tsaagan bones over the thick felt carpet, then tilted one small white anklebone with her fingers, the only one that had fallen upside down. "We would be unwise to kill them. There are strange movements about."

Meiramgul nodded. "We will do nothing. Watch them. Wait until they learn our tongue. Then discover what they know, where they hail from, and why they've come."

That is how the strangers came to lie on the cold hard dirt outside the warriors' yurt. That is how I began to know Timor.

14

WATCHING

We sheared the men like sheep—their heads and beards, even the hair on their strange, pale chests. One of them dared to glare as the Ak Kam held the fleecing blade. He shouted as he struggled, spitting as we held him down—"Oeorpata! Oeorpata!"—his spittle casting hatred, his harshest glances falling especially on our girls. We did not understand his words, but his look was pure revulsion.

Even shorn, the captives bared their teeth. All but the golden man, the blond one. Now smooth skinned as a child, he stayed unperturbed even as he knelt, hands tied. So Meiramgul went and stood before him. She reached and grasped his new, raw chin. He bristled, narrowed his gaze, jaw blunt as she tilted it from side to side. She surveyed him like a beast—his broad cheeks and narrow nose peaking slightly at the bridge. A gleam of sweat seeped from his temple. It dripped across Meiramgul's finger. She wiped it on her thigh.

With this last humiliation, our crowd finally dispersed. Again the blond man fixed his eyes on the horizon. I could not help but notice, as I came on guard: his interminable stare, as if he had seized upon a vision that, if he moved his gaze away, would simply disappear.

He stayed tied to his companions, backs pressed against the rugged post. The other two we saw at once were brothers. Their resemblance was in their close-set eyes and in the way they leaned, shoulders rounded at the same angle like a memory of the curl inside a single mother's womb. The elder had a craggy face and, after several days, again a crusted, prickly beard. The other bore thicker features, much akin but with a flat, pressed nose like one who had lost often at wrestling. These two were ruffians, anyone could see. But the fair-haired man—even with his wrists and ankles bound, even sitting in his own filth, his eyes retained their silent dignity. The other two leaned toward him too, and his whispers kept them calm. They drank his words and treated him with deference. That was how we came to understand he was their leader.

We made little of it, giving him the same gristly scraps as the others. Now at nights, they lay each tied to separate posts inside a threadbare yurt, the blond man pressed against the wall closest to the door. It was the lowliest position and a gesture of contempt, though one that he would little comprehend. Still, Erzhan said that it was not a place for prisoners. "He can almost reach the door-flap when it rustles in the wind." But Bayir reasoned it was worth the risk, that now we would see if the men were clever. So when we sensed some purpose in their gestures and whispered talk, Bayir assigned a second guard. And when they eyed us sharply for it, a third. But when it came my turn on watch, sometimes I sent the other guards away.

We had heard that Scythians do not train their women, that they leave them vulnerable, unable to defend themselves. We'd heard, too, that they knew our kind and called us despicable. So I sat with them alone, knowing that they took me lightly and looked at me with scorn, when all along it was they who were weak and at my mercy.

Then night would fall and the two dark dogs would sleep. I was left in the dull, dim silence with only the blond man's stare. Through the chill of those early midnights, we sat, hardly blinking, gazes locked, as if the blond man had no need for rest or had the will to remain eyes wide without wearying.

In the daytime we kept the captives outside like beasts. I would ride off with the herds and, when I returned, find the blond man sometimes watching me. His grim stare shifted from its distant focus, his eyes aglow like turquoise stones or the iridescent insides of the polished shells that the Ak Kam carried. His gaze grew bolder as I ambled, carrying my weapons and my tack still laden with my horse's sweaty sheen.

One day I took the blond man by the rope and led him, alone, inside Targitai's yurt. There I knelt beside the cooking fire and poured the tea that had been warming on the hearth. The blond man's lips were parched and cracked, a bit of blood dried black at the corners.

"Drink." I made his tied hands loose and gave him the bowl, dropping in milk and a pinch of salt that clouded, then merged into a creamy liquid. I watched him sip, his angled jaw set with hard shadows in the fire's light. His chin was stubbly, scaled with a dirty crust. One drop of tea dangled from his lower lip, threatening to turn the caked filth to mud.

"Wipe yourself." I handed him a cloth, sloshing closer the nearby bucket I had brought up from the stream. He dipped the felt and slowly rubbed. The dirt turned the cloth dull brown, in places tinged with crusted red.

Then a shadow filled the doorway. "Akmaral." Erzhan entered. "You treat him like a guest—give him koumiss and comfort?"

I eyed him harshly. "He must drink or he will die. Then what good will he be to us?" I pushed up from my knees, busying myself hanging my damp tack from the beams as Erzhan turned on the stranger. "Who are your people? Why have you come?"—the same barrage of questions that had gone unanswered for many days.

The blond man set the bowl back on the earth. He reached his slackened wrists toward his side, where a belt would have borne a bow and quiver, and mimed shooting arrows, shoving, the clash of arms.

Erzhan twisted the blond man's binds behind his back. "You provoke me, dog?"

"Erzhan, leave him. He is trying to speak." But the blond man was still again.

Erzhan shoved him to the ground, knocking his head into

the hearth-stones, his foot on the man's neck to hold him down. "Don't be fooled, Akmaral. He is Scythian. He can't be trusted." Then he stormed out through the wind-flapped door.

When I turned, already the man had tried to right himself again, struggling first onto his shoulder, then with all his strength pressing against the wasted hollows of his rope-raw wrists. All the while, he tried to hide a mocking grin.

So I stepped nearer, drew my dagger, and laid it flat against his cheek. His bare back tensed and he clenched as I pressed its tip but did not cut—just pulled back slowly, my gesture an unquestionable warning. Finally I released him, then knelt to check his skin for blood. The blond man caught my wrist and drew me close with his filthy fist. Before I could escape, he had tangled up his fingers in my hair.

15

BREATHING FIRE

That season brought its drop of foals. Lambs speckled the grasses, deep curling black or milky white through sprays of colored blooms. That spring I did not see what was to come. Timor had just arrived. It was only the beginning.

As youths, Erzhan and I had used each other as warriors often do, hoping to gain strange comfort from the joining, reassurance that we would live another day. I had longed to feel the power of my pounding blood and his, the thrill like another race as the one we'd run when we were barely more than children. But our joining had left me cold, longing for something still unfulfilled. Even when I'd done with him, still I knew nothing.

So when love began, I did not recognize it. Dangerous, uncertain, tentative, then vast, encompassing, stretching without stop—high and nearly silent as a flock of distant starlings which swell and break as great black clouds casting shadows across the steppe, all one and yet completely separate, fluttering apart, bound to be rejoined.

The blond man struck me with his silence, though I knew he'd begun to learn our words. Meiramgul had sent one of her sons to stay beside the strangers and badger them day and night, picking up sticks and naming them, stones and naming them, grasses and naming them. Riding in circles, the boy would shout out words for the horse's steps, and the felts we used for saddles or yurt cloths, and the poles and lattices that those would drape, and the kettles and cauldrons, and all the usual things until the men would speak them in their sleep, and we knew they'd begun to understand us.

Then came my turn. I brought weapons and taught them—"Quiver. Arrow."—holding each one in my hand.

"Bow." I raised mine up, stood, aimed, and shot. The target was on the far ridge. I pierced it at its center. The vibration of my bowstring warbled. The arrow's landing made a heavy thump. I raised my bow and aimed again. Even at that distance, the second hit the first with an audible *thwack*.

The rough strangers' eyes were dark coals shifting, swallowing the vibrant light. But the blond man looked at me and almost smiled.

We put them to work. They were thin and weak and could do little: mostly weaving, milking, cleaning wool for felts, collecting dung in sacks to burn for heat. The blond man was handier than the others, or at least more willing to try. After half a moon had gone, Meiramgul sent her youngest daughter to sit beside him. She taught him how to sew thin slivers of horses' hooves onto our leather vests. So the blond man became quite skilled at making armor.

In time they regained their strength and some little of their once taut form. But the more vigorous they grew, the more Erzhan mistreated them. "These Scythians—feeble, ignorant"—whipping, kicking them, handling them far worse than an unruly horse or a mongrel dog. Until Bayir came and told him he must stop. "They were strong once. As frail as they were when we found them, to have lasted on the steppes far from home and friendless—strong, indeed, to have survived at all."

Erzhan scowled. "We cannot hold them tied forever, captives within reach of our fires and arms. We should kill them and be done—"

"Erzhan, we have not learned yet what they know. The more you provoke them, the more they will refuse to speak. What words would you have for a captor who beat you?" Bayir spoke it sternly, then glanced across the grass at me. "Learn from Akmaral. She is patient with them."

I stared down at my boot, kicking at a clot of dirt to avoid Erzhan's gaze. He only grunted, but after that he kept away. Soon I alone was assigned as their jailer.

I sat high on horseback and harried them day by day. With

their wrists and ankles hobbled, I dragged them from place to place to do chores that no one else wanted. They carried heavy bundles on their backs, gathered horse dung, water sacks, or new-dried felts folded but not yet sewn. And when we moved to another field, they loaded our camels and trod beside them silently. They were useful and did little to resist. If they were thirsty, I made them milk the nanny goats or ewes, but not our horses.

Among themselves, when still they whispered, I curled my silver horsewhip around my palm in warning, though I rarely struck. I didn't have to understand their words: the blond man's eyes spoke ever toward the horizon's break. If that mountain cleft in the distance had been his aim, surely his arrow would have pierced its very center.

A moon had grown to full and passed away when there came a dawn of late spring storms. The air turned heavier and colder, then suddenly thick with snow. Then another melt and a second freeze that caked the snow with crust—ice so hard that our herds couldn't nuzzle through to find their grass. After a day watching the beasts' futile trials, our riders rallied to trample through the gloss before all the new foals and lambs were lost. Only I was left alone to guard the captives.

Just inside their yurt I sat, dagger at my hip, my long sword poised beside me. Each man was tied to a separate stake a good distance from his mates and the yurt's walls. Each lay on a thin wool mat with a blanket of worn felt covering his limbs, their places not too close to the dung fire. We'd grown used to each other like this, though still they rarely spoke while I was near. The blond man lay on his back, arms and feet still bound, staring silently up at the smoke-hole, awake while his brothers finally began to snore.

I busied myself tying sinews around the joints of a newly fashioned bow. Every now and then I glanced his way, noticing as the light grew dim how his skin glowed golden to match the ragged wisps that had sprouted on his scalp and the strange bright hair that had grown back across his chest, how it coiled into soft, amber curls. I set my bow aside when I was through, watching as he stared. He no longer seemed even aware of me.

Outside the aul was quiet with the mantle of thick snow muffling our distant horses' snorts. My hand rested at my collar, absently fingering my amulet on its thong, then drifting to my braid, its end tied with a strap of felt. I pulled off the tie, then gently smoothed the strands, bowing my head as I caught sight of its pale luster—how it caught Rada Mai's light with the same clear sparks that danced among the coals.

As if the blond man sensed my thoughts, all at once he turned his gaze on me. More than any time before, now his glance was a piercing arrow flung, an eagle's talons braced before a hurtling dive. My heart rose in my throat, so hard and swollen that I nearly choked. The stranger did not turn away, not even as my hand dropped down to seize my dagger.

My father's blade—feeling it against me calmed—as the man's breath rose and fell, slightly clouding the chilly air. His body tensed, aware as I edged close. My dagger firmly in my fist, I knelt at his side. I raised my blade and placed it on the thin, worn joining of his trousers. It was not hard to see his hunger rise.

I angled as if to pierce, but did not cut as I moved my dagger toward his belly and then his bristled neck. There I let it rest, absorbing his heat through the cold gray metal. His pulse inside those veins moved my iron rhythmically and very slightly. He stared without fear or contempt, his eyes so pale as if to fade into their own soft whites. His gaze was the heavy air; like a rising storm, it surrounded and clutched me. It pressed more powerfully than I'd ever thought—the only time before, when I had accepted Erzhan's touch so long ago. That had been a mistake. Yet here in this cold, dim yurt with the fire crackling softly and the air rattled by foreign snores, lay another.

I bent onto my knees with Rada Mai's fire burning behind me. My shadow stretched and towered. It engulfed him. Helpless, his hands bound by a long cord to his feet, his torso bare, arms clenched behind his back, his shoulders painfully bulging. Still his gaze remained, anxious, thirsty as the supine steppes, and I, the heavy cloud hovering above, withholding promise of a summer downpour.

I bent and touched his boots; their seams were worn to holes and their soles completely walked through. I drew them off, took them to the door, and threw them far out into the snow beyond the yurt. I said, "You will not kill me."

I knew he understood. The way he stared, how his eyes slipped down to where my hand lay still on my dagger's hilt. I untied it from my belt and hung it high above. The knot that held his wrists behind his back I loosened just enough, but added a second rope to the standing post. This one I tied around his throat. Then I straddled him and tugged at the sinew to draw apart his trousers.

His hips pressed toward me and I instantly took him in, my blood like thunder quaking. Such a passion, a fat-fed fire, the heat between us bursting hotter than the coals. The air around us crackled as on nights when lightning streaks across the sky: great bright scratches, wild, frightening. The blond man pulled at his binds, grunted, his hands clenched beside him as if he longed to take my hips, so I took his instead, raised them, pressed him deeper. His chest dappled with dampness, thick hair glistening. My fingers, then my face, pressed to his skin. Our breaths came hot and short and finally silent, his mouth pressed into my hair and my lips pressed to his breast. When I slipped away at last, he lay coated in a film of dust that had tufted from the felts our limbs had creased and scattered.

I stood and replaced my trousers, my tunic, regained my fox-lined jacket, my belt, my blade. Then I looked at him lying, his chest rising, falling with contented breath, his arms still tucked awkwardly beside his waist, his bare organ glistening and slowly shrinking from use and chill.

I bent, untied his throat, and laced his trousers up. "You will have your boots again," I said. "New ones, thick and dry, when it is morning."

I would have thought that would have been enough—repay-
ment for what we both had used. But suddenly the man rose up
with all the strength that was in his waist. His hands still bound,
he laid his lips over my mouth and kissed me fiercely.

That next dawn I beat him. I don't know why. I suppose it was
for fear, to show that I had taken him not as lover but as captor.
He was at my mercy and I made sure he felt my blows. But he
looked at me no differently, forever cool and penetrating. That
night I took him into me again, simply for my own pleasure,
though his back still bled from the hailstorm of my horse-whip.
I hung it just above, dangling from the roof-beams as I mounted, to remind him.

Then I watched him for a day from a distance, and then another night. I watched and did not come near, fearing the ache
inside me. On the third night, I did not resist, nor the fourth,
and by the end of the young moon's passage, I had untied his
wrists. Crusted, reddened circles, like bracelets, ringed where
the binds had cut—where each night he had struggled in our
passions.

I bound them up, this time in softer cloth, no longer tied
with a fastening strand between. As I drew back to my duty, he
reached for me. "Akmaral." He said it stiffly.

It was a triumph. I did not move. "Why did you attack?"

He gestured as if to take up meat and place it in his mouth.

"Are others coming? Scythians? We've heard—"

"Not—" He shook his head. "Not Skoloti!" He screwed
his face and spat. "Melanchlaeni." He pounded at his chest,
then reached for my tunic, gripping at the places made of black
sheep's wool. He struggled for some words. "Melanchlaeni—
black—"

"I don't understand—"

"Forests. Hills. Black Cloaks—Melanchlaeni." He bent and
etched with his bare, raw fingers a landscape in the rigid ground.
"Home—Skoloti take our lands." Then he furiously wiped the
scratches away.

After that, only in daylight did I keep him hobbled. At nights I took my fill of him. He told me his name—"Timor"—which means iron in their language. When I said the word, it rested on my tongue like honey.

There was talk that I had gone too far. Even Aigul came to question, though I found I had no answers.

"He is handsome," she said.

"It is not that—"

"Then what? Akmaral, to take a stranger—an enemy.... Our own warriors were not enough? There was no one in the cousin auls?"

I shook my head, though her opinion pained me.

Ruan stepped behind and brushed her shoulders. "Aigul, you of anyone should not condemn the whim of love." He clasped her hands in his broad grasp until she let her outrage fall. Lovers now for near a round of seasons, his patient sadness had softened her. "Marjan is not here," he said to me. "She watches from the heaven pasture. But if she could speak, I know, Akmaral, she would be happy for you."

There were others, too, who said that what I'd done had pleased the ancestors and gods. The sun came hot and all the snow had melted quickly. Through the muddy pools our beasts tramped and drank. The grasses returned greener than they'd been before. Our riders made their rounds, spreading wide our herds to take advantage of this new ripeness. Meanwhile Bayir sent Erzhan with a small band to patrol the outer hills. They encountered scouts from neighboring clans, all of them friends or cousins. But no more intruders. The dawn after their return, I took Timor before the elders.

"We come"—he gestured—"many days riding," then drew another map across the ground, this one vast with waving grass and finally short squiggles that were clearly hills. Through this, he drew a deep, wide line. "Rha." He pointed to the river. Then another. "This Danu. Danu—Greeks say Tanaïs."

He glanced toward me so that I knew this was the place

of which he'd dreamed, far beyond our mountain cleft. Then he drew a Scythian horse and rider. Spitting on the ground, "Skoloti!" he exclaimed, then rubbed the shapes away with his bare palms. "Take boys—not grown." He pulled the short hairs that twisted like rough fur across his chin. "We fight for Skoloti. Despise Skoloti. Treat us like beasts. Like you." He glared at Erzhan.

Bayir drew Timor's attention back. "Why not fight—drive the Skoloti off?"

"Fight or burn—Gelonus. Like Gelonus."

From the shadows, Meiramgul nodded. "Gelonus. Our grandmothers knew that name. It was a city in the north inhabited by Greeks. In the fight against the Persians, their army burned it to the ground so there would be nothing left for King Darius to seize."

"My home, forest cut." He drew a high hill and coated it with trees and heavy branches. "From here"—he gestured beyond the door-flap—"far away. These two—Bulat, Erbol—like brothers. Blood. The rest you killed, or dead before."

After they had talked, the elders seemed satisfied. "Let the captives live and become useful." Meiramgul ordered this decree before all the gathered aul. Then the Ak Kam scarred the strangers with hot dung ash in lines across their brows that matched my own. She read the tsaagan bones but did not mention much of what they'd told her.

So the three Black Cloaks would be kept as slaves. They were sheared again and for as many days as they stayed among us, they would walk beardless, without horses or warriors' arms. Meiramgul watched as Timor and I grew close. Her eyes said that she understood, but others in the aul did not. Especially Erzhan grumbled that I used the slave only to please myself, that Timor and the other two could not be trusted. His hatred was double-fold; I sensed it in the way he looked at me—his piercing mockery, as if my choice was an insult not just to him, but to everything Targitai's warriors should uphold.

෨

With the summer we returned to the high mountain pastures, following the geese that cast arrow shadows across the grassy hills. Farther above, late spring snow still clung, a blinding wash that cleaved earth from heaven. The Ak Kam warned of omens and often tossed her tsaagan bones. And once I saw the Kara Kam on a high hill watching as I rode to round our herds. She wore her tall, peaked cap, the same that I had seen when I was a child. I heard her drum, thrumming softly like a heartbeat, and once or twice felt the flash of her mirror on my skin.

But the pastures were still green then and our horses leapt across them, wild with abandon—all except for mine. She walked more slowly now with Timor tucked against my back. His hands stayed at my waist which was thickening with child.

16

THE DOGS

The women teased that they heard mostly laughter. It rang from within the yurt through the night when the old men and children slept. They must have stayed up late to listen, watching their own mates snoring on their cots. They were envious and admiring all the same. Such passion is rare, desired as hearth-fire after a long day hunting when the snows have come. Even from afar, it is never squandered.

Most evenings Timor lay beside me, and I would slowly teach him words.

"Rada Mai." I pointed. "Our hearth, our aul's protector."

"Tabiti." He told me his own people's name, his hand held close over the coals. Then, "Papaeus," and gestured toward my sword.

"Thunder. War god. We call him Targitai."

Timor nodded, rubbed the felt-draped ground. "Apia. Earth."

I stopped his palms. "Umai," running my fingers along the soft blond hairs that twisted just above his wrists. "She watches over children and brings new foals. She comes with spring when the goddess Argimpasa returns the birds."

"Argimpasa." Timor's eyes widened. "Melanchlaeni know this name." He touched inside my tunic's open sleeves. "Argimpasa brings birds and crackles ice—her footsteps—Danu flows. The trees—" He raised tight fists, then spread his fingers wide as leaf buds opening.

I smiled, clasped his hands, and moved them to my belly, enjoying their weight and warmth and the grazing kicks of our hidden child's limbs.

But he drew away to take the empty case that was strapped

onto my war belt. It lay on the ground beside us, made as both my quiver and to hold my bow.

"*Gorytoi*," I told him.

He nodded, turned it in his hands. "My people also know that name." Then he shook his head. "It is a man's thing." He laid it on the ground. In the way he looked, I sensed revulsion.

"*Oeorpata*. What does that mean?" I rose up on my elbows.

He turned away, and for a moment he would not look at me.

"*Oeorpata?*" I asked again, my palm pressed firmly against his sternum. "I've heard your men—Bulat, Erbol...one of them—say that word. I've heard it often since you came."

He struggled for explanation. "Your people—*oeorpata*—women riders with fierce bows. Skoloti say: man-killers. You know no shame, no mercy."

"Is that true? What do you think?" I reached to interlace our hands, then turned to place them on my aching breasts.

He shook his head and bent to kiss them tenderly.

The warming days wended mostly lightly as my belly grew. Timor's breath was soft against my neck as I guided my horse slowly across the steppes, only rushing when the herds began to stray. Sometimes we would lie together and take our pleasure in the grasses. And sometimes Timor would sing. He had a gentle voice, low and warm and softly pleasing. His songs, when I understood them, were of longing for his home which made me turn my eyes away.

"Your land is hard," he spoke as we lay naked beneath the sun. The wind's breath moved the air, heavy with downy seeds and insects buzzing. "To the west are hills, soft, thick. Shade is cool. You have no trees here." He swept his hand across the stubby clumps that lay beside us. A small cloud of dust drifted up and slipped onto the wind. "In my land, earth is moist. Tall larches, mosses, rain, bogs. Our rivers flow, coiled, black with fish and beasts. Bird sounds, pattering, paw prints—a man follows, hunts, kills. A woman plants, makes plentiful, protects the children."

I listened, nestling my cheek into his collarbone. His words—spoken in our tongue but with his foreign lilt—I closed my eyes to hear them, picturing this place he knew that I still could not imagine, dark and close and filled with noise while our world was windy, vast, always blinding white or brown or green.

Beneath my chin, his chest rose and fell, bare muscles etched with shapes of writhing rams and sharp-clawed beasts—lynxes, foxes, broad-winged eagles. I followed their tattooed clashes with my palms. "These are like our own. My friend Marjan bore one—a leopard like the one she'd killed. She was brave, a fighter. You would have liked her—"

"These are war brands"—he cut me off—"won in battle."

"You were a warrior then—and honored. Why did you leave?"

Timor sighed. "I did not leave. Escaped. I ran away."

I rose up to my elbows. "You abandoned your own people?"

"Not my people—not Melanchlaeni." He pressed me back, then wrapped my scalp with a heavy palm. "Skoloti—always fighting, always war, invading other camps, defeating lands, battling for pastures, herds—"

"It is no different from our lives here—"

"No. You do not serve Skoloti! Royals, like your elders, only cruel. Greedy. We go, fight where they say, feed their need—"

"For what?"

"Gold. Horses. Iron. Shiny things. Their yurts move with twenty ox carts pulling great palaces. Meat and drink they share with soft-armed Greeks. They press us to burn villages, murder children. We loot and slaughter, gather all the rest to sell as slaves. Skoloti claim the conquered are protected. But no. Never. Few survive. Men die, gorytois empty. Boys fall in their first fight—"

"Men and boys—"

Timor drew back. "Only."

"Your women do not defend themselves—"

"*Oeorpata!*" Timor spat, but then he stopped and said it

slowly, as if to teach. "It is not right—women who fight like men. *Oeorpata.*"

"But what happens to your women in an attack?"

"They shelter, tuck in carts, under blankets, hollows—"

"What if they are found?"

"Skoloti sell women as slaves, make concubines—" Timor paused. Hard memory washed his face. I pressed up and brushed his shoulders as he searched for words. "Upon Skoloti orders," he spoke dully, never letting go my gaze, "by my own hand…a woman is raped, cut apart but left alive. Then she is raped again."

At his answer, my stomach sickened. I pulled away, rose awkwardly, and put back on my clothes. For many hours we did not speak, our riding filled with thorny silence. But I went to him that evening and pressed until we both could take our joy. After that, I laid my head against his chest and gazed again at his tattooed brands—bare-toothed, tearing at the necks of cringing beasts—haunted by their darker meaning.

Timor shared no more of his life before. The aul had settled on the summer pasture, yurts scattered in an airy cluster ringed around with shining peaks. Our beasts roamed freely so that only the children worked the herds, playing as children do, practicing to become masters of the horse and then the sword and bow. Timor watched them, drawn to their petty battles, but more often to Targitai's warriors practicing on the distant fields. His fascination troubled me, his gaze the same as a hungry dog who is tied just outside the butchering. But he would not speak of it, even when I asked. Timor simply shook his head and turned away from me.

With the waning moon, the older warriors—those who had been injured or grown too frail to fight—went off with Paz-ylbek, Ruan's father, who recalled a village where a man knew how to work metal into sharp points as my father once had done. Erzhan rode out with them, taking the arrowheads the

Black Cloaks had brought. There, they would exchange the captives' golden plaques for more iron.

Timor seemed relieved with Erzhan gone. He laughed more and grew playful with the children. Before, whenever the two came close, they'd stalked as if ready for a brawl. Despite the Hewana's acceptance, Erzhan's contempt for Timor had only grown, swelling, it seemed, in equal proportions to my belly. At every chance he peppered him with insults, calling him "Hairy!" "Scythian!" "Brute!" kicking up dust as he drove his stallion too close outside our yurt on his way to the practice field. And nightly he spread his bile, his voice ringing around Targitai's fire: "The strangers cannot be trusted. They will betray us. Let them be sold on the trader's road. Or better, murdered." His voice rang loudest whenever Timor ventured close, as if he sensed his rival's impotence and reveled in abusing him.

Yet to Erzhan's intimidations, Timor answered nothing. He was still a slave and understood his state. He wisely kept away, though his stony gaze followed Erzhan always. He frightened me with his patience, stillness—a captive but still a lion, studying his prey. I sensed danger, though I could not guess how it would come. Only I knew Timor—he was not one to forget; nor would he forgive Erzhan his humiliations.

While the trading men were gone, our days passed in peace and ease, often staying close about the aul and joining the ana-women at their chores. For myself, I laid out my collection of arrow shafts and let Timor watch as I strung my bow. I cut fresh horsehairs and twisted them into a cord so taut that it felt almost like metal, yet flexible enough to sing when it was strummed. Timor reached and, though no prisoners were permitted weapons, I let him take it. He turned it slowly in his hand—admiring but cautious as if deciding what to do. In the end, he only played the bowstring, humming along softly. The ana-women smiled and soon we all had learned his tune. Everyone sang as they cleaned new fleece and matted it into rugs and cloth. I watched as Timor bent to help. Only his feet were bound now, very loosely, and that was just for show.

But for the other two of Timor's band, things were very different. I had learned by then to tell them apart: Erbol had the pitted face; Bulat was the one with the flattened nose. But no one else had tried or cared; and no one trusted them. They were treated less kindly than the herding dogs.

When they were let away from camp at all, they were closely watched, made to walk behind our horses, their waists fastened by thick cord. Their hard, bare soles oozed through fresh, hot dung which they gathered in sacks after it had dried. They were given cast-off rags to wear and scraps to eat that no one else could stomach. Timor begged me to plead for pity, but the elders would not budge, especially the Ak Kam, who had found among the tsaagan bones two small dark spots. When she tossed the sheeps' knuckles over and over, these would stack above the rest or bound off with sharp clacks and once nearly flipped some of the pure white bones into the fire.

I would toy with Timor sometimes, flashing my short sword or my dagger through the air, and he would try to catch my wrists. It was a game. Timor's hands were quick, his reflexes honed as finely as my own. Yet he never caught me—at least not firmly. I realized only later that I lived because he did love me in his way. If he had not, he could have killed me long before.

My pregnancy granted me the right to make an ana-woman's yurt. Timor's arms were strong as we cut the poles together and he found clever ways to shore them up. Meiramgul herself came when the frame was nearly done, carrying several wide white rolls of heavy felt. By summer's end I had woven the brightly colored straps that would secure them to our walls. There we would live together. We would raise our child. I would become an ana-woman. Though the thought brought Marjan's shadow, and her loss tempered my joy, still I sensed, even from the heaven pasture, that she watched and wanted only that we be happy.

Bulat and Erbol's eyes meanwhile grew hard, colder, their blackness tinged with threat. No woman would come near them, so they suffered. They were worked throughout the day and still tied at night in their old places in the captives' yurt with a watch now four arms thick—one warrior for each direction. Though sometimes they were let to walk under guard, to come at dusk and sit in our yurt's shadows, far from the light and warmth of the cooking hearth, and there they would whisper in their own tongue.

I kept my back turned, my hands busy at binding felts, and pretended not to listen. I still could not understand many of their words, but I understood their tone. Timor tried to keep them calm, no matter how they harangued and argued. Sometimes the brothers drew with sticks—strange markings on our dirt floor beneath the thick felt mats. They pointed as they talked, their faces reflecting the frenzied glow of Rada Mai's flame. I turned away so they would think I did not hear, but then I found the marks, erased but for dark smudges. I told Meiramgul. The elders came into our yurt, squatting to study them. They murmured among themselves. Bulat and Erbol were beaten.

It was dangerous. I felt it, but with Timor I could not be cold. "Why don't they understand?" I pleaded. "We have not killed them—they should be grateful."

"Grateful…?" he murmured, as if he had not understood. "You treat us like women—all of us."

"We treat you like ourselves."

"Our people are not like your people. Akmaral, our women wear no trousers. They do not ride or fight or shoot. Our men do not make cloth or milk the ewes."

"Perhaps they should." I leaned and kissed him on the neck where I knew it pleased him.

But he pushed me off. "*Oeorpata*, Skoloti say—man-killers. We are not men among you."

I should have known that this was not the end: Bulat and Erbol, just as Timor, turning an eye whenever our warriors worked their paces. Sometimes still I would lead the training, and while Timor watched, the Black Cloak brothers glared every time I galloped in my battle runs. It was true, my belly had grown large. It was harder to maneuver. Even my mare stepped cautiously, as if she knew my state. And the captives, gaunt and filthy, seemed enfeebled sitting in the open near the camp, their shoulders stooped, their limbs entwined. We had almost forgotten that they, too, had been warriors once. But they had not. Nor had Erzhan. When he returned from trading, he counseled that the strangers should not be kept alive.

17

PROMISE

The summer had grown old, the grasses trampled by a thousand hoof-steps, nibbled down to nubs and husks. The horses were restless. The sheep nuzzled about for food, but found mostly dust. The air grew colder. Then the first snow began to fall across the high mountains. That dawn the Ak Kam sprinkled the elders' fire with careful koumiss drops. With colored talc from the seashells fastened at her waist, she traced the shapes of flying deer that were tattooed on her arms, then raised her hands and cast the tsaagan bones. "Thagimasad has come. It is autumn—time to leave here."

She sacrificed an umber horse and shared its meat: "From the horse's neck to give us vigor. Here, the horse's stomach for our sustenance. Meat ground from its ribs—as it held the mare together, so it holds our aul." All the clan sat close inside the elders' yurt, Timor tucked in at my side. But nowhere were the Black Cloak dogs.

"It is time," Meiramgul murmured as the Ak Kam tossed the last of the koumiss into Rada Mai's fire.

"We will return to this place," I told Timor as we ducked beneath the yurt's beam and made our way to pack our goods. The small crowd scattered around us, murmuring softly, attending to their chores. Above, the sunrise caught hard shadows and burned rust patches onto the snow-draped peaks. "We have been happy here." I linked my arm with his. Timor nodded, though I sensed my gesture brought him small relief as, in the distance, Erzhan saddled up his horse. Timor watched as he joined the warriors, galloping off to round up the aul's stray herds.

"I will not leave you," Timor said that night, our last before we abandoned the highlands. Then he touched my belly, waiting until we both felt a kick. His hand followed the small round knob that was the baby's heel or elbow as it slid across my navel.

That dawn we began our march. Bayir ordered the watch on the captives doubled, but loosened their binds just enough so they wouldn't slow us down. We put them to work, packing yurts and many other possessions. They loaded our heavy felts and lattice poles onto the double-humps of our shaggy camels, then followed them on foot, tied close behind the warriors' horses, destined to walk from the summer pastures six days to the autumn fields. Timor shared fairly in the work, but then mounted at my back which had become his accustomed place, gently tied to my chestnut mare's haunches by a leather binding. His knees tucked close against my thighs. I enjoyed him there, his strength and warmth enfolding my body. Sometimes as we meandered, his Black Cloak brothers stumbled near: Erbol led by Madiyar's gelding, Bulat by Ruan's. Both brothers eyed Timor with their cold, hard darkness. Against my neck, I felt his breath as he turned his gaze away.

I should have known—as Erzhan somehow must have sensed. As we reached the steepest cliff, he positioned himself higher on the mountain scree. It was precisely there that Erbol tangled his rope-binds between Madiyar's horse hooves. We were halfway down the icy pass. Madiyar pulled against his gelding's bridle, and the steady beast panicked, fighting to keep his feet. Tilting into the tumble, horse and rider's shoulders skidded over short, sharp rocks. Erbol dragged behind, but had grabbed a jagged stone and already started cutting.

Whether it was chance or something planned, while Erbol worked, Bulat seized a pony. Now he cantered saddle-less across the rough terrain. His hobbles were still bound around his ankles but the frayed ropes dangled as he weaved expertly along the cliff. Suddenly from behind, carefully packed camels spilled their loads. Our homes and goods cascaded into the ravine.

The camels roared. Ponies bucked, throwing riders and

trampling them all along the narrow gap. Chaos took us in that instant, just as Erzhan skittered sideways down the high ridge's grade. He was the only one still in control. Sure-footed, determined, he raised his bow and shot. For once in a very long time, I was grateful to see him.

Soon the other warriors joined him as they rose from the confusion, though their arrows mostly bounded off the rocks and clattered toward the distant valley floor.

Now Erbol had broken free. He circled back, climbing hand and foot along the treacherous drop toward where Madiyar struggled. There he pulled Madiyar from his seat, bent, and stole his sword, tearing through Madiyar's belt to slash him at the waist. Madiyar rolled beyond his grasp, leaving a slick of blood gleaming on the stones, but Erbol followed, snatched him by the hair, then raised the blade and cleaved Madiyar's neck cleanly from his shoulders.

He tossed the bleeding head away, then mounted the riderless gelding and charged toward Bulat, who still lay hard against his stolen pony. Now the two dogs flew together, grasping sailing manes, dodging arrows with skill and speed as I had never seen, using the towering boulders tucked here and there along the narrow pass for shelter.

I turned to Timor. His gaze was guarded. Shocked or hidden, he made no move. I whirled my horse to join the pursuit.

"Stop," Timor whispered in my ear. He gripped my belly. "Stop," as I charged the brothers. He nearly shouted, "Akmaral"—his hands pulling against my wrists, tangling as he tried to retract my reins.

I fought him, thinking his goal was to protect them—his filthy clansmen—Scythian dogs. I swung my horsewhip high and back, felt Timor wince and clench as he took my strike. Once. Twice. After three times, Timor silenced, but he only held on harder. He moaned and I reveled in his pain.

I didn't—couldn't—understand that Timor feared I would harm our child.

I would not be made a fool. I shot and Timor no longer

tried to stop me. One arrow, two. My first struck Bulat's hip. He bent into his blood which poured sharp red across the creamy stolen pony. My second pierced Erbol's cheek. He choked on the arrow's point, lost his mount, and clattered toward the valley floor.

Timor stayed behind me. He made no move to divert my aim or to echo their escape. No sound as Erbol toppled. More arrows flew as Bulat veered, charging in my direction. He reached and nearly dragged me from my mount. I grappled for my sword but found it already missing. Behind me, Timor held it high, brandishing its threat. I ducked as Bulat shouted, "Traitor!" in his own language—I had heard the word before. Then he rode off. Timor gave me back my blade.

Already several of our aul surrounded us, bowstrings drawn, arrows poised for death. I raised my arms to stop them. "No!" I gasped. "Timor is still valuable to me."

Beyond, Bulat raced, riding low and darting to avoid our arrows. Soon he was well beyond our reach, and our party ruined—half our herd lost in the gorge and far too many of our warriors.

Erzhan rode to me at last. Behind him, all the elders. At Meiramgul's signal, the warriors lowered their bows. I sat in silence as they tore Timor from my seat and tied him backward against a saddle-less gelding, stripped bare as on the day when we'd first captured him.

"We were wrong to trust you." I bent over him and whispered, "I was wrong to trust you."

Timor would not meet my gaze, but I followed his into the distance. There Bulat still rode, dangling from his horse at the far edge of the ridge. He could barely keep his seat, his body pierced with bobbing arrows, his leg flopping at a useless, twisted angle. But he was alive.

18

AUTUMN GEESE

For four full days Timor traveled that way. He was carted through the mountain passes, sometimes slipping from the awkward mount toward an icy river's flow. Triumphant, Erzhan took no notice, leading Timor's horse roughly by the rein; and Timor tossed about, no better than a sack of felts or a pile of dented tea bowls.

Beside us, sheep were sluggish, goats stubborn, and horses skittish. Our camels plodded without complaint, their eyes black pools, jaws chewing absently. I said nothing as I rode. Timor's eyes glazed cold. No fury and no apology. Only a penetrating stare as if he could see beyond the mountain cliffs—that gaze that had beguiled me from the beginning.

After three days, I could bear no more and galloped hard from our churning mob, climbing high across the scree until I'd reached the headland. There I would not see, would not know Timor's degradation, and no one would know mine. I rode swiftly, flying along the ridge, pressing my mare with all the strength left in my shaking limbs. No tears—I would not let them fall as I plummeted from the heights to reach the autumn pasture— bronze and golden—the color of Timor's hair. And my own.

I tore across it, my horse's breath steaming, droplets of my sweat mixing with the thick strands of her mane. A sudden, blinding gust. The distance cut with a swath of bitter rain. I raced as it dropped broad, biting spears, not caring even as our child writhed within me. I raced, and in the thunder of my hooves, I did not hear the Kara Kam call my name.

She came to me as if from nowhere and rode at my side, cantering for a time, almost silent as she matched her rhythm with my own. Surprisingly agile, she sat tall upon her ashy horse, no longer stooped or seeming even very aged.

"Akmaral, you must stop," she said at last—the Kara Kam, Soyun, my mother's mother's sister. I gazed at her and she at me. Then the black witch let her glance fall mutely on my belly.

I turned my head away. I could not look at her for fear—my aunt, my blood, yet shunned, forbidden—charged with some offense I could not understand, that not even the Ak Kam or Meiramgul would explain to me.

The ground beneath our horses' hooves slipped with mud and ice, and yet the Kara Kam bounded lithely, rounding me once and then again—as if I were an untamed horse. I had no choice but to slow and stop. Both my mare and I stood motionless, panting, my belly cramping until she placed a hand across the breast-high rise and the child inside me calmed. The old woman showed her face, again cragged and withered with her nearly toothless grin. She reached and touched my cheek with her frail, thin hand, then turned and rode away again.

We camped at the autumn cliffs for many days. A vast blue veil had settled above the mountain clouds. The sun was stark even when it warmed. In the distance hog-nosed antelope clustered, scattered. Our own herds mimicked their movements spreading across the range. We sent our herders to follow. And our hunters. I did not travel with them. I sat alone beside our hearth. Timor had been taken from that gelding's back, hobbled at the ankles, tied to a pike in the middle of our camp just twenty lengths from me. Around him, the warriors' ponies bound him like a fence as they wandered, rested, grazed.

Soon the hunters returned, three beasts carried between them—a male stag and two doe antelope, gutted, flung across spare ponies' backs. We ate well that night with Rada Mai's dung coals sparking. The Ak Kam made great chants and sacrificed in sorrow for our dead. Most could not be recovered from the deep ravine; they would lie there, twisted, rotting, food for carrion crows. But some were carried on our camels—Madiyar's headless body wrapped tightly in thick felts. The blood had drained as we traveled, and dried to a round, brown spot the size of a warrior's shield. We would carry him that way to the winter shelters and then to the springtime lake. It would be many months before he would rest in a dusty kurgan on the heaven pasture.

Our clan huddled around the nighttime fires. We could hear the howls of wolves stalking in the highlands. After dark, the winter breathed its chill across our naked necks. Timor stayed tied to that pike, left outside day and night, guarded from afar, kept away from the comforting flames. From me. None of us knew what we should do with him.

At the second aging moon, our herders discovered wolf dung among the sheep. We listened at dusk as they prowled in the grasses, their low plaintive notes rising with the double-haloed moon. We set fires between the yurts to keep them from our camp. But I couldn't rest, a subtle fear rising in me.

Finally, when the stars were dim I stood and went outside. I crouched a horse's length away, the closest I had been to Timor since the attack. His back was bruised, his arms cut, in some places scarred from scraping along the mountain rocks, his skin rubbed bare against the wooden post, nipped raw by brutal winds. I knelt beside him and watched as, with his toes, Timor clawed a pebble, digging it from the dust, speck by speck, very slowly. His hands were still tied tightly behind his back.

"Why did you come?" he said at last. He would not even look at me.

"Because—" I had no words. I stretched my hand out. "I brought a healing salve."

"Take it away." His voice was low, caught in his throat. His head bowed as if it could hide inside his shoulders. He kicked the stone away. It rolled and skittered to a stop just an inch from where it had begun.

I reached, caught Timor's chin, raised it, its bristles already sharp though he'd been newly shorn. His eyes were pale, opaque as the clouded moon.

"I should have gone with them." He looked not at, but through…beyond me. "I should not have stayed."

"You would be dead."

"Better dead." Even wasted, strength rose in Timor's arms as he balled his fists. "I was their leader. We rode across grasses, mountains; we raided, took what we needed, killed those we would. We found that pasture rightly: empty, ripe, awaiting us. Then you came." He bit his lip. He tried to reach, wrenched his elbows toward me, the long pole shaking. His intent, perhaps, to kill, but I did not draw back. The sinew ropes caught his arms and held him.

I took the salve and touched it to his skin. Timor writhed but didn't speak. I rubbed as gently as I could. Though he winced, he didn't push away. He shuddered, but not for pleasure. When it was done, I spread myself beside him in the dust, pulling close my dagger for defense and a felt wrap that I had brought to cover us against the cold.

With the dawn, the elders' footsteps awakened us.

I rose up on my elbows, then my knees. "Timor is one with us," I told them, holding his hands against my belly. "Timor is one with me."

Three days more until we packed away our yurts, descending slowly into the narrow winter canyon. It was our secret place where no other clan had ever followed. A risk—to bring Timor here. The warriors tied his eyes with a swath of heavy cloth and kept hard watch on him. Throughout our trek, Erzhan was his only keeper. They no longer trusted me. Many spoke against him, called him "Betrayer!" "Scythian beast!" But from Erzhan, only silence, far worse now that he had been proven right. His eyes were stones, every glance pelting me.

Only when we arrived in the shadow of the icy southern cliff did Bayir call to remove Timor's blind. Then they wrenched him off his horse. Timor fell heavy to the earth. They left him to me.

He crouched, hands still bound, useless as I built our yurt.

Even if he had offered help, I would have refused it. Our winter shelter would be made only of felt, with no ancient wooden logs, nothing strong or sturdy to stand against the wind. It would face the east toward the wall where the sun-made waters drained into little pools, melting the snow just enough until it slipped with sudden, harmless avalanches. So many years ago, I had shown my skill here, using shining icicles as spears.

When it was done, I raised Timor from his crouch. He stood and stumbled inside where I'd built the fire high to keep from freezing. I dedicated our hearth to Rada Mai and pressed Timor to sit. Already outside snow had fallen twice. The earth beneath our rugs and blankets was frosty, hardened mud, softening to shining muck beside the fire's stones. From the rafters, only my warrior's arms, my horse whip, my tack and saddle hung.

I made milk tea with salt. Timor held the bowl with the heels of his hands above his fastened wrists. He did not sip, drinking in only the warmth and steam for a long, uneasy while. Finally I knelt and felt the new, tough sinews stretched between his ankles. They were cut from the same antelope we had sacri-ficed at the autumn camp, fortified doubly by the Ak Kam with chants, protective prayers, and offerings to Targitai to hold our enemy. With my knife I worked at the twisted strands. When they snapped, I turned the knife around and handed it to him.

Timor reached but did not touch it.

I asked, "Why did you not go?"

He took the blade and turned it, then worked it slowly through the rough cracks between the bands. When his hands were free, he looked at me over the lip of his tea bowl, sipping slowly.

He rose. We did not speak. I had laid our mats out separately, at one side and the other of the yurt. He bent, lifted one, then laid it by the first. Together we spread several felts across. There Timor fell asleep. When I finally lay beside him, he wrapped his arms around me, his hands cupped possessively on my belly.

☙

Once again we were as one, but a strange, hard sadness had come between us. The laughter that had once been ours had flown as the geese that streaked the autumn skies. Their formations aimed like arrows in hard fight; I could not retrieve them. I was tender, but Timor withdrew from my kindest touch. Still we lived. We drank. We ate. I curded milk to butter and made koumiss from the whey while Timor brought in sacks of frozen dung to heat the fire.

Our child was born with the first dawn cast when snows lay thick on the winter mountains. It was the shortest day—our valley lost in gloom, but the sun glowed somewhere far above, its hue a ruby flush, vibrant and warming.

Our son arrived screaming. He was healthy from the start, strong and bold, but our people do not count a child fully born until its hundredth day of breath. So we waited. Every morning Timor and I lay with the infant between us, tied to the hard-carved cradleboard as is our people's way to keep a child from the fire. Lying warm and safe, unharmed by sparks or in the path of beasts that trample, hunt, or roam—I even nursed him with that stiff, rough board pressed against my breast—and as coldly as I could, as the ana-women showed me.

"No fondling. No coddling," they chided sharply when I clucked or hummed even to myself. My mother had done the same. She had not cried at my own sister's two-moon death. When I'd asked, I recall she'd answered brusquely, "Why cry? That child was never born."

I learned to keep my wonder to myself, tucked quietly inside my bosom beside my wordless prayers. But not Timor. His people had no such inhibitions. In the dim light of our yurt where no one else could witness, he took the child in his arms, dandling it with sparkling bits of frost or balls of wrapped thin leather and soft gut twine. The baby watched them, reaching fruitlessly as they dangled just above. Then one morning the infant struck.

"Akmaral, he is practicing for battle!" Timor laughed and

kissed the child on the brow. I smiled. I could not help myself, though I tried.

Each dawn Timor marked our lattice wall with my dagger—one small cut for every passing day. On the rise of the hundredth sun, the snow dripped heavily from the cliffside. The air blew almost warm and the beasts seemed anxious for new pasture. Timor raised me from our mat. Together we counted off the marks. Then we unwrapped our infant from his cradle.

"He is Arman." I held him finally close, hugging and admiring, glancing back at Timor. "It means *dream—the most desired*."

Arman. His eyes were deep azure. When he laughed, they seemed to brighten to match the sky. Arman's hair was copper, flecked golden with the sun. His face was the color and shape of an unshelled almond.

At this second birth, the goddess Umai became Arman's protector. Laughter returned to our yurt, and color, warmth as all the aul flooded in with gifts: food, koumiss, fancy blankets, winter-made rugs, tapestries, and tiny felted clothes. Our meager hovel grew bright and festive, draped with shapes of beasts meant to bring prosperity. The finest was from Aigul: a rug that bore the prints of walking birds, circling sheep's horns, gold-stitched camels fighting, deer leaping over fields of boiled red-dyed wool, and at its center, a snow-white leopard—"so you will not forget Marjan."

"I never would," I said, pressing her hand.

Even Erzhan brought a gift—a small carved bow. "Fine work," I uttered as he handed it to me with a tiny gorytoi and a clutch of arrows. "Erzhan, I did not think—"

"Targitai says who should live and who should die. I am a warrior. I only follow."

The Ak Kam sacrificed a yearling colt, pure white, and made her offerings. "A bit of gut for the child's health, a bite of brain for wisdom, a shard of bone for strength." She threw each piece onto our hearth-fire, then passed the meat around. To Timor, she handed a fat mound of the colt's ground rib meat, then chanted in muted tones, "The horse's ribs to bind our aul."

Then she raised her bowl. "Rada Mai, accept this child, Arman. Umai, watch him who is newly born. See that he is loyal, cautious, wise, that he lives to pay Targitai's duty." Then she gave the yearling's hide to me. "When he is old enough, stitch a leather wrap to drape across his first saddle." We spread it on the ground and took Arman, untying him from his infant's board to lay him upon it, bare.

Just then Meiramgul ducked low inside our yurt. She had never stepped into our house before.

As keeper of our hearth, I rose and offered her the finest seat, then bent to stir the coals. I poured her a bowl of koumiss and another of salted tea. Then I bowed and squatted, my back blocking the woolen door-flap's chill. I was mother of this household. Ana-woman. I was its protector.

Meiramgul shifted on her cushion. The fire made her features dance. "Our people ride in many places. We drift with every season across these steppes and merge with other clans, then break. Like the great flocks of wild deer, this aul forever coming and going. So it was even in our great-great-grandmothers' time, when our people were called Amazons and lived without men's company. But we could not survive that way for very long. So we chose fair Scythian mates and together formed our people."

She breathed in the steam that rose from her salt-tea bowl. I shifted my weight, drawing Arman close. Timor's fists lay clenched over his knees.

"We have called your lover stranger, Akmaral. Yet perhaps he is more an echo of our past." Her voice was measured, fixed as she assessed the aul's response. "Timor," she called at last. My lover rose and knelt before her.

The Hewana took her hands, pressed them against his bright, curled scalp until his brow rested on the soft sewn felt before her knees. "You are one with Akmaral. Now take this oath and become one with us. Forsake your people. Embrace our aul. Or leave this place, Akmaral, your child, and do not return here."

Timor blinked as Meiramgul's hands lifted. Dark faces

flashed with the fire's gloom. From her pouch the Ak Kam took a clutch of tsaagan bones and tossed them before the fire. The priestess bent to study them, then nodded toward her sister.

"Give me your sword." The Hewana reached to Erzhan. He fumbled, hesitated, but she did not relent. Finally the heavy blade was passed through the dark as the Ak Kam held out to Meiramgul a bowl of blood from the sacrificial colt. The Hewana dipped the blade in the red, then drew it across Timor's open palm, then dripped his blood in also.

"This is the way of our ancient ancestors," she chimed, then murmured so only Timor and I could hear. "It is said the Scythians do this too?"

Timor nodded. The Hewana slightly smiled.

Then she held bowl and blade aloft. "By the spirits of our ancestors, we mix these bloods, distant and apart. The steppes are swept by the sands of a thousand, thousand passages." Then she took a bowl of milky koumiss, dipped the blade again, and stirred. Red swirled into white. Meiramgul poured the pinkish draft onto the fire.

What was left in the bowl was passed and all of us, even Erzhan, sipped; and Arman licked some with his small, soft mouth from my finger. Timor spoke allegiances to our ancestors and spoke out in our language the names of all our gods—"Rada Mai. Targitai. Umai…." I would never hear them from his lips in their bitter Scythian sounds again.

He became one with us. Amidst the women of the aul, there was rejoicing. Even a mother who had lost her son in the Black Cloaks' first attack brought back the heavy bear cloak she had taken and put it on Timor's shoulders. Aigul and Ruan came often to our yurt, and slowly distrust and doubt turned to friendship, laughter. Only Erzhan seemed disgruntled, watching with thick arms crossed. Whenever Timor neared, Erzhan worked his lips between his teeth. I resented it, but said nothing. Erzhan was no longer a friend to me, but I could not hate him. Even after all he'd done, his intent was to protect our aul. He, more than anyone, had done Targitai's duty.

19

The Cave

When our child was four months born, the spring snows released the earth to sucking mud and sudden, startling cracks echoed from hanging ice-shelves. Argimpasa's warmth came fast and rushing water slipped from narrow shafts. The Ak Kam's tsaagan throws showed that soon the aul would leave the winter valley.

Before we did, I knew I had to go to where I had ventured freely only once: to the yurt at the foot of the steep black cliff where my only true blood ancestor remained. To present a full-born child was the custom of our aul. Yet to go to the Kara Kam was forbidden. Now I understood the journey my parents had made with me so very long ago, furtively and in silence, when I was just a half-grown girl.

It was well before the dawn when I woke Timor. Just a few weary guards stood watch as we rode away. I waved to them and they did not stop us, me with my small family, though I told no one, not even Timor, where we were bound.

We traveled as best we could with Arman strapped to my mare's flank, his cradleboard tucked into a well-fastened basket. Try as I might to ride carefully and smoothly, the basket bounded as we moved across the steppe. The path was rugged, slick with ice as Timor rode beside me on his own horse, the first time that he had since I had known him.

I saw now fully what a waste it all had been: he was an excellent horseman, keen and subtle in sensing his beast. We rode close and I shadowed him in silence, admiring his skill which was far beyond even that of our finest riders. Timor seemed unconscious of it, as if the mare, though he had never ridden her before, were part of his own body.

"This way." I motioned as we started through the gap where the foothills descended to a swath of open pasture. No snow remained, the field fully exposed to the spring sun's touch. A clutch of wild horses grazed beside the ancient deer-stones. I led Timor, and in silence we stopped before them.

I sensed the same strong pull that I had felt when I'd first passed, that these stones connected to our ancestors. This time I'd brought with me one of the Ak Kam's shells pressed with pure white talc. Now I took it and slowly traced the stone deer's shapes with powder. White against the darkest patches—protection against evil.

We moved on. Coming onto dusk after riding many hours, our child had mostly been asleep. Now Arman stirred with soft, hungry whimpers. The sun slipped low, threatening to sear the new, short grass. Timor pointed toward the yurt tucked into the coal-black cliff. I held his wrist, pressed his forearm down. "Not until tomorrow."

I led him higher. We reached a shallow outcrop that stretched along the steepest ridge. A chill rattled my spine as I recognized the place where I had met the white snow leopard that mournful winter. Now I knew that she was Marjan—as I had only sensed before. The vision on Aigul's rug matched my vision on the cliff, as if she had visited with us both in waking dreams. Now I looked for her again, my gaze keen along the edges of those shiny, shadowed walls where every movement was a trick and the blinding glare betrayed. I looked for her, but I found nothing.

Still I followed as we reined our horses and tied them tight to some rooted stones. No trees and barely any grass or even bristle scrub were tucked among the windy jags. Timor carried Arman as we worked our way on foot along the faintest path, slippery still with ice and too narrow for the horses, until finally we came to a jutting ledge. There, among the recesses in the rock face, we found markings. Everywhere, people frozen

in strange rites—dancing, in places hunting among bounding
herds of mountain antelope, sheep, and deer, a snarling feline,
a presiding priestess dressed in black—the Kara Kam bent beneath her high peaked cap, her mirror poised before her.

We moved in silence, following the marks until we came
upon an open passage. Beyond, through a crevice in the rock
face, we found an empty cavern, sunlit through a narrow shaft.
Within, more images were struck as if with fire—a field of warriors charging, bearing lances, arrows, bows, heaving pointed
spears. Timor stepped into the glow and fingered the contoured
walls. At an image of a rider bearing an eagle on his wrist, he
paused, studying it intently.

"To these caves," I murmured, "it is said our ancestors return—here where their lives are etched into these stones. After
they have gone, they watch us through that hole above. They
can see us even from the heaven pasture."

"You have come here before?"

I shook my head. "Only close. It is sacred, forbidden."

"Why now?"

I bit my lip and turned. Even there I found her: Marjan behind me as if peering over my shoulder. I pointed—felt her
with my fingers on the wall. Deeply etched and seated on a fine
rust horse, her arrow case was full, one bolt already nocked and
ready to release, and there before her, the white snow leopard.
Freshly chalked, its face was drawn just as I recalled. I reached
to touch her arrow; then I traced its path. Across the narrow
gap, its point was raised too high. Just as I had thought—her
arrow could not pierce or injure; it only guided.

"Who made these markings?"

Even as Timor spoke, I realized that I knew. In the burning
glare of sunset, the narrow thread of the Kara Kam's black
smoke rose. I could smell it. And the polished stones along
the path—worn smooth by her constant footsteps. I let go my
breath, feeling as if someone watched us, even now, from the
cavern's depths. I shook my head and knew I could not tell him.
Instead I gazed at Timor as calmly as I could and took his hand.

"This is Marjan." I raised his fingers to touch the image of my absent friend.

As night began to fall, we made our camp within the cavern's hollow. While Arman slept, we watched the sunset's dance, the deer-stones on the plain below stretching their shadows like slender claws that softly scratched a path toward the horizon. After a time, Timor cupped his hands around his breath and out slipped the mournful tones that now I'd heard so often.

"Do you miss it?" I asked.

He quieted his sounds, reached to check Arman, then laid his arm around me where my waist was narrow again. "Miss what?"

I nearly laughed. "The fort of Melanchlaeni, the forests, darkness, trees?"

Sniffing slightly, he pressed my hands. "I return there any time I like. Melanchlaeni hills are just like this." He stroked the crease between my breasts. "And their darkness is the place that I treasure most between your thighs."

He touched me there now gently. So I pressed him back, laid my legs across his hips, and mounted him, my fingers grasping the little ringlets of his beard as I moved above. His hair had grown back in a golden thicket that flickered now in the fire's glow. Soft as a lion's pelt—a tamed lion, I thought—as my knees pressed into shadows where his bearskin cloak wrapped around my thighs.

With the dawn, we quenched our fire. I gathered up our things. Reaching into my saddle pouch, I withdrew my thigh-length blade. "My father's dagger." I handed it to him. "It was mine. Now it is yours."

Timor pressed its edge lightly across his thumb to test its sharpness, then tucked it into its sheath and tied it to his belt. "I will check the horses," he said, "make sure they are ready—"

"No." I put my hand over his wrist. "Only me. Only Arman. We must go to her alone."

I could see he didn't—couldn't—understand, to have lain

with him before the very vision of the dead, yet to hold him off from the Kara Kam, my own blood aunt. It made no sense; and in truth I had no plan to turn Timor away. But suddenly in my heart I felt the rising tremors. I was less afraid of those who'd passed than of that one who still remained.

As I led the way along the path, Timor held the cradleboard. He stroked Arman's soft bronze locks that spread like gentle fringe across his brow. Our child gazed up at his father, then beyond at the woolly clouds. Finally, his eyes pressed shut and his small lips parted. Timor set him sleeping in the basket as I fastened my saddle around my horse's girth, then swung my leg across my seat.

"Go back," I said. "Return to the aul. Stay away from Erzhan."

For a moment he glared, his face twisting as it sometimes did. "I am no woman," he blew under his breath.

"Of course." I bent down, smiling, and softly kissed him. "In two days' time, we will return. Stay away from him. I won't be long."

Timor wore his bearskin cloak and a fox pelt cap and the fine new leather boots that were an oath-taking gift from Ruan. The golden handle of my blade flashed against his hip as he mounted his borrowed horse and gently tapped her ribs. I listened to their hoof-falls beat softly until their sound faded. Then I turned. When I looked again from halfway down the cliff, the last speck that was Timor had already vanished into the valley's folds.

20

THUNDER

I saw the snow leopard's prints again, almost at the place where she'd stalked me once before. That cold season after Marjan's passing, she'd had her cub beside her; this time I had my own.

With Arman sleeping peaceful in his basket, I descended from the cave along the slick stone path. There I found her traces clutching at the cliff. I stilled my mare and studied them from a distance: the broad, distinctive pads hiding savage, tearing claws, the heavy brush of fur softening each deep-set toe. Her tracks did not cross the horse path or even travel far beside, but stayed on the sheltered ledge poised just beneath our cave. There was a hollow where her body had warmed the ice, a patch of rock still moist and glossy. If she had lain there, watching, gray-eyed, silent, she must have stayed for a very long time.

I moved on. By the sun's full height my chestnut mare had carried us to the far end of the valley. The Kara Kam's yurt stood like rough-edged coal abandoned from a passing nomad's fire. I tied my mare and raised Arman in my arms, footsteps sticking, snow-melt yanking at my boots. Before the Kara Kam's door, I paused. The air whipped around us, spring-nipped, chilling. I released my breath and watched it dissipate in a flimsy, listless cloud. Then I ducked inside.

"I have come." My voice slipped into dark silence. "Akmaral. You are my aunt Soyun, sister of my mother's mother."

I could barely see her even as my eyes adjusted to the gloom. She sat sucking at her teeth. Her hair was twisted back, unkempt, flying wisps of gray with naked patches. She wore a robe—thick black wool, cinched around the waist with reddish tasseled silk. Through the darkness she reached for her tall cap and pressed it to her brow. Only then the thin white beam of fragile light that filtered through the roof's eye caught the golden, dangling birds, the arrow-points and leaping horses. She looked at me and her gaze was numb. Then, at the infant in my arms, she smiled.

Black smoke swirled in a coiled twist rising from the just-stoked fire. There was a place for me to sit. With Arman still in his cradleboard, I put him to my breast and nursed him, silent for a time as the Kara Kam watched. Her face, unblinking, slowly drifting to a mindless gape. Then she bristled as if stunned, bent, poured tea from a small black pot. She offered me the bowl, sprinkled some black seeds over the fire. As she reached: "What is the child's name?"

"Arman." I swallowed.

The Kara Kam nodded. She showed her teeth again. "Give Arman to me."

My heart thudded as the woman clutched the cradleboard, her fingers raking deep into the wood, echoing the deer-stone scratches across the dusky pasture. "Do not be afraid!" Her voice chafed as the cradleboard slipped from me. She held Arman, coddling and cooing softly.

As she rocked him, my heart began to ease—until all at once she stood straight up and tipped the cradleboard above the fire. She waved Arman through the smoke, over and over, chanting, wailing. Terrified, my child coughed, then began to cry. Meanwhile, the Kara Kam moaned, "Kak! Ancestors. Kak! Ancient grandmothers. Great-grandmothers. Kak! Are you here? Kak! Bring my own mother. Kak! Bring my sister—Kak! All of us, dead. See this new one? Come! Yes, they come to see you. Kak, we are all here now! We are waiting for you. Kak! Kak! Come! Come! Come!"

Finally she stilled. She bent and gave Arman back to me. He whimpered. My heart was in my throat as the Kara Kam gaped her gummy grin. Her fingers had left bits of cinder in the salty runnels streaming down my child's cheeks. I cradled him to my breast. He latched and I felt him drink—the deep, hard sucks of certainty. He fell asleep still clinging to my bosom.

"You are my aunt," I said again. "Why does the Ak Kam fear you?" My voice was trembling, breathless, low. The Kara Kam said nothing. Her eyes flicked with spear-tip sharpness toward the pot now bubbling on the fire. She shifted closer to it, reached into her pouch, took out dried herbs, bits of seeds, and then a seashell filled with blue ash powder.

"You come to me," she ordered, not looking at me, her fingers busy fiddling at their work. I did not respond. She crushed the seeds, leaves, ore into rough grain in a small wood bowl that bore four legs and the gilded face of a grinning bear. She poured the dust into the pot. Humming as she worked, she stirred the thick blue paste with a carved bone spoon, then scooped and shook it until it dropped. The brew turned almost black, then, as it boiled, slowly smoother.

"Seeds blow. One tree grows. The land was barren. Now there is grass. Many beasts come to be beneath that tree. Many beasts fall to the warriors' arrows. Two entwine to make one child. This child. The child— Umai, protect Arman. Targitai, watch over Arman. Rada Mai, hold Arman in your arms."

Meanwhile she carved a feather to a needle's point, burning its tip briefly in the flame. It blackened with soot but did not spark. She dipped her bear bowl deep into the pot, set it carefully on a small, soft mat, then edged beside me. Arman lay asleep in my arms as she drew the long, close sleeve of my tunic from my shoulder.

"No markings?" she murmured, clucking with her tongue as she drew down the other sleeve. "I tell you, Mother, Rada Mai is not pleased. Look at her! Look! Quiet! Hush! She will hear you!" Her voice bounded from loud to soft, changing from shrills to husks, as if she spoke both for herself and for another.

She held my arm and, with surprising force, she pierced the skin. I flinched, but she didn't loosen her grip as she let the dark brew flow, mixing with my seeping blood. She took the quill away, blotted the blue tip neatly, dipped again, and pierced another point. Another and another. The Kara Kam drew with a patient hand. After a while I could no longer feel the pricking. Smoke drifted around us and Arman slept more soundly than before, and from somewhere in the night came a wolf's cry. Or it could have been the outside wind.

I did not try to understand. My eyes smarted from the seeds' smoke and the room shifted as subtly as the swaying flux of windswept reeds. Never once did the Kara Kam look up from her work—drawing, first, a deer across the rounding of my shoulder: leaping forelimbs, antlers, upraised, curved. Next to it, an eagle's dive—so much like Timor's own tattoo—and then, struggling in a sharp-toothed curl, the snow leopard who had stalked me. The Kara Kam smiled as she drew and murmured endlessly, words I could not understand, though sometimes I heard names I knew only from the stories of our ancient ancestors.

By daybreak I awoke with Arman in my arms, his tiny form unwrapped and tucked against my belly. We lay quiet on the floor of the Kara Kam's yurt on a thin felt mat laid over frozen mud. The old woman hovered above us, silent now but slowly waggling light from her bronze mirror. Its flitting reflected yellow ochre, rust, cinnabar curls like flames that burned my cheeks, then slipped down to light my neck, my shoulders, my forearms. There, chalky patches of muted hues completely covered my skin, even to my hands, my palms, my fingers. And deeper—thick, entwined and tangled—were the black-blue scrolls, the ingrained marks exactly like the drawings in the mountain cave. Yet these on me—their tiny piercings already scabbed over, but the skin beneath was raw and aching.

The Kara Kam stroked my hair, then helped me up to drink. Something strong this time, dark and smelling oddly. I doubted her intention; still, I did not resist. The drink was bitter, burning, but it revived me.

მ

I returned. In the time that had passed the little snow about had melted to dense, icy patches; the grass between was already etched where horses' hoofs had broken gashes through the mud. Yet the grass itself was empty—no mares or stallions grazing, no herders rounding the edges of the fields. I hurried, pausing only at a stream to wash the chalk and ores from my skin, though the deeper blue-black marks remained.

When I came in sight of the aul, our winter shelters were already vacant. Some yurts still stood, but most were bare or rolled, others already packed away. The aul was set to leave. I galloped faster toward the shifting crowd. Suddenly two riders cantered out to meet me: the Ak Kam and Meiramgul.

The others seemed to slow their chores as Meiramgul neared and slacked her pace, then stilled, stared, only her thin lips moving. "The ancestors have been kind. Akmaral, you are not dead."

I slid down from my horse, feeling strangely weary in my limbs. I began to crumple and Meiramgul reached to catch me.

"Seven days without food." The Ak Kam shook her head as she held my wrists, my arms, pried open my eyelids. She set her fingers on my temples, then on my dry, chapped lips. "No water and no rest." She sucked her own lips scornfully.

"Seven days?" I choked. "But it was only—"

The Ak Kam scoffed. Meiramgul stilled her with a hand, then slowly guided me.

I hadn't known I was so weak, or that so much time could pass without my knowing. "Where is Timor?" I begged, but neither woman answered me. "Where is Timor?" as a subtle rain dripped down. Behind us, the Ak Kam scooped Arman from his basket. She fed him milk from a sheepskin pouch. My child cried, but only for a moment, then fell silent, lapping.

Daniar came to lead my horse away. Now all the elders began to gather. They whispered among themselves as the Ak Kam called to the gods, "Rada Mai…Umai…Targitai…" her mumbled incantation oddly echoed by a rumble unsettling the earth just as gossamer lightning stretched across the sky.

"Where is Timor?" I asked again. Meiramgul held me close against her bosom as we ducked beneath her doorway.

Rainfall pelted heavy against the empty winter cabin's walls. Above, on the shallow roof, someone climbed to close the smoke-hole to keep the rain from dampening the fire. "Rada Mai…." The Ak Kam stoked the dung in the near-cool hearth. "Umai…." Meiramgul pressed her lips to Arman's silken brow, then kissed me too, as if I also were a child.

"Our aul's daughter has returned. She is safe. She lives. Praises to Rada Mai," the Ak Kam sang. "Here are gifts, Umai. Gifts of gratitude, Rada Mai." She threw milk, meat, cheese onto the fire. Then another thunder strike. She spoke out flatly. "Targitai is enraged."

Our shelters rattled as the wind pulled at the doorframes and rain turned into hail. Another crack of thunder, and Arman's blue eyes glowed, then filled with tears. I held him to my chest, stifling his wails, then reached inside my tunic and pressed him to my breast. Tiny clutching fingers. Small, cracked suckling lips. My tunic slipped below my shoulder. Meiramgul and the Ak Kam passed hands across my skin—shadows over darkness—the sinuous tattoos. Inside my head, I heard a roar.

"The Kara Kam did this to you," the Ak Kam murmured. She stooped, poured milk, raising smoke up from the hearth. So like the Kara Kam's, though this fire made me feel no different—only very, very tired.

From a felt pouch she withdrew broad leaves, soaked them in koumiss, then pressed them against my arms. She rubbed until they crackled, then scraped until the tattoos bled. Still they would not wash or fade.

"Kara—black! Soyun walks in blackness," the Ak Kam shouted, staring at the deep blue stains as if they could speak or dance. "The Kara Kam is no priestess. She turned from Rada Mai to ride where she was forbidden and follow the blackened spirits' path. She forgot her obligations. For this, she is forsaken—seven children dead. Even Umai could not protect them.

Akmaral, would you risk this? Risk Arman? You cannot choose another path."

For the first time, I felt our priestess's warnings spark my fear.

"I am a warrior," I mumbled. "I have always followed. Ak Kam, I could never—" But our priestess gripped my forearms, traced the blood-marks with her jagged nail-tips, digging until I winced, until Meiramgul pressed her sister's hands away.

"Khagan, stop."

"The Kara Kam has chosen her!"

"It is not her fault."

The two exchanged hard looks, then the Ak Kam flushed, turning to replace the poultices with more milk-soaked leaves.

Meiramgul handed me a small clay bowl. "Drink. Rid your body of the black kam's poisons."

I took it, slowly sipped. Steam caressed my upper lip, my nostrils, tongue. The tea, strong, salted, scalding.

Meiramgul stroked Arman's forehead. I drank another sip from the small clay bowl. Another crack. Lightning, then thunder—this time farther off; and the rain fell, cold but calmer.

Finally I asked again, "Where is Timor?"

Their eyes would not meet mine.

So I rose, leaving Arman with them in his cradleboard, warm beside their fire. I stepped outside into the frigid sleet, heading toward my own yurt's threshold. Its door-flap swung, oddly wild in the diminished wind. I stood there in the rain. Bitter. Freezing. Finally I pressed the curtain back. Inside: our bedding mats and tapestries, the birth gifts and oath offerings we'd been given. But the place smelled cold, empty. Rada Mai's small fire had gone out. It smelled of death. I turned around. The Hewana, the Ak Kam—they had followed me, quick and silent across the muck.

"He is dead?" I asked.

Meiramgul shook her head and touched my cheek. "Timor did not return."

I stared, uncomprehending. "He could not.... I told him.

We must find him…. He must be lost. Perhaps he's injured. I told him to go back…that I would meet him in two days! Only two—" Meiramgul shook her head, cupped my wrists in her hard palms. "I left him there. I gave him my father's dagger—"

Meiramgul's grip strengthened around my wrists. "We feared that you were killed."

Strange, cold shaking grew within me. "We must search—"

"We have," she said. "Ruan rode the valleys. Yerbol traveled on the cliffs. Jarakal and Aigul searched for you both to the open plain. Akmaral—"

I saw them now, there, all of them—Meiramgul, the Ak Kam, the elders, all the aul. Pity. Gray. Everything was gray, the color of the hard curtain of rain.

"And Erzhan?" I muttered. "Erzhan—where is he?"

"Here in camp. Erzhan stayed behind. In case—" She paused, but it didn't matter. Meiramgul's words meant nothing—a howl like the whipping wind.

Aigul stepped close and murmured softly, "We found no sign, not even on the steppes. Not even hoof-prints."

I stared, but I saw nothing. Not her, or the Ak Kam, or Meiramgul. Only in the distance, I heard Arman crying.

21

GOLDEN EAGLE

I remember the heat of my mother's winter cabin, and the color of the gold like the sun itself pouring from her pot. Red coals glowed beneath, and my mother's hand was deft as she moved it backward, forward, the sturdy pole long enough to keep her hands from burning. It was best to forge in winter when the heat from her fire was as welcome as its use. Her hands were rough, calloused from working at the grindstone. Her stone mortar and pestle were burnished, but the gold itself was bright, separated from the dust: quartz or pyrite pulverized to find the gleaming pebbles. She set me sometimes to sift the cast-off grains, and I held that gold between my fingers like a prize.

Her arms, bare sinews gleaming with her sweat; her skin, the same gold color as the ore she worked. My father, always by her, hammering in the shadows; their rhythms in tandem—pouring metal, casting clay, filing down to the keenest sword's edge, or incising supple spirals into the gilded deer's hind.

These were symbols of our people—the flying deer and the sword—always together, just as my parents working in harmony to make the blade I bore—twin-edged with griffins on its hilt and a gold-wrapped handle embossed with undulating threads. My parents had been proud of it, had showed it to me when I was just a child, and told how I would one day wield it when I pledged to serve Targitai.

When that day came, it was Meiramgul, not my mother, who passed the blade to me. And I gave it to Timor before the ancestors' vision. It was his—my gift. Now it was gone, as was he.

Infant breaths, quick, delicate as the scents of meadow flowers. Against my neck, they came in gentle puffs while my own came sharp, gasping as a warrior pierced by arrows on a bloody field. There was no explaining. No means of understanding. Timor's loss was the harsh gray light stabbing through the open roof's eye like a spear. Cold coals and gifts and woolen hangings dulled in the midday downpour. I drifted inside that hollow yurt, set Arman down within that icy circle. I lay beside him, pulling over us the thick felt mats. They smelled slightly of smoke, more of Timor's sweat. I set them off, enduring the hard sleet that pricked me with its barbs.

All that day it rained, and through the night. The earth turned to slush and mire. Wet crept beneath the yurt walls, soaking everything within. But then it stopped. The wind blew calm. The sun shone against the high cliffs' snows where the runoff drizzled down in seeps and gushes.

The Ak Kam gave the call. The aul would move at dawn.

I awoke and broke our house apart alone, leaving Arman in his cradle in the mud. Dogs barked and children peeped between the camels' bulbous knees as I lifted yurt poles, felt wraps, coiled tent straps, sacks of curded milk, and my second saddle. The ana-women kicked the dogs away, then pulled their children back. They chided them severely, but they didn't speak to me.

Meiramgul came before we left. My cheek was pressed against my mare's soft belly, warm as I milked her. Her sturdy hide glistened, damp from soaking up my tears. Arman's cradle lay settled at a safe distance. Meiramgul drew up a stool. Finding another pot, she began to milk another mare, its foal tied to a post not far away. "A warrior is never easy separated from his tribe." Her back was turned to me, but close enough to warm.

I listened to the spray falling hard into the pot, the steamy hiss and dribble through the funnel of my fingers.

"Akmaral—" She turned her chin. In the purple half-light, Meiramgul's hard-boned face seemed softer.

"He betrayed Rada Mai," I murmured. "Timor betrayed our clan—"

She shook her head. "He was no longer a prisoner. Taken in haste, now in haste he has returned. You do not know his reasons."

"Targitai's angry." I bit my lip.

"Yes, the thunder god was furious. Now, you see, he's calmed."

I looked hard at the looming mountains. The sky glowed gold above the ebony. The cliffs were etched in fire. Meiramgul reached and took my baby, held Arman close against her chest—as natural to her as if her bosoms still made milk, though it had been some years since she'd borne a breathing child. She sat as if there were no other pose, while I'd struggled many days just to learn to feed him. "A hearty boy." She smiled. "He has the piercing eyes of a hunter."

"So Timor says…" Then I paused. Timor's talk meant nothing now.

With her rough knuckle, Meiramgul brushed a speck of dirt from Arman's cheek. Then she placed him down and turned back to the mare's teats, squeezing slowly, firmly, one after another. Then she bent and raised her milk pot, holding steady as I braced a sack for her to pour. She did the same for me. We wiped mare's milk from our palms and carried the sack together to a waiting camel. There we tied it tight. Nearby the horses stood already saddled to depart. Erzhan and some other warriors stooped over a game of tsaagan bones.

He turned and eyed us both. It was the first time he had faced me since I had returned without Timor. Erzhan raised his elbow to his knee and twisted the anklebones over and over in his fist. They clacked against each other, a soft-toned mimic of Targitai's cracks. I adjusted Arman on my hip. The gift Erzhan had given us at Arman's true birth dangled—the arrows and the bow of Umai's protection.

Before the dawn brightened, we collected all our things. We left little trace—a swath of hoof-prints in thick melt-water and scattered piles of dung. As we made our way, Erzhan rode as captain, far at the front beside Bayir, and proud, riding in that place we once had shared while I tucked in with the ana-wom-en, infants, children perched on ponies, old or injured men. I still carried my long sword, my bow and arrows, though de-fense was no longer my first duty. Meanwhile the air rang with the ana-women's laughter, gossip, complaints of aches, bronze bowls clanging, and shouted warnings against the children's mischief. I rode in silence, the rhythmic clop of my mare's dull hooves like the steady echo of the Kara Kam's drum that no one else could hear.

Arman lay in his cradleboard, heavy blankets tucked around his cheeks. Strapped tightly into his sinew basket, he gazed up at the sky, reflecting his own eyes' blue that opened wider as the cliffs parted. His tiny nose sniffled at living scents—fresh moss, the crisp of dripping ice releasing frozen scrub. He gurgled, played at forming words. I murmured back to him. Senseless. I could not tell him why his father was not there. I had no answer.

Seven days across the steppes, dark and light, the shadowed grays of shale and granite gave way to yellow turf and last year's sunbaked mud. The snow-melt lake had already formed in its shallow basin. At its edges, the earth softened, bloom-ing with a heavy band of red-tipped buds. We set our camp there beside its shores. The light fell low and the night was still but for the coming of insects and frogs to creak a ca-dence to our sleep. I tried to settle, alone in my yurt but for Arman's breathing. But at every footstep or horse's whinny, I drew awake, thinking perhaps the door-flap's felt would part and there would be his shape, his face, shadowed, grizzly, cow-eyed, apologetic, and I would punish him with slaps and kicks before I embraced him.

Until a low, sharp grunt. A boot kicked soft into the hard-ened mud. Outside, a rustling that was not the wind. I choked as I rose and pressed the curtain back to find Erzhan standing. Half turned, he looked as if he could not decide to stay or go.

"Come." I said it harshly—a concession, not invitation—then pressed the drape to make way for him and set a cushion by the fire, new made but barely warm. I stirred the coals and gestured for Erzhan to sit—the routine courtesies of a woman of the hearth, but with no welcome.

He crossed his legs, said nothing, only watched as I made tea. After he had sipped the bowl I'd passed, Erzhan placed it near the hearth to keep it warm. "I am sorry," he tried.

"No, Erzhan, you are not. You, of anyone, are grateful he is gone."

Erzhan sucked his lip, bunched his fists around the worn creases of his leather trousers. His hands were meaty, crusted with calluses from working reins and pulling at his bow. Timor's once must have been that way, long ago before he was captured. Now they were softer, gentler, and smooth. The thought set my heart to grip, but I quelled it, remembering that Erzhan's hands had once touched me too.

"You were wrong to trust an outsider. A Scythian," he said.

"Timor was no Scythian."

"I don't care what he called himself. I warned you of those dogs. Now Madiyar, dead, and all those others. Yet still you chose him—Akmaral? When all of us—even Meiramgul—"

"She knew better. She understood." But the thought only made me choke. I held my breath. "Do not gloat," I said at last. "Erzhan, leave. It is hard enough."

But he did not go. For a time he sat sifting dust from the felt by scraping his short-nailed fingers until the cloth showed ragged, angry lines. I reached to make him stop, but suddenly he grabbed my shoulders with a hard, fierce grip.

I thrust him off. "Erzhan, you have never trusted me."

"Trust?" His breath caught low. "When I have ridden beside you, have lain down with you, faced death with you in battle? But you—" His fingers worked like claws, tearing at my arms to show the Kara Kam's markings; and when I shoved him off, he seized the amulet at my neck. "This, Akmaral—no one else would ever dare—"

But his fierceness suddenly dwindled. He coughed and his cruel hands fell. His face tucked into shadows as he reached

again to touch my collarbones, this time brushing only fingertips gently. "Akmaral, all I want—"

"Erzhan, get out." I tucked the amulet deep inside my tunic.
"You are not welcome here."

Some days hence, the pain had dulled but not yet gone. I was
helping with the herds, Arman strapped to his cradleboard,
basking in the sun. Aigul rode beside me, Ruan with her. She
was pregnant now, showing at last the proper weight of their
melancholy joinings. Then, from the distance of the milling
herd I saw a rider coming: one man moving slowly, alone along
the water's edge, bearing no shelter and a single horse. In the
shallow lake, he reflected like a double-pointed spear.

I rose slightly in my seat. Aigul laid her hand against my
thigh. "Look," she whispered, "it is Timor."

The man's cloak was woolly, dark, but not his head, his
beard. I nodded but did not move, working my fingers through
the tangles in my horse's mane.

Suddenly Yerbol and Jarakal came charging toward me, then
some younger riders moving fast behind. Finally Erzhan cut me
from the crowd as deftly as he'd cull a new colt out for clipped-
ear branding. He tucked up close and spoke through bitten
teeth, "Will you go to him now or shoot him as he deserves?"
gesturing roughly at the gorytoi fastened to my belt.

I shook my head and touched my arrows. "Arman is my son,
Erzhan. Timor is a part. I cannot cut that part away; I cannot
kill his father."

"Then I will." He raised his bow, drew an arrow, and set it
on his strand.

"No." I pressed it down, feeling him resist; but then he set
the weapon on his thigh. I heeled my horse and started down
the slope, the breadth of distance growing behind me.

In the gusty stillness, Arman cooed in his cushioned basket,
lulled by our movements gently into dreams. I paused just out
of arrows' range, fingering the weapons at my hip—my bow,
my heavy quiver, my long, straight sword, the place where my

dagger would have hung. I steadied my horse, loosely settling the reins.

Golden, sparkling, Timor's crown tipped low as he gazed at me. As I approached, he raised his sight and then his arm. Silhouetted against the lake, on his wrist something emerged, heavy winged and fluttering. A massive bird from his thick black robe. A wild golden eagle.

I gasped, afraid, but then the great bird calmed.

He called to me. "Akmaral, I have been a prisoner for too long. With this, I can be a man. I can be useful!"

It was only a nestling, barely free of its soft brown fluff, but with a sharp, curved beak and cutting talons. Timor smiled, raised the bird to ruff its feathers, its claws clinging hard to Timor's arm.

The images came to me of what we'd seen in the ancients' cave—the broad-winged bird Timor had studied so intently. I remembered softly touching that very shape etched into his skin. And now on my own forearms and my shoulders, the three figures the Kara Kam had carved—the flying deer, the snow leopard, and the eagle.

Timor trotted toward me carrying the raptor on his wrist. He wore a fingered sleeve stitched from uncured pelts, rough-honed and hefty. The eagle bristled. Barely a fledgling, one day it would be huge. And ferocious. Eagles stalk from above, piercing prey with their four-fold barbs, their eyes narrowed with better sight than Erzhan's battle-aim. They carry foxes in their talons, take full-grown antelopes, or wolves from a pack with a single strike. On Timor's thick, protected arm, the eagle started flapping.

I backed my horse away, bent over Arman's basket. But I couldn't shield him. The bird's shadow hovered, then rose with menace up above. Then the bird stopped short. It fluttered, fell heavy to the ground. A wooden branch and a long, taut rein were tied to the eagle's ankles.

"She is mine." He smiled softly. Slipping from his mount, he knelt and kissed the bird to quell its shame. "Her name is

Garah—*lightning*—for the fire of her eyes. You will like her, Akmaral. She will be an excellent hunter."

Garah pecked at Timor's hard, gloved fingers. The strangled carcass of a goose lay tied behind his saddle. Timor loosed and tossed it on the ground, then drew my father's dagger to butcher and take the entrails to feed the beast. Immediately Garah stabbed and tore at the fresh, dark, bloody strands.

He anchored the eagle to a nearby boulder, then finally he stepped toward me. He drew me from my horse and took my face into his hands. They were cut, covered with scabs, scars, dark, deep lines, and thick red gouges. I touched them, felt their roughness, but avoided Timor's eyes until he raised my chin and kissed me, so deep and softly that I began to cry. He held me in his arms for a long, long time.

Finally, reaching one hand to Arman in his basket, he cupped his tiny face, his calloused thumb stroking Arman's silken cheeks. Timor's eyes welled, too, but his softened temper did not mask what I saw behind: the glistening, sharp-edged fierceness. All that had been lost when he'd first been captured had finally returned.

There was joy, but also strangeness—Timor's attention shifting from Arman and me always to that bird, and even more to Erzhan, who watched from an outpost on a rocky perch. It was the only hill in that vast green pasture, the last frail crumble of the peaks from which we'd come. Mostly used for scouting and defense, now Erzhan made it his favorite station, turning as the sun to follow wherever Timor roamed. And Timor watched him too. I sensed it as I rode, briskly shadowing our herds with Arman by my side, or sometimes nestling together on a blanket in the grass while Timor ambled farther, working with his eagle. His gestures never pointed toward the cliff, yet his movements—so alert; his stride, broad and firm, slightly wider than before, stabbing the hard-packed earth as if to stake his claim—as if, even from far off, Erzhan would sense Timor's newfound power and be wary of him.

For the first half-moon it went like that: Erzhan and Timor, bound like two ends of a well-strung bow, drawn by force yet pulling mightily to see which side would break. All the while, Timor trained the bird.

With the eagle on his wrist, he taught Garah to fly only when he raised her up, every day slightly higher and farther. He fed her well-rinsed rabbit or raw sheep's lung, dangling bits so Garah could snatch them from his hand. She gobbled them hungrily, but the meat gave little sustenance, so lean that the bird grew gaunt and fierce even as she grew large. But for all her starving fierceness, Garah was as patient as a pet, permitting Timor to coddle and stroke her and to cloak her with a leather hood which he tied and untied seemingly at random.

"Keep her lean and blinded, hungry so she knows her place. If she depends on me for everything, she will obey me."

I nodded, but I did not like it. To me, his way of training her seemed cruel. And dangerous—a wild bird with beak and talons fearsome as any dagger—but Timor would not stop, keeping on day by day until Argimpasa's warmth was at its height, every night tying Garah to a rope perch tucked beside our yurt, so rickety that she could not rest even in her sleep, which kept us all awake and exhausted her.

Until at last Timor took Garah to the rocky hill—the very one where Erzhan hovered. It was dawn when Timor approached, using Erzhan's hoof-worn path, riding boldly to the hill's stone crest, then pausing at the cliff a few lengths from where Erzhan stood.

All the aul came out to gape at them: there, both men high on horseback, one carrying a golden dare. Timor settled on the ridge, looking down across the spring-bright steppe, the endless grass swaying in the gentle breeze. He raised his arm. Garah bristled. Instinctively Erzhan staggered back. But Timor's motion was a signal. Just then three small boys ran to beat the brush with sticks, just the way Timor had trained them.

Soon a large brown hare startled from its burrow. All at once, Timor drew off Garah's hood and pressed her hard up toward the sky. She shot into the air, flapped and hung, then suddenly dropped, her body locked into the shape of a well-wrought arrow. She fell at such a speed, marked her aim against the rabbit's dash, then landed with a soundless pounce. When she arose, in her talons the rabbit dangled motionless as a woolen rag.

The children whooped and all went running, but Timor galloped down the crest, scattering them before they reached her. He swooped upon Garah just as she had done the hare and hooded her before she could tear her claim to tatters.

Oddly, she seemed only slightly affronted as he kissed her, cosseted her, gave her another skinny string of meat. She seemed satisfied, even grateful, though it was the last that she would eat until the next day's hunt. Meanwhile, the aul had gathered round them, muttering, amazed. Only Erzhan stayed above, his broad arms crossed before his chest, his stance set wide.

That night we offered the rabbit's meat—its flesh and bone and stomach—to Rada Mai. Then with the dawn, they hunted again: every day until Garah learned that Timor's hand was the only source of food. She left her prey unnaturally untouched— as if it was not meat at all. In time she learned to obey Timor even without the rein and block. But she never once dove upon our herds, until I began almost to trust that she would also never harm our child.

Amidst new lambs and rutting goats and spindle-legged foals, Timor strode about the aul, a ready sight carrying his golden eagle. Garah was as fierce as any hunter but steady on his wrist, as if awaiting his command. Everywhere he'd go, up and down among the yurts and gnawing camels, a circle would draw around them, curious but wary. Timor would hold the bird quite firmly, smiling, even beckoning the children near. And Garah would never strike. Only once I noticed Timor stiffen as Erzhan approached, his blue eyes narrowed like the slits of Garah's gold. Timor held the great bird steady and allowed his foe to look while Garah's tail feathers roused and peaked as if a heavy wind had blown. Finally Erzhan moved away with a sullen grunt while Timor watched his rival go.

It was difficult and awkward, this hostility between them. Timor, clearly with an aim to taunt Erzhan—though he would never admit it or dare to do so directly. And Erzhan, standing hard above, relentless before his rival. To Erzhan, Timor had no rights. He was still a stranger, no better than a dog waiting to be kicked, deserving scraps we should deign to leave him and no more. Yet to parade round the campground flaunting his mighty bird and visibly adored! To Erzhan, Timor stood within a void, neither friend nor foe, not warrior, leader, or elder. No longer captive. Not guest or slave. Timor was nothing and no one except to me. Yet Meiramgul and all the elders had accepted him. And now he charmed the aul.

I saw, too, how Timor followed Erzhan at a distance, taking up his perch high on the very hill where Erzhan had made such claim. From there the sweep of the steppe-lands spread and nothing could pass below that he could not see. So he watched wherever Erzhan went, these days mostly leading the warriors in their drills. Now he was in charge, ever since last winter when Bayir had grown too weak. It was clear that Erzhan would take his place as war-master as soon as Bayir rode the heaven pasture.

Nearly every dawn I came out of our yurt, leaving Arman to toddle in the dust as I joined the ana-women at some felting. From there I watched them both: Timor gazing toward the fields where the warriors charged; and Erzhan driving them even harder, knowing Timor was there. He would shout more fiercely, fight or bully some new recruit with more vehemence than before.

Still Timor bore no weapons beyond my father's blade. He was allowed no bow or arrows, no practice at the sword. Though sometimes Timor would let Garah off his glove and she would soar for no other reason than to cast her shadow across the practice grounds. There she'd drift above the aul's yurt domes. I would shield my gaze, knowing Garah for what she was: a fine, carved spike carefully aimed and honed, hovering but not yet set upon its mark. Timor waited only for his chance to strike, and I lived holding my breath with anticipation.

22

ALLIES

It was Umai's time again, the season for gathering and joining, a time to renew our ties and obligations, to breed our beasts, marry off our kin, celebrate new births and victories, and to mourn our dead. That season we laid in the kurgan mound the many lost in the Black Cloak dogs' attack. Standing distant with Garah on his wrist, Timor did not try to dig. He was wise, knowing that his own blood kindred had made these deaths, though many of our aul offered him their picks and axes.

After the mound was closed, drumbeats roared and horse-meat boiled. Riders raced their horses, archers shot, and wrestlers fought on the practice fields. Arman was two seasons old, and I had regained some semblance of my form. I'd grown strong again from carrying and milking, from riding on the steppes and wrangling the herds. So one dawn I retrieved my bow, preparing to join the archers in their match.

As I left our yurt, I found Timor stooping low to watch the games. He dandled Arman on one crooked arm while Garah preened on her perch behind. "You will come and watch me?" I asked.

He shook his head. "I have seen what you can do. Akmaral, you're a better shot even than the men."

"Must you always judge me by their measure?" I sighed. "Well, this time you may be wrong. I have lost my archer's sight. Look, my fingertips—they have softened." I held my bow hand out to him, but he barely looked.

"You have never missed your mark, Akmaral. You are as eagle-eyed as Garah. No wonder both of you are female." He sniffed, but his gaze stayed fixed across the field.

I followed to where Erzhan stood among the wrestlers, his skin glowing rusty in the sun. Bare down to his waist, his smooth, coiled strength rippled in stark light and shadows.

"Cheering Erzhan, then?"

Timor bristled and even Garah roused her wings. "He will have watchers enough."

I studied him curiously, but he looked beyond me. "You will not fight him. Timor, you cannot—"

"No, of course. I am content to stay away. Better here than tied backward to a post or saddle." He reached to stroke Garah's feathered head, then adjusted Arman on his knee.

"Fair enough," I said, but did not move. Together we watched Erzhan's distant swagger. Rage seemed to fill each step as it always had, but here was something more: he would not look this way. His eyes almost skirted past our yurt as if some menace lurked in our felt wrappings. As he won another round, our warriors paddled him with cheers and slaps. Only then did Erzhan raise his eyes—a cold, indignant glare that seemed no brighter for his victory.

Next to fight was the toughest of that season's champions, a cousin from an aul that had traveled from the distant west. Kurai had a burly thrust that none of the rest could match. He had won in every round since Umai's feast's beginning.

Kurai took the field and Erzhan joined him, strangely, coldly, his gaze grazing the matted earth before it drifted toward his challenger.

"Should I bring Arman to the ana-women to be watched?" I mumbled, sensing something I could not express. I wanted to leave, but couldn't. Timor nodded distractedly, keeping Erzhan in his sights. I bent to pick up our boy, but suddenly Timor pulled my arm, drew me close, and kissed me hard across my lips, his hunger mixed with a kind of grappling as if he pawed the empty air for an arm that he had lost in battle.

I scooped Arman up and held him until I could no longer find a fair excuse to stay. Halfway to the archers' field, I turned.

Timor had already headed toward the wrestling. I stopped to watch him, Arman propped upon my hip. Timor moved first to the crowd's edge, then hovered slowly, closer to the field. Soon he was nearly at the fore, his head pressed between the others. Everyone was shouting, but Timor stood calm. Though I could see some motion—his arms and hands and feet—waving as if they knew some better tactic.

"To the right. To the right!" finally he cried aloud. But Erzhan tilted left and Kurai quickly felled him.

Erzhan stumbled from the field, muddied by the dust mixed with his sweat. Timor followed close, and for a moment my heart pressed into my throat. Erzhan's head hung heavy with frustration as Timor approached. "Erzhan, you are leaning against your balance."

Erzhan's fists were balls, his muscles strained. "What do you know?" he growled, loud enough for me to hear. But Timor stayed his ground. I adjusted Arman higher on my waist and moved closer.

Timor raised his arm above and grabbed at Erzhan's back— this time with no eagle on his wrist, nothing to protect him from Erzhan's ire.

Erzhan whirled around, the fighter in his eyes. The two men wrestled, and my heart seized hard as Timor heaved and tipped his weight. In a moment, Erzhan lay on the ground.

Gasping, he scrambled to his feet. He pinned Timor with his eyes, choking as if he'd swallowed dust. Finally he spoke. "Show me."

"Do not use your strength. Use your weight to pull him down."

Erzhan paused and listened as if to a cunning wind. Then he let his arms drop as Timor placed them. "Let the earth be your advantage. Here," he said. "Again."

The two men struggled. A small crowd gathered round. This time Erzhan tossed Timor and he fell, breathless.

"Good!" Timor coughed. "That was good! Now try against your rival."

Erzhan stepped again onto the wrestling field. He was smaller by far than Kurai who was thick about the middle and very tall with great arms and legs to match his girth. But something about Erzhan's manner, if not his stature, had suddenly transformed. Erzhan locked onto Kurai and for a long while they stood almost frozen in hard motion—the look on Kurai's face, red and twisted and a bit surprised. Finally Erzhan moved his foot, shifting balance only slightly, and Kurai struck the ground. There was a tremendous roar as Kurai rolled and pressed up on his knees to glare at Erzhan standing above him. He seemed stunned, but then his belly shook and laughter spread across the field. Kurai reached to Erzhan who raised him up. All the auls gathered around with whoops, clashing swords, and hollers.

Erzhan took the winner's prize—a golden plaque of wrestlers clenched. When the award was passed, it was Timor's eyes he caught, chin tilted slightly in odd respect, before he showed the plaque to Meiramgul and the other elders.

That night Erzhan came into our yurt again, only the third time since Arman was born. His silhouette in our doorway sent a nauseous choke that burned my throat, but I calmed myself, turned my back, and stoked our fire.

Timor met him. "You are welcome, Erzhan," he said as I watched them both from beneath my brows. "Woman, offer tea," he commanded.

I had never heard Timor speak that way, ordering me as if I were a slave. Neither did I trust why Erzhan had come as I set out salt milk tea, warm flat bread, koumiss, cheese, and the last of that night's share of Umai's feast meats. Timor gave Erzhan the honored place at our western wall as I pressed my back against the lattice's curve and nursed Arman.

The two men sat in silence. I listened as Erzhan chewed. Timor pressed his hands against his knees so that his chest showed tall and taut, and the light from our hearth cast broad shadows. At his back, Garah perched and occasionally stretched, echoing Timor's girth with her full wingspan.

Finally Timor pointed to the plaque on Erzhan's belt. Erzhan unfastened it to place in Timor's hand.

Timor turned it curiously, holding it close to see it well beyond its gilt. Then he handed it back. "It is Scythian," he said. "Crafted in the fashion of the Greeks."

The two men's eyes met, glowing with a kind of fierceness that I'd never seen before, like two flames joining together in the middle of the fire. No longer was it only Erzhan's gaze that frightened me; as he handed back the plaque, suddenly it was Timor's.

23

GAMES

To watch Timor and Erzhan was to study two fine lions sizing up their prey, each choosing when to grapple and when to hold. That first dawn after the wrestling match, Erzhan came to our yurt leading a dappled gelding. Bronze stains mottled its pure white coat. The horse's back was fitted with a saddle and a blanket made of felt, leather, and dangling horsehair.

"A gift," Erzhan said, though I'd never known Erzhan to offer thanks before.

Timor didn't take the kindness lightly. He mounted the horse and rode it round. The gelding was not tame and only barely bore the saddle's weight, bucking under Timor's bulk, though he controlled him.

It was a challenge—anyone could see—as they rode together and headed toward the lonely hill. Erzhan carried his blades and bow and arrows while Timor carried nothing but his thick, hard glove with Garah's talons wrapped around his fist. I watched until they disappeared, then appeared again on that stony outcrop. I waited, heart clutching, certain that, at any moment—fearful of a push and fall—but it seemed they only sat and perhaps talked. From so far off among the yurts, I could not hear.

After a time, arrows snapped, flying level, landing in some distant grass. Then Timor slipped off Garah's hood and sent her soaring. High above the greenish pasture, she traced dark circles that overspread our milling flocks. Goats and sheep protested with raucous bleats till, all at once, Garah tipped her wings. The beasts below her scattered as when a pebble breaks a low, still pool. The ripples raced across the grassy surface,

troubling the waters, doing little harm. Then she climbed right
back and landed, fluttering, on Timor's sleeve.

It was then I understood: the two men were weighing up
their odds, as much competitors as if they'd joined the wrestling
games. But theirs was no friendly contest; and of their compe-
tition, only they would be the judge. There was nothing I could
do. So I stayed, taking Arman into my arms. For the first time
in his life, he brought little comfort. Still I sang, rocking slowly
the child who had taken more than my strength. I remembered
Marjan now—how she'd longed to stand by the ana-woman's
hearth; and, after she had gone, how I'd felt the pointlessness
of a warrior's duty. Holding Arman to my breast, I sensed that
my fire had indeed gone out. I had not missed it until then, but
now I missed it sorely.

A day later, they went riding. Their dust drifted higher, moving
far beyond our camp. I saddled up my mare and tried to follow,
taking Arman, but I arrived too late. I found only their tracks
dug into the earth. Their speed was like two darts aimed to
pierce the horizon.

Bayir must have seen me. He rode up quietly and warned
me not to interfere. "It is for them to say if they'll be enemies
or friends."

I nodded, though still I doubted that anything but enmity
could grow between them. I stood there, fully torn, with Arman
tucked up at my saddle's bow. His feet dangled, scarcely reaching the edges of my felted blankets. He could barely walk, yet
had already learned to keep his seat. I sighed, and Bayir cupped
Arman's head in his ragged palm.

"Timor is a man." He seemed to understand my thoughts.
"Perhaps he does not need your protection."

So it went for several days: the two men leaving, coming back at
dusk, often sweaty, and sometimes bruised. Their hair was thick
with dust and mire—even in Timor's ears. As he lay beside me,
he'd caress me in the dark and I'd feel new scrapes and scabs,

some hard, torn calluses. He would smile, mostly to himself, but would not explain.

Soon the arrows in Erzhan's quiver were a hefty number short and there were broken shafts and a deep chink in his iron sword. Still, Timor bore no weapons besides my dagger, though that did not seem to stop them. Where they went and what armaments they used mattered less than that they fought and neither one, so far, was killed.

Then one dusk they returned carrying on their saddle-straps the carcasses of hares. "Rada Mai has guided Garah to meat." Timor smiled and invited Erzhan to join our meal.

It blew distinctly cold as Erzhan ducked beneath our woolen flap and took a place at Timor's right while I knelt beside the dung fire to stir the coals. The two men sat gravely silent while the heat around me formed a fragile, shimmering pool. Our bronze cauldron soon was boiling as I cleaned the rabbits and set them in the pot. All the while Arman toddled loosely at the end of the cord tied to keep him safely from the fire. He almost tumbled on the edge of a woolen rug, then babbled as he crossed and climbed into his father's arms. I turned just enough to cheer him, but then saw Timor aim our boy toward Erzhan who sat crouched, tempting him to come. I could do nothing as Arman giggled, oddly trusting this hard man who had been his father's bane—his high, sweet laughter, the chiming innocence of a child.

They shared few words. At least, few I ever heard.

When I asked Timor, he would say, "We are the same."

"He would have gladly murdered you only months ago."

"As would I, if I had been his captor."

I stared as Timor bent to brush away some grass that had tangled in his boot.

"We are two sides of the same mountain," he said. "One faces north. The other south. Both are high and cold, struck by winds and snow and darkness. At times the sun shines. That light is you, Akmaral. If not for you, we might both be dead."

❧

By the end of Umai's games, our shallow lake had drained to
a muddy pool. Only the wading storks and herons could find
a feast there. The other auls remained only long enough to see
the pastures turn from bristle to nubs. Then they traveled off,
spreading across the distant steppes or to the highlands.

Through those empty days before we left, Timor slept apart
from me. I did not ask where he had laid his head. But with the
dawn, I saw that he came from Targitai's yurt with Erzhan at
his side. Too, he started riding with the warriors who watched
him when he'd charge or fight, then raced to him to teach them
what he knew.

On the day that we departed, I found Timor sitting with
Erzhan. The light outside had barely crept up the arch of the
morning sky. Women were already emptying their cauldrons,
washing off the bottom soot with handfuls of grit and sand.
Small tables from inside their yurts were separated from their
legs and stuffed into bundles to hang from the ragged humps
of camels. And children played nearby, the youngest practicing
how to saddle our smallest ponies for our long passage to the
mountain pastures.

I crossed before the warriors' yurt where Timor sat stripping
bark from a long, straight sapling—a limb of dogwood that
would be perfect for a bow. Erzhan squatted near him. They
would not look at me. I put Arman down and let him wander, staying close between my child and the last of the cooking
smoke. When the sun rose to the heaven's brow, the men had
already tipped the limb with two sleek ibex prongs. They glued
them tightly, wrapped each length in horse sinew, then tied it all
into a graceful curve to let it dry. It lay for many months, carefully fixed in that position. When it was complete, it became
Timor's bow, the finest that any of us had ever seen.

24

Blood Oath

The highland pastures wafted cool with summer's breath. The grazing lands were rich, rippling, misty in the dawn. A sinuous river meandered through the flatlands where I rode with Arman tucked into my saddle, driving our herds.

He'd grown thick and red-cheeked, sturdy and babbling. A small boy, but strongly built with dense russet hair like a fox kit's pelt. Sometimes Timor would join us riding, taking Arman on his mount, sending Garah flying with a toss of his bounding wrist. Her circles would track us along a coiling spiral, then she'd light with wings spread wide onto Timor's outstretched glove. At times like these, all was as before, the three of us unhindered, joy rushing forward as a gushing spring. But then Erzhan would come and the two of them would go. We would not see them until night fell, dark and brooding.

That season Timor and Erzhan took Arman often from our camp, staying out for many days on the far side of the valley hunting. Garah brought them foxes, marmots, antelope, and once even a wolf. I cured their many skins and pelts, stitched them up for winter, cleaned the bones for tools, and dried their meat. Our yurt grew rich with the smell of fat, but for me there was no longer comfort with Erzhan always near.

He came mostly at night, playing tsaagan bones with Timor, then stayed until dawn to teach Arman how to ride. Arman loved Erzhan and squealed whenever he lifted him onto his saddle; then they rode full force across the open fields.

I felt their rhythm retreating from my body, felt it beating long after his white stallion's fading strides. I stood there in their dust, unmoved as the wind whipped hard around me. The stray ends of my long hair flailed, the open panels of my tunic thrashed, the sun burned my face even as the brisk air cooled until finally the dust rose again and they returned through the ashen cloud, breathless, hollering, and laughing.

Timor was little better. Even strolling through the camp, he would grab our son, flinging him about while Arman sang, "Mama, look! I am Garah!" Then he would stumble across the dust, his arms outstretched: "Mama, did you see me? I was flying!"

Sometimes the three would ride away to the highland's edge and climb the highest peak. They stood: two thorny silhouettes, one slightly taller, double-armed, and squirming with Arman propped on someone's shoulders. Against the cobalt sky their forms would merge into the mountain's back, fierce as dragon's scales, while I was kept apart, not expected to understand them.

I forced down my anger, fought my fright. I strained against the narrow bounds of an ana-woman's duty, never expecting that my warrior's arms would grow so quickly stiff, my movements dull from pouring milk and cleaning wool. My arrows, when I shot them now, fell short and angled from lack of aim; and my close-thrown spear barely stuck into the earth before it toppled.

When Erzhan called the warriors' practice, Timor joined them now, calling out orders from Erzhan's side. Together they worked them harder than they'd ever worked before; and the warriors' aim grew sharper, their attacks swifter and more deadly. I was envious and avoided watching, staying among the women for as long as I could bear. But daily Arman begged to see his father ride, and finally, one dusk, I yielded.

At the edge of the practice fields, we found Bayir sitting with his back pressed against the base of a large boulder.

"You shouldn't be here," I told him, for he had been ill again.

"Nor should you." Bayir shook his head and pointed to Arman.

I put my hand on his shoulder. "Hush. You should rest.

Meiramgul will worry." His cough of late had grown to a constant growl.

"I am resting, you see? No horse beneath my seat. No weapons at my hand. I am sitting on the ground, as rooted as this stone." He clapped the boulder as Arman romped in the grass around us, copying the riders in a clumsy trot. He'd tucked a broken reed-stalk between his thighs and clutched at torn up grasses to pretend at reins. Bayir smiled, but quickly his gaze drifted back toward the arcing cloud of warriors' arrows.

At the far end of the field, Erzhan called another round of drills: each rider was to charge, one after another, their game to stay on saddle, riding hard across the dusty tract, seizing their horses with only firm-drawn limbs while grasping shaft after shaft, strumming bowstrings, striking the center of small, distant horse-hide scraps. Several missed and one new warrior fell. She rolled quickly from the path, but still was nearly trampled.

"They are tired," Bayir murmured. "They've been at this since dawn."

"She hasn't mastered the hugging grip. Her ankles dangle. Erzhan should show her how to hold with both her calves and thighs."

Bayir nodded. In his fingers, he twisted up a sturdy length of grass. Its juice bled, scented, yellowing his skin. One after the next, more riders raced across the practice field, hammering at the dangling targets, twisting their backs as they fired a retreating charge.

"Better," Bayir mumbled almost to himself. "That was better."

The horses panted clouds into the cooling dusk. The shadow of the mountains stretched behind them. Timor hovered, watching at the practice's edge. Finally, the round was through and Erzhan took his turn. From a distance, he pressed his horse and galloped toward the shooting ground. The other riders parted as Erzhan drew his bow, hitting each cloth at full gallop, reaching for arrows from his quiver until it was empty.

"He is very strong," I murmured.

"He has always been. One of our best. As were you, Akmaral. Perhaps you should join them."

I smiled, my gaze bemused. "I am an ana-woman now, as you said—"

"Try as you may to believe that," Bayir sniffed, "there is still the warrior in you."

I shook my head. "I am no longer wanted."

"Wanted, no. But perhaps needed."

I looked after Arman and avoided Bayir's gaze. He sighed and said no more, turning back toward the field.

At the farthest range now Erzhan stared across at Timor. His was a look of purpose, a subtle challenge as if the wind itself provoked. Timor saw it and leaned back smugly. Tossing off his rein, he almost sauntered, controlling his horse's movement only with his legs. He reached slowly toward his belt, his quiver, his bow and arrows as he turned.

"What are they doing?" I asked.

Bayir stroked his eyebrows with thick fingers. "I don't know."

I tucked Arman between my knees. We watched as each man took aim, then charged full force directly toward the other. They wore only leather armor and soft wool caps. Erzhan shot first, drawing hard, his strikes as certain as they had ever been. Then Timor took his tack, holding close, his horse's mane clutched between his forearms. Jabbing his horse's flanks, Timor joined with a steady, rising thunder. Finally he let go his rein and raised up to stand. With his calves holding steady, he reached for his bow, then shaft, aiming short and tight. I had never seen such precision—from my gentle husband to fiercest warrior, striking his targets again, again, again.

They took their rounds, circling back and forth without stop, and never once did either wobble, nick each other, or miss their marks. The other warriors spread around, setting a boundary like a living fence. They watched them, breathless. Finally Erzhan called a truce. Drawing up to Timor's gelding, he grabbed his rival by the wrist, raising both their fists into the air.

The warriors cheered. The air streamed thick with dusty

gossamer that caught the last of sunset. The sky around them shone livid red. Arman cried out for his father but I held him back.

Bayir crushed the last grass blades, letting them fall to the ground, lost among the half-gnawed thatch. He mumbled, "Now we have two."

I knew well what Bayir meant. Their friendship was a dare. Each time they rode together, smiling like seeming brothers. But brothers are well known to fight; I remembered, and knew to beware.

That night when they returned, I served them food and salt milk tea, then, after Arman slept, sat quietly, slipping into the shadows, stitching felts for boots.

Garah bristled on her perch as Timor dangled lean meat from his downturned palm. Then he took his place beside Erzhan and picked up the tsaagan bones.

"Bulat was a hunter." Timor rattled them in his fist. "He taught me how to capture eagles." It was the first time since the black dogs' attack that any of us had heard that name.

Erzhan nodded, then took the bones from him.

"He taught me how to train them," Timor went on, "how to make them docile and useful. Erbol was his brother. They were good men, Erzhan. You should not have abused them. We were desperate on the steppes, alone and friendless. We only took that pasture to survive."

Erzhan rolled the bones and watched them spread across the felt. Timor pulled the heavy hairs of his now bushy golden beard. "When the Skoloti conscripted us, we were little more than boys. We could barely hold the dull end of a spear. The Skoloti treated us with less regard than cattle. We learned to ride, learned to fight to a cracking whip. We protected one another. They were my brothers—sworn by blood, loyal until death. We cut our arms and soaked our swords and drank from the same cup, mixing it with wine."

"We have no wine here." Erzhan raised a brow and gathered

the anklebones. He passed them across. Timor held out his hand to catch them.

"We grew to be fine warriors—the finest, though the Skoloti made little of our capabilities. We were Black Cloaks—Melanchlaeni—and they, with their arrogant commanders sitting under gilded tents, sending orders through narrow-armed Greek servants, heeding visions from the mouths of soothsayers, the foul, womanish *enarees*—" Timor shook his head. "They were useless—all of them. They knew nothing of blood or courage or sweat or the faces of those they sent us off to kill. They knew only pomp and privilege. They were soft, but for them we had learned to be fierce and ruthless." He sighed. "Wherever the Skoloti sent us, we ravaged. Still we gained nothing for ourselves. The spoils went on wagons to Skoloti camps, then in massive caravans to the Skoloti king. His palace yurts often rested by the sea in Greek market towns like Chersonesos or Gorgippia."

"You have seen those places?" Erzhan mumbled.

"Never. Melanchlaeni are not sent. They call us savages and keep us back. Though it's said Skoloti lie fat and rich there with so much silk and gold and scents and Greek refinements that twice their kings have succumbed to worshipping their foreign gods. Their own soldiers murdered them for it, but their successors were no better. Another king takes up the dead one's stance, while we are still drenched in sweat and blood, bent over our horses' necks, forever bearing the wounds of battle. We were nothing—Melanchlaeni—but we were finer than the rest. Though the Skoloti captains treated us only more brutally for it. Jealous or afraid, they would never let us lead."

Timor dropped the anklebones one by one onto the mat, watching their fall.

Erzhan scooped them up. "Tell me of the Scythians' country."

"Their lands are much like these." Timor pointed vaguely toward the door-flap. "Open places fit with grass. But there are also stands of trees, sometimes forests, and many rivers. The land is rich, made richer by trade—always with the glut of farmers, merchants, crafters pouring in, bringing all their goods, all begging to serve the Skoloti royals. But that is just a part. Erzhan, the Scythians' domain is vast, greater than any place you know, anything you can imagine."

Erzhan's eyes turned dark, a mix of envy and calculation. He sucked his upper lip, glanced toward the low dung fire, then leaned across the felts and tossed the bones hard across the mat. They rolled in a wide sweep. One landed by my foot. I picked it up and turned it in my hand.

I went to sleep while they still talked, but toward dawn I awoke to a softly chanted drone. I found them sitting, now with their weapons all gathered round them. An empty jar of koumiss lay toppled on the felts, and both men had cut their arms. Their blood dripped from their elbows into a small bronze bowl. Timor took Erzhan's sword to stir the blood and koumiss. They added arrow tips, spear tips, even my father's dagger, then they drew them out. Finally Timor dipped in a long, curved ram's horn—a rhyton, like a cup—and raised it up. The men pressed their heads together awkwardly as they drank. When they were through, their lips shone slightly pink and glistening.

The next evening Erzhan called our warriors into the private of Targitai's yurt. They spoke for many hours, long into the dark. By the rising sun, all of them were gone. They gave no sign, no reason, leaving behind only those who were too old or callow or who had no fire left within.

"They want more iron," Aigul whispered. "Something I overheard of how the Scythians would laugh at our weak bronze—"

"Scythians?" I shook my head. "Is that their aim?"

"Ruan would not tell me, but he didn't like it. They wouldn't let me in, even when I tried. I don't know where they are bound," she said. "They brought few mares for drink, so it can't be far."

She was right. In two days' time, our warrior band returned.

It had been a raid, we saw at once. Their booty took nearly half a day to enter, rounding fifty horses, twice as many sheep and goats, camels, gold—both worked and ore—and wools, felts, even tent-clothes they had not burned. There was an air of shock as the elders circled around the spoils while Erzhan boasted, "We destroyed a village, took everything of worth— even these trade silks just bargained for from a passing caravan."

He pressed the nubbled fabric brashly into Meiramgul's fingers, but still as stone, she simply stared while the Ak Kam scraped a finger over a polished golden beaker, then passed some clattering horse tack into Daniar's hands.

Bayir's voice came hoarse, yet he nearly screamed, "What use are these, Erzhan?" kicking at a pile of axes, hoes, and tined pointed rakes to stir the soil. "We keep no crops."

"They can be sharpened, melted, shaped into better weapons," Timor answered from where he stood quietly watching.

"There is no one in our aul who has such skill. We must turn to the very villagers from whom you stole them."

From the crowd, Erzhan thrust a man with rope-bound, muscled arms. "We have brought you their gold-maker." He pressed the quivering man until he fell onto his knees.

Bayir stepped forward and stood above him. "Is he gifted in weapons too?" He yanked the man's head back by his matted hair.

"He has shown that he's a master. It saved his life. Otherwise he would lie in his own blood with the other villagers."

Erzhan handed him a long leather satchel. Within it was a dagger finely turned, its handle scored with griffins' heads, its sides edged with twisted stags bearing towering antlers. Bayir drew it out and ran his thumb along its flat, then pressed gently over the sharp, honed blade. "You made this?"

The man nodded, quivering.

Bayir handed the blade to Meiramgul who examined it slowly, keenly. "It is your father's art," she said to me, "married with your mother's. Akmaral, come, look." She passed me the blade, then turned to Erzhan. "If he makes another under guard, the gold-maker may live. Your raid, Erzhan, would prove we need someone with such skill."

But in the private of the elders' yurt, Meiramgul did not contain her fury: "It is unwise to provoke hostility. We lack for nothing. Rada Mai has been generous and kind. Targitai has had no cause to storm," while the Ak Kam mumbled out some prayers and poured milk and small white seeds onto the coals. Erzhan shifted his weight. Timor caught his eye, but would not look at me.

That night I tended to our hearth in silence. It was late and Arman slept, but Timor woke him. Bent onto his knees, he pulled a rag from his belt which I saw at once was a hank of human hair. Barely washed, Timor held a small round skull. He offered it to our child.

"We will make of it a cup. Line it with smooth leather and perhaps a little gold—"

I watched Arman's face, his small hand reaching for the small, dead thing.

"No." I slapped it from him.

Timor dared a vicious glare at me. "This is my child's birth-right, the practice of a mighty warring people. To hold an ene-my in his hands—would you deny him his heritage too?"

"I deny him nothing. Or you. You were prisoner and now you are free. You are father to my child. You ride a fine horse and have the pleasure of shooting arrows."

"Pleasure? I defend you with those arrows, and our son."

I glared at him. "This raid was no defense."

Timor burned, his eyes drawn sharp and narrow at me.

"I told you she wouldn't like it," Erzhan mocked as he dropped our door-flap and settled by our hearth as if he be-longed there, smiling, seeming to enjoy my rage.

"I have another gift," Timor tried. He withdrew a filthy cloth from his belt, unfolded it; and there was a spiral bracelet twined three times, headed by two well-formed beasts. "For you." He pressed it into my hand.

I picked it up and turned it, examined it—then I stopped. Its shape showed a lion devouring a many-antlered deer.

I handed it back. "Do what you will, Timor. Take the bracelet and that skull. I want neither." I walked away, leaving Arman with his father to grapple with the ruthlessness of men.

They went that night to share the warriors' celebrations. Scattered voices drifted to me, singing, recounting stories, boasting raucous claims of their reckless raiding, riotous with laughter at the village cowards and their shrinking deaths. But no regrets—all of it as familiar as if I'd joined them.

I remembered Marjan, how she'd trembled at the thought of battle, no matter her great skill. "To kill a beast is different than to kill a man." Now the scent of burning milk had turned to blood—the warriors' offering to Targitai. The fragrance wafted across the camp, slightly sweet and darkly tinged. It seeped through our yurt cloths, hanging above me, smothering. When they returned, it was nearly daylight—Arman tucking in beside me, his skin cold where it had always been cozy at my breast. Timor's arm draped heavily across my waist, but I could not rest. His scent had changed. Timor had turned wild again.

25

THE GOLD-MAKER

For many days, I heard the sound of metal pounding—this new music rekindling my past. Though the memories, from so very long ago…. There were only scents and noises, no true words or even thoughts that I could fashion.

Inside a flimsy yurt, the gold-maker worked at a makeshift forge. After the passing of the quarter moon, I went to see him. I had with me my bow, my sword, my dagger, and my child. We watched him work, my hard breath shuddering in my throat as he touched his tools, taking from a heavy sack that Erzhan and Timor had stolen. There were pounded clays for molds, long turning tongs, hammers, chisels, pliers, and soft stone files, so like my parents' tools as I recalled them. And his handling of the fire, so distantly familiar. He watched me, too, I noticed, fascination masked only by shadows.

We returned again, again, Arman and I, though I made no explanation, my lips pursed and always my weapons well at hand, though I had no cause to use them. The gold-maker went on working. Finally he finished at the waning of the moon. The blade he'd made, even better than the first, and longer, a sword rather than a dagger.

Then he bent his head, his scorched hands shaking. "For you." His offering—I reached for it—was a small gold deer. He raised his eyes and dared to point to the one dangling at my chest. "For your child." The gold-maker's glance was eager, urgent, as if I held his only hope for mercy in my hand.

I tucked the shape into my fist, then murmured, "Rest," and left him.

Outside, I handed it to Arman standing in twilight beyond

the forge. My child's chubby fingers wound around the deer. He toyed with it, then smiled. "Mama, just like yours!" He pulled the cord tied around my neck. I took it, tucked it back inside my tunic, hushing him as we returned to our own yurt. There I found another thong and laced his deer so that it hung down at his sternum. Arman stroked the fine gold antlers, then put them into his mouth. I pulled them out and scolded him gently.

The dawn was brisk when they brought the gold-maker finally from his forge and pressed him before the warriors and the elders. The autumn wind roughed the hair at the gold-maker's collar. Erzhan bent him down, his brawny arms bound tightly behind his back. Gripping either side of the man's broad neck, Erzhan ground his forehead hard into the dust. As the gold-maker cowered, I stepped before them both and offered out the blade he'd made.

It bore all the fine-wrought images that I had always known, the same art of entwined beasts, a coil of grace and unleashed power. We waited as Erzhan studied it, then released his grip and stepped forward, holding out the blade to the Hewana.

She took it, turned it, nodded, then passed the sword to Bayir who raised it for its heft, then walked to the nearest field. There a sheep lay readied. The Ak Kam held it down like the gold-maker himself, a bowl of bronze for blood and a tall jug of mare's milk by her side. Bayir heaved the heavy sword, then brought the beast down swiftly. In one stroke, he raised the mutton's head dripping, dangling gore. While the Ak Kam sanctified the meat, Meiramgul called to have the gold-maker's wrists unbound.

"He has proved his worth," she said. "The villager may live."

That night the new weapon was laid in Rada Mai's hearth, wrapped in coals to gather up her strength, preparing it to guarantee Targitai's power. But as the sickle moon climbed higher, its light slipped away behind a sudden cloud. The storm moved quickly to cover up the stars. Then lightning etched the sky and a heavy rain flooded down as if the ancestors had spilled all the heavens' waters.

I awoke, spattered by the downpour, and quickly pulled the heavy flap over our smoke-hole, tying it down with a sturdy cord. Our lattice walls held steady as the wind tore at the felts. Arman whimpered beside me while Timor slept. "Clutch your gold," I whispered. "Your deer is not afraid to fly." Then I coaxed the yellow brightness between his fingers as my mother had often done; the warmth of her touch came suddenly back as a shiver.

Not in many years had our aul seen such a storm. The pool of mud seeped like a slinking fox beneath our canopy, stealthy and then quick. I woke Timor and we rolled our rugs to keep the mud from spreading to the hearth. After that, we did not sleep at all; and Arman's rest between the mats was fitful.

By dawn the storm had waned, but the Ak Kam's footsteps slapped across the mud. She pounded her drum low and shook her mirror in the muted light. "Targitai's blows have cut our people deep. War-master Bayir is dead!"

Her words struck like lightning as the sky hung still heavy as a shroud. Far off it thundered, but the rain had stopped as the aul gathered, stunned, around the elders' hearth.

I tucked Arman tightly in my arms as Meiramgul called Erzhan. He led the gold-maker lashed like a beast. The finely crafted sword was clutched in Erzhan's fist. He shook it as the Ak Kam poured libations, but the dung fire goddess only sputtered and sparked. She refused to raise a flame.

I couldn't hold my tongue. "Lower your blade, Erzhan, I beg you. It is not his fault. The gold-maker did only what we demanded under threat of death. If Targitai rages, it is for the warriors' unprovoked attack. The villagers posed no threat—"

But with a mirror's flash, the Ak Kam warned me off. "Silence, ana-woman! It is not your place."

The hearth's pitiable sparks caught her mirror's bronze reflection, shaking, shivering until the Ak Kam tossed some ochre dust, and suddenly the fire blazed. At the sight Meiramgul shook her head, closed her eyes, then gazed at Erzhan and sharply nodded.

At her signal, Erzhan swung the sword. The gold and iron

slashed its maker's neck. The poor man's head hung briefly by a strand, then flopped heavily against his shoulders.

26

Black Crow

We buried Bayir in the sacred mound. He was lucky to have died in summer. High on the grass plateau, his journey would be short to where our ancestors waited, grazing their vast herds on the heaven pasture.

While the kurgan pit was dug, the Ak Kam embalmed the war-master's body in beeswax and honey; pressed his hollowed chest full with grasses, moss, and herbs; and sanctified his grave goods—his dagger, sword, and horses, his bow and quiver of our finest iron arrows. All but the new-wrought blade. Mei-ramgul insisted that Erzhan take that back. "You had wrought for him this gift of death, Erzhan. You yourself have earned it." She passed it into his hand along with Bayir's horse-hoof armor. In this way, Erzhan became one of our elders, war-master of our clan.

But the gold-maker's body was dragged and left on the open steppe. Great flocks of vultures descended, their wings spread wide and fluttering. They swooped and jostled, pecking at his cold, stiff flesh while a few gaunt birds stood guard. The greatest of the scavengers fought the rest for purchase, pulling back the gold-maker's chest, long strings of muscle dangling from pincer beaks. By the setting sun on the day of the man's murder, there was little left but hair, tattered cloth, and gnawed whitish bone.

Still the raids did not stop, not with Bayir's death or the gold-maker's murder or any of the elders' warnings. The taste of blood was savory, fresh, hot on our warriors' tongues. Even Targitai's thunder no longer frightened them. If anything, each time the heaven warriors pounded across the sky, our own rode out more recklessly to join them.

And our aul grew rich. Our captured sheep and horses now ranged to the farthest edges of the mountain pasture. We scarcely had enough spare riders to mind them; and the beasts gave milk, so much that we ana-women hurried to strain it into cheese, and pounded arm-sore, making wool into felts so thick that with the autumn our camels could barely carry them.

That summer our riders traveled so often to the traders' road that when we moved to the autumn steppe, we found two caravans already waiting there. The merchants had sought us out, grown bold enough to ride up to our camp, having heard we had so many goods to sell.

But the rains did not come. Our swelling herds tramped the drying straw to shreds. And a stifling heat lay across the autumn pasture, heavy as a warrior fallen from his horse. At night the darkness whispered: sounds of wings, scratching, creaks, wolves' steps louder than the windy grasses. The Ak Kam warned that Rada Mai was not pleased.

"She reins Targitai like an unruly horse. She holds back his storms so no rain comes. She is ill with the wrongdoings of our warriors—"

"No." Erzhan refused to listen. "The god of storms has stood long enough feeding Rada Mai's pathetic fire. All these seasons, these generations, protecting her dull coals." Erzhan stepped before the priestess, face to face as no one should have dared. "The sword bears Targitai's strength. Now *he* will lead. Targitai has stood far too long in Rada Mai's shadow."

Raising up his blade—the very one that had ushered Bayir's death—Erzhan thrust the weapon hard into the center of the elders' fire. "Targitai's power rises here." Dung coals tumbled, startling the flames. They burst like falling stars as Erzhan pulled the sword out and held it close beside his shoulder. "Follow me if you serve him."

Thunder struck again its drum. The dry ground shook. But no rain fell. Erzhan was war-master now. There was little anyone could do. The Ak Kam murmured beneath her breath, "The gods above are arguing, unquiet lovers."

I knew where Erzhan had learned these words—knew, though I had never heard them spoken out before—knew as I turned my gaze to where Timor stood hidden in the flickering shadows.

Now at nights in the warriors' yurt, new armor was meticulously fashioned: wool and boiled leather, molded iron plates to replace horse-hoof scales, and golden adornments, each warrior sewing plaques until they covered every rounding of their muscled shoulders. Erzhan stood now a glittering, polished general. And amulets were passed, spoils of their raids. Timor's was a stalwart griffin shaped with an eagle's beak and the body of a lion. He fastened it to his belt—the plaque that made him Erzhan's second.

They rode together—two turned into one—with Garah always steady on Timor's leathered sleeve. Meanwhile Meiramgul sat, dumbstruck, shrunken amidst the stolen luxuries. I went to her for comfort and found her, awkward in a silken dress, beaded earrings dangling beside fallen cheeks. I bent before her and she cupped my hands. "The other clans that once were our cousins—now they fear us," she said. Her eyes were rheumy, red from weeping. "We need no more beasts. What we need is grass. And that, these great herds trample. No warrior can ride two horses with one saddle."

I tried to speak to Timor, but even he refused to hear, treating me less these days as partner than as keeper; and somehow I was transformed into a precious thing. I rode beside him, weighted down by his unwanted gifts: three hefty golden bracelets clanging stridently upon each wrist, and a three-ringed torque choking at my neck, binding like a horse's ill-fitting bridle.

The only care Timor did not shrug away was his son, swept along with these men's ambitions. Still far too young to fight, Arman imitated the warrior's savage stance, swinging viciously with a sword made of bone, not bronze or iron; and keen-eyed with his wooden spear, sure of his aim though his small arm bore little force. He played at fighting and mirrored Erzhan's clout, ordering the younger children to war. But he also wielded Timor's quiet composure, and for this the children mostly obeyed him.

Only when dusk fell, soft as a cloak of trader's silk, Arman would run back to our yurt and be my sweet child again. Quick to tuck into my arms, he would tell me of his exploits. But his shining eyes drifted ever toward his father. Timor would often praise him as he bent to raise the embers' flame. "You are brave as any Scythian, Arman. Commanding as a Skoloti prince."

So I asked, "You would press him to be like those who so oppressed you?"

"I did not say that." Timor bristled, then bit into his meat and would say no more.

On the days when they were away on raids, Arman waited for his father, his eyes straining into sunset until the warriors' silhouettes etched against the cobalt sky. Strong enough at last to ride alone, he would mount his pony and gallop across the rooty ruts. "Mama, they are coming!" he would shout as he heeled into his pony's girth, scampering breathless toward the oncoming riders. I would race my mare to catch him, then grab his rein up short. But one day Arman yanked and broke away, bounding toward his father's stallion. Timor barely saw him, then reared up hard to stop, his own feet clinging fiercely to the beast's wide barrel. As I choked against his dust, Arman leaped from his startled horse, fearless as Timor caught him, then heaved and tucked him close onto his saddle's arch, charging off before I could speak a word. I stood silent, aghast, my hand still clutching the lead of Arman's abandoned pony.

After a time, the two returned. Timor handed Arman down to me. In my small son's grip was the hilt of a handsome sword. Raid's bounty.

"He is far too young," I said. "Arman has not outgrown Umai's protection."

But Timor shook his head as Arman raised the hefty blade. Even with both his hands, he could hardly lift it, his eyes bulg-

ing broad and blue as he tried. Still, our son's excitement caught
the last of sunset's flash reflected in his father's spangled armor.

When next they rode, we waited far too long—longer than
for any raid before. Thagimisad's breath turned cold and the
herds went hungry. But we dared not cross the plain without
the warriors' safeguard. We had made too many enemies, even
those we had once called friends. So Meiramgul set out guards
drawn from among the warrior girls—neglected and shunned
since the rise in Targitai's power—and called up scouts from
our older women warriors who had eased caring for their
young. Though Aigul still nursed her newborn daughter on a
cradleboard, Arman these days rarely begged to suck. So when
it came my turn, I left him in Aigul's charge and traced along
our paths, spying for safe passage between our autumn camp
and the winter gorge.

I discovered none. Instead, I found the Kara Kam—
Soyun—watching me from a great distance. She wandered very
slowly, but no matter how I raced, she stayed far off and I could
not catch her.

Between us both stretched the withered, dusty grass. At in-
tervals lay countless piles of scattered, blackened bones. Some
still smoldered, though I'd never seen their fires, not even in
the dark of night when there had been no moon. I bent when
I came near one and smelled its scent. It was peppered with the
tinge of harvest seeds, coriander, hemp, also something very
different from any offerings that the Ak Kam poured. Just embers now, but their tang still drifted. And the smoke, rising in
wiry, sturdy tendrils. Black. The smoke was like the headdress
that the Kara Kam always wore: reaching up to trace the path
toward the distant heavens.

27

Wind

With the blackened moon, the warriors did return, bringing with them such plunder: foodstuffs, weapons, clothing, pots and tools and finery—so much that no one could dispute Targitai's power. There was a crowd of countless beasts, even some of kinds we had never seen before, that Timor said were mules and donkeys.

"Such were left behind by Persians in the Scythians' ancient war. They are sturdier than pack horses—"

"But their braying—it's unbearable. It will startle the herds!" The elders complained until Pazylbek promised to rid us of them as quickly as he could, as soon as he found another traveler along the trade road.

But there were also slaves driven from some distant land: women, half-grown men, and children, footsore, gaunt. I couldn't tell from where they'd come—their dress caked in dust, perhaps once beige or white, flimsy and sleeveless in the looming frost. Others wore torn felts or tattered woven wools, but I saw some black bear pelts like the ones only Timor wore. The women were mostly thick and stocky, but some were pale or even fair, their bodies slight to the point of frailty, their hands uncalloused as if they'd never milked a camel or touched a rein or a butcher's blade.

"Those are Greeks," Erzhan gloated, "captured from beside the sea. Merchants' daughters, some concubines or slaves. Those fought with us the least, having already been indentured. But these others—" He chucked one fine girl's chin. She closed her eyes and tensed until he released her. "All from Gorgippia, from prosperous households built beside the city walls. Seizing them was like opening a simple pit trap teeming with witless prey."

Timor spoke more softly. "Akmaral, remember what I told you about the Scythians' slaves, ready on traders' ships to be sold at the farthest reaches of the Black Sea—"

Erzhan cut him off. "We broke over the city's ramparts, marched right down to the Scythian royals' port. We stole them from beneath the Skoloti's noses!"

Timor's face should have shone with pride, but instead he turned red and oddly silent. Scanning the foot-worn slaves, there was something in his eyes. I went to him, longing to understand, but Meiramgul broke into our midst.

"You defy Rada Mai. You broke your oath. Now you return flaunting your spoils?" She scanned the rows of strangers tied with lengthy leather cords and horsehair ropes. "And draw the wrath of the mighty Scythian army behind you!"

I had never heard the Hewana's voice so raw before, her whole body quivering as she signaled the Ak Kam, who spread milk and ochre dust in a widening round until Erzhan caught her arm. He shook it and the dry dust fell.

"We are warriors." Erzhan bore the priestess's glare. "We have listened to the god of storms. We have heard his battle cries and followed them to victory. Now we bring Targitai's bounty and lay our tribute before Rada Mai's weak hearth. Would she refuse it?" He dared to speak directly into the sacred fire.

Then Erzhan loosed his grip and stormed across the dust-cloaked field to the saddle of his stallion. He pulled a mounted sack and yanked a dangling tie. Out poured gold onto the ground like water. Glittering chalices, molded pole-tops, sword hilts, scabbards engraved with beasts. One golden plaque was carved as a bare-toothed panther while a comb was topped with a battle scene. "All Timor told is true," he said. "The Scythians' lands are far better than our own, vast with riches beyond anyone's imagining."

Timor stepped into the clutter of shining loot. He bent, chose a bright round bowl, and handed it to me.

I twisted it about, realizing at once that this was far beyond
my parents' craft—that what I had so admired and cherished
for so long must have seemed to Timor artless, backward,
crude. My heart strained, my ears ringing; I passed the vessel
back, afraid to be caught in Timor's glare while all these Scythian captives looked on in disgust, as if they'd been abducted not
by humans but by a pack of wolves.

"Load the camels," Meiramgul ordered. "Make the horses
ready. We will break at dawn—"

"No." Erzhan defied her. "We will stay until the captives can
be traded."

She stared. "Rada Mai did not require this raid or any other. This gold you bring bears no honor. It is shaped of vanity.
These slaves come only with the promise of retribution. We
will leave here now. Thagimasad's time is done. If Rada Mai
intends it, then by the fire of her hearth, perhaps these hapless
prisoners will find their way home again."

The Ak Kam poured another rain of milk and a storm
of ochre dust over the sputtering dung coals; but her chants
throughout the night were lost in the defiant air. All across the
aul and long into the moonset, we could hear the warriors taking oaths in blood and milk, promising that they would serve
only Targitai.

Except Timor, who stood strangely subdued. He took his
part in gold when it was passed, then handed it to me and left
us, saying almost nothing. Arman was in despair, calling for his
father, crying that he would not sleep. But after the days' long
wait and such excitement, he was resting soundly when Timor
returned. It was long past dark. Timor did not say where he
had gone as he tucked beside me on our cot, his arms wrapped
around my waist as they always had been, but, it seemed to me,
not as tightly as before.

That next morning we did not leave. Instead, we found two
dozen horses slaughtered, healthy cattle killed, their meat left to

rot in the autumn sun if we did not stay long enough to butcher and preserve it.

So the warriors made their stand. Again the Ak Kam called. Again Erzhan was censured—all his gold and goods forfeited, and the slaughtered horses to be counted from his own. But there was little more that the elders dared to do. They seemed almost to fear him.

Meanwhile the aul remained, working mournfully at butchering, so much meat that we could not waste with so many strangers' mouths to feed. We stayed at the autumn camp, tanning skins and cleaning bones. We were captive to our warriors' will. And Erzhan stood unashamed while the warriors reveled in cold defiance beside their leader.

But Timor stood between. Since the coming of the Scythian captives, he seemed to long only to join them. "It is my watch," he would say as he slipped off. "My duty. I am best equipped to manage them. Only I understand their tongue."

And it was true. When he was near, the captives grew calmer, more cooperative, or at least more resigned. Timor told that, on their march, half the slaves had fallen on the path, the others stumbling and feeble by the time they arrived here. Now the strongest of them tried hard to escape, until our scouts were forced to shoot them down like prey. But when Timor neared, they calmed.

Sometimes I would join him on patrol at the edges of the captives' camp. The place was flat and dusty, open, without even the thinnest brittle carpet of grass to ease their steps or sleep; and no shelter from the wind or sun. Only our kurgan mounds in the distance spread low shadows. The captives' sounds were as the milling herds, moaning, guttural, their language punctuated by hacking spits. Though when I asked, Timor said, "Their words are forgotten music to me."

Once he insisted that we bring Arman. Unarmed, Timor said, the captives offered little menace. Still I kept Arman tucked close into my saddle's arch and my hand upon my sword. Raised up on our saddle, even my child towered above the captives' heads while they watched us through dust-caked eyebrows, murmuring and plodding. The scent of their hatred mixed with the rising stench of human sweat. Their gazes were tendrilled curses, reaching, intent to strangle.

Arman must have sensed it, for he lifted up my shirt even as we rode and pressed his lips against my breast as he had not done in many days.

"*Sauromata!*" one woman spat in her twisted tongue. "Amazon!" Though I didn't understand her words, I understood her eyes.

Timor rode between us. Leaning down, he spoke a few soft words. The woman's fierce glare cooled to a simmer, still burning hot, but she did not speak again. Her forehead furrowed, tight beneath her graying brow. When she turned away, her movements were firm and oddly clipped as she whispered to the others whatever she had heard.

Over time Timor's stays with them grew later, longer. Sometimes he only returned at early dawn. Clearly he had not slept— his eyes red-rimmed and thick as if he'd stared into a fire's smoke or stood face on in a dusty wind. Through those days he barely spoke except in thanks for food, or to answer Arman's childish prattle.

Then one day he appeared bearing several thick, straight branches across his saddle. "It is time we fixed our yurt," he said. "Its frame is sagging."

He was right; and through the next few days he spent his hours cutting them into new lattice walls. Then we lashed them up together. It was dull work compared with the thrill of battle, yet Timor seemed content, taking comfort in simply tying the binding thongs. He stayed quiet and apart, his blue eyes soft, following me and often Arman. He had not been so attentive since our child was first born.

Then, when we were through and our yurt stood firm, Timor

left to ride far across the fields. There he sat for hours, hardly moving amidst the brittle, broken brush. If not for his grazing horse, I barely would have noticed him.

I did not follow, not until that dusk when I heard the sound that I had not heard in many seasons: whistling like the wind but softer, like the breeze when it is caught between my winter fox cap and my ears—a cross between night's breath and a dove's cooing. I rode out finally to find Timor sitting on a broad, flat stone, his fists tucked against his lips and his face distorted by the air he held carefully in his cheeks. In the dark, for a time, he did not even sense that I looked on. When he did, he dropped his hands. His eyes would not meet mine; they were glazed with falling light, glistening with sorrow.

Late that night sleep came, but with such weight from Timor's sound, such heaviness as he pressed his body into me. I felt his thickened muscle, so strong again with all the riding and raids—strong as he must have been long ago, but no longer joyous. No longer singing songs or laughing. Between us, Arman rested, well covered with felt mats. The arch of our yurt rose gently above us, sturdy again and finely framed. I picked Arman up and moved him to the side. Then I reached and touched Timor's shoulder, so brawny that it could no longer fit into my palm. He stirred in his sleep as I brushed his lips, his chin, his chest, between his thighs, longing for our dwindled passion. Timor barely stirred even when I mounted him. And though he spent his seed as men are bound to do, when he slept again he did not reach for me.

With daylight he left early, taking Arman out to the cliffs to practice with Garah. No longer for the hunt, it seemed Timor trained her now only for battle. As I rode among the herds I kept my distance, watching as the great bird rose, circled slowly, plummeted. Even the eagle's target had transformed: still a meat-stuffed pelt, but now its shape was a small model of a man. The method was still gruesome as the eagle's claws grew caked with blood, her ankle feathers stained and stiff with it, her beak gripping, tearing, slashing. But over time she grew more subtle, only lifting up the mannequin to carry it away. And Arman, beside his father, raced on his own small pony to keep up. My boy watched, rapt, as Garah caught the lure, then curiously, gently set down her untouched prey.

Erzhan came that night to admire Garah's savage points, honed as deadly as our finest arrows. Timor offered him few words—far less than he had before. He only released the great bird from her leather cuffs and hood, listening through the first crushing flaps for the steady whisper of the wind. Garah rose, magnificent, then was gone for many miles, reaching to the distant ring of wintry cliffs with her great broad strokes, then turning back, hovering to touch the indigo canopy of the sky.

Timor showed such faith, an absolute certainty in Garah's training, even when she swooped down a mere arrow's length from Arman's chest. It startled me and even Erzhan. But Timor praised our son, nodding proudly at his calm, his glistening gaze, the trusting azure of his eyes.

28

Armor

That final evening Timor sat beside our fire, stitching up a leather tunic, fixing it with small gold scales. They were the finest of Erzhan's hoard, given to honor Timor's fidelity. Beneath them Timor slipped in bits of thicker iron—true armor for protection like his own. I didn't think much of them at first: the tunic suited Arman well and he was anxious, proud to wear the gift his father made for him.

Meanwhile Erzhan mocked. "You sew like an ana-woman."

"Like a slave," Timor said. "Like a captive, as I have been."

"I haven't forgotten." But Erzhan's gaze turned cloudy. He seemed almost remorseful, an emotion extremely rare for him.

Timor teased. "You would do well to learn this skill, Erzhan. Look." He showed him the sturdy stitches pulled through the molded leather. "It's true, these days we have new captives for such work. But I wouldn't trust an enemy." He shook his head. Reaching for his own hard shell, he plucked at a loosening patch of metal. "I prefer my own stitches to preserve my breath."

I did not think much of the iron scales at all.

It was dark that night as I moved about the yurt, bending to scoop up bits of boiled horse meat from the cauldron, pouring salt milk tea into hammered silver bowls and laying cubes of soaked hard cheese. The men sipped koumiss. Arman should have slept, but he stayed awake leaning against Erzhan like an uncle.

"It was a good raid at Gorgippia," Erzhan murmured. "Sixty-five at last count, of all the slaves that have survived."

"Sixty-five out of two hundred. Those are heavy losses."

"But fewer mouths to feed. And with gold and herds and goods—you'll see. Pazylbek will make a fine trade of them."

Timor sighed. "We did not raid even at Gorgippia's heart. Erzhan, we barely breached the city's walls. The Skoloti's power lies farther to the west, at the port where the slaves were bound."

"Next time." Erzhan's eyes were sharp. "Next time, I promise, we will slaughter them completely."

There was weight to Erzhan's words, some meaning in his promise that I could not understand. And from Timor's laden grunt, I sensed that more than treasure lay behind Gorgippia's walls—

"Next time." Timor pulled at the long locks of his beard. "We could never penetrate that far with so few warriors and the whole of the Scythian army watching. We took them by surprise. This time we were lucky."

"We've made a start. A worthy foray. Timor, we have shown the Scythians we are a force—"

Timor shook his head. "Next time, you're right, we will do better." Then he looked absently away, reached into the woven basket, and let the golden scales fall like yellow rain. The leather shirt was finished. Timor stretched arms out for Arman. "Stand, my little eagle. Put this on."

Arman loved when his father called him that, as if he and Garah were true beast kin. Arman tried and the shirt fit perfectly. He danced about, posing, preening. "Mama, look! Come fight me, if you dare!"

I smiled and reached, but before I could embrace him Arman scurried into the shadows, digging through sacks and jars tucked against our wood yurt frame until he found a trunk that held our few forgotten things. He drew out his old cradleboard with Umai's bow and arrows still dangling from its corner. So long we'd held that board, hoping it would be filled again. After traveling back and forth with the changing seasons, the cradle's wood had a long, thin crack. Its leather straps needed refitting. Arman worked clumsily to untie the crusted thong.

"My gorytoi." He used the word that Timor and I had shared when he was still a captive. The quiver had been sewn of gut and scraps of leather by Erzhan's inexpert hand, though the bow and arrows were fitted masterfully—perfect replicas of a warrior's weapons. Finally Arman loosened the ties and tucked the leather quiver cockeyed on his belt. Then he drew an arrow, nocked it on the strand, and raised the tiny bow. He aimed at Erzhan's brow. Erzhan laughed a bit, pressing down the shot.

"Outside, Arman. It is time. You are old enough." Timor beckoned and both men rose.

I followed them into that milling dusk, walking softly among the sheep and goats and glow-lit yurts until we reached the empty practice ground.

"You will need more than air to lift your shot." His father knelt. "You will need sight and strength and vision." Then he handed him the bow—a duty I'd always thought was mine, but here, now, neither man looked toward me.

I stood silent as Erzhan murmured, "For all these years, these arms have protected you in Umai's name. I gave them upon your birth. Now use them for the purpose they were made."

"Arman," I tried, "show us what you can do." But my child looked on me with a resentful gaze, as if a mother's voice was an intrusion.

Finally he reached for one of the three small arrows bound into the narrow leather sleeve. He lifted up the bow, tiny fingers fat around the shaft. Seizing at his grip, Arman was small but strongly handed. He plucked the bowstring once as he'd often seen, strumming for its tone and tautness. Then he placed the arrow—awkwardly at first so that it almost dropped. I bent to snatch it up, but Arman waved me off. "Mother, I can do it."

Such brazen disrespect I'd never heard except when Erzhan and Timor were near. But from my son—for Arman's sake, I dropped my arms and backed away.

Timor helped him truss the string and hold the arrow better. Then the boy took in his breath. He drew and shot—my child—the arrow fell hard, short, and dug into the turf. But the two men cheered and Arman beamed at both of them.

"It is late," I said, turning toward our yurt. "The cook pot will be boiling off the last of our fresh water."

It was true. When I returned, I took the cauldron from the coals and held my hands above the rising steam to warm them—hands that had lost their grip, their aim, grown useless but for sewing felts and making cheese.

When they returned, it was well past moonrise. "Arman must rest." I aimed Erzhan toward the door. He reached for Arman's arms and hugged him, then held Timor tight against his chest. The sound of hands roughly slapping backs was dull and hollow.

From outside there came a constant shush—footsteps and hoof-falls, mewling, camels' constant gnaws and snorts, the cries of children from the captives' camp. Set off at a distance, it was just a patch of dust, circled around by arid flatness and guarded night and day by six complements of warriors.

"You will patrol tonight?" I asked Timor as Erzhan walked away, a little drunk, not with koumiss but with an uncle's pride.

Timor's fist clung loosely to our doorframe. "You know I will." He scraped his boot across the pounded dirt.

"You do not have to. You could be exempt. Erzhan is war-master and you are his general."

"I want no special privilege, Akmaral. To watch the slaves—I will take my turn." Timor leaned his forearm across the low, rough lintel, and then his forehead against his arm.

"Must I sleep?" Arman pressed between us. "I'm old enough. I will ride out with my father."

"It's late, Arman," I said.

He began to pout, but Timor knelt and held him. "Tomorrow, Arman, I promise you will ride along with me."

Arman brightened. "You will teach me how to shoot?" He poised his bow and arrow.

"Your mother is the finer archer. She should teach you. I'm better at the sword."

Arman's face twisted. "My mother is a girl." Then he tried his shot. The arrow fell before it even flew beyond the threshold.

"Go to bed, Arman," I said.

Timor took him to his mat and tucked him between the heavy felting.

"His armor." I pointed. "He should take it off."

"No!" Arman clutched his chest and screwed his cheeks for tears.

"Let him wear it," Timor said, but his gaze was strange, as if he longed to speak again but found no words.

"I am a warrior in the field, Mama. I sleep in my war shirt and wait for dawn to strike!" He said it fiercely; and I saw in Arman's eyes how much he longed to be so.

"In the field," I warned, "no one ever rests." I tucked him tighter between the mats, bent to kiss him, then sat beside the coals working at some felt, waiting until Arman's breath took on the steady rhythm of a child's dreams.

Timor had stepped outside to give Garah her meat. I sat listening to her sturdy wing flaps, then the rustling of the wind. When he returned, Timor's hands were cold.

"Winter is nearly here," I said. "Pazylbek must rid us of these slaves soon. Then we'll go to the winter gorge. There will be no raids there. It will be as it was before." I took Timor's hands to warm between my palms—his fingers hard, nails encrusted with earth and the tanning fats we use for leathers.

"When I was a captive?" he murmured. "I think you liked me better that way."

"No." I held his fingers to my cheek. Timor smiled, but there was sadness in his eyes, as if, for all his pride in what he had become, he also missed those early days. I laughed and bit the tip of his thumb gently, then took his palm and placed it on my belly, slipping down between my thighs. "You do not have to go." I reached for him. He clutched my jaw and pressed his lips against mine with sudden hunger. Then he pulled away. Strangely. Awkwardly, with all his might.

"When I return," he promised, cupping my chin, tender as a

child's. He slipped into the dark. I heard him mount and press his horse in the direction of the captives' camp. His hoof-steps sounded like his heart, pounding wild as if I held my ear against his chest and listened through the thickness of his battle armor.

There had been movements in the hills. For many days dust rose with the early dawn; though when our warriors rode out to scout, they'd found nothing. Rarely even hoof-prints or scuffs among the loosened stones. If there'd been any riders near, they must have counted our great host, our arms and well-bridled horses, and turned away.

But there were also sounds. We heard them: low, soft echoes coming from great distances. They were sometimes almost whistles like the ones Timor made upon his fists—that I'd heard at his first hard capture. Now they came from all around—from the distant hills and near the captives' camp, rising, falling like starlings calling to their mates until the great, broad steppe is swept by the sharp black wings of a murmuration.

Too, there was the woman in the captive camp—the one who'd shouted, "Amazon." I saw her when I rode: she was younger than I'd thought, but big boned and meaty with the arms of a village laborer who pulled great beams. Timor told me once that his people built their auls within wood fences and that all of them—men and women both—felled the great larch trees of their forests and dragged them to their camps, only sometimes strapping them onto cattle-driven wagons. This captive seemed just such a woman; the collar of her threadbare dress was as black and furred as Timor's old bear cloak had been.

I did not think much of her tunic then. I think of it too often now.

That woman watched me every time I rode through the captive camp, more harshly when I was with Timor, and especially when I dandled Arman. Her eyes were sharp amidst bland features, like shards of basalt poking through dull clay. Hard, unyielding as the winds that blow cold but bring no useful snow. I couldn't understand the venom of her gaze. Once she even dared to spit, her saliva falling short of me, soaking into dust—small white bubbles that sank to nothing and had no power.

When Timor went that night to the captives' camp, he spoke long with that harsh woman. Or so Erzhan told me after.

I smelled the fat smoke first, so familiar it would have gone unquestioned except for the gentlest whinny—the sound of a horse tossing its mane, the soft slap of leather braid against a war-horse's withers. Timor had returned. He lay beside me, his warm skin pressed against my neck. His eyes were open when I awoke, catching the slivered light of the waning moon through the roof's eye. Beyond, it was very dark and turning clouded.

The intruders' horses were well trained. Their hoof-falls barely hinted at each strike of earth. Across the nibbled grass, they slipped as softly as saiga antelope among our milling sheep. Timor folded back our felts and sat upright. The chill air cut around our sleep mat as he rose and pulled on his trousers and his battle gear. I crawled over Arman, crouched beside Timor, stooped to pick my dagger up, reached to take down my bow and quiver, belted on my heavy battle sword. Timor also took up arms, then rose and tucked back our woolen doorway.

The first arrows fell like stones. All at once, roaring, pounding, anchoring their flames into our thick felt roof. Already it stank of fire. Not very long before the darts burned through and dropped, flickering brighter than our dwindled hearth-light, gnawing at our rugs and mats, scattering sparks that rushed along the yurt's new lattice ribs.

I turned and scooped up Arman, wrapped still in sleeping wools. When he woke, his eyes grew wide, his arms clutched around my neck. Choking, I whispered, "Don't let go," as I reached behind me to set my bow, my arrows.

Timor stood at our yurt's gap, shooting shaft after shaft. The stranger-warriors raced past—heavy men in long black cloaks and leather riding boots, their heads capped with metal battle helmets. They bore no scales, though their leather shirts were sturdy and thick. They veered this way and that, shrouded in darkness, smoke, the fire's flash, racing through the aul, dodging our strikes, whooping and screeching like falcons, then swooping in at us like a noose intent to strangle.

Around us, our own people rushed. They dragged groggy children, half undressed, through the smoke. Our own shots rained defiant, ana-women and old men donning arms in our defense. Already the battle had turned to blood. Several of our warriors lay pitted with thick black clots, faces slashed, chests pierced, no longer breathing.

Over bloodied earth I carried Arman, barely able to shield him, finding my way behind the whip and slice of Timor's blade. He fought wildly, cutting horses through their tendons as they charged, diving low to avoid the slash of an iron sword, tripping up a warrior's spear with his swinging bear cloak, distracting the veering horses.

Musty, moldering—the cloak he had been captured in, that we had tucked away as a cushion on our cot. His black bear cloak. Now, again, he wore it proudly.

The invaders wound around us and then moved on, leaving us in tatters but not all dead. Instead they charged toward the captives' camp. Some drove horses dragging wagons. Others broke away, rounding our stolen herds which ran to the strangers' calls as if they already knew them.

In the distance, our sentries were already toppled. The captives spilled from their prison, running or riding if they could, spreading out in all directions. Great dust clouds sprayed as horses skittered, slowed, or turned. The captives mounted, riding without blankets or saddles, clinging to tangled manes, two and sometimes three on a single mare. Those that could piled onto the wagon flats and clung. This was no raid. It was a rescue.

Our own mounts were tied not far, but I couldn't make my

way—not quickly, holding Arman tight. Timor raced ahead until a rider cut him close, then swung around and cut Timor's path again.

The warrior sat on a strange dun mare but also drove another pony; and on its back, that same woman with the look of blood and hatred and now of triumph. She stared at me, but only briefly, like a shot, as she said his name—

"Timor."

I looked from her to him.

"Timor!" she said again. And then the stranger warrior offered down his hand. Insistent. Both of them speaking in that language that I barely understood.

"Timor, come," the man demanded. And then I recognized his timbre and the grizzle on his chin, the hard black eyes and his twisted leg, once very badly broken: Bulat. He was Bulat, Timor's Black Cloak brother who had survived the murderous escape. Now he rode with surprising firmness, holding his horse expertly against old pain.

Bulat galloped close and reached again. Timor flustered, his hand held out but not close enough to grasp. His sword raised high—high enough to strike, yet he did not. Nor did he turn away. He stood like a pillar, firm between us all, his sword a glimmering sharp-edged shield. His glance, hard against the man who had been his brother. Hard upon the blood-soaked earth, his own feet bearing stains from both his peoples. Finally his gaze fell on me: his blue eyes shadows; their frost lost in flash and fire, lost in the fear that choked his voice and shattered mine.

"Don't—" I barely breathed.

But I could not be heard above the rouse and battle. "Don't—" I gasped again, breathing harder.

Timor reached for me. The grief that was in his face seared me with its passion and its coldness. Then Bulat reached and, in a blinking, Timor leapt. He threw himself behind, clutching first Bulat's waist, then the high arch of his saddle. Gripping hard, they kicked the horse's flanks together with both their

heels. The horse's muscles rippled with the sting. The woman's
pony followed—all three racing away across the steppe. I cried
out, but Timor did not turn, did not look, not toward me or
even Arman.

Away.

Nothing—I heard…I could sense nothing. The smoke and
fire, the battle all around. Hard enough to see with Arman at
my neck. Impossible to aim. I placed him down on the gory
ground and groped, found my bow, my arrows. My aim was
slow, though my arm knew its target and my eyes took their
sight and my fingers almost plucked the strand. My heart
pounded thunder—Targitai in my ears—a sort of screaming
from behind—then suddenly Arman rushed toward his father.

"No!" I shouted, dust and fire in my throat, throwing down
my bow, reaching, dragging Arman back, pulling him hard
against me. "Timor!" I called out hoarsely. Arman fought, his
heels and elbows stabbing at my knees.

From somewhere on the ground, I scraped and found my
bow again. My bowstring trembled against the arrow's shaft.
My finger slipped. The sharp point dropped into the muck—a
mistake like a child barely started on his training. I bit my lip,
set the shaft, and drew again. Timor and that woman and Bulat
all riding harder, slipping out of range. Then, from somewhere
close behind, an arrow flew. Another. And again. Timor fell
from their horse, his body rolling, heavy, flailing in the mud.

I turned. Erzhan, thighs pressed against his stallion's shoulders, lowered his aim.

Then a great dark stroke. Windy air. A screech from up
above. Garah swooped, startling me so that I stumbled back,
slipped, and fell into the mud.

Arman pulled from me as the bird descended. Her broad
fringed wings hovered close, beat hard. Closing and opening.
Talons like hooks. Spears. Needles. Darts suspended above me.
Her beak a tearing point. Her eyes the color of sunset glinting
on a blade.

In the distance, Timor's body trembled once, then stilled as

Garah rose, her great wings spanning far beyond the width of Arman's tender shoulders. Her piercing grasp plunged hard into that leather. Talons clutched and held their grip. Metal scales flashed protection, glittering gold and gray. Arman's small legs dangled. His fingers wiggled wide as if at play. He called out, "Mama, look, I am a bird!" laughing, joyous as he lifted up and flew away.

PART III

THE FLYING DEER

29

REALM OF THE DEAD

We left Timor's body for the birds. It seemed only right for one who'd been their close familiar. They stood and tore at him—just one of many who had fallen in that fight. I watched. I stood and made myself watch until all that was left were bones and dangling shreds of hair and tasteless cartilage dusted with fallen fluff of feathers sticking to the drying gore.

It was a gruesome act, but I endured it while, all around me, our kindred gathered pieces from the ground: forearms and fingers, broken bits of knees, limbs and hooves from our finest mounts. They washed them of their battle blood, wrapped them rightly, preparing them to travel. We would bury them in the kurgan mounds. After that, we would leave. We were lesser, shattered by the loss, but still an aul. Winter would come. Our herds required shelter.

But my child—my sweet child—still I did not know if he had lived or died. I returned in my mind again, again, to the sight of that horrid flight—my Arman dangling, a small dot on the horizon, rising higher, ever higher, far above the dust and battle, though within an arrow's reach—if any had thought enough to shoot. The sudden stillness, all of us looking, even the Black Cloaks slowing their retreat. But not for very long. Bulat and that woman rearing up, then galloping harder.

Garah flew above them all, and my child's cries—his laughter like tinkling metal—already so far gone, muffled by the clouds that cloak the highest mountains at winter's start. Still I heard him—hear him, even now in another eagle's squawk. Her shadow crosses me, dark until she wings above, gliding upward as if she has no other purpose than to remind me.

Erzhan sent a search party, but it was no use. All the while came the Ak Kam's curses: "Betraying spirit, keep your evil from our people. May your soul rise no higher than a dung pile. May your memory be forgotten like the bitter shafts that waste across these fields. You betrayed our hearth, betrayed your oath, betrayed Rada Mai, Umai, Targitai. You betrayed blood kin. You betrayed our aul. We are one fire—we are one hearth! Go into the darkest realm where there is no pasture, where the fields are thick with winter ice and in summer turn to dust, where all your horses and herds will parch and starve. Go where the milk of foaling mares always runs dry."

Meiramgul came and stood beside me. She said nothing, though it seemed she'd always known that this would come. I could sense it in her touch as she turned me, guided me away. Fire and cinnabar, ochre, and drifting, powdered talc. Blood and death. I longed to cuddle Arman at my hip, but my arms were empty.

I packed my yurt alone, left behind my broken hearth, the gray smoke coiling upward like unraveling thread: Rada Mai's embittered breath. She had drifted from my coals, caught on the chilly wind, once protected by latticework and the warmth of laughter—a happy family. Now my hearth grew cold.

Our camp walked slowly to the kurgan mounds, picking out our way. I listened. I heard nothing. Only the crackle of new ice crusts breaking beneath our horses' gait, the litters that dragged our dead scraping and hopping across the grassland.

We buried them, though the earth was almost too stiff to dig, too dry to pack away again. Then we turned and rode toward the wintering place that had been our home since the earliest beginning.

As we traveled, Arman's face emerged from the gravel path, but then the horses kicked the stones away. Only dust and a few rough pebbles. That face, taken swiftly from my sight. But from my memory, it would never fade.

In the winter canyon where we settled, we made our nights as we always had on Meiramgul's stories of our greatest glo-

ries, hot tea, koumiss, hard cheese, dried chewy meat, and quiet
song. Ruan had learned the horsehead fiddle, though he played
it badly and he could not sing. Aigul was big again with child
and their first daughter, Nishan, had survived the Black Cloaks'
attack. They offered that I stay with them so that I would not
be alone, but I refused them.

"*Alel bam, alal bam*," I sang over my winter hearth, though I
could not raise its warmth. My cold breath moved over Rada
Mai's coals, hovering, keeping her alive—alive while, in the end,
I would have snuffed them out. In that cold, damp dark, I sang
songs, praises begging Umai to protect my child—now long
lost, long gone—"*Alel bam*"—he was no more. My child had
flown away.

For a while every child's features became his own, with
his guileless eyes, nose crusted and ruddy, lips the shade of
rare, ripe cherries gained from a caravan trader for the price
of a hand-sack full of gold. Small pearl teeth, polished as
the inner surface of one of the Ak Kam's precious seashells.
Hands the texture of new combed wool brushing against my
cheeks. Breath warmed my chin, forming quiet, mumbled puffs.
"Mama, are you there?" Then the screech of nightjars. Owls. I
covered his head beneath our matted quilt. A rustle in our yurt
from up above—I awoke—

He was never there.

Our people watched me—our warriors sitting outside their
winter cabins sharpening arrows and restringing bows as I
went about my winter chores. None would meet my gaze as
I milked my mare, then some of our other horses, then the
goats, and then the sheep. Each time my jars were full, one
of the ana-women helped me pour, but we barely spoke. If I
joined them, kneeling in the Hewana's cabin to sort a sack of
unwashed wool, I kept my head down at my task and cleaned
more fastidiously than before; the pile of bits of grass and dry,
caked dung that I combed away grew slowly beside me.

After a time, Aigul sat at my side, awkward, so pregnant now
that she could barely stoop or kneel. She placed her hand over

my own—hers so smooth and warm, mine cold as the hand of the dying. But she did not stay. Needing help to rise, she murmured, "Nishan is crying. I hear her. Ruan cannot nurse her by himself." As she said her husband's name, I felt the parched, dry memory of Marjan, so close, so lost, so beloved, so long ago.

A warrior's carcass is left for carrion, Marjan once had said, *wasted on the battlefield.* We had been young and I'd thought her wrong, but now I knew that it was true—all that I had lost, such life, such love, now futile. Wasted. I raised my hands, smelling thick and oily with the fatty wool. When Aigul was gone, I placed them on my face to shroud my eyes.

Then Erzhan came. Alone in my yurt, I had not—did not—want to see him. Not since the raid. Yet now he stood like a shadow in my doorway that I could not see beyond. So I let him in. He sat. I could hear his breathing. Neither of us spoke—what was there to say? Yet he stayed there for a long, long time. Finally he reached and took my hand. I pulled away, resentment, disgust, nausea all seething through me. I hated Erzhan almost as much as I did myself. Now he gripped my palm and held it firmly.

Words came—bile in my throat, burning so I longed only to swallow, but instead I spat them out: "You killed him."

"Yes. There was nothing I could do—"

"Yes. Of course." I knew. I had nearly shot the dart myself, though I had not. Erzhan had. He had done his duty.

I hung my head. All my life, devoted to Targitai—and here I was, alone, left hating what I'd loved, longing for my hatred. "Timor—"

"I know. I loved him too."

Such words had never fallen from those lips. I gaped at him.

"Timor was a brother."

I could not help but think what a brother was to him—of how he'd tortured Timor when he'd first been captured. "You hated him."

"I loved him. We were as a broken arrow—two halves that

cannot be mended, a blade that has been cut. I cut it, Akmaral. I, not you. I cut him down—" All at once, Erzhan broke as he never had before, gasping with tears that had never been shed, not even when he was a child. "He told me long ago why he'd run from the Scythians—such words, that he loved his people—those Black Cloaks, rough beasts, that woman in the crowd. She was family—some kind of kin. And all those raids—Gorgippia—all of it, just to find a way to steal them back, to outwit the Skoloti, make them pay for what they'd done, to finally avenge his people."

I stared at him, juggling his words that came at me like stones until they made slow sense: Timor had tried to help me understand. He had said these things, though I'd barely listened, my hearing clouded by love and pride. I remembered how those captives watched while we passed them on our mounts. And those many days before—Timor and Erzhan on that hilltop—talking, riding off, raising up a force, leaving me behind.

"But my son—you knew he would go? You knew he would take my child?"

"No, Akmaral. Timor did not say. But I sensed—I saw. You saw him, too, stitching up the scales for armor, teaching Garah to raise a body without harm. We both should have seen it. But neither of us thought—"

His words sank in like the first drops of rain after a long, harsh drought. After a time, my tears flowed silently to join his. "We both should have known, for clearly…." But I could say no more as Erzhan let his hard grip on my hand soften to a touch, the tenderest that I had ever known from him even in those few short days when we had been lovers.

Then came the first hard snows. Until winter's end, we would huddle together behind clay-log walls. We would portion out our dry stripped meat strung on nettle cords and our heavy lumps of cheese. The cliffs would whisper with the sounds of horse hooves scratching through the snow and the snuffling of goats and sheep desperate for the grass beneath. The only footsteps then would be our own: Erzhan sending out patrols in twos and threes.

And I would join them as I was meant to. No longer serving Rada Mai's hearth—no longer an ana-woman—my duty was to take my place, to protect our clan, my kindred, my own people—they who knew my pain, though I would beg that they did not—that they had never heard of Arman, Timor, shared our laughter, seen our joy. Amidst thorny compassion, I stood anguished. Lost.

Better to nurse that bitter taste of sorrow alone.

I turned away. On a day of storms, Erzhan sent us one final time to check the herds and I went too. I was unwise to drift apart, but I could not bear to travel with them.

By the time the blizzard was at its height, I had ridden far across the driven snow. Then, when the storm was through, I tracked by moonlight—that bright orb shining like a torch, glinting on rocks. Frozen rivulets were silver floss; crevasses concealed by the crusted drape of ice. I rode, cautious of their trickery, toward the high ground, following buried paths, though they were scant at best, dwindling to snowdrifts, wind picking up another glittering hailstorm that pelted my face, leaving long red scratches that would never fade.

There was a hush in the peaks, as if the earth were barely breathing. I rode, patient, knowing my mare suffered, taking her toward the rising passes, ankles slipping, cut by ice, leaving a trickling trail of blood and pain. When she could stand no more, I let her go. She knew the way to return. She did not need me to lead her.

I set out on foot. Two days through drifts, traveling only by darkness, sleeping through the light in a hollowed bowl filled with blinding glare. My skin burned and stained with frost, my fingers icy beneath heavy gloves of camel's hide turned inside out, oiled into strong, soft leather.

Finally I stood below the cave's mouth—there where I had stood before. But then the sun had been bright, the sky cloudless, and I had not been alone. Now my feet lay lost in snow.

I scanned the ground, found fox prints, small, rushed depressions. A fluttering of birds. Where hare's feet scratched the powdery surface. The moon—a hollow maw now swallowing the dark. My shadow grew gray and long. I could see where I would go.

High above me on an outcrop, the snow leopard arched her spine. Her paws crossed; she settled, then gazed as if she had been waiting all along, knowing that I would come. Her great pale eyes, nothing like my own, and yet they were—the way they stared at me.

In her heavy winter coat she looked bigger than before—softer, fiercer, and more gentle. Her breath steamed puffs, dissipating, rising up. My own breath drifted to nothing. Clear, unmoving. Suspended like crystal.

I called to her, "Why do you not kill me?" My voice echoed, drifting over distance, reaching no one else's ears. A subtle purr floated across whiteness. The slanted field between us crackled and sparked. She refused to speak, refused to move. I took one step and she craned her neck, giving me a sidelong grimace. I plucked my bow, carefully readied my shot. The leopard stretched her limbs, yawned, placid as if I were a pebble barely balanced on a perch, susceptible to wind. She turned to go.

I climbed to where she'd been, but found no sign. Only the cave's mouth: gaping, black as coal. I stumbled in. Full dark. I staggered. Fell. Asleep. For many days, it seemed, I did not waken.

Or if I did, I could not sense that I was awake at all. In a dream, I found a fire, a pile of softened meat, a bowl of milk still warm from a mare who could not have been there. I set the meat aside, spilled the milk to quench the flame. Then I slept. When I awoke, the food was there again.

Three days. Four. Many more. I did not count them. If the light penetrated, I would not see it, wrapping my cloak tightly around me, heavy as the cave's dark—thicker than a black sheep's wool matted into tent cloths. But again the meat, well dried this time as if it had stood many weeks in the autumn breeze. I took it up, turned it in my fist—barely a claw now, blistered with frostbite, shriveling to blackness on the tips. I did not stop myself this time. I took the meat, tore it with my teeth, and chewed.

In the dark, I ate and drank. The milk was tinged with ferment, sour or spoiled—the shallow cup resembling a skull the size that Arman's drinking cup had been. I was grateful I could not see it, though I felt it—wrapped in skin, edged with cold metal, strange shapes smooth and carved, barely warming in my hands, and the inside polished until it must have glistened.

In the dark I sensed I was not alone, welcoming every twitch, every crumbling of dust, every soft breath that could not have been the consequence of humans. Demons or predators. The spirits of the dead or the shapes of wolves. Perhaps the leopardess herself in the gloom that lay beyond, where the walls grew narrow and jagged. Bats flew fearlessly now that my embers had turned from graying coals to ash. They hovered above, so close that I could feel their wind.

"Kak! From the white cloud, Kak! From the black dark, Kak!"—echoes of the Kara Kam's calls; and her seed smoke filled my head, drifting from nowhere. They lifted me, though I did not want them. Another sip. I knew it was the drink she made—libation of the goddess of death and life and vision: the Flying Deer.

I soared. It was delusion, starvation, delirium, vivid in the grip of cold. If there was thunder, it was a drum struck far above by an unseen hand. But no light. No lightning. Now one spark—a mirror's flash—

Night with its sharp, small stars.

Arrow-points pierced an ebon midnight's ceiling. No moon to light my way along the mountain's edge. The yurt stopped me in my path, set alone in the dark with its single smoke rising up toward heaven—drawn by the ancestors—a slim, fine thread. It twined up with the peaks and joined the clouds on the heaven pasture. There the dead roam, hidden, driving their stately, boundless herds.

I crossed the threshold, sniffed the yurt. Inside the Kara Kam—her face was my own mother's. She sat, offered me tea, smiling as if she had been waiting. The bowl was small. It barely fit into my fingers but I held it to my lips. The liquid drained, slipped back beyond my tongue. I couldn't taste. Too hot. Its fire burned me.

The Kara Kam wore her high peaked cap. It dangled with glitter as she sat before her hearth. Her teeth were black, her skin crawling with winged snow leopards, deer with griffin heads and endless, curling, tangled antlers. Her hands walked across the thick felt mat before her, over white and black felt, then gray, then gold and bronze, then red that spread beneath, the color of blood. They crept toward mine, her fingers showing me direction. The Kara Kam whispered, "Akmaral. Welcome."

Her lips did not move when she spoke. Her arms didn't move as she offered out her hands. Across them draped the ash-dot pelt of the snow-white leopard. The leopard rose and regained her flesh. She blinked at me once, then turned to leave.

I awoke and the dream was gone. I lay inside my own yurt now with my husband and my child. We had slept all through that night together, naked beneath our felts, Timor's skin against mine, Arman's softness. Our bodies touching.

I withdrew, pulled on trousers, tied my tunic with a thick, hard belt close against my waist. It was small again. Too narrow. I touched it, longed for it to grow thick once more with child.

I shook my head, pressed the door ajar, walked down to the spring lake. The water shallow, in places the earth was mostly mud. I bent and pressed my hands through the murky still. Grasses pierced the surface, distorting the ripples that scurried away from me. Looking up, I followed the blackened arrow of a flock of geese. It would not be long before the elders called for us to travel.

When I turned, Timor stood at our doorway. Sun was on his face, burning its gold-reflected rise. I looked out to where the hard edges of the horizon blazed, watched the great compass of the sky. A thin layer of clouds hovered—the heaven steppe, uncoupled from the earth, where only the ancestors ride.

"Akmaral." Timor was beside me now, his footsteps silent in the spattered dew. His hand against my neck, his shoulder warm and musky.

"I had the dream again," I said. He wrapped me in his arms. His body's heat enveloped me like his black bear cloak.

"Will you go to her?" His gaze floated toward the south, toward the single line of smoke—a thin gray spike piercing the heavens. The Kara Kam's place lay beyond the spring plain at an almost vertical drop near the narrow path where Madiyar had once been murdered.

I shook my head.

"You cannot escape a dream."

Suddenly I awoke again and was finally alone inside that black cave. The fire was cold: a sin against Rada Mai to neglect the hearth. I groped in the dark. This time I found a birch twig beside me, freshly cut, hung with a knot of horsehair. I stumbled, barely steady on my knees, tripping on a heap of sheep's dung that had been piled there, dried so long that it was beyond even frost, turned stony and ageless. This I set alight and burned for the next few days.

It was spring. I hadn't noticed. Time awash with timelessness, and the shadows shifted, meaningless to me. I didn't want to welcome the daylight to my breast, only the constant dusk that would fall to dark forever. But the livid sun refused to set, relentless, bringing back the vital flush when all within me should have quenched its fire.

A shriek. A golden eagle. I heard its fluttering wings above, heavy and striking. I looked up and saw it through a small, bright crevice—two tiny cracks spreading radiant beams. The brilliance brought the cavern's marks alive: dark spirits etched in red, black, brown, flecked by sulfur moss and peeling lichen. Hunters on horseback wielding bows and arrows—the walls were flush with them, and pounding antelope, camels, deer,

leopards fighting, the lion-headed griffin, and a horse-beast
with the hump-nosed saiga's horns. Over great swirling grasses,
the beasts churned and cantered. Arrows flying. And spears.
And the greatest of them: antlers curled, forelimbs tucked for
flight—a single white flying deer.

Timor stood beside me once again. We passed our hands
together across the dim, finding one and then another of the
wall's stone figures. Finally he touched the antlered deer and
drew my hand across. Behind there flew a hundred of their
kind, but this one's antlers were the largest, each tipped with a
griffin's head. Part deer, part eagle, part the snow-white leopard.
Timor whispered, "Akmaral, this is you. You are transformed."

The cave filled up. Blinding light. Hundreds dancing. Laughter. Buckets with lake-damp clay molding into more: children
walked toward my fire and warmed themselves. Small ones,
dark with the scent of soil. Light ones like sunlit rain. The waters flowed. Flooded. I stepped out among them.

The wind blew from above. With my birch twig I drew a
circle, singing the chants as I could recall them: "Welcome
Targitai, Kak! Rada Mai—hearth-mother, Kak! Umai, protector
of all children, Kak!" Another shrill, this time softer, fading
to a whisper. The sound of breath pushed through a strong
man's hands. Timor's hands pressed against his lips. His sky
eyes piercing blue, high above the cave, breathing into me.

When dawn came, I rose and wrapped my cloak. I tied my quiver to my belt—my fingers too damaged by frost to do it well. I
could barely lift my sword—almost cut myself as I placed it in
its scabbard. Beyond the cave's mouth, the spring melt gathered
its flow and set off down its course. The small, bright stream
chattered as if to escort me.

I came into the thawing valley and she was there. Stooped
on her haunches, wizened, ancient, hung with tattered pelts and
cloth. Woolly threads, barely twisted into twine, fell from her
tangled hair. Her fingernails were gray like the stones she'd gathered. She held them up, spread her arms, fists turned downward

as she gazed across the broad horizon. Then she dropped them, one by one, in many places.

"Akmaral, can you find my camels?" the old woman croaked. "My sheep? My herds? Where are my mares?"

Her eyes were milky, squinted, the color of blindness. The woman turned and smiled broadly.

She stretched her arms again, tried to rise, but tottered. So I helped her. She gripped my hands, studying the swelling joints with her own shriveled claws. "Come." She hobbled off, sometimes tripping, her feet crooked as if caught between hard stones and broken when she was very young. If she was in pain, I could not tell. She stepped swiftly far ahead of me, dodging slippery places, unsteady footing, crevices too broad to jump. She squeezed behind a boulder into a crack so small she could not have fit. From its dark entrance, her eyes blinked twice, then disappeared.

At the foot of the stone, I found a healing herb mixed with fat into a salve. Through some few days, I stayed by that rock and nursed my wounds. My hands grew fit enough to fletch my arrows. When I was well enough, I returned, winding along the exposed path now cluttered with horse dung, sheep pellets, clear black ice, great tufts of just-shed wool. The aul was packing up to go. Another day and I would have missed them.

Meiramgul did not speak at first, and when she did, she held her voice willfully steady. "Khagan," she called to her sister, "Akmaral has returned."

The Ak Kam stepped from the elders' hut, took my hands, turned them over, twisted them from side to side. "Hideous as an old man's feet"—she shook her head—"mangled forever."

I drew them back and held them at my sides. They were my prize for what I'd come to know. "I would have perished," I answered, "but the Kara Kam would not let me."

The women looked at one another. "Akmaral," Meiramgul spoke, "before midwinter, the Kara Kam—Soyun, your mother's mother's sister—died."

I looked at the ground. My boots, worn to skin and cord, my leggings and tunic in tatters.

"Find a horse," the Ak Kam ordered. "You must ride if you are able. Strap your hunting spear and gather up your arrows."

I went without speaking and found my yurt tucked into the sheltered cliff as it had been. Inside, all was as I'd left it except for a small round bowl etched in gold, decorated with flying deer, eagles, leopards. It smelled of the white fermented drink and the hard black seeds, a crust of their remains still fixed within. I knew its weight and shape, closing my eyes. I had sipped out of that bowl only in a dream. The spoon beside it was scorched with milk; and a mirror lay, freshly polished bronze, and a drum, and a clutch of seashells wrapped to a post to make a rattle. All of these, the Kara Kam's sacred things.

30

RETURN

I tucked the mirror, cold against my chest. It dangled, took its place beside my flying deer. My ancient amulet, another weight hanging heavy from my neck. That one old and small, yet still it shined, brighter with the thought: still it reminded me of my mother. But then, before her, how the deer had come to me— again through the strange smoke, through the Kara Kam's seeing. And now the mirror, cold and anxious—the pain brought comfort, lying flat against my skin. The hard round disk, too small to be a shield, and yet somehow I sensed that it protected me.

Outside, the Hewana knelt before the last of the hearth goddess's fire, gathering the glowing embers carefully into her broad clay pot while her sister chanted praises in slow measure: "We are one fire. We are one hearth," as each ana-woman dropped in her own last coals.

My hands were empty. I had nothing now to offer as I sat, mounted upright on my horse. My head raised high, but between two stations of our aul, I did not know which way I should turn.

Erzhan came to me after he'd surveyed the warriors. "Akmaral, it is good to have you back."

I studied him, nodded mutely. I did not know what Erzhan meant: if he was glad I was alive, returned, or glad I was no longer an ana-woman—could not be now with no child, no husband, no longer one with the man who had cut us both so deeply. Erzhan's arms pressed hard against his leather war vest, his face a beaten mask, both forceful and remote, so unlike the tear-glossed visage he had shown that night before I'd gone.

He rode off. Around me, the ana-women scurried. Their eldest children tucked their ponies into droves. Wielding urga poles and silver whips, they nudged the herds over loosened stones while shouting at the dogs who darted and raced to start the crowds toward the water's edge—the same rough stream that I had followed to the ancestors' cave. That winter it had lain like a dead man's blood clotting in cold veins. Yet now it was alive again, gushing to lead us from our winter shelter. Here it turned into a narrow torrent, and further on, would grow into a calm, wide span. After a time we would leave it, turning north toward fresh spring pastures. There the lake would shimmer, crystal clear, pricked with knobby storks' knees, its quiet shattered by harsh goose shrieks as it had been every springtime since the beginning.

I stood alone and watched the whirl of them. Shaggy, shedding camels loaded down with household goods. Even the youngest of us dragging heavy satchels from the river filled with drink—something my own child had not lingered long enough to do. Meiramgul came beside me. Her lucid gaze, high cheeks rough and winter-tinged. "You cannot go back."

"I know," I said.

The Hewana reached her broad hand out to touch my chin. Bare and calloused from endless work, still her palm was warm as she tucked me close against the scratchy wool of her winter tunic. It smelled of cook smoke, dung coals, and fermented milk, comforting scents I remembered from when I was an orphaned child—whiffs of a forgotten memory.

We went from our winter place up through the valley's throat and reached the springtime steppe just as the lake filled high with snowmelt. The black storks had indeed returned. All was as it had been. Before Arman. Before Timor.

After we buried our winter dead, a line was hung for shooting arrows. Our warriors turned to drills on the spring plain, charging, brandishing battle swords, practicing cloud shots, and aiming rearward. All was as before. I rode up to Erzhan quietly and watched.

"You will join us, Akmaral?"

I did not answer.

His eyes leveled at the dirt, then raised toward the distant cleft, that place between the mountains from which Timor's first raid had come.

"You would go there?" I asked him.

He would not look at me. "Not for bounty. To find our enemy. To see his face."

I looked beyond that narrow pass. "You would seek out the Black Cloaks? The Melanchlaeni?"

"And their masters." Erzhan nodded. "The Scythians."

"The Scythians." The word caught on my tongue like tangled wool. I dropped my lance point, slowly drilling until a small round hole formed in the tender soil.

Erzhan reached around my neck and pulled the mirror on its cord. "What is this?" He stared at his own face in the distorted surface.

I gently took it back and tucked it again beside my chest. "If you go, Erzhan, I will go with you."

This time Erzhan asked and the elders gave their consent. After all our people's anger, betrayal, loss, this time Targitai's charge was justified. Even Meiramgul approved. The Ak Kam poured colored dust and scorching milk while she prayed: "Rada Mai, six generations we have stayed. Six generations in our mountain refuge, the ancestors' mounds beside us, resting peaceful, left mostly to ourselves. Here, no Scythians have ever dwelled…." When all was done, we plunged our blades into the coals, digging deep to stir Targitai's sparks from Rada Mai's fire.

For the next few days Erzhan and I stood, shoulders nearly touching, drilling our fighters as we prepared for war. We knew little of the place where the Black Cloaks dwelled. Only hints from Timor's stories and that there were trees. Trees here grew only along the lake's close edges, their roots jutting out for us to trip or dodge. So we turned our warriors from the hard-packed earth and made them slosh through muck along the shore. Our warriors racked those roots so many times that the leaves soon yellowed; then the branches withered, and then the trunks rotted and died. Never again would anything so hearty grow there, not even when the melt-waters flowed fresh and at their highest.

For me, too, the drills were rough and tripping. So long had it been since I'd played at war, since I'd wielded weapons aimed at anything but sport. But this was not like Umai's feast, not like when I'd practiced as a child. Now every time I drew my bow, I knew my aim was charged with death. Finally I understood why ana-women are rarely called to fight. Once you have loved with all your heart, you cannot kill idly again.

Sometimes Aigul trotted close to watch Ruan. That first day I rode across to greet her. We had barely spoken since my return. Her arms stretched wide to welcome me. Squeezed into her saddle arch was her eldest girl, Nishan.

"She can already hold her seat," Aigul said.

I reached and patted smooth the child's thick, dark hair. "Soon she'll learn to ride her own horse—you'll see." I tried to smile.

Strapped to Aigul's saddle was a well-worn cradle basket bearing another sleeping girl. "She is Marjan," Aigul whispered as if she did not wish to offend me.

I tousled the infant's wisps, so soft, and her scalp—a cup of warmth tucked safely into felted wool.

"I brought a gift." Aigul handed me something wrapped in cloth. "New riding trousers. I made them for Ruan, but the leather was too short. And if you give me your tunic, I'll mend it and tighten up the scales."

"I can do it."

"Not with those." She took my hands, almost gawking at their frost scars. "You took pitiful care of yourself while you were away."

"They are fine." I raised my bow and set an arrow flying to prove it.

"You are a warrior again. I am pleased for you. But you are

no green recruit as we once were. Akmaral, it isn't right that you should fix this for yourself. Let me do something for you."

Finally I nodded and passed my shredded tunic, filthier than I'd thought with only a handful of my golden plaques still dangling at the collar's edges.

She fondled them gently. "You'll soon earn back more. Ruan's gained fistfuls of gold from every battle."

"Yes," I choked. "I know."

"Of course." Aigul backed away, though I had not meant to silence her. Only I could not bear recalling Timor with his gold griffin tied onto his belt, how he'd worn it proudly.

31

BLACK FOREST

I have never seen the sea, but I have seen forests—vast where the sky is shut away and the horizon is stabbed with the sun's sharp spears like gold plunging down through countless tent poles. There were larches with their draping branches, as Timor once told me. Barely a bit of light filtered through that heavy canopy and every sound echoed like an enemy stalking. If a branch dropped down, it startled. Or when the wind blew two tree trunks close together, they sounded like the cries of eagles—a noisy screech. Or the scurry of some tiny creature, so small it was barely seen, would warn of a stranger's step and send the heart racing.

We moved forward in a pack toward those unseen forests so far across the steppe. Erzhan led while I held back, claiming to protect our rear. But that was not the fact—only I preferred to stay where I could hear my heart beat its dark, unsteady rhythm. All across these rolling pastures, I sensed it like a drum. And the starlight and the moon each night were bright, sharp mirrors striking me with their beams.

First the new moon, then the full moon, then the old moon, then the moon of death. All our lives we had ridden far, but never without the aul. Now we followed the cold spring winds and sunsets' dark into unknown regions. We settled down each night, exposed beneath those boundless stars: the distant ancestors' fires. In their shadows, the young warriors played tsaagan bones, rolling the polished knuckles over dusty grass. They laughed, drank koumiss, dabbled at the carnal lusts that are a warrior's right. I could see already who would survive and who would likely die in battle and who would bear a child by next winter's thaw. Most of those I'd known before were long since changed or lost, grown too old to fight, or killed, or, like Aigul, found their place among the aul doing finer things. But I had lost that place and had no purpose. I was a warrior once and now again, riding alone among children.

When they dared, those young ones stared across the grass camp at me in curiosity or blame. None dared mention my dead husband directly. The elders had long claimed that he had fallen prisoner in the Melanchlaeni raid, that Erzhan's shot had been to save him from a captive's fate. But no one believed them. Everyone recalled that Timor had lain after that battle beneath those vultures' wings wearing the same black bear cloak as the fallen raiders.

I stayed apart, keeping watch along the night camp's edges until the other warriors mostly slept. Then Erzhan came and sat beside me—now with no shiver of desire, no hatred or resentment, and no rivalry. We sat as if our backs were the only parts of us that dared still touch. Erzhan's youthful rage had long since cooled to a warrior's iron, while mine had smothered in the dark, cold winter of my mourning.

We traveled on. We sang mostly dull chants to our horses' rhythms or rode in silence as we swept each day farther from our familiar mountain pasture across those endless plains. Finally the grasslands turned to shallow foothills covered in forests, as deep and black as the colors of our enemies' cloaks, shadowy with piney growth and outcrops of hard granite. We searched them, looking for a place that Timor had described: *where a river bends into the shape of a ram's horn*. He had said it more than once as I'd traced it on his skin: an echo of that spiral carved into an indigo tattoo, one of many across his shoulders and his chest—signs of a strong man rising.

As I thought of him, he spoke to me, his voice as clear as if he rode beside me. *I was a leader once among my men. They were my blood brothers. I will not betray them.* But he also said, *I will not leave you.* I tried to hush him up. His words were tricks, turning left instead of right. They would not guide me.

When I found a shape I recognized, I rode to Erzhan and pointed out the path. He looked into the dark pit of the valley and shook his head against hard memory. "Akmaral—" He pointed. "You take the lead."

My face into the wind, I spread hands wide across the high curve of my saddle. "No," I answered.

"You know Timor's stories best."

I gazed at him. "You know his stories too."

So we rode together. Our horses' feet grew tender on the restless stones and tripping roots, nervous in the forest valley clutched by darkness though it was not yet even dusk. So different from our broad plain where the light broke free and played among drifting clouds. Those trees beside our lake were nothing. Laughable. They had not prepared us.

Timor had told me it was so, that our world was bright, so bright that it sometimes left him breathless. *In my land, the earth is the dark between two breasts, or the place that I treasure most between your thighs.*

There were settlements among these rises: tiny farms in the angled dirt, strange crops wasting in rocky, half-cleared patches. The surface of Timor's river rippled and the narrow waters opened into lakes, deep and black even in the shallows. On their shores clustered villages sheltering people wearing rags of drabbest browns, the colors of the earth, as were their houses: log and plank, daubed with cakey mud, and roofs of sod or grasses. But they wore no cloaks of black bear's fur. These could not be Melanchlaeni.

We were hungry, so we raided but found little of real worth. These people had few horses—sometimes only one or two of the heavy sort bred for pulling. Still we took our kill and the farmers with it if they showed too much resistance. Some just stood as we ransacked stores and butchered sheep, as if they'd seen such raids before and had learned to endure them.

We passed on. After another quarter of the moon, we found a wider valley where herds of horses were scattered on a grassy pasture. Many were blanketed and primed with bronze-clasped bridles, saddled, ready to ride or already mounted. All were men upon the horses' backs and most wore shaggy cloaks the color of coal.

We stopped at a distance, using the wood as shelter. We could barely see their faces—only their hair like matted manes tucked close beneath metal helmets or soft felt caps with blunted peaks that bent almost to their woolly brows. As the hard dusk draped the forest, the Black Cloaks' language drifted with their cooking fires' scents, too twisted to decipher from birds' squawks and the lowing of cattle that hung about their inner yards.

Our warriors looked across to me, and I toward Erzhan. We nodded, moved a little closer.

It was a clustered place, assembled with quarters sometimes one against the next. Their huts were dug into the earth or underneath, rooted as deep as the nearby trees. And set around the whole was an earthen wall erected high with wooden ramparts. The river ran beneath, wrapping the broad fort with its curved embrace. Only the fields beyond were open to attack, and these were ringed with tents somewhat like our yurts, and many armored warriors.

"Those are Scythians." Erzhan pointed toward the men wearing hard bronze helmets. "Probably one hundred on horseback, and half as many others lingering about, plus untrained women, children, wasted men. We can take them only if we trap them. We must wrap a ring about, a noose for catching beasts—use their own valley as a pit to ensnare them."

The other warriors nodded, though I found it suddenly hard to breathe.

Erzhan sniffed. "Akmaral, have you so forgotten Targitai's duty?"

My glance fell upon my sword's hilt. "No." I swallowed, my mare's hooves shifting as if she too felt the lingering weight of Timor's specter, his arms clutched around my waist as if he rode there still, as he had throughout our early, happy days.

The Black Cloak women wandered from their houses far below us. They tended to their goats and sheep, bending broad,

strong backs to milk their cows. They wore braids beside their
cheeks and their deep-set eyes were shadowed. Their long skirts
were cause for tripping, as Timor had once told: "Our women
rarely mount. They travel in wagons pulled by horses or oxen."
I had mocked this until I'd seen such wagons racing toward our
captives' camp, taking off even the weakest among them. But I
had seen that woman—Bulat's woman, or perhaps Timor's—I
didn't know who she was, but I recalled that she had ridden on
that stolen pony like a proper horseman.

I would never learn the answer. Our warriors spread out
through the brush, using the forest cover and the night for safe
passage. There were only thirty of us—not many when the
ramparts were dotted with warriors well armed, and so many
cattle and horses, and trees like sentries, their branches aimed
low enough to strike us down.

We lay flat against our horses' manes and waited for the
wind to blow away our scents. Then Erzhan split our ranks:
several through the underbrush, rustling back behind the ramparts; others linking like a dull glint chain around these Black
Cloaks' fields. The rest took to the river, staying close beneath
the banks. They emerged dripping, cold, to tie their horses'
reins to the wood wall's anchored pillars. In the dark, their armor scales glistened to match the fractured light of the Black
Cloaks' torches on the rippling stream.

With the final squad, Erzhan signaled me to follow. We kept
our horses still as the waving branches—kept watch on the
fortress gate, waiting for the dawn. Erzhan and I stood side by
side, two eagles perched, eyes peeled for prey. The sickle moon
made slow progress across the narrow slit of sky. *In my land,
the earth is the dark between two breasts.* I felt it rise and fall and
breathing.

When the dawn did break, the sky toned gray for so long,
it seemed it never would turn blue. A thickness wrapped the
forest, a foggy mist and a heavy gloom that held us like the
aching bones of a rising fever.

"Can you shoot?" Erzhan asked me.

"I haven't tried." Though I knew he was not referring to my hands; he meant my will.

Down the length of my leather quiver, I felt for my arrows. Iron tipped, triple lobed, they were as the Black Cloaks' own, formed in the style of the enemy. We had learned from them already, stolen their thoughts to gird our strength. We knew them in a way they could not know us. As I had known Timor.

Mama! Mama! Look at me riding! Arman, bounding on his pony, his saddle legs soft and slightly dimpled. Timor riding up, pulling Arman's reins. "Take your aim as a Black Cloak does," he said, his elbow bent and cocked, using his cloak as masking. Timor's skill had matched my own, but his aim was short and sharp while mine was always long and high. Perhaps these forest hills had made it that way.

We crept up close—close enough to see the sentries' breaths before they faded into wisps and disappeared.

Then came Erzhan's call: the sound of a raven's caw as we had heard in these parts. Then an owl. Three hoots. Then stop. Three hoots and another caw.

The Black Cloak warriors noticed nothing as their women served them food. I drew my bowstring slowly, felt my heart flutter as it had not since I was a girl—foolish child on her first hunt alone with Marjan: she had killed the boar while I had not even maimed it in my fright.

My arms trembled. Erzhan noticed. "You must charge or turn, Akmaral. You cannot falter."

"I know it. I will not betray you"—but Timor's whisper was in my ear. I believe he meant it. He could have killed me, burned our yurts. He could have left at any time. And once he did, returning with the golden eagle. Garah, soaring far above.

Through the trees, I surveyed the dense, dark thicket for any movement—then a raven's shriek—I aimed my arrow between the boughs and let it fly.

The others aimed and the battle started, felling warriors just beyond the wall. The Black Cloaks charged to collect their weapons while more mounted in the pasture, darted, and gave chase. We charged into their confusion, yammering battle cries, springing from the brush to aim, then scattering into the woods' protection.

But this terrain the Black Cloaks knew far better than we ever could. They pursued us, using the woods as we used our arms. Our warriors toppled, many struck beneath low branches, leaving their horses panicked, thrashing through the forest jumble. But Erzhan quickly found our bearings and rallied those who remained.

I shot as our company raised its voices—shrills rising with the battle's heat. I had not known how much I raged, but with each shot I landed, I murmured coolly, "For Arman." "For myself." "For Timor." For my sorrow, lying in blood on that distant steppe. For my love pecked to pulp by vultures on an abandoned field.

I drew and shot and took pleasure in each man I murdered. I felt no piercing as their arrows stuck feebly between the horse-hoof scales on my chest and thighs. I pulled the arrows out, then turned their darts against them.

Erzhan sent some warriors to set the Black Cloaks' carts ablaze. Suddenly came rocking, shrilling, bodies jumping, cloaked in flame. Most were women who had taken refuge in those wagons. They darted out, rolled in the dirt, setting more of the grass to smoke. Several stumbled to the river's edge. They dived into the water where our river-hidden warriors finished them.

When all was through, only the log-walled fort remained. From the blood-steeped water, our warriors clambered up the banks, their horses pulling hard against the rooted posts. First one plank, then one whole side of the wooden girdle fell, forming a makeshift bridge. We drove across it, scattering sheep and cows and pigs and woolly goats, then into the earthen pits that were these people's houses.

"Targitai triumphs!" Erzhan roared as he shot arrows caked with fat and dung set alight from the Black Cloaks' fires. "Let Rada Mai's flames feast on this enemy's blood and bones."

Then we dove into their pit houses. Chambers harbored mothers holding infants' heads against their bosoms. Swaying, shaking, shouting curses, pleas, hands raised against our swords so that we cut them and they dropped off at their elbows. Their few defenses were fire logs raised as clubs, crumbling or fumbled from scorched fingers; cauldrons of hot broth lifted and poured where it turned to mud before it could burn.

I drew my sword like any other. I severed heads from bodies, arms from shoulders, knees from thighs. I felt nothing until I saw her: heels dug into dirt, eyes that I had known before, deep and dark and full of hatred. Now her arms wrung about a dark-haired boy. The woman from our prisoners' camp who had ridden like a warrior—she stared at me with loathing choking her last breath. Too late. I'd slit her throat before I'd even recognized her.

But the man beside her was not Bulat. He was old. But even twisted, he was Timor's shadow—his sword held at the same strong angle, striking as I came, surely, swift, and sharp. Then drawing cold—his eyes the brittle blue of the sky in early winter. There were claw-marks on his arms and wrists, a strike across his cheekbone, forehead—scars of a great eagle, just as Timor had from Garah—but this old man's scars had healed.

I searched about the room for a perch and found it. Tiny hood and cuffs both empty, fallen on the ground, but some talon cuts fresh across the rutty wood. The old man eyed me as I held him at a distance.

"Timor," I said firmly, then I felt his strike. It caught my breath. Again I said, "Timor."

He did not stop, nor did I. The old man slashed and I blocked him. He cut and I shoved his blade swiftly aside. He struck me on my arm, but I pushed him back and cleaved his thigh. When he stumbled, I chopped him sideways, first on the left of his waist, then on its right. His eyes bloomed bright with rage and anguish, a sort of knowing that transcends fear. But just as quickly, he squelched them and heaved one last blow against me. High and hard—the strike of a dying man. I raised my arms but couldn't hold him off. With all his weight, the old man knocked me from my feet, then tottered and thudded to the ground.

For a moment, all I heard was my own breathing. The world spun and my eyes saw sparks. Then the old man groaned. Dizzy, shaken, I rolled to him and clutched his chest. "Did you know Timor?" I begged in a pitiful smatter of his language. "Was he your kin?"

The man's eyes hardened into glass, then went cold.

Outside I could hear the fighting, low like a rumble of thunder in the dark. I pressed up and peered about, all alone among the dead but for that child—the boy covered in his own mother's blood. He gazed at me. A little younger than Arman. Perhaps not even three years old.

He looked with the same bold fierceness as his father— grandfather—uncle—who he was I would never know. I bent to the boy and took him from his dead mother. The child fought me, tore at me, clinging to her gory limbs, beating at my stomach with small feet, squirming from my grasp, kicking harder than the long, pounding ride or this clash of swords and arrows that should have killed me. His tiny feet, wrapped in thick, dark, blood-stained boots, more painful than all the blades and arrows I had suffered. I let him beat me, tear at my face with his plump, soft claws, watched as the small blood began to cake under his nails: my blood and his, mixed with his own mother's.

I took him shrieking, and wrapped him in a cloak that hung against the wall. Dark, black as the night without a moon, that pelt of thickest bear fur. I took the child and went out of the hut, found a broken post, and with my one free arm, lifted it and set it in the cook-fire blaze. Then I left the place to burn.

The child cried no more. He did not fight me. His face softened with the color of the flames. But his tears—though their moisture vanished in the instant of that burning wood—left long, slow stains, two shadows just beneath his eyes that would not wash or ever fade.

32

DRINKING TEARS

This child was the first. There would be more—mother of a thousand children!—but I knew then I would not conceive again—as if my womb had shut, but my heart left wounded, bleeding. Like the flying deer, pierced while high above: just an arrow's prick, but the blood flows down, a bright red blot to mar its pure perfection.

"She brings the enemy again into our midst," the Ak Kam protested. And Erzhan stood behind her with the elders and many more. Angriest were the warriors, though they'd dared say nothing on our long return. Only Meiramgul understood—she and the ana-women. Somehow they must have sensed that no child should ever die.

"We are one hearth. We are one fire. That child has no place here!" the Ak Kam called. "We have made this mistake before. His blood is not our blood. His aul cannot be our aul. That was our fault, Akmaral, allowing you to join with that stranger. We will not be so lax again."

But I held him just the same, just as I had all the way on that hard journey, all those days riding through the forest, up and down those rocky hills, then spreading out across the open grassland. He was a sturdy child, but I held him like an infant: head pressed into my elbow, feet resting on my lap, not strad- dled across my saddle upright as Arman had learned to ride. The boy was old enough, but shivering, frightened, this child of the forests who knew little more than wagon wheels and houses dug in dirt. I laid him as a baby in my arms.

After some time, he stopped his choked-back sobs and shivering. He clutched and squirmed, but no longer cried. The edges of my horse-hoof armor pressed against his tear-stained cheeks, leaving livid, arching indentations. He rubbed them sometimes, his small hands groping close against my unyielding bosom. He looked at me rarely. Mostly he looked through me, his gaze like a frozen springtime lake where something has broken through, the ice just barely crusted over.

I held him, riding until the trees fell away and the sky's dome opened. So bright and blue, it made the child squint. I covered him against the glare with the cloak I'd taken from his mother's hut. Hung on a twig pierced through hardened mud, it had dangled against the wall spattered with his mother's blood and the old man's, too—and on the cloak. I hadn't noticed the stains in the forest-dappled twilight. But I saw them here, only now in this blazing sun. So bright I could not help but see.

I came to our encampment with that child in my arms. I took the final place in line after our stolen war goods—horses, sheep, and milling cattle. More cows among our herds than there had ever been before. They looked lumbering and boxy like knobby boulders rooted in the mottled fields, so forlorn and thin after their long journey, graceless beside the useful, elegant ponies. Our warriors meandered, only grimly triumphant—not as they had been after Erzhan and Timor's strikes whose only purpose had been gain and a show of might. This raid had been far different, laced with anger and revenge. Our ana-women first came forward, all those who had lost in the Black Cloak attack. They gathered around Erzhan, who told them, as if in benediction, "Now you may lay your final stones across the kurgan's niche. Their deaths have been avenged. Targitai is satisfied."

I slid down from my mare's back awkwardly so as not to disturb the child sleeping in my arms. Meiramgul came to look at the bundle breathing.

"It is not Arman," she warned.

I nodded. "He is not meant to be."

She set a grimace that answered nothing, spoke neither sanction nor censure.

I walked to where my yurt was settled, near enough to the

warrior's quarters but alone and empty now. Burned were all those things that reminded me of Timor—that had once made it a relief to enter. There was only a blanket laid for sleep, and a rug—barely more than a mat to veil the ground. I set my boots and saddle on it. Otherwise, the floor was earth, bits of grass, in places stones. I hung my armor from the lattice and laid the child in the place farthest from the open door-flap. Then I draped the blanket over the roof's eye like a shroud.

I watched him sleeping—nameless, speechless—unsure whether to kill the boy. Unsure why he had the right to live—

"He will rise against us," Erzhan had accused. We'd stood among the drifting ashes of the Black Cloaks' fires. Their charred bodies, broken into bits, cluttered the bloody fields. "He will betray us, just as Timor—"

"Timor did not. You said yourself, he had no choice—"

"He had a choice," Erzhan spat. "That is why he's dead."

I stared at him: such a change from the broken man who had once talked of love. Now it seemed he had swallowed all his loss, his pain. He could only seek revenge.

He tried to seize the boy, to wrench him from my arms. "One last death," he struggled, "to make an end to it."

But I pulled the child back. "There will never be an end. Erzhan, we were both betrayed."

Now we settled around the elders' coals, the first time all together since the raid. The child lay on my lap, no longer asleep, but strapped against a cradleboard, immobile as we keep our infants, insensible to his fate. But watching, wide-eyed. Limbs too hefty for the cradle, pressed awkwardly against their wraps, bulging at the sides.

"The child's danger is in his blood," the Ak Kam warned. "It is in his very nature."

"I've made my promise."

"Your promise to whom? To this child or to our aul? To Umai or Targitai? To your dead lover, your lost son? You brought misery upon us once. Now you'll do it again?"

"I will not—I swear it. I give my word upon this hearth." I

fell upon my knees and took up her bowl of milk, pouring it as an offering to Rada Mai. "He will betray us only if he knows his past. He will not. I will not tell him."

Meiramgul knelt and stayed my hand. "Your word?" She gazed at me thoughtfully, in a way I'd rarely felt since I was young. "The promise of a lifetime is not easily kept. A truth withheld is the truth betrayed." She said it steadily and without chiding.

"Better he be a slave," Pazylbek proposed, "that he know his place and fear us. When he grows strong, we can sell him at the trader's road."

"And that has served us well before?" My tone cracked; my eyes penetrated the fire's shadows. "You know what I say is true, that our business in raids and trading slaves has only brought us death and sorrow. This boy's people are already dead—a fair exchange for our losses. Isn't that enough?"

Erzhan muttered, "Timor once swore that he was one with us—blood brothers who could not be betrayed."

"Timor was a man," I shot him with my gaze. "This is a child."

When I rose to go, it was far past midnight. Already the stars had drifted with the waning moon. The others' eyes darted as they watched me walking—awkward with a child so heavy, not an infant at all. But no one stopped me. Not Meiramgul. Not Erzhan. Not even the Ak Kam.

That night I rekindled my small hearth and made my yurt glow with perilous warmth again. "Child of my wound," I whispered to him from my savaged heart, barely staunched with this clotted blood that brought no healing. I lay beside him—this nameless, speechless child—every day and every evening, holding him as if he were my infant son. I pressed him toward my breast and begged his lips to suck, but there was no milk and he made no effort. If he had been a just-born child, he would have died, but as it was, he lost only some of his milk-flesh and grew gaunt circles in the hollows above his cheeks. In time he ate some of the hard white cheese that I softened for him.

The air fell still except for the rising creak of frogs and insects. The hot season loosed its breath, spreading day by day across the high mountains. But then it passed. The nights grew cold and clear. We moved on to our autumn pastures. And the great sky stretched above us, its blackness a mat of loosely woven reeds; and between its fronds the speckled starlight shone. Through the roof's eye, he and I watched it. Silent, sparkling with so many distant fires lit by the ancestors, as Meiramgul's stories told.

It was the hundredth dawn.

I lay beside him feeling soft breath shifting around me through the air. A subtle movement that barely touched my cheek. An awareness of someone near where there should have been only darkness. *Kara Kam. Ak Kam.* A sound of scratching. I closed my eyes again and saw her: the same old woman, gnarled hands, and in them, etching tools: a sharp, incising point, dark soot mixed with sheep's tallow. Across her skin, on knuckles and forearms, wrinkled, blackened marks. Intertwined, broad sketches—camels in fiercest clutch, arch-backed lions fraught with conflict, power. They writhed on her skin, wrestling eternally. A spotted leopard poised above a ram. Griffins pecked at the ends of branches, so many ordered, sharp-hooked beaks. Then the sun broke and I saw more clearly: starting on the old woman's shoulder, traveling certainly across her breast, the sinuous portent—not branches but antlers. The shape of the flying deer.

I awoke. The scratching was the splintered cradleboard pressed against my cheek. It creaked as the child stirred. He opened his eyes. He stared at me as he had every dawn since I first held him: wary, vigilant, presuming nothing.

I didn't smile. He had come to understand and reflect my indifference.

The light was dim, but it poked into my yurt like a burnished blade carving around the outline of my darkness. Sometimes the breeze swept in, backward, forward gently, or it would blow wildly around our lattice cloths in an angry gale.

I leaned upon my elbow, then shifted to my knees. I took my knife—the two-edged dagger. The same blade I had wrested from Timor's fingers, bloody from his death but before the vultures' beaks. From my parents' hands to mine, then his. Now here it was again. It was never meant to leave me.

Now, the hundredth day. I set my heart aside. I lowered my blade and pressed it close beside the boy's flesh. The child did not wince or even grimace as I sliced away his wraps one by one until they fell.

He lay there for a time, strangely shaped and helpless. His legs were shriveled, weak from atrophy. When I stood him on them, he clutched around my neck to catch his balance. I pressed him to my shoulder and we stayed there, clinging, breathing. Then I whispered cautiously, "I give you a name. Bekzat. My child. Bekzat is your name."

33

THE FRAGILE CORD

The name meant almost nothing. Simply "boy child." But it spoke in our aul's language and could not be denied. I took Bekzat in my arms and laid before him a gift that I had made: a simple bow, a quiver full of tiny arrows.

"Umai, protect this child. I put Bekzat into your care." I said it knowing that my very prayers were contradiction. If Umai could hear my plea, would she not have helped this child— struck me down or blocked my blows to keep me from killing his hard-eyed mother? Or kept Timor alive to me and loyal to his promise to our aul? Or left Arman beside me instead of caught up in a wind, swallowed by a maelstrom, dark shadow in the night, the ambush that sent him flying?

Still I said it, "Protect this child." Again. Again. Again. If Bekzat did not know the words, he must have understood them. He watched me solemnly as I sprinkled mare's milk, spattered it on the ground and toward the rising sun and where the moon had set, toward the steppe lands and the ringing mountains, toward the river and the distant lake bed, empty now but bright and cool when the spring waters flow, and toward the sky and the clouds and the vicious, fickle winds that, at that moment, whipped around our yurt as if in warning.

I emptied my small bowl, dribbling my offering's dregs into the fire's smoke. In the cold, hard light, I scooped up the ash and made a pigment and slowly pressed it into my skin. Just as in my dream: great deer antlers crowned by sharp-beaked griffins. Then I cooked Bekzat a meal.

Clots of softened cheese, a rare paste made of trader's flour mixed with fat and fried. A bit of meat—not horse's meat as for a rightful birth. But this was not a birth, so I gave him a slab of mutton, old and fatty, tough but bearing strength. Bekzat must have known it as he took it to his lips and chewed, watching me intently.

The scents circled and spread around us—an oily, widening vapor hovering in crisp air. The sun had risen a little higher, though still it brought no heat. But a sliver, a silver beam, split our dirt-grass floor. We sat on two felt mats, one opposite the other.

The boy remained, at first barely moving, then slowly, uncertain of his balance, awkward on his limbs. Thin as twigs, they seemed almost as fragile, shriveled and frail after so long wasting in their wraps. I brought some heated water, poured it in a pot, added some of the powdered salts I'd found among the dead Kara Kam's bundles. Bekzat did not fight me as I lifted and placed him in. Steam dulled the sun's sharp blade, mixing with thin smoke that swathed him. The rest of the yurt was dark and cold and very still.

From outside came the usual morning movements—herders heading toward their beasts, hunters waking, lifting up their bows and strapping quivers to their hips. Already the sky through the roof's eye shone a glaring white: Targitai watching. We sat beneath it, in its beam.

Soon enough I rose, knowing there were sheep and cattle to be tended, and nursing cows and mares who would be full with milk. I looked at the boy, finally legged and armed and trying to find his feet, edging toward the fire. Awkward. So I dug into my riding rig and withdrew a herding rope of braided camel hair, strong enough to hold, soft so it would not scratch. I tugged it around his tender belly, then anchored it to the doorpost of my yurt. Then I pointed toward the fire. "Hot!"

Bekzat nodded. "Hot." He said it in his own language—a word I understood. I bent and kissed him. It was impulse more than plan. Then we both stood before one another, staring.

I went to tend the mares, but before the sun had crested the eastern hills, I heard pattering feet, some strange stumbles and small grunts drawing closer. I turned and found Bekzat plopped in the grass, his knees covered with mud and scrapes and bits of sheep's dung. He looked at me, eyes coy and prideful. The camel hair braid was frayed and charred where he had burned it. It dragged behind him like a tail.

The nearby milkers saw him, watched us, but said little. Bekzat followed like a pup, dutiful and distracted, at once relishing his new freedom and feeling its strangeness. While I worked, he sat gazing toward the milling sea of sheep and horses or at the camels whose shaggy humps jiggled and flopped as they grazed. He reached to touch one that sat dispassionately chewing its cud. So I paused to lift him into the two humps' hollow. He groped the thick, soft fur, explored the spongy flesh. Then he slid away to stare into the glassy, bottomless eyes. The beast sniffed, yawned, and continued chewing.

With my milk sacks full, I brought them to the ana-women. The boy stumbled through the camp behind me, our pace favoring weak legs. Outside the elders' yurt, a cauldron had been set for making cheese. I held Bekzat off, tying up his cord again. He looked at me, his gaze subtly defiant. Already I knew it was futile. As I poured my mare's milk into the women's cauldron, I sensed their speaking eyes on me, but mostly on the stranger child determinedly prying at the rope. So I set aside my empty sacks and joined their staring. It was many minutes long, but at last Bekzat pried loose the knot.

"Bekzat, come." I stood up, reaching for him.

The ana-women raised their brows, their silence booming as I tucked the boy against my knees.

"Bekzat?" Aigul finally murmured as she spooned up curds that were forming in the milk.

I nodded. She smiled at me softly, only with her eyes.

But I knew I no longer belonged beside their fire: I was not an ana-woman. Bekzat was not my son. So I saddled my mare to join the warriors at their practice, taking Bekzat with me. I tied him to a boulder where he could watch me ride and shoot.

By the dull, cold afternoon, I rode back to check on him. His head was bowed between his knees, arms clutched, shoulders shuddering at each warrior's whoop, at each clash of swords and the sound of our arrows piercing targets. I slipped down from my saddle and pressed my cold palm against his neck. He raised his eyes, shadowed and bleak with half-buried recollection. He shivered as I placed him on my horse and took him back to Aigul's yurt and left him there.

It was dusk when I returned to find him fast asleep beside a makeshift sheepfold near the sheltered lambs and skinny kids and a colt with rheumy eyes. Nishan, Aigul's daughter, had laid a blanket across Bekzat's back. She sat close to his head, gently rustling his pitch-black, curling hair.

"He wouldn't go inside," she said, "no matter how we begged him."

His cheek was dented from resting on stiff grass. His breath shifted the tall stalks softly. Barely older than the boy herself, yet Nishan understood.

Through all this time, the child stayed mostly unspeaking, though we knew his voice, for sometimes he sang soft verses to himself when he thought no one would hear. I didn't remember Timor's tongue well enough to understand the child's meaning, but the tune had the gentle cadence of a lullaby.

It was not long before Bekzat learned to laugh. The first I heard, it came like a shrill, sounding far too much like Arman. I bristled at it, tried to shut it out, but then I saw that light was in his eyes. And a sense of belonging.

It was mid-spring and the melt-lake was again with us. Nishan had been teaching Bekzat how to ride, though his legs were barely strong enough and far too short to reach beyond the saddle's blanket. Still she helped him, coaxing, guiding his horse with clicks and gentle tugs, begging him to kick with all his strength until at last he did and discovered his first hard gallop. Bekzat gasped, clinging to the pony's mane, terrified while Nishan raced to catch him, coaxing him to canter, then to trot. Only then did Bekzat burst out, "More! Nishan, again!"—peals of glee amidst his few words, still awkward with their foreign inflection.

I tried not to listen. His crack of delight was like a stone, sharp, turned on its edge, cutting into me.

That winter there'd been little snow and then no rain. Now the streams all dried and the shallow lake was a thick brown puddle. Few lambs were born and fewer foals. Their mothers' milk flowed thin and weakly. Only the camels seemed unperturbed. When we rode to the highlands, even there the grasses reached barely to the horses' knees and the broad steppe cracked, patched with dust, and would not green. Then one dawn, the dust arose to fill the mountains' bowl—a storm so thick and black that we could not see. A *dev*, my people called it, a sandstorm formed of a demon's sleep. For as long as the demon snores, the dark sands whirl; and it seemed this demon refused to waken.

The dust dropped heavy upon us, smothering as dung-soiled wool. Through it, the Ak Kam trembled, chanted, made her offerings: a ewe, a nanny goat, a mare. She scraped pale chalk from her seashell using a thin bone spoon with a flying deer's grip. Still the black dust swarmed. All the while the ana-women whispered that this was not a *dev* at all, but Arman who cast his vengeance—my true child still high up in the clouds, blowing all his fury, holding back his tears, kicking angry feet to stir the dust at his mother's betrayal.

Bekzat—they meant Bekzat, who could never take Arman's place and was not meant to. They could not understand and I had no words or strength to try to tell: my child was gone and this child had no mother. That was all.

It was early morning, quiet for the din, the third day of the demon's raging. Grit penetrated everything; our eyes raw and red; our skin shone gray. I lay inside my yurt taking refuge from the storm. I had not slept, listening long into the night to the *dev*'s fitful breathing. In that dim, I watched the child sleep—a twisted silhouette in the shallow light of the meager hearth I'd raised. Though the Ak Kam had objected when Meiramgul passed Rada Mai's dung coals to me. I was no ana-woman and Bekzat was not my child.

There was movement beyond my doorway. The wool flap opened, letting in a sooty shade. "Who is there?" I could barely see.

"Akmaral"—Erzhan's voice. His figure blocked the wind as he let the flap fall limply. He wore his battle tunic; the gold-maker's sword hung heavy at his hip. It caught the low, dull glint of my nearly smothered coals.

"Akmaral, this child should be dead." His hand was on his hilt, though he did not draw.

I rose and stirred the embers, filled the cooking pot for tea. In the half-drawn bucket, the muddy water churned. Silt rose and fell gently with the sudden heat. I took dried leaves from a small felt sack and spread them in the pot. I knelt and poured, brought Erzhan a bowl, then sat and sipped from one myself.

"He should be dead," he said again, forgetting or not caring that I had not answered.

"His death would bring us nothing," I murmured calmly. "It would not wake the *dev*."

"That is not what the ana-women say, or the elders, or even the Ak Kam. They all know why this *dev* has come."

"Do they? If that is true, then this is your fault—yours and Timor's. First for the raids, then the slaves, and then the deaths. This *dev* is punishment for your conceit. Bekzat is blameless."

Erzhan shook his head. "Bekzat," he mumbled beneath his breath, "is an abomination."

At his words, I felt the child rouse, trembling slightly, his body just behind my back. I turned and stroked his cheek. With a shudder, Bekzat got up to his knees. He eyed Erzhan with wary defiance, bold for a boy so small. Erzhan began to raise his blade, but I ignored it. Instead I gave Bekzat a strip of meat. As he chewed, I moved aside a stack of cooking pots and dusty, threadbare sheets and found him a clump of sheep's wool I'd protected from the storm. Immediately the boy began to comb it, diligently, neatly.

"You defend that child against your own?" Erzhan charged.

"My own child is lost or dead. What does it matter? Everything I had or loved is gone. I have sworn Bekzat to Umai's protection. He will be protected."

Erzhan pursed his lips, breathed low. Finally he turned and went away. I sat with the boy in silence. Bekzat put down the wool and tucked up close. Suddenly choking in my own yurt, I pulled a blanket over us both just so that we could breathe.

Beneath, I tugged the Kara Kam's mirror at my neck. Pressed close against my bosom, it was dewy with my sweat. I squinted hard into its surface; its warped reflection showed what no one else could see: my face, my eyes, golden in the bronze, and weeping.

Just then I raised my gaze toward the bundle lying beneath my sleeping cot, where I'd barely looked in all these passing days. I crawled out and took it, folded back its tattered felts, and stared at the seeds, the drum, the Kara Kam's rattle, the small etched bowl coated with a filthy sheen. I took them from their wraps and set them on the gray-tinged carpet. Finally I lifted up the drum. It was the first time I had held it: the well-oiled handle heavy in my hand, carrying the bristling vibrations across the tight skin as I struck, turning it from side to side as Soyun had once done. Its sound reverberated in my heart like far-off thunder.

You cannot choose another path—the Ak Kam's words.

In the dim, the child watched me, rocking slightly to the beat as I murmured all the Kara Kam's chants I could recall. I closed my eyes, and after a time the rhythm took me.

I dreamed that I galloped hard on horseback, drifting farther. Far away. Suddenly a broad new valley stretched before me, peopled with great swarms brimming over hilltops, spilling down steep gorges, slopes of grass, waterfalls, and scree. People assembled at great stone courses—places of carved pillars and kurgan mounds. Yurts lined the valley's sides. Fires burned. And singing, chants. Horses raced across the open steppe amidst great rounds of wrestling, cheers in a common tongue, and war-horses' tails wrapped in gold. Their bits were shaped from iron.

I opened my eyes but the vision did not leave me—the sense of many crowding in my yurt where there had been only one, then none, before. I blinked and saw Bekzat staring. I tried to recall my own child's face: Arman—slightly faded, it had only grown more lovely. But Bekzat's visage was nothing like Arman's—dark and mostly dull with eyes that hid beneath low brows—sunken hollows as the ancient caves concealing spirits etched in stone—

Suddenly, I sensed those spirits—all of them, rising all at once—the fine snow leopard, the eagle flying, and the many antlered deer roaming solemn across the steppe. I blinked and saw them still, but suddenly transformed—the eagle now was Timor, his gold hair gleaming, his fist pressed tight against his lips. To his whistling breath, like wind through the eagle's wings, the leopard joined softly with words, as certain as the promise that Marjan had whispered at her death—*Akmaral, there is still life within you.*

I awoke to sparks dancing from the smoldering fire—the Kara Kam's seeds from her alabaster jar that I hadn't known I'd poured. Bekzat tucked into my stomach's curl on the woolen mat beneath the filthy cloth. Outside, the Ak Kam's rants had softened to low murmurs.

I pressed the child and raised him up, tugging straight his sleep-wrinkled tunic, tucking back his tousled curls. I pressed aside the felt flap doorway. Then we went outside—me and the small dark boy.

The sun had barely broken. I squinted hard into its rising blaze. From crest to crest, shimmering gold had burned away the storm. Leading Bekzat by the hand, we stepped over sands that pooled and banked against my yurt's walls. Faint footprints rippled across the wastes where our herds had turned and fled.

We looked but could not find them, not across the whole expanse. Even the distant mountains bore an ashen rime, as if their snowcaps had been soiled by the *dev's* harsh snores.

We crossed the dusty foot-track until we saw, in the middle of the pasture, the Ak Kam stoking Rada Mai's coals. Her sacrifice—a pure black stallion—one of our finest, cut to bits and laid across the desiccated grass. From its neck, blood seeped into a shallow bowl. The Ak Kam lifted up its heart and fed it whole into a cauldron's gullet.

We approached, and I bent to touch my fingers to the bloody pool.

"The demon has wakened. Look, the air has cleared. With the stallion's sacrifice, the sleeping *dev* is gone." She said it calmly, as if the air itself were proof of her wisdom's triumph. But her tone bore the twinge of uncertainty—the way she looked at me. I reached and took up Bekzat's hand. It fitted rightly in my own.

Just then I understood that the Ak Kam had no wisdom. Nor the strength to travel to the heaven realm. Nor to summon up the ancestors for guidance as the Kara Kam once had done. She knew only simple healing, superstition, some ways to read the seasons' signs, and enough of tsaagan bones to tell us of the spirits' discontent. But not enough to change things, to bargain with the gods. I found my spirit wafting toward the distant hollow high in the ashen cliff, toward the place where the Kara Kam's black yurt had once stood. I felt her absence, where I'd barely felt her presence before.

34

THE CHILD SEA

"We will travel to the valley—there." Meiramgul pointed as we packed our goods. The highland pasture was ruined. We all knew that we must go. By the sun's height, we plodded through the sandstorm's devastation.

Everywhere we rode, we rounded up our scattered beasts—the horses, sheep—but the Black Cloaks' cows lay sideways, more like ill-shaped rocks than creatures that had ever been alive. And most were not: carcasses already. Along the way, our ana-women set upon them, skinning hides, taking limbs and chunks of clotted meat. In the end, all that remained were bones and sinew; we would gather these after scavengers had picked them clean.

We loaded the meat onto our camels' humps, then coaxed them slowly onward, leaving the highlands well behind. Still along our track the ground was pebble and dust. What grass there was shone shriveled, gray, splayed tufts that our stray goats ravaged.

We took our rest at a pinnacle before a cliff. Far below, across the steppe, the trade road's tracks were empty. Only a gritty plume bent its spiral to destroy itself, picking up the chalky dust that should have been rich soil.

"Where will we go if there is no pasture?" people wondered.

"There." Ruan pointed toward a mottled patch of green. A handful of mud huts lay scattered like hard sheep's dung. "There must be water—wells dug in the dirt. There will be grass and meat and a store-pit high with winter supplies."

Erzhan nodded. "We will raid there."

The Ak Kam threw her bones. When she was through, even

Meiramgul agreed. "Let it be as it has always been. Our herds must have grass. We must have milk and meat to live."

Erzhan drew his stallion to the edge of the descending cliff. He raised his sword and waved it so that its shadow fell across the distance. "We will drive the people out. When the land is ours, the aul will follow."

My stomach churned as I raised mine too. I was a warrior once again, battle and defense my only charge, and death my best reward if I betrayed Targitai.

"Bekzat, come." Aigul clutched my forearm, then signaled Nishan to guide the boy away. "We will keep him safe, I promise." I watched them go, bit my lip to calm my heart.

I moved to take my post, but Meiramgul galloped close and laid her hands against my reins. "Akmaral, you will ride beside Erzhan and be his equal."

I gaped, not fully understanding. But then she turned to the others and raised her voice. "This will be no vengeance's raid. We must return to the ways of our ancestors. But recall that the wolf attacks out of hunger, not anger, greed. The snow leopard kills to eat, its claws and teeth so much sharper than our own. We have seen even an eagle can be trained to do man's work. But on its own, it circles high above and dives only to sate its need."

She released my bridle and briefly pressed her palm over my wind-chapped hand. "Bring them back to peace." Then she bounded on her mare, her thighs broad and flat as she steadied in her seat, rounding to take her place among our ana-women and children.

I went to Erzhan's side as she'd commanded. He and I stood silent, watching one another, twisted like two opposing cords. But when we turned to lead, the warriors did not question. They followed.

We headed toward the settled plain, as quietly as we could with forty warriors on horses and twice as many arms. So early before the dawn, not even the village women were awake. There were pens for beasts but they were empty. A heavy ox yoke abandoned in the dirt. A broken plow. Between the mud-daub huts, a flock of squatting, black-barred geese. We used their startled clamor to mask our advance. Then we circled and poised our aim. At Erzhan's sign, we made a wild ululation, drew our bowstrings back, and sent up a cloud. Our arrows fell in a clattered heap. From the houses and in the fields, no movement came, no sound.

Erzhan and I exchanged hard glances, then prepared a second volley, easing closer but still beyond retaliation's reach. Cautious. We had known such ploys used as ambushes before: a silent pause and then sudden attack, just as the wild boar had done so long ago. My memory of Marjan and how she'd sensed the sow would come…again and always, the instincts of a mother.

Our second arrows fell, and then our third. Finally the silence broke with a muffled whimper. A withered hand creaked back one of the mud huts' doors, showing the corner of a reddened sleeve, the only color in the aimless shades of ash and umber.

Then it was gone and all was still. Erzhan tried to move but I restrained him. Suddenly out slipped a small, bronzed boy dressed in rags, no more than a wisp, wide-eyed with the look of fright I had seen so many times in Bekzat. He tore recklessly across the compound, and Erzhan chased him at his fastest charge. Reaching down, he scooped him up and held his dagger against the child's fragile neck. Then he turned his horse and bellowed, "Come out or this will be the first to die!"

My own heart fluttered as if the cold iron pierced my skin. We all waited as the unseen sun burnished the sky. Then an old man emerged, eyes swollen and murky. His face bore a stubble of gray and dark, dull hair, thick and wiry, tied up in a knot. More silence. Then a woman. It was her sleeve we'd seen, red but torn and tattered. She stumbled some few steps, then fell onto her knees and laid her forehead in the dirt.

"I beg you," she stammered, "please don't hurt my son!"

Erzhan's dagger pressed a notch beneath the child's chin. Tears streamed down the boy's gaunt face with the slim trickling of blood. The woman scraped at the earth and cast dust onto her head in small, pale heaps. She crawled to clutch Erzhan's boot. "Let him go, I beg you!"

"The rest," Erzhan demanded. "Make them come."

But no others emerged. Erzhan kicked the woman off, angled his blade, and yanked back the boy's thin shoulders. The mother raised her head and whimpered like an injured sheep. "Please." Her mouth gaped in twisted agony. "Please—"

I drew my sword. "Erzhan, leave him be."

He turned, dumbfounded. I raised my blade and said again, "Erzhan, let the child go."

From the half-cracked doors, I sensed some movement.

Stunned, Erzhan mouthed, "Targitai's oath—" But I had heard such vows before and witnessed their effect: the leavings, mangled corpses, slaughtered children littering Umai's breast, and the soiled stench of blood among Rada Mai's ashes. All of it and more—the death of worthy warriors, of our own kin—

Bring our warriors back to peace, Meiramgul had said.

"No." I rode up closer and aimed my arrow point at Erzhan. Our warriors stirred and raised their bows. But I did not flinch as I took his hand and stretched it back. Twisting his wrist, I took his dagger away.

"No more death," I breathed, then turned to the village watchers. Holding both blades in my fists, I called in my calmest tone. "Come and do not fear. We will not harm you."

I turned my horse's nose and reached over Erzhan's saddle. He stared but did not resist as I took the boy's thin arms. I drew him from Erzhan's mount and handed him down to his mother. The boy crumpled to the ground. The woman whimpered, cradled him, shielding his shape with the threadbare cloth that barely covered her.

"Take us as slaves!" the woman begged. "At least then we may live." Her gaze pressed down to the grayish dust, tears spattering the soil.

Our warriors stared. Erzhan's outrage—masked as he

worked his stallion's bit. The beast would not be still, its impatience mirroring its master's. But he held it back, signaling our warriors to settle down their aim. They obeyed, but kept their arrows nocked and ready.

"Come." I swallowed hard the knot that seized my throat. "Come," I called just as dawn pierced the earth's dry crust. In its light, the plowed fields beyond shone brittle, broken. The subtle green we'd seen from high above looked wan. Their lands were no better than our own.

Squinting into the glare, the old man shaded his forehead. "You must go from here. We have nothing for you." He spoke it boldly but wearily, as if he had no fear of death. He was feeble and decrepit, but a second woman peered around the door, younger than the first. The low daub walls cast shadows on her sallow face as, from behind her ragged skirt, the shades of several scrawny, dust-cloaked children appeared.

"You, come out." I aimed the tip of my long sword.

She tugged on children's limbs, sending them squeezing through the doorway. They came forward reluctantly, each as frail as the first who'd run: three bow-legged daughters, bruised as if recently beaten, and three child-sons whose bellies bloated beneath their rags. The eldest bore a bandage on his head and held a narrow, shattered stick as if he would wield it as a weapon. It could have been a hoe, except it no longer had a blade. Another mother stayed tucked inside the hut, sheltering a hapless infant.

I called, "Only these? How many more?"

"All that you see, and mostly broken."

I knew the man was lying by the way he gaped at me.

"Another horse clan. Another raid two days ago. There is nothing, I tell you"—he glared at Erzhan, then back at me—"except to eat our flesh. Will you do as all your kind— pick at us like vultures?"

The image of Timor struck me like a blow.

I said nothing, turned, then murmured calmly, "Our people

suffer also. Our pastures have turned to dust. Our horses are starving. Let our people come and set our yurts around you. We will protect you from other clans and our horses will graze on the ruined stubble of your grain. We will share what milk and meat we can from our own herds."

The old man gawked, as did the mothers and the children. Our warriors rustled on their mounts and grumbled among themselves. Erzhan could no longer hold his peace. He rode up close to grab my arm. "Akmaral, you have no right to make this pact," he whispered harshly.

"Rada Mai gives me the right for all that I have suffered." I glared at him, then eyed our riders all around. "I have been a warrior and also an ana-woman. Now I am both. A warrior's duty is to protect; an ana-woman's is to nurture."

I shook him off, then turned again to the mother of the boy. "Have you water? My riders and horses are thirsty."

She glanced at the old man, begging with her silence.

"No water." The old man balked.

But the woman caught my eye. Nodding, she tapped her child's shoulder. "Baltabek, show them." Slightly shaking, and with the trickle of blood not yet dried where the blade had touched, Baltabek ran off toward a flattened rock behind a distant hut. He pushed it with all his might until it slid away. It revealed a hidden well.

"Trust," I mouthed and saw her frightened tears cut streams across her cheeks. So I said again, this time loudly: "Trust." I heeled my horse, reached down, and urged the woman up. "Mother, rise and come with me."

Now we moved together, walking slowly toward her boy. At the well he held out a dripping bowl. I tipped it to my lips. The water was sweet and cool. I handed it down to her. "Ana-woman, drink." Then I called to the mother standing by the door. "Woman, bring me your child, that one in your arms."

Trembling, she came and held her up—a tiny girl still with a newborn's curling limbs. I cradled her and let her sip the mare's

milk from a sack tied to my saddle. The child drank, staring up
at me.

I looked ahead and noticed shadows: more hands holding
doors and pelt flaps shifting at the other huts.

"All of you, come out!"

One doorway parted and then another. Fifteen huts around
the tattered cluster, and from each emerged a few. They peered
at me—some forty in all, though most were ravaged, wasted.
Their eyes gaped warily as I roused my horse's muzzle. Already
she'd started nibbling at a clump of drifting straw.

I handed Baltabek my reins, slipped down from my horse to
give the new mother back her daughter, then went to the older
children, fingering their chins, rolling their thin wrists in my
hand. Their arms were slender but hard as stone from heavy
labor. Their backs and shoulders—slightly bent, though muscled, strong.

So I called, "One more thing," eying Erzhan, though his
look was brittle. "We will take one tenth—the strongest, smart-
est among your youths—to train in defense. Yours and ours.
They will ride with us when we require. They will bind you to
us and us to you. We will take you as our own—make you our
own people. And you will pay your debt in tribute, whatever we
need that you can offer and whatever we can offer when you
have need."

I mounted back on my horse and moved a little farther.
There, another flattened rock. I reached my lance and pried it
up, then shoved the slab away. A second hidden well. I let my
mare's neck down and she began to drink.

"Agree to our terms or die here, as you wish. Either way, we
will take what we need. I offer you a bargain. All who pass will
know by our yurts that we lend you our support. But do not lie
to us again, old man, or our rage will equal our mercy."

The old man's eyes drooped, as did his shoulders. His head
slightly shook. "Why should we trust you?"

"Because you live."

Just then Erzhan raised his bow. The other warriors shifted, shuffled, uncertain which way his aim would choose—until finally he shot out far into the distance. The clutch of geese flew up in a sudden, frantic curtain where his arrow fell. Erzhan shot again and one goose faltered. He shot another and then another swiftly from the sky.

"Go. Fetch them." He gestured toward Baltabek. "Cook those for our meat—a paltry feast to Rada Mai to seal our pact."

Then he sent a rider to summon the aul.

As our people neared, I shouted across the barren field, "I have made new allies and brought new warriors to serve Targitai."

Through the clearing dust, I felt the Hewana's pensive gaze; but the Ak Kam's pierced like a hurtled bolt. Erzhan parted our warriors at my flanks as if he'd caught her aim.

Now I stood alone with only the hopeless villagers behind me. A trembling grew beneath my skin, cold wetness seeping from the warmest hollows.

"You do not know what you have done," the Ak Kam called.

"No," I said. "Perhaps I don't. Only that we cannot kill aimlessly again."

At my words, I sensed movement in the throng. Aigul and Nishan, with Bekzat close behind. Seated on his speckled colt, his face controlled, his stance seemed little like a child's. Such sturdiness, and a gaze as dark and resolute as any warrior's. Aigul whispered and Nishan nodded, then Bekzat eased his colt ahead. The aul and all the village stared as Bekzat took his place beside me. His presence gave me courage. "I bring you grass," I called again. "There is water here, and stalks to feed our herds." I spread my arms out broadly.

"What have you brought but more mouths for us to feed?" The Ak Kam spoke. "It is a mistake to share Rada Mai's coals, as you should have learned already. First with Timor, then Bekzat, and now—there is no place for strangers beside our hearth. You are no ana-woman. You have no right—"

It was true, I knew. Yet she was wrong: I felt it as strongly as my heart beating beneath my leather armor—as strongly as pounding at a clump of wool to turn it into useful felt—

"We are one fire," the Ak Kam shouted. "We are one hearth."

"Yes"—I choked—"but a hearth can grow."

The Ak Kam stammered as I fingered the hot bronze disk that hung against my breasts. I dug it out and showed the Kara Kam's mirror. I peered and saw Marjan's face rising from its shadows, so placid before my eyes in the grip of death; then, all at once, Timor torn apart by vultures.

"We are alone," the Ak Kam chanted, "between earth and death, between the mountains and the sky. Our ancestors are watching, with Rada Mai and the heaven gods—"

"You, Khagan"—I flashed the mirror to stop her speech—"you have never borne a child. Never known the beat of a lover's heart. You have never held your child in your arms or watched one die. As this woman has." I gestured toward the mother at my back. "As all these women here. And so have I."

I raised my mirror, held it shaking high, and let it spark. "I have seen this vision cross before my eyes: a great expanse, and churning; cattle, horses, yurt smoke rising; and around me, behind me, spreads a child sea. Small and young, large and strong, they sweep to the far horizon. Wave after wave rushing forth to drench our land, and in their wake, they will leave this dust-grass green. It will come to pass. It presses me and I will heed it. The Ak Kam says, 'We are one fire. We are one hearth.' She says that we cannot choose. But I say that these children must be saved—Bekzat and Baltabek and many more. To embrace these strangers, to become a greater nation." I shook the mirror, tossing its glint to spark the crowd. "Hear me! Blood is not the only way. Marjan knew. And Timor. To protect, to love—there is no greater course. So these children will be bound. They will serve us. They will fight and, when they are ready, they will die. I promise you, they will die defending us. Defending all of you."

Then I turned on my mount, very slowly beneath the sun's hot glare before all the gaping crowd, but it did not burn. In the searing heat and dust and thirst, I felt refreshed. Mended. It was then I understood that this was Timor's gift—his strength. And the Kara Kam's wisdom. And Marjan's love. And finally, my own forgiveness. So many cold base metals finely smelted in a keen, hot forge. Now I held them in my hand, made stronger for their amalgamation; and I would wield them like a knife—a carver's blade carefully crafted for small, fine work, to make something beautiful and useful.

By evening, our yurts ringed the wasted farmland as a latticed, woolen barricade. There were fires between the huts and a wary mingling, mostly of children surveying one another expectantly while their parents exchanged distrustful glances. Sheep roamed in bleating herds and goats passed; camels' grunts broke with occasional bursts of ire among the horses and sharp dogs' barks. But even the warriors' mounts had wandered half a length toward the dusty stubble, the bare remains of six-rowed barley and emmer wheat, and begun to graze.

So there was a wary peace, and I had brought it. But now I faced the movement I'd begun. There, five village children waited. Their twisted silhouettes stretched long in the shallow glow of the half-lit moon, away from the warriors' tents at the encampment's outer course. In the distance I heard the voices of the elders arguing, harsh tones hurtled over the dry, cracked earth with no gentleness to mollify their sounds. But I closed my mind to them. Bending to my camel's pack, I took out felts. Not my own. These ones were black—the Kara Kam's yurt wrappings.

I shook them from their bundle and motioned for the children to help me spread them out. They obeyed without a pause. The musty smell was strong with memory—oily dung smoke and the patter of small black seeds—a cloud that drifted and engulfed me.

We dragged them wide across the dry cracked soil. We lifted them and stretched them over my dead aunt's lattice frame, grunting, pulling, tightening the woven straps until they lay firm around the yurt's broad belly. At last I climbed above and peeled the roof's eye back. Cold, hard moonlight dropped into the darkness like a stone.

Our doorway faced the east, toward the tattered hoof path which cut across the shadowed field, rutted, dusty, lined with ashen grains. I climbed down from the roof and turned. There Meiramgul stood, pulling aside the yurt's thick door-flap. The children gazed from her to me, questioning. I nodded, and the children bent and stepped inside. The eldest girl knelt before the hearth. Already she knew to light the fire.

Bekzat brought her the dried dung sack. From a clay bowl that Meiramgul laid beside a ring of stones, the child took the smoldering coals and worked until the fire flared. She had clearly done so often before.

Then she whispered, "I dedicate this hearth—" and almost spoke the name of the village goddess, but then she stopped and turned to me. So I set my hand across her wrist, nodded, whispered. Then she spoke the name I'd murmured, slowly and very clearly: "I dedicate this hearth to Rada Mai."

35

THE GOOD GRASS

For those many seasons, we followed the good grass, as had ever been our people's course. For a time it stretched out wide and bristling. Our sheep and countless horses surged across the verdant steppes like a tide lapping at a hapless shore. We never questioned our good fortune, only moved within it, guided by its ebb and swell. But every season since that last, the sleeping *dev* returned, until the lake's edge turned to dust and drought drove us so far to the west that we no longer knew the mountains we once called the heaven pasture.

We moved onward, pushing farther, leaving behind our winter shelters and even the kurgan mounds where our ancestors slept. All across the grasslands, the sun brought heat that seared the pastures to brittle husks. With each spring we crossed another river and did not return.

On strangers' banks, our herds nibbled quick blades into nubs until their hooves scuffed an ashen waste that could not sustain us. Just so, we trespassed over settlements, but did no malice unless we were attacked. We protected what was ours, fought only reluctantly, made alliances where we could. Even when we killed, at my command we took the children with us.

Over time more cousin auls joined us, and begging villagers escaping brutal strife, sometimes whole encampments burned for a bit of food. Together we raised new kurgan mounds to lodge the many dead, then set scouts scouring the hill-slopes for signs of more attacks. At the villages we left sentries to guard the farmers' hidden wells.

This was what I'd begun, and now it spread out wide before me. Standing in my dark wool yurt, the daylight streamed from up above. Dust hung in a column through the open roof's eye, glittering like sparks from an ironmonger's forge. Merciless and hot, the vista roiled before my eyes: the earth, a great, wide disk without the slightest undulation; and our people filled the barren course to the farthest rim of the boundless world.

Yet there was food enough, with such offerings and gifts as each new envoy or settlers' band would bring. Outside my lattice walls, our people prepared our winter stores: sun-parched cheese, fermented milk, dangling shreds of meat, and now fine meal, seeds, even sweet rare fruits which we had to neither steal nor bargain for.

"It is the way of things. Dust drifts up and falls; and where it settles, new grass grows and our herds prosper"—so the Hewana had learned to say. Even the Ak Kam had embraced it. For each new alliance, she chose an acolyte to join her train until our camp rattled with their chants and chimes and drums. They were heard to the far horizon; their offerings' smoke touched the edges of the clouds. And she drew a new tattoo upon my arm after each new truce until they crawled with beasts of fury and savage might, cut with the sharpened tip of the Kara Kam's own reed and the ash from my dead aunt's ancient shell.

So, through those many suns—ten full seasons' rounds in passing—still each dawn, I picked up my iron sword, stained but the blood turned rust. I scraped the muddy crust away and laid it in its sheath. "Go forward!" I called, mounting on my horse, and my people followed. They swore allegiance to me. Some called me war mistress, others priestess, Kara Kam, healer. Though I have never healed another in all my life except perhaps myself, and done so badly.

Bekzat, my not-quite-son, stood proudly among our warriors. He was one of my captains now, having long ago made first battle kills in those early days when my recruits stood apart, uncertain, mocked, even unwanted. But he had earned his place, showing courage in battle, faith and loyalty to me. Though he never wholly earned Erzhan's trust. Despite all those who had ridden into our fold, the enmity between them was dark, restrained, as if Bekzat's very nature was Erzhan's foe. Openly Erzhan was courteous, or at least he could be civil. His contempt was crafted in neglect. Bekzat—fiercest at all his weapons, a magnificent rider, fearless in attack—but still Erzhan held him back. He would never let him lead.

Nishan, too, stood beside me watching. In her saddle's pack, a basket soft with wool bore Bekzat's firstborn son. It was no surprise, as she hovered at his side through all those seasons, a constant presence he took for granted. And how she'd played at kesh-kumay on those springtime fields; Nishan's yearning showed in every blink of the young girl's eyes. Aigul and I had said nothing, though we'd both hoped; clearly Nishan had chosen Bekzat from the beginning.

But now her eyes looked old and her face furrowed, full of worry. Their child brought her joy, but my stepson did not. Always brooding, just as Timor once had done, as if Bekzat knew or sensed that this place was not his own. Surely he could not remember, but his gaze was ever toward the west; and secretly he gloried in every dawn that drew us closer.

Perhaps that was Erzhan's reason, though only once did he dare to speak it openly. "Akmaral—that boy—he was never one of us."

I dismissed him, called him foolish. "Erzhan, what does it matter now? The ways of others are the ways of the aul—we are all one fire, all one hearth," using the Ak Kam's words to silence him. But I sensed that his muted discontent veiled another buried truth—a memory of Timor, suspicion turned to love, unquestioned trust betrayed—something we once had shared and that both of us had lost. A pain that neither he nor I had ever truly conquered.

Erzhan never spoke of it again. He continued training villagers as warriors. Now the practice field was filled with them, the soil beside the settlers' huts pounded hard as clay beneath the tromping of ponies' hooves, the falls of wrestlers' muscled backs, and the sturdy stance of archers. In the cooling dusk, the ana-women worked their fingers shaping felts for saddle shawls and fashioning boiled leather tunics to fit their kin. Meanwhile, their children practiced turning hay-bales into shreds. The thunder god seemed pleased. Our fighters' prowess surpassed even our steady, growing ranks. Erzhan saw to it, training my young recruits, turning them one by one into warriors. And I was proud of them, every springtime blossoming in will and fierceness, fearless to protect our swelling tribe.

Together we built a mighty army, and Erzhan became the general he had always strived to be. Still, he prickled when we left a battlefield unbloodied. But he said nothing, threatened me not once, patient as I rode out grandly to make new allies. And he held back, seeming satisfied to linger in my shadow. It was unlike him—a place he could not want, against his very nature—but he deferred, beseeched, lent credence to my purpose. And I have relied on him and held him in my trust like the upper reach of my own arm, weighty now, fastened with a thousand golden plaques cut into the shapes of arrowheads and stalking panthers.

Most nights I lay awake. Or if I dreamed, it was of our distant winter canyon, of its low wood cabins, our yurts tucked under ledges glistening with ice. Again I threw wet spears made of icicles and laughter, and slept in the warm, dark closeness beside lost companions—Marjan, and then Timor, and so many left so long and far behind, so small and meager and nearly forgotten.

Then one dawn, I awoke. Beyond my yurt's flap, from the west, I saw a cloud obscure the distant stretch. It drifted across the pasture waving amber and golden. Moving slowly, another band—no surprise, for we'd found hoof paths across the steppes, as we had so many times before, and known that we'd been watched, every day and every hour through the ages of the moon since we'd arrived here.

My warriors stirred as a scout rode to my broad yurt to report. Their glances shifted tellingly among themselves—all the young ones anxious to have their battles, eager for blood and thrill and even pain. They whispered among themselves, reluctant to settle if no attack should come and the days pass again into tedium. They reminded me of Erzhan and myself when we were young.

The scout bowed low as he stepped across my threshold. Gone were the Kara Kam's charred black felts. Now my yurt was a palace that must be carried on the backs of seven camels. It took twenty men to raise it up, with its lattice framework draped with tapestries, its grass floors laid thick with piled carpets. I had resisted it at first, but the people and even the elders had insisted. Now at its western edge stood a great carved throne. There I sat amidst its resolute enfolding.

But what the scout foretold brought me little comfort—this was no traders' caravan or an aul of familiar kin: the cloud that came showed the shape of an oncoming storm. I had seen such clouds before, frantic gales that threatened, only to dissipate to gust and breeze. Still, we could not tell yet if they came for peace or conflict. I nodded to the scout, then begged the boy to go. Turning, I prepared to welcome them alone.

From a clutter of splintered trunks tucked in the shadow of my yurt, I withdrew the very last of the Kara Kam's things. Long ago I had donned her garments, for their shape and air were as much a shield as our arrows or sharpest blades. First the tussah silk—I spread it out, removed my tunic, and let hers fall. As a winter snow, the fabric draped me, pale, light, and slightly cold after the weight of my battle vest. I shivered as its broad sleeves cloaked my arms, etched already from shoulder to wrist with the blackened shapes I'd earned.

Then, from her felt bag's dark, I drew out the Kara Kam's tools, tied her seashell at my waist, hung her sack of brittle leaves and the dangling jar of well-dried seeds. Finally I held the Kara Kam's mirror. This I polished, mixing koumiss with powdered talc until its bronze light flashed across the shadowed lattice walls. I tied it to my belt. Then I set her tall, peaked cap upon my brow.

So odd and rare, and yet it bore the shape of wisdom, inviting question instead of warring, stopping enemies as they drew close enough to see. Rising to touch the sky, I bore its weight and heard her music, her chanting, smelled her black ash smoke as if it had infused the very fibers of her gift. Her touch was in the ripple of the tussah silk against my skin; and through its whisper, the Kara Kam spoke to me.

So it had been many times before, so long that I had ceased to ask my questions, recalling only when, in the distance, I had seen her—in darkness and in flesh forever watching. Perhaps she was the leopard on the cliff, perhaps the rustle in the shadowed cave. Perhaps she held my loss and felt my anguished longing. The old woman looking for her camels—was that her? Or was that me?

Just so, I felt her beside me now as I stepped out of my yurt and stood to greet them. I parted my way, walking slowly toward the gathering swarm. My people stopped and stared. Suddenly silent. Listening. I mounted my horse, raised my hand to my brow, dangling with small, crafted birds bound to the band of the woolen headdress, heavy, tall, and wound with gold, spiked with shafted arrows, winged rams, and sinuous, narrow leaves. The center stalk rose from my crown, a massive tree trunk, strongly rooted, towering above me. If I held my arms wide, the sea of my warriors would tumble out before me. If I opened up my lips, I would utter great flocks of birds. If I lifted up my limbs and studied them closely, they would be no longer legs or arms but hooves and slim, taut tendons covered with short, bright fur. I had become—as I had always been—the flying deer.

My children—warriors—stood as one before me, a battalion heavily laden, peering gravely toward the nearing cloud. Their hollers pierced the vaulted sky. At my signal, Erzhan rode to confront the strangers while Bekzat stayed full center at my right, formidable, while several of my captains flanked him. And still there were more, all those leaders from other auls and clans who had joined our ranks. They ringed around me, a double arc of protection, their bowstrings primed with arrows drawn from their gorytoi. We waited as the cloud descended, seeming slow in the distorting distance but gaining speed, then rearing to a stop at the farthest reach of even Erzhan's arrows.

As the cloud dispersed I saw that the strangers came in an odd array for war: in wooden wagons pulled by oxen, trailing scrawny goats and motley sheep. Some carted children, gaunt, holding to their mothers in stiff, shaken stillness. In some of the carts were men and boys, but many of these seemed injured or badly healed. Those who walked showed a weariness that spoke no threat. Their stance seemed humble. An entreaty.

I held our warriors' call, all of the strangers silent now as their leader, dressed in gray and woolly black, rode forward on a too-small pony. He alone came within our arrows' span, awkward, though his figure held a grace despite his coarseness. He slipped from his beast and bowed. Then he reached toward his saddle's pack and withdrew a thick rolled tapestry. Even from afar, the carpet's angled bands of vibrant colors took my breath. He spread it elegantly across his elbows, then knelt again on the ground. Erzhan signaled two recruits to ride together to take the rug away. They prodded the man back roughly, just as they'd been taught, then unfurled the mat to ensure that it held no serpents or other tricks. When they signaled with bows upraised, I pressed my horse forward calmly.

When I was close enough for my blade to slit his neck, their leader pressed his head into the dust. I reached my sword's point and turned it flat to tap him up. He lifted his dark brow, now caked in grime and sweat, then answered in a tongue I had not heard in a long, long time:

"War mistress, Sauromata, we submit ourselves to you."

His eyes were Timor's blue, but nothing else about him recalled that past except for his mangy cloak which was wolf pelt instead of bear.

"Why do you come?" I demanded.

"The Skoloti drove us. They have fettered us for seasons, forced our people to pay heavy tribute, taken our men as boys, turning them to serve at war."

I had heard the tale before. I closed my eyes and, with a

gesture, ordered him to stop. He bowed his head, afraid, until I nodded. "Please, continue."

"Only few of us survive"—he gestured with scarred hands— "tucked into the forest highlands. Our people are Budini. I am Asokomas. We heard rumor of a tribe rising in the east with a strong, wise woman at its fore. We traded everything we had of worth for this one fine carpet so that you would know we are humble, that we praise and will obey you."

So no new attack did come. Together we made offerings to Rada Mai whom these strangers, just like Timor, called Tabi-ti; and they swore our oaths and gave in sacrifice what small wealth they had. That night our hearth-fires glowed as the Ak Kam nursed the wounds of those who had survived the Sko-loti's razings. Soon the parched air quivered with the sounds of the horsehead fiddle until the strangers joined their voices to our songs.

Meanwhile I stood alone. Their tones, their speech—all that I'd known and nearly had forgotten—now they strained re-membrance: Timor's voice, Timor's touch, soothing in its rush; and yet I closed my eyes and saw him, torn apart by vultures.

I could not stand by to dwell in memory. I called one of my captains: "Bring him to me—the stranger…leader, Asokomas." Even as I said his name, the tastes of blood and iron cut my tongue. But I did not call the herald back, and soon the stranger was before me.

He seemed younger than I'd first seen, but worn and frail, as Timor once had been. He cowered in my hearth-fire's shadow, his head bowed low, eyes steady on the rug that he had brought. Now it spread beneath his feet at the center of my broad black yurt. This stranger dropped down to the mat and would not lift his eyes.

So I laid my birch bough gently, carefully against his shoul-der. Only then he dared to glance up. I almost smiled, offered him the hospitality of my hearth: milk and meat. He could hardly eat, as if his mouth had forgotten how to chew and his throat to swallow.

On the fire a cauldron boiled my mare's milk down to cheese. Several servants stirred the pot. Leather sacks dripped milk whey into jars. Strewn about were all the apparatus for fermenting koumiss—all an ana-woman's dealings.

He looked about them oddly.

"You think a warrior cannot also long for a woman's chores?"

"I think nothing." Asokomas cowered down again.

"You must look up if we are to speak." At that I raised myself from my fine silk bolster and sat upon his rug, brushing my hand over the magnificent fibers. "You have given me a finer place to rest. Come. Sit by me."

He did as I commanded, nearly crawling, awkward on his knees. I watched him for a time, searching for some hint that I should know him. But there was nothing.

"Where is your country?"

"It rises"—Asokomas pointed—"there, across the River Rha. It is a place of hills and forests. Though there are mines and gold that the Skoloti covet. Our people do not bring it out—others do. Our camp is known for crafts and carvers. We are gentle people, not prone to fight. But the Scythians do not care. They send to battle any body that still can bleed."

I said nothing, my hand stroking the consoling yarn. The twisted wool was dyed with shapes of grazing deer, griffins, and mounted horsemen. One bore upon his wrist a golden eagle.

"You say your people hide up in those hills?"

"That is how we endure—those who remain. You must come there, mistress. The Budini will give you shelter." I heard a tremor in his voice.

"You call us to a place of Scythians?"

"No. We have hidden ourselves well. War mistress, come! The winds blow colder every sunrise—join our people in the hills. We will give you food and fire, and you will give protection. Come, I beg. Our people are humble—fearful. But Sauromatae are good and strong—so the people say—and we will serve you—"

"What people?" I eyed him, suddenly wary of his plea.

Asokomas did not talk, so finally I asked what had long trembled on my tongue. "What do you know of Black Cloaks—Melanchlaeni?"

Asokomas stammered when I spoke the word. "Nothing. They were cousins, sufferers like us. Only one captain urged them to resist. It was foolish. The Scythian army cannot be coerced. So the Skoloti enslaved them."

I knew what he said was true, recalling the woman among the captives—her brittle voice, harsh as she spat and pierced me with hateful eyes.

"But Budini are clever," Asokomas continued. "We hide where no enemy can see—"

"But the Black Cloaks"—I cut him off—"do any of them remain?"

"No, war mistress. They are no more. Only traitors and slaves."

I listened and I tried to believe, but there was something in the way he spoke, a quiver in his lip, the bleary focus of his gaze. All at once I saw that fire—I recalled those flames—those forests, dense with shadows and piercing light where my arms grew heavy bearing life out of the death that I had caused there. Asokomas did not seem to know, or if he did, he would not say. Still the smoke, the stench of death that stabbed my gut—I quenched it well with coldness: "I will consider your offer," like tossing hefty wool coated in frost. Then, to the guard, "Send for Erzhan. Asokomas, you may go."

Just so, I dismissed him and the man went out. My black felts grappled with the breeze—the wind picked up when he was gone, this man who was not beautiful, who dared not stare back, bearing no defiance as Timor once had done, only quivering with passiveness and terror. Still, the black fur, mangy cloak—for a breath, I'd thought to place my hand upon his shoulder, perhaps to hold him close, to lay my mouth across his own. Instead, I stood staring at his half-drunk tea. I bent and picked up the bowl, raised the rim to touch my lips. The last quick sip was cold and left a milky droplet across my upper lip; I wiped it away with calloused knuckles, awkwardly.

❧

The sun had passed its height when Erzhan finally came to me. He bowed down deeply, but it was just for show as, without a word, he took a seat and watched as one of my new minions poured a bowl of koumiss to make the proper oblations. "To Targitai. To Rada Mai," the young girl murmured, so like that first and many others who had served that place before. The child passed the bowl to me. I drained my own mute offerings. Then I nodded for her—for all of them—to leave. Finally there was stillness. Erzhan would not look at me.

"There is trouble?" I asked.

He savored his first tart sip. "At the nearby auls, no roving bands, no blunt attacks. But we caught two spies; and foreign scouts left footpaths through the grasses."

"When?"

"Soon after the Budini came."

"From what direction?"

He nodded toward the west.

"Scythians. We draw closer." I told him of Asokomas's offer.

Erzhan sighed. "We cannot turn back. We must move forward. The grasses to the west are green. Not far, there lies a great wide river, and beyond there is no sign of drought."

"But settlements—"

He bit his lip.

"Settlements, Erzhan?"

"There are some—with warriors."

"Scythians." My breath dropped to my belly.

"Akmaral, we cannot avoid them. Behind us, to the east, there is only gray and dust. We must travel west or die."

I did not look at him, fingering my birch bough, softly polished where for so long I had gripped it. It was a thing of majesty, a symbol of peace, its branches rising toward the heavens like antlers. I did not long to brandish it in strife. "The spies, Erzhan, where did you leave them?"

"We sent them to their kin."

"Alive?"

He shook his head.

I pinched my brow. "Slaughtered—Erzhan—"

"A show of force—a warning! Akmaral, you cannot nurse these Scythians at your breast as you've done with all these other petty tribes. They are skilled and vast and mighty. We must show them we are strong. You don't understand. You do not know them—"

I stopped him, gripped his wrist. "Yes, I do. I knew Timor."

He shook me off, a scowl heavy on his lips. "You did not know him, Akmaral. You only loved him."

His counsel stung, but still I took it. Erzhan had never lied to me, never misled me even in those early, angry days. Still, in my heart I worried at Erzhan's random fierceness. "Next time, Erzhan, bring them to me alive."

36

BLACK FELTS, BLOOD MOON

Thagimasad—the dying season. The autumn moon loomed up above. We camped on dry grass pasture among shallow, rolling vales. Winter was in the wind's breath, gnashing its bitter teeth, promising frost and sickness if our people did not find shelter.

Erzhan was right: we could not turn back. That way for us was gone forever, as if we'd carved our course through a swollen stream: as soon as it was crossed, the path was swallowed. And now even the stream itself, dried up and lost completely.

That dawn I awoke while there still were stars. I parted my wool flap to gaze over our yurts spread out beyond me. Their glow was rich with softened shapes and shadows, their scents of boiling meat, talk drifting on early light, murmurs thick with surviving death and stories of ancestors' mighty battles. Still the moon hung full, her broad face gazing larger than the sun. She loitered on the hill, glowing rosy, almost red—blood moon, my mother had called her long ago, and told that she promised many great and terrible things. If she'd said my great-aunt could read such signs, I was young and had not understood then. Now I watched the moon myself, lighting softly on the shallow hills, remembering the distant mountains' veil—fog above unmelting snow. The world I saw was breath, soft on dying coals, the edges lightly filigreed and glowing. Then a whisper moved the ash: Erzhan gave out the call. The stricken embers smoldered; our people's laughter tripped upon the breeze as they began to break our camp—its touch, delicate and passing.

In that early stir, Bekzat came to me. His face still smooth about the eyes though his cheeks were hidden behind thick black bristles—so like Erbol and Bulat, though without their vengeful gaze. He had never heard those names, but perhaps somehow he sensed—Bekzat cropped his whiskers short, trimming every day with a dagger's blade.

I set a cushion for him and climbed down from my wooden throne. Sending my servants off, I bent before our hearth and dipped a dull bronze ladle to serve him as I had when he was a child. "We will go forward?" Bekzat questioned, slowly chewing on fresh meat—a sacrifice: the fine white mare the Ak Kam had offered at dawn to bless our journey.

"Erzhan says we must. Bekzat, do you agree?"

He nodded, fed Rada Mai another draft of koumiss, then a thread of meat, and then passed the bowl to me. I pressed it off. I had eaten quite enough. The scent of food already reminded me of blood.

"These people across the river—" He hesitated. "They are Scythians?"

I sighed. "Some of them, perhaps. We do not know which clans—what alliances we'll find."

"And we will fight?"

"I do not know. Targitai rules this path. Perhaps we will not have to fight at all."

He gazed at me skeptically—"If they are Scythians, Hewana, then we will fight"—softly sucking a bit of mare's juice from his thumb.

"Then perhaps this time you will have your chance."

He barely muted his disgust. "Why should this charge be any different from the rest? I have begged to prove myself. Still Erzhan ignores me."

I poked back a dung coal that threatened to tumble from my hearth. Suddenly Bekzat pressed up to his knees. "You are our leader, our Hewana."

"No. Still there is Meiramgul. And the Ak Kam is our priest—"

"They are old. The auls, the new clans, the villagers—all of them follow you—only you, Hewana. Not even Erzhan, though he'd like—"

"Erzhan is war-master—"

"They speak of you as queen!"

I sniffed. "I am nothing, Bekzat. A warrior, rider, archer, little more than that, for all these trappings." I tossed the thought away with a brisk brush of my hand, but Bekzat caught it, held it in his own—strong and sturdy, as was his bearing.

He gazed at me with fierceness. "Make me a general, Hewana. No one would oppose you."

"Except Erzhan." I wrapped my palm around his bristled cheek. "That would be enough."

He breathed, heavy through his nostrils.

"Your chance will come. I promise you—"

He stared, only for a moment, before he turned from me.

"Later we will ride." I tried one last time to calm him. "I will need you by me."

He bent again, raised his bowl to pour one last drop of koumiss onto the coals. Then he put it gently down and gazed into my face. "Hewana, I will stay by you forever."

Soon he was lost amid the bustle of our people packing up their goods. The sun had breached the steppes; the waning warmth and lurid hues of dawn-touched grass had returned to ash and coal and dun. Erzhan assigned a few old warriors, leaving them behind with horses and arms enough to guard the nearby villages and auls. The rest of us rode out across the steppes, heading west with Asokomas toward the River Rha.

It was two days' journey with his people guiding, mostly injured but still on foot. Even when we offered horses, Asokomas said they could not ride. "We are no horse-people. Even if we were, Skoloti steal the beasts. In our forest, riding is dangerous, but here we have advantage—we hide among the trees and boulders in places the Scythian warriors cannot find. We shelter in low hollows, dig our houses in the earth—"

"Yes, I know—" But then I stopped. I did not say that I had seen such a place before.

I rode in silence as Asokomas rambled, talking of the riches of his woods, of rivers thick with fishes, of hills with game.

"We trap foxes, rabbits, squirrels. There will be hearty feasting. All winter, I assure you, you will sleep well fed under our canopy of trees."

"What of wolves and bears?" I asked.

He smiled. "I speared this one myself." Then he pried the mangy cloak from across his back to show its savage teeth still gleaming from its skull, and its dead, dark eyes.

I was little reassured, gazing off for a time toward the looming highland. Somewhere along its crest was the very peak where we had been before. As we drew closer I sensed again its crushing dark, the moss-bound branches, the earthen huts, the filthy, pelt-worn people. All of them pressed upon me now as if to clutch my heart—squeezing in the empty spaces that could not be filled, not even by Bekzat. Still he rode just beside me, his muscled shoulder always at my right, so close I could feel his heat, silent, faithful, ever my ward and now my life's protector—Bekzat, stolen long ago to save us both. Yet he could not. Once again, I felt the fever of those fires rising.

That third dawn, we found the river. Asokomas led us down a rugged bank, then along a shallow stretch littered with boulders. The course was rough. Our horses balked as they pressed across; our children clung by fists to their horses' manes.

By the somber light, through those waters' iron gray, our people crossed at last into Scythian lands. We were vulnerable and knew it—so large a crowd was impossible to hide, stealing grass in gloomy fog like thieves. The Scythians' trails and trappings were everywhere, fortified and strongly manned. At Asokomas's urging, we moved quickly through the mist, anxious until we tucked into the forest, longing for the Budini's promised shelter.

Even there, we choked and tangled amid larches, birches, underbrush, our people threading in long, thin columns and occasionally caught on a thicket's thorns. My palace camels stumbled and soon were left behind. I would sleep in a common yurt like all the others. Our horses, sheep, and goats filled the forest like a black ant swarm. We carried onward, leaving a ragged trail of trampled brush and half-gnawed leaves. Finally we reached an upland outcrop. From there a deep-cut glen and a snaking river tucked into the gap. Erzhan glanced at me, then at Bekzat riding at my flank. We knew that we had found again the Black Cloaks' land.

When last Bekzat had passed this way, he had been only an infant who could not possibly recall. But Erzhan, just as I, remembered the twisting path, the woodland dark with forest ferns, dangling moss, briar, and blood—the old antipathy.

We descended and the forest dwellers climbed out of their huts to greet us. They came bearing gifts—berries and wild meat, paying homage with woolly pelts of beaver, otter, fox, and carved boar's teeth like the ones Marjan had saved me from when we were both just children.

"They are grateful you have come," Asokomas explained. "They know you will protect us from the Skoloti." But then he slunk down to his knees. It was the first he'd shown that he was not his people's leader. As he cowered, a man came forth, twisted and stooped with wild hair, half white, half flaming red.

"We are not afraid of you," the old man blustered. "We have seen far worse than you before. Some years ago strangers burned our neighbors to the ground. We are Budini." He pounded at his chest. "They were Melanchlaeni, allied with the Skoloti and thus forsaken. The stranger warriors left our camp untouched. We are protected by our gods."

I heard his words and felt the fire rise again beneath my battle vest. If he recognized our horses or our garb, I could not tell. He said nothing, only perused our company with squinted gaze, pausing at Bekzat for perhaps too long. Finally his lips cracked a half-toothed grin. "You—Sauromatae. You are not Skoloti. You are welcome here."

His name was Skudxa, and he was the Budini's chief, while Asokomas, I learned, was a messenger and little more. I thought again of that first time when he'd come, his brow bent upon the gift of that fine wool rug—what I'd thought, and what I'd longed to do—but even then I'd sensed that he was quivering and small, nothing like Timor.

Still Skudxa honored Asokomas's promise—he offered us a place to settle among the upland's trees. Though they were stripped to bony branches. Only the darkling pines lent a bit of shade against the glare of clouds looming with the weight of winter. Here the cold was damp and our bodies ached as if a beast gnawed at our bones. The Budini's wooden huts were rough, dug into the ground just as the Black Cloaks' had been, though they were warm and dry inside. Still, despite the chill, I could not bear to step within—remembering what I'd seen, what I had done in such a place before. Instead we found a clearing and set our yurts among the trees. Even there, our camp looked out upon the place that I could not bear to see— the black coal pit set in the forest's heart—the remnants of the Black Cloaks' fortress.

After all these seasons, still the trees were scorched or lay in piled heaps where they had fallen. I slept and faced it, woke and faced it, watching as our camp made its way across the frost cuts of my scars. In the mournful shriek of tree trunk against tree, I heard the echo of what had been. At night, when I slept at all, I dreamed of that last hard raid and those vultures tearing Timor's flesh, pecking at his eyes that once had pierced me with their beauty—until I heard my child's cries, louder than they had ever been. Not shrieks of fear or death but of laughter, joy—of the thrill of lifting up in flight. So I reached my arms and Arman came—alive—returned to me—

But then I woke there in our camp: dull gray covered with wet snow that melted before full light to slush and mud. I raised up from my cot, wiped the longing from my senses, and donned again my thick wool cloak, now lined with dark mink fur to bear the Budini winter.

Bekzat, too, must have sensed the murdered calls. In time he took to riding along the ridge, peering down through the thick-set fog upon the Black Cloaks' ruin. He said nothing, asked nothing as he stared at the great dark sweep, the forest

larches rising round it, lifting up like spears. I longed to follow
but had no courage. I could find no words or dared not speak
them out. In all these years I had kept my promise: I had never
shared his past. But Bekzat was no fool. If he could not recall
what had been, now the Budini stirred those phantoms. The
way they watched him: he looked nothing like my son with his
dark, thick hair, his lips full between rough whiskers, and his
deep-set eyes, blacker than my own, overhung with brows like
the forest's branches. Before him, the Budini's hush was louder
than their words. But among themselves, the forest crackled
with brute taunts—"Black Cloak bastard!" "Melanchlaeni!"—
hovering among the ice-cloaked boughs.

Then one dawn, I found Nishan cowering in their yurt. The
unwrapped cradleboard lay abandoned on the rug and she held
their infant, naked chest to naked breast, beside their hearth's
failing embers. "He is lost," she murmured, her gaze vacant
beyond the yurt's felt flap, a helpless stare from a woman who
had been a warrior.

I saddled up my horse and found Bekzat down the icy slope.
Before him stretched the charred expanse: remnants of fallen
ramparts, small dark pits dug low into the earth, the shapes
of the Black Cloaks' stronghold still visible beneath a drape
of snow. Bekzat slipped down from his mount, then stepped
beyond the fire's ring. Among the Black Cloaks' hearths, he
wandered, slowly, softly so as not to disturb their ash. Then
he knelt to touch damp soot. Blackened fingertips lifted nearly
to his lips. Keen memory could know no faces, no names, no
thoughts, no words; but the pungent scent he sniffed and must
have found familiar.

I left my horse and walked to his side. "Here, child, I murdered your own grandfather."

Bekzat stayed stooped, working his tongue slowly over
wind-burned lips. So I told him again. "Here I took you out of
the blood of your dead mother's arms."

Finally he turned, staring as if the sun had flashed and left
him blinded. He raised his bow, took an arrow, set it on the

strand. He could have pierced me. I bore no weapon; I would
have let him. Bekzat stayed quite still, drawing back with all his
force, his brow furrowed and glistening sweat like dew. Finally,
he raised his aim and released his arrow, high and fast as if to
slay the heavens. It came down hard and pierced where the ash
lay spread between our feet. Bekzat did not look at me, only
stepped before it, raised his boot, and cracked the shaft against
a rooted stone.

Some days more and Bekzat abandoned us completely. He
took up with a woman of the Budini called Surum. She was
no Black Cloak, but something near enough. One of Skudxa's
nieces, she was a beauty with long scarlet hair and eyes as cold
as winter frost. Bekzat spent long hours in Surum's hut, earth-
bound and covert compared with our bare encampment. That
he took his pleasure with her troubled me far less than his cold
retreat, the way he barely glanced at Nishan or their child or any
of our kind, but followed Surum's path, almost counting all her
footsteps, and she, wearing a dark red dress the color of blood.

"I told you this would come." Erzhan's eyes darted back and
forth as if to knit me to my foster child's beguiling. "Akmaral,
he was never one of us. Long ago, I warned that we would be
betrayed."

I hushed him and endured my shame, loving Bekzat as my
son but also needing Skudxa's support to sustain us. Now I
understood why he had been keen to keep our warriors close.
The Budini did indeed need our protection. Through that cold,
damp dark, the forest was plagued by rogues—unprovoked
attacks of two or three or sometimes several. Most were Scythian deserters, villains who lived by wiles and preyed on other
men—as Timor once had done, though I did not say it. I did
not want to remember.

Skudxa long ago had barely lived through an attack. "I lost
this eye," he pointed, "and the strength in both my knees when
some Skoloti brute charged his horse and shattered them." It
was true: he was hard to look at, hobbling and bent, but clever
in his way. Through the cold, he often joined us in my tent,

eating heartily of our meat as he told of the Scythians' abuses. "They raze our forests, seize what they can in wood and stock and slaves. Our people are fine carvers whom the Skoloti use to shape their weaponry. Shields, handles for axes, bridles, saddles, spear shafts, even the idols of their gods. The Scythians covet our craft, but not those who have no skill...." He shook his head. "So many of our people carried off—"

"Like me?"

We all looked up. It was Bekzat who interrupted—the first that he had spoken, standing dark and chill at my yurt's door-flap. Skudxa turned his eye away, the odd one watering as he worked cracked lips between rotted teeth.

"Bekzat—my son—my child—you do not understand—"

"Don't I, ana-mother? How are we any different? How better than the Scythian brutes? We take these people's kin, turn them into warriors, train them to fight, to die, their own camps left far behind, their own people abandoned."

I gaped, but could shape no words. His charges were points of one hundred stabbing daggers. But Erzhan rose to my defense. He gestured beyond the Budini strangers toward the leaders of our allied clans. "All of these are coerced? Forced to fight against their will? To die?" He reached hard to slap Bekzat's cheek. "Ungrateful dog!"

But then Surum appeared behind my son and laid her face jauntily on Bekzat's shoulder. "Come now! Really?" She burst a loud guffaw. "Have we no greater foe than to fight among ourselves?"

Her laughter twisted both men from their rancor. Just then Skudxa took advantage, slipping one hand to his belt. He untied a leather pouch and passed something to Erzhan.

"Better you than them," he said as Erzhan examined a fine gold-hammered plaque carved in an eagle's shape with outstretched wings. "Now that you are here, the Skoloti will be afraid of the great warriors who protect us."

Erzhan fondled the plaque, then passed the gift to me.

37

THE FLIGHT OF SWALLOWS

So we defended Skudxa's clan, and after each attack, they turned their allegiance to us more firmly. Soon the snows came hard and the forest shut us in. Beneath those towering trunks, as dense as bars of a wooden cage, I traveled along forest paths with my retinue of warriors. Asokomas always accompanied us, ushering me to every hearth. There the people cried their fear and praised us as if we were Targitai's warriors descended from the heaven realm. Still, through the winter, even with our protection, some of their smaller camps were badly breached: fires smoldered; cattle roasted on picket gates or scattered far across the hills. In places it seemed as if a great black storm had swept each patch and left the land covered in ash, dilapidated, ruined.

Finally the snows began to melt. At dawn, gray-necked cranes returned to cast long shadows. Our people welcomed them as we did each spring, the first of many gifts to fly from Argimpasa's sleeves. But here above, the sight was snagged against a tangle of hard branches, delicate and studded with small red buds among the filigree. Each day their grasp grew broader, denser, enclosing our yurt domes like a trap until finally they burst into clustered, incarcerating leaves.

At night a blue-gray fog hung about our yurts. If I dared to drift asleep, odd sounds would wake me: a scratch; a ruffle as an eagle roused its wings; horse hooves grazing earth in a distant glade; the soft, dark snuffling of boar among thorny shrubs; a fleeting toss of antlers rubbing against bark; and then finally the swishing of a tail—in my dreams I saw it, long, white, spotted with hints of shadow, dangling from some narrow chasm in midair.

"We must leave this place," I warned Erzhan at dawn. "We cannot stay. Our people do not belong here."

Erzhan sighed, but did not question me. He spread word about our camp. Before full light, our goods were packed, prepared to leave.

"Do not go, war mistress. Our people need you!" When I went to Skudxa, he feigned regret, but in truth he seemed relieved. "There is a passage," he offered. "Asokomas can lead you—beyond our river, just beneath the western cliff. It travels low through the last thin wood where it sweeps to open meadows. There the Melanchlaeni once taught their captured birds to hunt. Now that they are gone, the pasture is abandoned." He smiled at me wryly, his small, cracked teeth hanging crooked from his gums. "Go there. Your horses will grow strong and your sheep fat. And if the Scythians come this way, still you can defend us."

We shared a bowl of koumiss to pledge our faith, but there was something in his voice, guarded halts that I had not sensed since our first meeting; and when I rose to go, the strong clutch of his gnarled fingers, like claws against my wrist, biting into me.

Surum shed no tear when Bekzat told her we would leave. She seemed at ease to see her winter comfort gone. But Bekzat's gaze was beleaguered as he took his place beside Nishan and their child. There hung a heavy pall, a family bound and yet estranged.

I myself took up my station and led our people from the Budini wood. Asokomas stayed beside me, constant as before. He was quiet as we traveled, barely at a horse's trot when I turned to see the place its last. Already the Budini had slipped among the trunks and stones and shrubs. The woods we left were silent and deserted.

Down from the high hills and across a frigid stream, finally there before us stretched an open plain. After so long in the forest's haunt, the unveiled sun was blinding. New steppes stretched unbroken, lush, slightly greening with the springtime melt and lit with the last spark of the morning's dew. Geese rose in startled flocks as Erzhan gave the call and we raced across. Our herds flooded the last low slopes while swallows dove among us, sweeping, rising open-beaked, snatching their feast from drifting insect clouds while falcons circled high, scanning through the brush for prey.

Our many households were soon as scattered as our sheep, unfurling yurt cloths across the pasture. I breathed in deeply; the long winter's ache melted from my bones like ice from a mountain stream. We were finally at ease, escaped from the forest's gloom into glorious freedom. But our felts were not yet set even upon their lattice frames when we saw on the horizon sudden glints and sparks—sunlight from so many bright bronze helmets.

We heard a distant beat of drums, and then we saw them clearly: Scythians—mounted horsemen rising up from the distance like a wall. They kept their march at the farthest periphery, but the whole expanse was lined with them as far as our scouts could see. Behind them lay the river Timor had called Danu that he'd said the Greeks had named Tanaïs. From there the Scythians stretched to close a narrow gap toward the river at our backs, bending west, then south again, just as Timor had described—how once it had served to hold the Scythians off, but after they were vanquished, it acted as a fence to circumscribe his people.

Erzhan gathered all our captains, who sent a ring of warriors out to form a fragile barricade.

"We must pull back," I said as we took shelter, squatting in the last cramped brush beside the Rha's cold flow. Already the Scythians had unsheathed their swords and now battered them against their leather-covered shields. The sound rose hollow like the roll of distant thunder. It reached us even this far across the open plain.

Erzhan rallied all our horses. We retreated to the cliff where, from above, I had often watched the sun descend: facing hard away from the Budini camp, longing for a stretch of open sky away from the Melanchlaeni ruin, away from all my past. Yet now I faced the west unbarred and knew that they had sent us to our fate—Skudxa, the Budini, even Timor. All of them.

Erzhan's shadow soon blocked my doorframe. "We are safe here, but only for a time. The cliffs will not mask our smoke. The horses cannot graze on rock."

"We must pull back," I said again.

Erzhan gazed at me. Still well-muscled but now wiry with age, a hint of gray smoke coloring his temples, he looked tired, fraught as I had never seen before. "Pull back, Akmaral, to what? The Scythians are before us. Chaff and dust are at our backs. The forest dwellers are between."

"The Budini gave us shelter. They are allied with us—"

"Akmaral, no. We have been deceived." He gestured gruffly toward where our camp had gathered. Our crowd stood unsettled, small children clinging closely to their ponies.

I nodded, pinched my brow just upon its ridge. "Send a party back to Skudxa's camp. If there is a traitor, find him—bring him—"

But Erzhan only moved my door-flap, holding wider the dangling wool. "Where is your foster son?" he murmured. "Akmaral, where is Bekzat?"

In the distance, our captains hurried, but Bekzat was nowhere to be seen.

"He must be—he is somewhere—"

"We have seen no sign—not of him or Asokomas."

"They have gone in search—to find another route—"

But Erzhan pinned my gaze. "Wherever he has gone, we cannot trust what we have left behind."

I waved him off harshly. "Erzhan, leave me. Go!" My heart reared back like a fine horse maimed.

He bowed and backed away—all my servants leaving me in silence as had not been in my yurt in countless days. Not in all the seasons since Arman and Timor's deaths. Not since I had stolen Bekzat and brought him back with me. *He will betray us*— how many times had Erzhan warned? Now my breaths were low exhales like racking bursts of wind. Even with the noon-time glare, my yurt turned dark as if clouds had dropped, intent to smother my hearth with their threat of storm. I lingered in the half-light pallor, bending to stir the coals so the fire would not go out. "*Alel bam*—ancestors, watch—Rada Mai, protect—we are one fire; we are one—" Nearly choking, I scooped the still-burning ash, then let it fall with a dusty heave that scorched my leather-covered knees.

Finally I crawled into the yurt's dark shadows, groping among forgotten things. I dug until I found it: a scrap of felt and my own child's bow within. Not Bekzat's, but Arman's, the one Erzhan had given at his second birth. I set it on the earth and carefully removed its wrappings.

Its limbs and handle rising, worn at the very center by his small, sweet hand—this had been my child's and he was lost to me. And Bekzat—ever of dark and death and shadows; never, though he tried, to take his place. I clutched it to my stomach, fighting for a girding breath against its small, smooth shape, but my shoulders shuddered, betraying me.

By nightfall we heard horses, their steps stumbling over the forest's roots, then sharp on cracking scree. As they came into our camp, we saw at once Asokomas riding, his arms strapped behind and tied to the saddle's bow; then two more horses, each dragging its own pale prisoner: Skudxa and Surum.

Finally from the shadows came Bekzat, mounted and armed. "They made fine trade at our expense," he charged. "Seven prisoners suddenly returned to the Budini camp, and twenty new head of cattle and a sack of Scythian gold. Skudxa may have given our direction, but Surum, it seems, gave the Skoloti more."

All the while the aul drew close. Erzhan hovered, his eyes narrow with distrust as Bekzat cut Surum from her horse and wrapped the leather cord from her wrists around her neck.

"Harlot," he hissed. "Witch!" Tugging as if to choke, he yanked her to the ground.

Surum glared. "Did you think I cared for you? You filthy Black Cloak mongrel!"

Bekzat dropped from his mount and drew his sword. "I trusted you. What I told you in my pain…all our strategies, all our strengths"—the anguish in his eyes as impenetrable as his rage.

I stepped forward and tried to stop him. "Bekzat, it is not your fault—"

"Isn't it?" Erzhan moved between us. Blocking Bekzat's sword, he raised his own and, with one grim thrust, pierced the siren traitor's throat. Then he turned and slaughtered Skudxa where he stood and toppled Asokomas from his mount, stabbing him in the core as he dangled there.

Bekzat stood speechless, shaking—my boy, my almost-son. The heat of him. The shadowy darkness even of his strange, thick beard. As if I'd brought some part of that murky forest with me, full of trickery and confusion. I did not know which way to turn. I reached, but Bekzat swept away, heaving savage breaths, clench-fisted, staring.

"Come back!" I cried, as helpless as if my child had been caught in a rapids' flow. Then silence. Erzhan led me from the bleeding corpses back into my yurt. There, together, we listened for Bekzat's horse—the sound of galloping fury—but it did not come. Only footsteps. Hush. And then the moon—a silver scythe that stabbed sharp light into my yurt's eye as if opening a sore.

I started quietly. "Whatever loyalty we might have gained from the Budini is lost now with these murders."

Erzhan showed no regret. "We cannot retreat. We never could. The forest lands are valuable to the Scythians. They will fight to keep them."

I swallowed. A sudden wind rustled outside my yurt, shaking slightly the lattice frame. "What should we do?"

"War mistress, you know well."

I nodded, bent to warm my hands before the dung-coal fire.

Though the night was mild, my fingers ached as with a winter's frost. When they were warm enough to move, I opened my dangling pouch to pinch white talc from an ancient shell and slowly etch it across my limbs and shoulders. I poured libations of fermented mare's milk to liven Rada Mai's smoke—then, from the alabaster jar, the very last of the Kara Kam's small black seeds.

Erzhan pointed. "Beyond that bend lies a great salt sea, southward, and along it, all the Scythians' strongholds. Their trading posts are fat and weak with gold and Greeks—"

"You have crossed this way before?"

He nodded. "On our raid of Gorgippia. With Timor." Erzhan had not said that name aloud in so many years, the sound coming from his mouth seemed strange. "There are fortresses not far beyond, with all the Skoloti wealth. Their clans will turn to us if we defeat them."

"Defeat? The Skoloti? Erzhan, and risk our aul?"

"An aul, Akmaral?" He sniffed and grabbed my wrists. "You lead a massive army! We could split our forces, attack on several fronts. We have the might to face them now as we never had before. In Timor's day, we were a roving band. We could do little more than sting the Scythians like bees—"

I shook him off. "You have planned this all along"—my heart cracking like a battered, skin-torn drum.

"No." Erzhan looked unrepentant. "But I have not avoided it. The gods have led us here, and the grasslands, and you. We both have followed Timor's path. Don't you see? This is what he wanted—how Timor led each charge, always bearing to the west, targeting the Scythians' allies, raiding their small camps—and even after, while our warriors claimed the Skoloti's wealth, he took nothing for himself—a trinket or two for you and Arman. But he never aimed for gold. What he savored most were those Scythian deaths, riding back to the bloodied ground long after their retreat, standing above their shattered bodies, staring."

"Revenge."

Erzhan shook his head. "He never found it—at least, not until the end."

"Those Black Cloak captives—the way he hovered—as if he had awakened from a dream." All at once, I stumbled. Erzhan caught and clutched me awkwardly by my shoulders.

"You are not the only one Timor betrayed. It was my arrow that brought him down. Not yours."

I nodded, gently pushed him off, and regained my calm. "We could ride farther to the north, away from here—" But I knew it was a frail attempt, even as I spoke the words. We had no other choice. To the north were cold, dark, hostile mountains. To the east was dust and death. To the south, the sea. But to the west was war.

38

Eagle's Grip

We set our watch that night without a fire. The winds blew cold. Loose earth pelted us from above. It crackled against our warriors' armor and smarted on exposed skin—no yurts for our shelters; better to sink down and disappear among the grasses, all of us hunched, arms ready, arrows fletched and spiked, poised through the murk toward any flash of white-bared teeth, any glistening eye, any sound of snuffling or a scratching paw. Wolves and bears surely lurked nearby, no more dreadful than men.

In the distance we could hear the Scythians' drummers.

For a time I tried to sleep, but there was little purpose. In the dark I listened as someone sharpened a dagger against stone. I drifted off again and when I roused, found Erzhan next to me. "It is time, Akmaral," he whispered, eyes open to the purple gloom.

I rose up to my elbows, reached for my sword. I stood and shouldered my bow, adjusted my quiver on my hip. I felt the cold of the Kara Kam's mirror and, above it, the small gold amulet at my neck: my mother's flying deer rising, falling with my breathing.

"This will be no hasty skirmish, Akmaral. No calculated dawn attack. This will be a battle as our warriors cannot imagine—not even you."

I nodded understanding, but there was eagerness in Erzhan's eye in equal measure with his warning.

I waited until he'd gone, then gazed across at the Scythians' fires. The sky was clear but for a few thin clouds. Black vultures swooped, then perched on the river's wooded banks. As

I watched, they raised their beaks, strutted, preened their ruffs, rustled tattered wings. I prayed for a single golden eagle's pass, but there was nothing.

I turned at a gentle whinny.

"Hush, child." It was Meiramgul, tall astride her horse. Her thick ash hair pulled back from cheeks that had sunken in the passing years; her body still held the power that had once led raids, her eyes never succumbing to the veils of age. Whether she rode or walked or spoke or sat in silence, Meiramgul seemed both ageless and immovable.

I stepped nearer, groped for the Kara Kam's mirror, and raised it up. "Have I your sanction to lead this battle?"

She nodded and lifted up her palm. From a fist, her fingers stretched and cast long shadows on the ground: branches rising, then fingers bending into the shape of the flying deer's curled antlers.

Soon the field was teeming with our warriors, firm on horseback, armored with scales of gleaming iron or hardened hoof. Battle plaques and bridles gilded in gold or bronze or silver. Around me like a sea—this rising horde that was now our clan. They spread across the river's edge, overflowing its banks toward the steppe beyond. Arrows and bowstrings, helmets, heavy javelins and sheer wrought swords. Erzhan was right—now we were a mighty nation. A great confederacy. Our clans marshaled from every point: from where the steppe-lands lapped the desert dunes to this place, here beside the inland waters. Now was not the time for regret. Now was the time for celebration, to praise the gods who had joined our clans—one thousand different auls bound together.

Praise to Umai who would bless us with a fruitful season.

Praise to Rada Mai who warms our hearths and keeps the wolves at bay.

But the loudest praise of all to Targitai. Thunder!

The warriors' drums beat in loud succession. Our archers

primed their arrows, tied strength into their bows. Our warriors' laughter was muted, anxious. Our horses galloped, too pent up to slow. So many young, so many dark or pale, so many not old enough to remember when it had not been so. We were a tiny aul drifting across this land as tufted seeds in the waning season. Now we were no longer seeds, but the mighty, sweeping wind itself.

I gave the call to arms: "We confront a massive army—those who call themselves Skoloti and will not yield. We have known their kind before. We have witnessed their brutality. Their time for reckoning finally has come. May Targitai pour rain and thunder upon our enemies!"

But even as I said the words, my heart reared back. How much had I lost? Bekzat—Arman, my only child—and Timor, dead on a forgotten field.

I turned away as Erzhan addressed our throng, more of what strategies would win this battle and this plain. He spoke the truth: I had never planned more than a skirmish or a raid before, in all these years counseling against conflict except in defense, riding into so many strangers' camps with my arms extended. "We will lead this charge to defeat these Scythian enemies, corrupt enslavers, brute oppressors of fine, good men!" Now I watched our generals, captains, untried youths, all rising to these fighting words. I had drawn them here with promises of peace and protection. As I gazed across the war field at the Scythians' spears and battle barbs, their strong curved bows and war helmets' peaks, I knew the Scythians simply for what they were—murderers. Like me.

Our captains readied—all the leaders of our archers and our cavalry. But nowhere was Bekzat among this tribe's great spread. Nowhere, until I saw him riding, tall above his horse's shoulders, knees tucked tight into his saddle curves. I barely recognized him. He had shaved away the thick forest of his beard.

When he stilled, I reached and touched his naked cheeks.

"Bekzat," I murmured, "you have returned." He was the young man I had always known, though somehow older now, thick about the brows with a broad, square chin.

"I would never leave my people." His eyes were brooding with their heavy nature, not the small bright stars that once had shined from Arman's own.

I questioned gently: "These are your people?"

Bekzat clutched my hands. His fingers curled around my wrists, moved along my arms following the intricate tattoos. "Hewana, what people are one's own but those who feed and clothe and teach you?"

But Erzhan would not hear his words. "And those traitors in these forests? Those savages across this field? What people are they to you?"

Bekzat refused to speak.

"You will not fight," Erzhan ordered. "You have no place among us."

"Erzhan," I whispered, "leave Bekzat where he stands. It is not his fault. The Budini's vows were false. Their intent was never to ally with us, only to use us."

"The Budini bow to any lord they must. They are wise. We should learn from their example. Bekzat made his choice."

"Erzhan—"

"Akmaral, I will not risk this tribe to suit your guilt."

"It is not guilt. It is truth. Bekzat is one with us, as are any of these people. Look around you. Look what this truth has made."

Erzhan scanned the crowd, chewed his lip, spit softly at the ground. Finally he glowered toward where the rising dawn had already faded the Scythians' fires. "Truth has made an army, and I intend to use it." He pressed his stallion and left us in the rising wind.

"Bekzat," I turned, "you must take the rear—"

"Hewana, I will show you—I will protect you—"

"Yes." I closed my eyes. "I know you will." But I stiffened.

"Take the last defense. Protect our herds and households. Keep our people ready and our beasts moving."

He bristled at my command, but did not protest again. Tugging at his rein, Bekzat turned his horse and set roughly toward the edge of our great force, gathering up his own small band.

"Are you ready?" Erzhan pointed far across the steppe to where the Scythians' front guard had closed its edges, gathering strength for the first attack. We had waited long enough. Too soon the dawn would blaze against their arms and the glare would leave us blinded.

I prompted my mare forward, finally swallowing my dread. "Align your horses!" I called. "Prepare your arms!"

Then Erzhan shouted, louder than I ever could: "Charge!"

Our warriors shrilled, high and sharp above their snorting beasts and the rattle of bronze tack against leather reins. We pressed and galloped, gathering speed that stirred a cloud of dust and pelted clots into a filthy spray. Our herds, our households, our safety, and our past, all left behind. The thunder of our hooves and the hammer of our hearts became the mighty storm Targitai had for so long been denied.

We drew closer. The Scythians stood just along the Danu's edge and watched as we approached. We were nearly within arrow's reach when their ranks thickened, then focused to a point. A front of battle horses galloped to break our charge while each side showered the other with a deadly hail of arrows.

Erzhan called out orders that I echoed with a nod of my helmet's peak. We split and spread to circle them. Our plan was to catch them at the rear and force them into a tangled noose, then pierce again and again within their swelling center. But another skirmish broke us. Row upon row of Scythians washed us back like crashing waves. Our horses scattered in a mass of confusion as we drove beyond their arrows, riding tight and blind. Then we turned, clinging thighs to mounts, aiming backward, high into the sky, hurling bolts down on them like falling shards.

I called to regroup, but from somewhere through the dust, another front of archers swarmed. This Scythian throng wore dense black fur, the same that once had piqued my eye for all its tattered filth. I looked again. But these Black Cloaks could not be Melanchlaeni.

Still, these archers wedged their horses and nocked their arrows hard against their bows. They fired again, again, faster than I could fathom. Their pall engulfed us. We tripped over grassy fields torn and littered with bloodied bodies, horses slipping, and toppled men, limbs cut, chests firmly pierced by arrows from both sides.

I cried out to my warriors. We rallied and sortied. They charged beside, around. Beneath, my mare's blood, her sweat, her unswerving fierceness. Our hearts pounded a frantic tempo as we galloped through the hail. I swung left, right, my shield above, backward, sideways, all while firing until my quivers both were empty, then stabbing with my spear. Finally, even its strong shaft broke. I had nothing left but my blades.

Suddenly there was Bekzat, riding at my side.

"You defy my order! Bekzat, you betray our charge!" But there was nothing I could do. The Scythians' ranks closed tighter around us—they, too, re-arming without bowstrings, readying for blades and flesh attacks. Soon we struck iron amidst showers: blood and falling limbs, horses down and fighters, so many dead beasts, dead women, men.

I anchored my thighs into my horse's chest, clung close to her mane, taking worthless shelter between my helmet and her darting neck. I raised my battle arm, certain of my aim as we drove harder, deeper into the clash. We were hand to hand now in the thick of death.

I am the flying deer. The ground passes before me, beneath me. I set my thighs. My blade has passed from its scabbard, thirsty for blood. The clanking rhythm resounds like thunder. Sparks like lightning. Then a sudden shriek. A shadow passing over dimness. A golden eagle amidst the filth and blood. It shrills so close; it whispers in my ear.

They came at us and struck. Bekzat anchored, fighting to

protect me. I cut his horse's path to send him off, but he jostled hard again. I turned my blade just as a Black Cloak's sword fell, heavy at its edge. It caught against my own. It cut a jagged furrow but I thrust it off. I sliced and the warrior's leather armor tore.

The Black Cloak jerked away. Beneath his helmet's flap I saw his azure eyes. Hair the color of bronze. Shoulders bared revealed the scars: deep, brighter than the rush of blood—my own blood from my own slashes—and the amulet at his neck, so like the one given to Arman by the long dead goldsmith. It was the same. It was my flying deer.

I should have known that he would grow to be a warrior, that he would be tall and amber-haired with blue eyes like his father but a brooding glance that was so much like my own. I should have recognized him by the shadow of his face, the glitter of his vision, and by the eagle's scars: hidden beneath hard-boiled leather, small, red hollows at his collarbones, scratches scoring muscled shoulders, anchoring the broadness of his chest—the marks Garah had left, that proved my child had survived.

Even injured, Arman raised up his blade. It sliced again, carving into mine. I reached and parried, but my true blood son was young and strong. I called his name—he did not hear me—I called his name again. My son's arms were thick like his father's and his aim was just as true. Arman cut me at my shoulder, deep across my breast. I tumbled from my horse, but Bekzat caught me. He carried me as the battle raged—as I fought him, reaching backward, gasping. But then the jouncing of my horse, the rising dust amidst the jumble of broken chests, screeches, stomachs open, moaning, cracking bones.

When Erzhan saw me, he shouted our retreat. Our horses turned and raced away. But there were whispers in my ears, so still, I could not tell the voice—was it Bekzat's? Or Arman's?

39

SWANS

I awaken from a dream. A black crow perches on the lip of the open smoke-hole. It clings to that stretch of felt, clutching between sharp talons, shifting with its weight, pecking at the soft, dark wool.

My hair is tied in knots, caked with talc and cinnabar the Ak Kam has laid upon me. Across my broken body—balms and salves and wrappings meant to heal. Still my limbs do not obey me, nor my bowels. It hurts even to breathe.

"Hewana? Ana-mother?" Bekzat calls out softly. He lifts my fingers, caresses where the wounds have barely scabbed. He raises up my head—his thumbs against my temples. Life still throbs in them, surrounded by coarse, disheveled wisps. He strokes away the blood-encrusted hair that has fallen across my eyes.

"Can she rise yet? Can she move?" Erzhan stands, still wearing the filth and gore of battle.

"She isn't strong enough."

"I am," I say. "I will." But I cannot. My amulet lies immobile, balanced on my bandaged chest, barely troubled even by my breathing.

"The battle?" I beg, but Erzhan hushes with a softness I have never heard from him before.

"It is won, Akmaral. The Scythians have withdrawn."

"It cannot be—they are Scythians—"

But he pulls away the dark felt flap so I can see their bronze helmets fallen, blood-stained weapons scoured by our ana-women's hands, our smallest children leading away their horses.

I close my eyes.

"Hewana, we are safe here."

But the world outside is still and hushed. I long to force the ancient mirror to my face, but I cannot reach it. My limbs, limp against my sides, heavy with the grip of pain. "No—" I struggle. "Sunlight is only brief. The shadows will return. Go up to the high valley. Find sweet grass. Erzhan, lay me among the weeds."

We retreat across the river, away from the battleground and blood, back into the protected hills, avoiding those who regaled us through the winter. We know we cannot trust them. Still, we are grateful for the stealth we've learned. We move silent through their forest's shelter until we reach the open steppe. It is brown and cracked and everywhere turned to dust. They use a stolen Scythian cart to transport my body's broken pieces.

At each small settlement some warriors bow and leave us. They return to their own people who cry misery at my demise. No longer do the ana-women hide or fight or shriek or even cry as our warriors ride into their camps. Instead they set a feast and make way for my great tent. They lay me inside to give me shade, nestled upon a cushioned cot. From there I hold council on my back, and their elders bow before me. They show me all their ready children anxious to join our force. This will be the last time that I will choose.

When I die, Erzhan will make of them an army in praise of me.

"We return Akmaral to the place of our ancestors." Erzhan cheers them. "To the mountains, the heaven pasture."

"Mother of our tribe!" they cry between their tears.

"When it is time," Erzhan promises, "we will camp again on the Rha's far banks. We will look across those fields and raise our arms. You will join us in bloody retribution."

Retribution for my death. How can I tell them that this death is of my own making? That my son, the child that I have ever always loved—that my death came at my own son's hand? Even now, the feeling rises above my anguish—the gift of Arman's final blow, that I should know him still alive. I cannot hate him for it—cannot condemn him for what he could not know. That dark flush through my body, bittersweet, that I will cherish until my death. Even for these last few breaths, these few remaining days.

Outside it is never quiet. Everywhere there is wind, insects buzzing, birds flapping, diving down, flying close, passing on. The mewling of our herds mixes with the rustle of broad grasses. My ears grow deaf beneath the muffle of close death. Yet I hear their quivering chatter, loud as if I am walking close, grazing among them.

After countless days, we rise into the mountains. It is our finest place, hidden high in a wide, cool gap. It is the last I will see of this narrow pass with its sharp black spines dusted with powdery blindness. Here the goddess Argimpasa's breath has barely broken through the upland crust. Beyond, the high grasses are lit by sunlight. Here the water has returned, great trickling pools and streams like silvery, twisted ribbons. We settle down on open pasture among mounds filled with our ancient dead. Here flowers bud, undisturbed among the grasses. We take our many fallen and lay them down in small dug pits. For me they will do the same, but they will raise a mountain. For me, fill me up with moss and anise, grasses, seeds of coriander, thistle, thyme. Already now, the petals drop from their blooms, waiting, drying in the sun. The wax already mixes with the honey.

They say the wind resembles mischief, though none have ever seen it. It is a brawling horse who will not take the rein. It is violent in its character, reckless, sometimes coy and gentle, then as quickly bent upon destruction. Some people, just like horses, are said to be born of wind.

  There is a northern wind tonight, touched by cold and things that are passing. Death comes often of a northern wind.

"Akmaral."

Comes a call from somewhere close. I hadn't realized it was dark. "Yes," I answer, wondering what time it is and why no one has called me for the evening meal—

"Your son would see you."

"Arman, yes...."

"No," says the voice, a little timid for such a simple answer. "Not Arman. Your son. Bekzat."

"Bekzat—" Arman is not here. I had forgotten.

I almost say it, but hold my breath. It is hard, this breathing. Torchlights glisten, coming nearer. A little quiet, though their flames whip, hiss, and sometimes writhe.

"Bekzat, welcome." My voice is drifting. I stare into the rising smoke. It is brighter now. Its moving shapes cast small shadows above me through the open roof's eye. If I close my own, I can travel where they float. I can see the distant mountains.

Bekzat's face is grave as he bends over my cot. "You are better, Hewana?" He tries to smile. "Enjoying the sunshine?"

So that is sun upon my face? I feel it now, gentle when the wind stops its constant thrashing.

Bekzat sits and sings above me, strumming a heavy note on the horsehair strands. His tones dangle. Some fall onto the ground. Others catch above as if on sharp, bright stars. He does his best, but he has never had a lovely voice. Not as did Arman's father.

I reach to him, but my hand won't move. I whisper, though my words are no longer precisely lucid.

"Rest, Hewana—mother." Bekzat stops his playing and presses me back. His hands are gentle but compelling.

"I am no mother—" I look up at him. "No Hewana. I am—" I break—I say these things, though Bekzat knows them already. He has known them all along, since the first day he came to me, a stolen infant in my arms.

"Hush, Hewana. Calm."

He lifts my hands, warms them between his own while I am almost numb. His face unmoving, but the anguish, tucked deep behind his eyes.

There is a trickle on his cheek; it is dark, yet this shines clearly. I wonder why Bekzat cries.

༃

The Ak Kam leads the line of elders: some from every aul and village and priestesses dressed in somber felts. Bronze mirrors flash in their hands—smaller, finer than my own. From their fingers, seashells sprinkle offerings. Milk and dust pour onto the fire. Rada Mai drinks and is fed. The Ak Kam's healing smoke eases my pains but clouds the shallow light....

Last light. I would want it brighter.

Outside the pyres burn. Butchered meats boil in great bronze cauldrons. I scent them on the air. Our aul will eat well tonight. Generous is the feast for the dying.

"One woeful dawn, the world was ravaged by Chaos." Meiramgul's face, long pitted, etched as the chiseled steppe itself. "Sky pressed down on Earth and Earth was split in two." She sits stiffly in my yurt's shadow, her eyes unblinking as the bonfires burn. The well-carved seat is the place of highest honor, which all these years I've reserved for her. "Three rounds of seasons, Chaos reigned. Three years Rada Mai endured such suffering. All was misery, grief, confusion, until finally she cried out, 'Targitai, go! Make war on Chaos!'" Meiramgul bows her head and hums. Her sister joins her and all the priestesses tinkle their small bronze bells.

Meiramgul tells the tale because she must. This is what is done when a great leader lies dying: Targitai's spear has lost its grip; the sky shakes and the whole of the earth and all the heavens rattle. It is enough to say the words, as if they themselves have the strength to still and fasten.

But I think that they do not. No. This time, they do not have the strength at all.

Now my cot is raised up high. There are shouts, drumbeats hammered, ululations. Around me, their mourning claps are Targitai's thunder. Rattles and shrills. Their dances riffle the grasslands, bounding toward the snow-capped mountains, ricocheting back. The jingle of our horses' heavy bridles, their mantles of many-colored felts. Seven of them are sacrificed in my honor, including my own mare. In death she wears a tall, carved mask tipped with curving, coiled antlers. She has become the flying deer.

"My people," I say, though my voice no longer carries. "I greet you." I am clothed in a heavy gown of crimson wool and tussah silk. My legs are clad in soft white felt to hide their dissipation; my knees, bent in the shape of a warrior's horseback bow. I can no longer ride. I will never ride again—except on these dead horses who will accompany me on my journey.

The priestesses and ana-women throw grass and dung to raise the fires. From a sacred bowl they pour milk from a just foaled mare. *Praise the goddess of the hearth.* Sixty cauldrons cooking. *Alel bam. Alal bam...* Scents of horse meat and mutton drifting, thick. *Alel bam. Alal bam...* Sacrifices to Rada Mai.

We burn the pyres up to ash, but more and more our people serve the blade. Targitai reigns supreme. He is the strongest god, the savage one, and we are a mighty nation. Erzhan prepares to drive our enemies to the west. A great confederation poised as a single spear. My death delays them only as a summer wind. When I am in the earth, they will ride back, sharp, pounding hard to where Arman waits; black sands blowing across the meadows toward the west, destroying everything.

I look up to the sky and see a vision of birds. First swans, then storks, then geese, then falcons. Eagles. They are flying toward the sun, and the radiant light sets each of them on fire. At the distant edge of the land where the great peaks rise and are touched with snow, a leopard rests on a cliff. Its heavy tail curls and drifts and dangles.

I enter from a dream.

In my yurt I rise, wearing the high headdress of my stature. I do not sit upon a throne. I step out to walk among my people.

I am encrusted in gold. I bear the trappings of a warrior. My arrows, my bow, my lance, my spear, my blades. My mirror dangles from my chest, fastened with a seashell. I raise the sacred bronze to catch the sun and see it flicker like a dove and touch the yurts that spread about the fields like small piles of unmelted snow. The steppe is covered with them; their roof's eyes spew the smoke of sacred mourning, white like the frothy streams that flow from the mountaintops in spring.

Bekzat is beside me. And Erzhan. And Timor. All hold my hands. They lead me forward, but I walk alone.

I step out of my yurt surrounded by children. They are not my own—not one of all these offspring have come from my womb. They grow from a hundred clans joined together like a chain across these grasses.

Wherever we cross, the contract of my vision spawns more murder.

They adorn me now with a towering headdress and, on my warrior's garb, one thousand sparkling arrowheads knit against my bosom. But the birds dangling at my earlobes still speak their whispers; their feathers rise up in a round, encircling the tree of seven limbs, seven branches and, on each, a beast that guides me—a horse, a boar, a fox, a camel, an eagle, a leopard, and on the top, rising from the central stave: the flying deer.

The flying deer—the Kara Kam. She takes the great deer's form, powerful and white with her antlers falling back in swift, dark curves. She lays her head against her breast and plies the grass with curving antlers. They drape her shoulders, and as she reaches to touch them to her back, she drifts and floats away. And I float with her.

There is a thunderous sound, the pounding of many hooves. They rattle across the steppe lands, filling the hollow of the sky with their terror. I join them, yelping the high, frantic bark of the oncoming rider. My quiver is filled with arrows, mostly iron. Some are bronze. My bow is strapped against my hip, taut and at the ready. My dagger and my sword bound against my thighs, on the right and on the left, their sheaths laced to the leather belt cinched around my waist. My helmet is thick felt, peaked and pointed, my armor clattering with shaven horse-hoof scales. They make a rhythm as I gallop like the beating of many hearts pressing me onward.

Around me, sisters, brothers: at once we all draw our bows. Our arrows arc like a yurt's round canopy. In the distance, a cloud of dust marks our rivals' hoof-falls. We charge the grassy plateau and strike them down. Bodies fall from their mounts; reins tangle around broken limbs. Limp fingers release, setting free our stolen horses. The beasts return to us. They are racing, grateful, obedient children, some of them trampling or dragging their captors. Under one heavy step, a skull is burst like a fruit turned to juice by a crushing stone.

In the thick of the fray, my bow hurls away my arrows. They spring, flinging, flying. Charging close, I stab and kick and slash. With the wrenching of my body shaping powerful, swift strokes, here on the heaven pasture I am utterly alive.

HISTORICAL NOTES

Piecing together the past from a pile of bones is never easy, though archaeologists do it all the time. It's an unrelenting and arduous effort of digging, notating, and contextualizing bits and pieces, the tiny cast-off hints that remain of long ago.

Akmaral was constructed in much the same manner. Its culture is obscure, its geography remote, and yet these fierce, ancient women warriors existed. The evidence lies in kurgan mounds, the countless burials that dot the Central Asian steppes. Within them, women warriors lie at rest beside their daggers, swords, and arrowheads, their thighs bowed from lives spent on horseback, their bones betraying battle injuries. Yet, there are also more typically feminine effects: earrings, beads from necklaces, spindle whorls, as well as vivid remnants of a deep connection to the spiritual world.

Although numerous classical texts mention the Amazons, only scant passages refer to the Sauromatae or their (possibly) later incarnation, the Sarmatians. Herodotus's *Histories* (IV:110-117, excerpted in précis at the beginning of this novel), provides the most detail; while Pausanias (*Description of Greece*, 1:21) describes the making of Saurmatae breastplates using horse-hoofs "as if they were python scales;" and Hippocrates (*De aere aquis et locis*, Pt. XVII), after repeating some of Herodotus's story, adds the myth that these virgin women warriors cut off their right breasts to divert all their strength into their shooting arms. Rather than taking this hyperbolic turn, I chose to follow Herodotus's original legend beyond its end in my search for the authentic, living people the Sauromatae became.

I started on the Ukok Plateau, today called the "Pasture of Heaven" by the people of Tuva, a small state in the Altai Mountains of southern Siberia. There, in 1996, near the village of Pazyryk, archaeologist Natalia Polosmak uncovered the ex-

traordinary remains of the Ice Maiden. She had lain encased
in permafrost for 2,400 years, adorned in a wild tussah silk
blouse, a crimson wool skirt, and white felt stockings. She bore
an elaborate headdress, so tall that her coffin was nine feet long
to accommodate it. She had died young, her hair still blond,
her skin well preserved and covered in elaborate animal tattoos. Her grave goods included six sacrificed horses, a generous
feast, gold jewelry and, among other personal effects, the telling
ornamentation of a shaman or priestess: a small bronze mirror.

The Ice Maiden's burial is tied to the wider culture of the
Scythians that ranged from the Black Sea to the Altai Mountains that border Kazakhstan, Mongolia, China, and Siberia.
Perhaps her burial, at the outermost edge of that context, was
indeed that sacred place many days to the east where, legend
tells, the Sauromatae buried their dead.

That a people of such antiquity and technological simplicity
could have traveled over such vast stretches is easier to believe
when you consider that six days' travel on horseback would
cover about 240 miles. In a month, one might travel 1,000
miles. In a season, one could cross half the Asian continent. In
one researcher's parlance, these many tribes swept across the
steppes like waves across a shallow sea.

The Scythians themselves were a semi-nomadic people of
Iranian origin. Though they shared many traits and traditions,
they were far more vast and powerful than the Sauromatae,
with stronger ties to the more familiar Greek culture across
the Black Sea. Herodotus himself was Greek, and his observa-
tions of the Amazons and Sauromatae clearly favored ancient
Greek ideals. Particularly, he disdained the Amazons for their
unwomanly penchant for warfare. As such, his reliability on this
obscure culture is questionable as much as his details are scant.
To fill in the many missing facets of Akmaral's story, I turned
to archaeology and anthropology.

The work of the late archaeologist Jeannine Davis-Kimball,
PhD, led me to a number of women warrior burials in Central Asia and provided proof of a definitive genetic link to the

West. Using DNA taken from kurgan burials, Davis-Kimball traced these ancient warriors to contemporary nomadic herders in Western Mongolia. Among the modern nomads she tested was a young blond girl. Her name, like the leader of Akmaral's band, was Meiramgul.

This DNA connection confirmed the breadth of the Sauromatae sphere. My characters could indeed have been descendants of the Amazons. Thus Akmaral became golden haired and intrigued by the foreign stranger, Timor, who resembled a lion.

I followed Davis-Kimball's research further into the authenticity of the woman warrior legend and discovered her radical speculation about another famous Central Asian burial, the "Issyk Gold Man." Discovered in southeast Kazakhstan, the Issyk Gold Man was buried in leather trousers with an iron dagger and long sword at his side, but his body was also adorned with an elaborate, peaked hat very similar in shape and ornamentation to the one that accompanied the Pazyryk Ice Maiden and also to the peaked *saukele* that contemporary Kazakh brides wear to this day. Davis-Kimball speculated that the "Gold Man" was quite possibly a woman.

In the end, I decided to conjure a woman warrior who embodied both the Gold Man and the Ice Maiden, a warrior and a feminine leader, perhaps even a priestess. Akmaral became clearer to me still when I discovered the ancient deer-stones, a prominent symbol found across the Central Asian steppes but attributed to a much earlier culture. Tall, carved deer-stones dot the landscape at what appear to be ritual or burial sites, and are adorned with the shapes of leaping deer with curling antlers. Connected directly to the "Scythian Animal Style," but also to the nomadic reindeer herders of Siberia to the north and east, this symbol became a spiritual connection for Akmaral through her mysterious priestess aunt, the Kara Kam.

From these deer-stones, I also chose Akmaral's name, which means "White Deer" in the Kazakh language. Many other names I chose from a list of Kazakh first names found at a now defunct website, *http://kazakhadoptivefamilies.com/*. In a similar fashion, I looked to contemporary sources to develop Akmaral's culture and the daily lives of her nomad band.

Though the herders who still live on the open grasslands of Mongolia and Kazakhstan are far removed from these ancient, warlike people, there are clear ties. I adopted their portable houses—called "gers" in Mongolian, though I chose to use the more familiar word, "yurts." I also adapted their methods and tools for herding horses, making cheese and koumiss—fermented mare's milk—and for methods to keep young children safe, including strapping infants to a wooden cradleboard and using a cord to tie a toddler a safe distance from the yurt's central fire. For Umai's spring gathering, I borrowed from Nadaam—a traditional festival of horse racing, archery, and wrestling that still occurs annually in modern Mongolia. The traditional music of Mongolia, including the horsehead fiddle—*morin khuur*—and Tuvan throat-singing inspired and accompanied the writing of many passages of this novel.

For the art of training captive eagles, I learned much from *Eagle Dreams* by Stephen J. Bodio, who spent time with Kazakh and Mongolian eagle hunters learning their traditional methods, which differ somewhat from those of the West. The name of Timor's eagle, Garah, meaning "lightning," is taken from the legend of Chor, the first Kazakh eagle hunter whose bird bore the same name. I found this origin particularly intriguing because, in Mongolian, the word *garah* also means both "to go out" and "to go up."

Traditional shamanic practices gave me a pathway to form the Sauromatae's lost beliefs. "Ak Kam" and "Kara Kam" (White Shaman and Black Shaman, respectively) are both terms for Altaic shamans, and much of the ritual practice, especially the Kara Kam's, is drawn from Mircea Eliade's rendering of Altaic shamanic practices in his classic study, *Shamanism: Archaic Techniques of Ecstasy*. I borrowed persistent Mongolian and Kazakh traditions for rituals such as tossing mare's milk in all the cardinal directions as a blessing or prayer. I also adapted shamanic rites and specific details from Barbara Tedlock's book *The Woman in the Shaman's Body* and the work of Dr. Alma Kunanbaeva.

For the myths of Akmaral's aul, I turned to Central Asian folktales. The Mongolian tale "Erkhii mergen or why the marmot doesn't have a thumb" became the basis for the story of the warrior who shot down the seven suns. I also borrowed bits of story from *Tales Told in Tents* by Sally Pomme Clayton, *Stories of the Steppes* by Mary Lou Masey, and *Mongolian Folktales* by Hilary Roe Metternich. The symbolic phases of the moon are borrowed from Tengrism, the religion of the Turks and Mongols who postdate the Sauromatae, but who inhabited the same landscape and whose descendants still retain faint remnants of these ancient beliefs.

For the Sauromatae's own unique deities, I was hard pressed to find reliable information. There is virtually no record of their gods, practices, or beliefs, though Herodotus (IV:59) links Scythian gods to their Greek counterparts, particularly their primary goddess, Tabiti, equivalent to Hestia, goddess of the hearth. My Sauromatae deities would not share the same names, thanks to Sergei Rjabchikov's 2005 paper, "On Some Names of the Scythians, Sarmatians and Meotians." Though I'd come to understand that there are virtually no inscriptions of either the Scythians or Sarmatians/Sauromatae, I gratefully took literary license to use Rjabchikov's interpretations to name Rada Mai, Targitai, and Umai, while sharing the Scythian goddess of spring, Argimpasa, and other lesser deities to imply cultural connection.

For other aspects of Sauromatae belief, I reached forward instead of back, finding inspiration in the rituals of several Siberian reindeer-herding tribes. Art historian Esther Jacobson's excellent work, *The Deer Goddess of Ancient Siberia: a study in the ecology of belief*, provided me with Akmaral's mourning chant, "Alel bam, alal bam." Jacobson writes, "In the Ket culture of Siberia, 'alel' (alal, alel bam, bam) were protecting spirits of the hearth and family left over from pre-shamanic times. They were believed to be special protectors of children, to watch over and caress them as they slept." (Jacobson, p. 186.) The Ak Kam's frequent refrain, "We are one fire. We are one hearth," is adapted from the traditions of the Evenk who reside in northern Russia, parts of China, and Mongolia. The concept of sickness as a hungry beast that feeds on souls is based on Khosedam, a raging, malevolent demon of Ket mythology.

Descriptions of the rock art in the cave near the Kara Kam's yurt are combined from various sites including Tamgaly and Tangbaletas. Esther Jacobson's analysis of these sites also led me to the perception of these caves as portals for the dead.

The many specific artifacts that litter *Akmaral* are shared via my website (*https://judithlindbergh.com*) and social media. Among them, Akmaral's dagger, Timor's golden plaque, the wooden carriage in which Akmaral is transported to her death, and the magnificent Pazyryk carpet—perhaps the most well-known artifact from this period—which Asokomas gives to Akmaral in supplication and to lure her people to their fate.

In the end, *Akmaral* is a story of matriarchy versus patriarchy and which power would ultimately prevail. Several aspects of the archaeological record indicate a clear shift from female leadership to male, including the transfer of worship from the female hearth goddess to the god of war, burial placement in kurgan mounds, and the existence of the stirrup. Though scholars debate the precise date of the stirrup's invention, one theory is that matriarchy was overrun by male domination because the stirrup enabled better warfare on horseback. I applied this presumption more broadly to pave the way for the confrontation between the Sauromatae and the Scythians. As Erik Hildinger relates in his *Warriors of the Steppes*, the Sarmatians eventually drove the Scythians out of the Black Sea area except from a small enclave. Although this would happen long after my novel's close, hints of that future are implicit in Erzhan's determination to avenge Akmaral's death.

❧

GLOSSARY

Ak Kam: white shaman; from Altaic South Siberia.

Akmaral: white deer; traditional Kazakh name.

Ana-woman: a woman who has borne a child.

Argimpasa: Scythian goddess of spring, equivalent to Aphrodite (Herodotus IV:59).

Arman: dream; traditional Kazakh name usually given to a long-expected firstborn male in the family.

Aul: a small nomadic enclave or encampment.

Baltabek: "balta" is Kazakh and Turkish for "an ax," and "bek" means "chieftain."

Bayir: traditional Kazakh name; meaning unknown.

Bekzat: boy child; traditional Kazakh name.

Budini: an ancient tribe living in the Scythian forest zone beyond the Black Sea (Herodotus IV:21).

Bulat: strong, powerful, hardy; traditional Kazakh name.

Chersonesos: a Scythian trading port on the Black Sea located near modern day Sevastopol on the Crimean Peninsula.

Daniar: traditional Kazakh name; meaning unknown.

Danu: the Scythians' Danu River, called the Tanaïs by the Greeks, known today as the Don River.

Dev: a violent dust storm often lasting several days, believed to be a vengeful demon spirit.

Enarees: androgynes; ones that are neither specifically feminine nor masculine (Herodotus I:105 and IV:67).

Erbol: "Be a man!" (as an implied prophecy); traditional Kazakh name.

Erzhan: soul of hero, strong, "manly" soul; traditional Kazakh name.

Garah: in Kazakh, lightning; in Mongolian, both "to go out" and "to go up."

Gorgippia: a Scythian trading port on the Black Sea located near modern day Anapa, Russia.

Gorytoi: combination bow carrier and quiver holder.

Gulnara: juice of flower; a sweet girl; traditional Kazakh name.

Hewana: "mother of our people," the leader of the aul.

Jarakal: traditional Kazakh name; meaning unknown.

Kara Kam: black shaman, from Altaic South Siberia.

Kesh-kumay: "Kiss-Chase," a horse-racing game also used for courtship and still practiced in modern-day Central Asia.

Koumiss: fermented mare's milk, also called *airag* in modern Mongolia.

Kurgan: a burial mound.

Madiyar: honest; traditional Kazakh name.

Marjan: star of the sea. Marjan was named for a Mongolian female shaman in the Altai Mountains discovered in my research.

Meiramgul: the female leader of Akmaral's aul, named for the fair-haired Mongolian girl whose DNA tied her people to the ancient female warrior burials.

Melanchlaeni: Black Cloaks, an ancient tribe located approximately twenty days' journey from the Black Sea (Herodotus IV:20, 100-103, 107).

Meruert: pearl; traditional Kazakh name.

Oeorpata: man-killers, a term used to describe the Amazon women warriors (Herodotus IV:110).

Rada Mai (Scythian: "Tabiti"): goddess of the hearth.

Rha: Scythian name for the Volga River. I placed the location of Akmaral's final battle along the Volga River at modern-day Samara, Russia.

Rhyton: a curved drinking vessel shaped somewhat like a ram's horn.

Riphean Peaks: the Ural Mountains, although scholars dispute their exact location.

Sauromatae: the descendants of a band of Amazon and Scythian warriors reputed to have lived on the Central Asian steppes to the north and east of the Black Sea from the fifth century BCE to the fourth century CE.

Scythians (Scythian: "Skoloti"): a loosely related group of equestrian nomad tribes who inhabited the steppes from Eastern Europe to Central Asia from the seventh century BCE until the fourth century CE.

Soyun: the proper name of the Kara Kam, Akmaral's great-aunt, who is named for a 100-year-old shaman woman who was living among the nomadic herders of northern Mongolia at the time of my research.

Steppe: extensive, open grassland; specifically the grasslands that stretch from Eastern Europe to Asia which are bounded on the north by Russia and Siberia.

Surum: riddle, secret, mystery; traditional Kazakh name.

Targitai (Scythian: "Papaeus"): the war god, associated with lightning, thunder, and storms.

Thagimisad: Scythian god, the harbinger of autumn, equivalent to Poseidon (Herodotus IV:59).

Timor: iron; traditional Kazakh name.

Tsaagan bones: astragal; sheep's anklebones. "Tsaagan mod" is sometimes spoken aloud when the bones are tossed for games or prophecy.

Umai (Scythian: "Apia"): goddess protector of mothers and especially children. Her name, from Tengrism, means womb, uterus, or placenta.

Yerbol: traditional Kazakh name; meaning unknown.

Yurt: a portable, round, domed tent used as shelter by nomadic peoples in Central Asia. Also called a "ger" in modern Mongolia.

ACKNOWLEDGMENTS

This book would not exist if not for my younger son. When he was two years old, I took him to the Metropolitan Museum of Art in New York City, a frequent, favorite adventure. We decided, for a change of pace, to visit the Medieval wing. From the moment he stood before the sharp and shining glory of those mounted medieval warriors, our family's life changed. He instantly became an impassioned knight in shining armor and there was nothing I could do to convince him otherwise.

Suddenly his toddling, diapered days were spent running with a foam-rubber swimming noodle as a pretend lance as he charged at the dangling hollow of our backyard tire swing, falling on impact from his stick-horse onto the ground. How could I process this improbable, emotional conflict—a mother in love with a son, but also a nature-loving pacifist who did not approve of her sweet baby playing with weapons, even if they were toys? Like any reasonable author, I wrote a novel.

My story moved fairly quickly from medieval Europe to Central Asia when I learned about the discovery of the Pazyryk Ice Maiden in the Altai Mountains of southern Siberia. However, it took me years to fully understand my theme: "a woman warrior making peace with making war." To do that, internally and in Akmaral's world, I had to embrace what I had previously shunned.

This work also would not exist without the scholars whose efforts informed every step of my journey, particularly the late Dr. Jeannine Davis-Kimball, who responded to several vital queries early in my research and set me on the right path; and Dr. William Fitzhugh, whose research seems to intersect with my interests, project after project. I am also grateful to Adrienne Mayor, whose research informed later drafts of my novel.

My years of writing were constantly buoyed by the encouragement and critique of countless dear friends and writers. My gratitude goes to Laurie Lico Albanese, Marc Aronson, Dorothy Berinstein-Kelly, Marina Budhos, Lois Cantwell, Karen David-Chilowicz, Maude Chilton, Stephanie Cowell, Chet Ensign, Sunita Jaffrey, Sandra Joseph, Christina Baker Kline, Sarah Lyman Kravits, Stuart Lutz, Gloria Malter, Catherine Pagliuca, Donna Piken, and all the students—adults, children, teens, and their parents—at The Writers Circle. (I know you'd be really disappointed in me if I didn't finish my book after harping at all of you to do the same!) And to Jaynie Royal, Pam Van Dyk, and all the Regal House team, thank you for believing in a novel about a time, place, and people both obscure and, to my mind, beautiful. To my business partner and fellow novelist, Michelle Cameron, thank you for making every day worth looking forward to without (too much!) dread. And finally to Chip, Colin, and Cooper Davis, without whom there would be no joy at all.